THE
GOLDEN
SCALES

PARKER BILAL is the pseudonym of Jamal Mahjoub. Mahjoub has published seven critically acclaimed literary novels, which have been widely translated. Born in London, he has lived at various times in the UK, Sudan, Cairo and Denmark. He currently lives in Barcelona.

THE
GOLDEN
SCALES

PARKER BILAL

B L O O M S B U R Y

LONDON • NEW DELHI • NEW YORK • SYDNEY

First published in Great Britain 2012
This paperback edition published 2013

Copyright © 2012 by Jamal Mahjoub

The moral right of the author has been asserted

Bloomsbury Publishing, London, New Delhi, New York and Sydney

50 Bedford Square, London WC1B 3DP

A CIP catalogue record for this book is available from the British Library

ISBN 978 1 4088 3036 9
10 9 8 7 6 5 4 3 2 1

Typeset by Hewer Text UK Ltd, Edinburgh

Printed and bound in Great Britain by CPI Group (UK) Ltd, Croydon CR0 4YY

www.bloomsbury.com/parkerbilal

How doth the little crocodile
Improve his shining tail,
And pour the waters of the Nile
On every golden scale!
How cheerfully he seems to grin,
How neatly spreads his claws,
And welcomes little fishes in
With gently smiling jaws!

Lewis Carroll

Let the caller and the called disappear;
Be lost in the call

Jalal al-Din Rumi

Prologue

Cairo, 1981

The bright light struck her full in the eyes and for an instant she was blinded, as if struck by some ancient curse. Liz Markham reared back, completely stalled by the human mass that confronted her. Her heart racing, she began to run. Her child was somewhere out there, lost in this madness.

She stumbled. Behind her she heard someone make a remark that she couldn't understand. Several other people laughed. Darting away from the eyes that seemed fixed on her, closing in from every angle, she ran on. Glancing back, certain that someone was behind her, she moved away from the hotel, pushing impatiently through the crowd of tourists and tea boys, pushing at everything, knocking over tables, sending glasses and trays flying, hearing cries of astonishment and curses. But she didn't care. All she cared about at this moment was Alice.

Where had it all gone wrong? Her life, this trip? Everything that had happened since she had arrived in Cairo had turned out differently from the way she had expected. From the moment she'd stepped off the plane and been hit by the oppressive heat, the clothes instantly sticking to her back. It was supposed to be the end of September, for Christ's sake, and it felt like the middle of July in sunny Spain. It had seemed such a good idea at the time: get away from London, with all its weary habits and old accomplices. A chance to get clean, to start a new life. But what did she know about him, really? When she first met Alice's father he was just another of those listless young men hanging round the bazaar shops selling trinkets, or so it seemed. He and his friend had trailed behind them, her and Sylvia, calling out to them. It was irritating at first, and then it became a game, a challenge. Sylvia was always up for a challenge. And where was she now? Gone. Swept away in the urgent blue clamour of an ambulance that led to the dead end of a cold, impersonal corridor in the Accident and Emergency unit. Liz knew she didn't want to end like that.

He had been so charming, so confident. For three weeks they had been inseparable. That should have been the end of it, only it wasn't. Liz had been careless. When had she not been? The entire course of her life was marked by reckless impulses. She remembered how he had led her round the city and doors fell open before them. She liked that. As if she was somebody, as if they were important. They walked into a crowded café or restaurant and a table would be cleared for them in an instant. People bobbed their heads in respect. He had drugs too, in easy supply, and in those days that was something to consider. It wasn't meant to last. That was five years ago. It wasn't meant to change her life, but it did.

When she got back to England and discovered she was pregnant, Liz had straightened herself out for the first time in years. No booze, no smack. Clean living. She had seen enough horrors – children born without fingers – to know that she didn't want to run the risk. It didn't last, but it was something. A start, proof that she could do it if she wanted to. Alice was the best thing that had happened to her. Liz knew that it was worth it, that despite the difficulties of taking care of a small child – the tantrums, the constant demands – despite all of that, Alice made her mother want to be a better person. But she couldn't manage it in London. Too many temptations, too many open doors. Then it came to her, like a window opening in the darkness. Cairo. A new life. Why not? 'Any time you need anything, Liz, you come to me,' he had told her.

All around her the little figures spun. Monkey kings and gods shaped like dogs, baboons, crocodiles and birds, all carved from green stone, or obsidian. A window stuffed with jewellery, silver crosses – *ankh*, the symbol of life. Miniature pyramids; some so big you couldn't lift them with both hands and others small enough to dangle from your ears. Turquoise scarabs. A window full of chessboards. Silvery blue mother-of-pearl, shooting arrows of sparkling light. A mad funfair.

'Alice!'

Liz rushed on, her mind reeling. She turned, crashing into the arms of a woman balancing a tower of tin jugs on her head. Liz wheeled round. Nothing was as she recalled it. The streets, the noise, the leering men. It felt like a different country. Had she been so blind five years ago? So off her head that it didn't register? The bazaar she had recalled as an Aladdin's cave of glittering wonders. Now all she saw was row after row of cheap trinkets, clumsily fashioned artefacts designed to seduce the eye. To dupe rather than to satisfy the soul. The place made her sick, literally. At first she'd thought she must have eaten something that disagreed with her because she'd spent the first night crouched over the toilet bowl. Only it wasn't the food, of course, it was the drugs, or lack of them. Withdrawal symptoms. This was the first time she had really been clean since Alice was born. She'd lain in bed, feverish and weak but determined to carry on, the child tugging at her arm.

The only kindness she'd experienced here was in the warm reception given to her little girl. It was as if they recognised something in her, as if they knew Alice belonged here. Everywhere they went people smiled at the little golden-haired girl. Women, old and young, clucked and pinched her cheeks, tugged her pigtails. Men made swooping motions with their hands like birds darting around her head, making her squeal with delight. She was something of a novelty. Those were the moments when Liz had told herself everything was going to be all right. But there were other moments: when anxiety made her pace the room sleeplessly, scratching her arms, clawing at her throat, struggling to breathe in the oppressive air as the wail of yet another call to prayer echoed over the square. Moments when she thought her mission hopeless. She would never find him, or even if she did, what then? Liz was beginning to get the feeling that there was a limit to how long she could keep this up. Alice was impatient with her. As if she sensed her mother was out on a limb. Always asking questions, refusing to move, asking to be carried, clinging to her, dragging her down like a dead weight.

Then, yesterday afternoon, a man had walked straight up to Liz. No hesitation. Had he been following her? 'I help you.' He led her to a narrow doorway opening into a shadowy interior. Narrow darts of light cut through slits set high in the walls, bouncing off the polished brass and tarnished mirrors. The place was deserted but for a man sitting against the far wall. His thick, lumpy features put her in mind of a bullfrog she had once dissected in the school biology lab years ago. His eyes were like hard black rivets, almost lost in the swollen face. His hair was smoothed straight back with scented oil. His whole body gave off an aromatic air, like an ancient eastern king. On the table in front of him stood a heap of tangerines on a huge round tray of beaten bronze, like the disc of Ra the Sun God as it travels westwards across the sky.

It couldn't have been that big a place, but to her mind the distance between the door and the far corner where he sat, waiting, stretched before her into infinity, as if she was shrinking and the room growing longer even as she walked. There was movement flitting through the shadows behind him. A couple of louts hung round by a counter on the left. Nasty-looking, but Liz knew the type and wasn't particularly afraid. She caught sight of herself in the mirror above his head, and despite the dim light could see that she looked terrible. Her hair was lank and lifeless, her face filmed with sweat and the sooty grime of the streets, which turned the towels in her hotel room black every night. Her eyes were ringed with red and swollen like eggs. He gestured for her to sit and so she did. Alice pressed herself to her side. The man's ugly face creased in a smile that made her blood churn.

'Hello, little girl,' he said in English, stretching out a hand towards her daughter, fingers like plump dates. Alice shied away, pulling back, pressing herself in towards her mother. The smile waned. The fingers withdrew. The black eyes turned to Liz.

'Tell me, why do you want to find this man so badly?'

'Do you know him?'

'Yes, of course. He is . . . an associate.'

His English was not bad. In itself, this was not surprising. Everyone in the Khan al-Khalili had at least one foreign language. It was a veritable Tower of Babel.

'Associate?' Liz repeated, thinking it an odd word to use. 'Where can I find him?'

'He works for me. Or rather, he used to. Now he has . . . gone into business for himself.'

He bared his teeth in what might otherwise have been a smile and Liz felt a cold shiver run through her. Holding her gaze as the smile faded, he plucked a tangerine from the pile in front of him and handed it to the child. As she began to eat, sucking the little lobes of fruit contentedly, Liz felt uncomfortable that her daughter could so easily trust a stranger they had only just met.

'This is not your first time in Egypt?'

Liz shook her head, feeling his eyes scrutinise her, lingering on her fingernails, bitten to the quick. The raw hunger in her stare, the desperation she was unable to hide. She was reaching the end of her meagre funds. Her patience was running out. She was climbing the walls. And then there was Alice, with her constant demands for attention, for reassurances that Liz couldn't give her. The only thing that would make sense of any of this was finding him. She didn't care who helped her find him, so long as somebody did. The dark, sunken eyes met hers.

'Is he the father of this child?'

Liz hesitated, sensing that any information she gave this man would place her further in his power, but she had no choice. If she wanted to enlist his help, she had to trust him. She nodded.

'Ah.' He sat back. 'Then she is a valuable child indeed.'

'Valuable?' Liz placed an arm protectively around Alice's shoulders. 'I don't understand.'

'You don't trust me,' he smiled. It wasn't a question, and she detected the steel underlying his voice.

'I don't know you.' She didn't want to offend him, but by now Liz could hardly breathe. She was beginning to sense that this had been a big mistake.

'What is there to know? I am a man of simple tastes. Ask anyone.' He reached for another tangerine and broke it into segments. She watched him, helpless to stop him feeding her child; wanting, more than anything, to leave, but finding herself unable to.

'What is it you really came for?' The deep-set eyes flickered upward, catching her off balance. 'If you need money, all you have to do is tell me.' Again the toothy grin. 'People come to me all the time because they know I will help them.'

'It's not money.'

'No? Something else then?'

Without warning he seized her wrist and held it firmly, almost without effort. She struggled to pull back, but couldn't move. With ease he tugged up the long sleeve of her blouse, past the elbow. Relentless eyes searched for the telltale tracks. She wriggled helplessly. When he was satisfied, he let go. Liz pulled her arm back, massaging her painful wrist. A segment of tangerine fell from Alice's mouth as she watched in silence, eyes wide. She crawled on to her mother's lap.

'You have no right . . .' Liz began, struggling to control her voice. It was futile, but he tilted his head understandingly.

'This is Cairo. Everyone's business is common knowledge.' He gestured with a wide sweep of the hand that encompassed their entire surroundings. It was true. Life was lived on the streets here. Hadn't she once admired the carved wooden *mashrabiyya* screens over the old windows, and wondered at the veils covering the faces of some of the women on the street, feeling their eyes sear through her flimsy clothes like hot pokers? She understood now this obsession with secrecy, the value of preserving a private space.

'She's my daughter,' Liz whispered hoarsely.

'But of course.'

'I want the best for her.'

'That's only natural.' He inclined his head.

Then Liz had managed to make her excuses, pull Alice into her arms and flee. Later that evening there was a knock at the door of the hotel room. It was late; she had been dozing, and rose from the bed half asleep. She opened the door a crack to peer round it. In the hallway stood a young boy, no more than twelve years old. He had a keen intelligent gaze despite his grimy appearance and an ear that was swollen and misshapen. They stared at one another for what felt like hours but was really only a matter of seconds.

'Yes? What do you want?' asked Liz.

Without a word he thrust forward an envelope. It was thick and heavy and she turned it over in her hands. There was nothing written on it. No name or address. Nothing. When she looked up the boy was gone.

Alice slept on blissfully, her damp hair stuck to her forehead with perspiration. Liz sat on the bed and opened the envelope. Inside was a bundle of banknotes. Dollars. A lot of them. So many she couldn't count. She rifled through quickly – fifties, hundreds, tens, twenties, no sense of order to them at all. And there was something else, something that shifted around at the bottom of the envelope. Throwing the money on to the bed, she tipped the rest of the contents out into her hand. A simple twist of paper. Liz stared at it. She knew what it was. She could feel her heart start to beat. It was fear, excitement, or both mixed up together, that coursed through her veins then. She knew what this was. It was what she had come here to get away from. Or had she really? Her first instinct was to throw it away. Don't even think about it, Liz. Just flush it down the toilet. And with that intention she got up and headed for the bathroom. She locked the door behind her and leaned against it, the wrap clenched between her fingers. All she had to do was take it one day at a time . . . But she was tired. Tired of the pain in her limbs, the dull ache behind her eyes. Tired of sleeplessness and weariness.

Lowering the toilet cover, she sat down and unfolded the wrap. She stared at the contents, feeling her pulse accelerate. She dipped in a finger and touched it to her tongue. Still there was a moment's hesitation, in which she saw the road to ruin laid out before her in that single brown thread tapering across her hand. Then the despair rolled back over her like a thick carpet of cloud blotting out the sun, and there was no alternative. Kneeling on the floor, she tipped the heroin on to the seat cover and used the edge of the paper to divide it into narrow lines. She rolled the wrap into a tight tube, pushed it into her left nostril and leaned over. It was like sinking into a warm bath. She felt weightless and free, sliding back to the floor and slumping against the wall. Time stopped. Someone cut the safety line and she watched the blue world floating off into the dark void.

When she opened her eyes she realised it was light outside. Her head felt fuzzy and unclear. She struggled to her feet, her eyes going to the empty wrap on the floor beside her. She threw it aside as she wrestled with the door latch. The first thing she noticed was the money lying on the bed where she had left it. The second thing was that Alice was nowhere to be seen.

She checked the windows, the wardrobe, under the bed. Each option offered a fleeting, absurd ray of hope before the inevitable realisation. Then she was running. Along hallways, down stairwells, through the narrow arteries of the bazaar. She ran in disbelief, in shock, numbed, crying the name of her child. Alice. She walked until she was ready to drop. She was lost herself by then, delirious, finding herself reflected back in pieces, divided into strips by shards of mirrored glass, slivers of shiny metal. The men hanging around, leaning in doorways, called out as she went by, again and again, like a game.

'Hello, welcome!'

'Where you from?'

A gust of cold air wafted from a dark passage, making the hairs on the back of her neck stand up. She spun round, seized by the strange sensation that somebody was watching her, and found herself staring into the fierce gaze of Anubis the jackal, guardian of the Underworld. Or rather, an ebony carving decorated in gold leaf, of exactly the same height as her.

Alice was hidden somewhere in this nightmare . . . but where? Turning a corner and then another, not stopping, Liz ran left, right, left again. She paused for breath, looking back, only now she was not sure which way she had come. It all looked the same; the stalls, the narrow streets, the vegetable peelings on the ground, the discarded newspapers. Another corner brought her to a shop filled with junk no one would ever want: old rusty copper trays, wooden tables, strange tablets covered with letters that looked like no language she had ever seen before. Clusters of oil lamps dangled from the rafters. Centuries old. The kind a genie might fly out of if you rubbed them. A man shuffled out of the shadows. Liz looked at his wizened face, the wrinkles inscribed like hieroglyphics. Eyes filled with a very old light, in which she seemed to see her fate written. He smiled, revealing a row of stained yellow teeth. She closed her eyes tightly, then opened her mouth and screamed, 'Alice!'

1

The Missing

1998

Chapter One

Being something of an optimist, it had always struck Makana that it made a good start to the day to wake up in the morning and find himself still afloat. One of the little pleasures of life on an *awama*. He thought of it as a boat, but of course it wasn't, not really, just a flimsy plywood construction nailed haphazardly on to a rusty pontoon. Still, it was a nice thought. A comfort to think that if he wished to he could one day simply cut the moorings and sail off around the world. The truth was that the thing would probably sink like a stone. It was only a raft with walls, to keep the world out. A dream. A trick of the mind. But it is the little things in life that keep us going, as he often told himself.

There aren't too many people capable of sleeping soundly on such an unreliable craft, night after night, not knowing if they will ever live to see another day, or might in fact wake up to find themselves swimming, or even (better or worse?) simply drown in their sleep. But then, Makana wasn't most people. Such worries never bothered him. He had long since come to accept that if it did go down one night there was not really a great deal he could do about it; that it might even be a relief in some way. And besides, he had no real choice in the matter. The risks of

3

living on an *awama* were a fact of life for a man in his precarious financial situation. And even then, he was already four months in arrears with the rent on his flimsy home and didn't need a soothsayer to tell him there was little prospect of any more money coming into his pocket in the near future. On this particular morning, peace of mind was a luxury he couldn't afford.

Makana was a solitary man. The few friends he had tended to be drawn from among the community of his exiled compatriots: writers, painters, musicians, men and women forced to leave their country or else face the consequences of a repressive regime. Although he saw them infrequently he valued their company and they in turn seemed to appreciate his peripheral presence.

Most days, all Makana had to contend with was the steady stream of traffic that swept without cease along the tarmac artery skirting the west bank of the Nile. He had learned to ignore the fact that if he chose to throw open the grimy shutters, he could look up and see the whirling constellation of flying metal and machinery orbiting his flimsy sanctuary.

The familiar rumble of heavy traffic was already in full swing when he looked down from the upper deck that morning to see his only real neighbours: his landlady Umm Ali and her family. They lived in a shack made of stencilled wooden crates and flattened jerrycans, that clung precariously to the crumbling embankment, rising up like a muddy wave from the water's edge. The long, drooping branches of a huge eucalyptus tree curled down over them like a protective hand.

Makana had not yet unravelled how exactly the *awama* had come into the possession of Umm Ali. There was a long, complicated story involving her late husband, without mention of whom no conversation was ever complete, as well as the village in some obscure part of the *rif* where she hailed from, several brothers and sisters, a piece of land, and a wayward father who gambled. Makana had long since given up hope of fully understanding the process and as a general rule he steered well clear of the subject. Since it could not be moved and presumably could not be turned to any other kind of profit short of chopping it into firewood, Umm Ali chose to rent the houseboat out. She could have lived on it with her children, of course, but either they needed the money more than Makana did, or they had less faith in its ability to float. Still, so long as she was happy having him as her only tenant, despite the rather irregular manner of his payments, then he had nothing to complain about. There were times when Makana had the impression that they were all clinging to this pile of matchwood as if it actually was a raft adrift far out to sea.

Considering his options for the day, he set about reheating the coffee grounds left in the brass pot on the stove. He gazed out at the river as he waited for the trickle of water from the tap to fill the pot. The tiny cubicle that passed for a kitchen was so narrow that he had to back out of it the same way he went in. If he turned around too quickly his coffee would go flying out of the low window to the fish. The facilities were basic: one small gas cylinder and a rusty metal ring. Since gas was a major expense he used it sparingly, although even when lit it generated little more heat than a candle. As he waited for the murky liquid to boil, Makana wondered if it was worth the trouble, putting off the moment when he could allow himself his first cigarette.

When it had bubbled away for a while and showed no signs of growing any more palatable, Makana poured his coffee into a cup and took it back upstairs. The upper deck was one open space with a set of rusty metal stairs leading up to it from below. The rear wall was missing, having fallen off at some point in history and never been replaced, which meant that he had an unrestricted view of the river beyond where the wall used to be. This was the place he spent most of his time. He usually preferred to sleep up here in the open air, even when it was cold. Old habits die hard and he couldn't stand being cooped up inside. The furniture was an unremarkable collection he had accumulated over the years. A trestle table, covered in thick pools of dried pigment, that had once belonged to a painter. A creaky old wicker armchair which was his favourite place to sit and where he often slept, his feet propped on the small plastic crate that doubled as a low table. Scattered around the deck lay a collection of cardboard boxes filled with case files and unruly heaps of newspaper – his archives. The boxes were weighted down with stones to stop their contents from flying away, but the fluttering of paper in the river breeze sounded like a forest full of dry leaves.

From here he enjoyed a clear view of the city in all its glory. The pyramids were somewhere out there to the south, buried under a pensive cloud of smog more turgid than centuries of tomb dust, and out of which the pale orb of the sun was now struggling to lift itself. If he stepped to the wooden railings and looked up he saw a jumble of high-rise apartment blocks arranged like an ugly row of broken teeth, blotting out that corner of the sky. People looked out of their windows every day and wondered who on earth would ever think of living on that heap of floating driftwood, and he looked up at them and wondered his own thoughts.

Makana still felt like a stranger in this city. The river he gazed down upon provided a tenuous link to Khartoum, far upstream, the place he still thought of as home even though he had fled it some seven years earlier and had no plan to return there any time soon. He had not had any choice in the matter. It was either leave, or die.

For seven years Makana had managed to find enough work to survive on through his few friends and acquaintances – you got nowhere in Cairo without knowing people. Usually his clients thought they could get him to work a little more cheaply and discreetly than a local investigator might. Still, in recent months he had found himself struggling. The work had dried up, no one had any money, and Makana was faced with the fact that if things did not improve soon he would have to think about finding some other kind of gainful employment. His needs were not excessive, his one vice being tobacco; other than that he lived the kind of frugal existence that would have shamed a wandering Sufi.

Ahead of him lay the prospect of trawling once more round his usual contacts in search of an opening of some kind. That and avoiding Umm Ali, whose patience regarding her long-overdue rent was beginning to wear thin.

Somewhere far away, he heard a voice calling him back to the present. Stirring finally, and realising that he was not going to be able to avoid his landlady, Makana tried to think what excuse he might possibly use this time. In all likelihood she had heard every one of his stories before, many of them more than once. With a sigh, he crossed the deck and peered down at the small, happily plump woman wearing faded, raggedy clothes and a grubby scarf tied around her hair. Umm Ali stood barefoot in the muddy field holding an armful of fat aubergines to her ample bosom.

'You have visitors, *ya bash-muhandis*,' she sang out, with all the ceremony of a courtier making an announcement in the palace of Haroun al-Rashid. Makana could tell that she was excited about something. The rather giddy pitch to her voice suggested she could smell money, which was not a bad thing, generally, as it would have to go past him before it got to her. With a wave of gratitude, Makana walked down the stairs to the lower deck. He stepped through the cabin door to find his living space had shrunk.

Nasser's High Dam at Aswan had marked an end to the annual flooding of the Nile, but some years, when it was particularly dry and the river level dropped, Makana's floor was somewhat less than flat. It meant looking at the world from rather a strange tilt, although he reflected that this was not such a bad thing altogether. Today, however, the floor was affected by a factor it had never encountered before.

The man standing in the middle of the room had clearly been well fed since birth. He had a sizeable girth and a very stout neck, on top of which was a rather small and perfectly spherical head. It looked like a stone about to roll down a very large hill. Underneath all that corpulence, however, Makana suspected there was a good deal of solid muscle. He looked like he could have eaten the boat for breakfast. Also, he was wearing a suit. Not many people stepped on to the *awama* wearing a suit. Makana began to understand the reason for Umm Ali's excitement. It wasn't much of a suit, the kind you might pick off the rack at Omar Effendi's – the state-run department stores. Makana had one himself somewhere. But this man looked uneasy, as if his bulk was about to burst the seams at any moment. His expression said he would have been more at home directing a donkey to and from a muddy field. He was cultivating a rather silly little moustache to lend him an air of sophistication, but the stains on his trousers said he had eaten fava beans with olive oil for breakfast, just like the rest of the country.

'Would you mind standing further over to that side?' Makana asked. 'Only the boat tilts if there is too much weight on the outside.'

The gorilla stared back at him impassively. Either he did not understand or he didn't like being told what to do. The thick brows furrowed angrily and he glared back as though pondering a profound metaphysical dilemma. It was such an alarming expression that Makana burned his finger on the lit match he was holding. The man's fists were balled up tightly – clearly he was the type who resorted to words only when physical violence was ruled out. Before either of them could move or speak, however, another man stepped in over the threshold.

His suit was in an entirely different category and certainly not purchased at Omar Effendi's. A more likely guess might have been one of the fancy boutiques of Paris or London. For the price of that suit Makana could have bought the whole house-boat, sent Umm Ali home to her village a happy woman, and still had enough change to buy himself a whole new wardrobe. The man inside this suit was slim and naturally elegant. Around sixty, Makana guessed, with his hair combed back from his fine, even features in a smooth white wave. He glanced around the place with the curiosity of a man who finds himself inexplicably inside the monkey cage at the zoo. Then he snapped his fingers and the big man turned and left without a word, which was good news for a number of reasons, mostly because the floorboards seemed to heave a sigh of relief. In place of the blank expression of the big man, the new arrival was wearing a thin, unpleasant smile that Makana realised wasn't a smile at all, but a grimace of distaste. Whatever he was smoking actually had tobacco in it by the smell of it. Makana took a step sideways and flicked his valuable second Cleopatra of the day through the low window out of pure shame.

'Why the dramatic entrance?'

'It's his job,' said the slim man, distractedly. 'You are alone, I

9

take it?' He circled a hand in the air. There was a lot of gold on that hand. Makana had a frying pan hanging in the kitchen about the size of that wristwatch. It answered any nagging queries he still had about the purpose of the gorilla. If you were going to walk around with that much gold on display, you would need a big friend.

'I'm alone. Are you going to explain what this is all about?'

The slim man seemed to be in a hurry to leave, now that he had seen the place.

'I am just the messenger. Mr Hanafi himself will explain.'

Makana kept his mouth shut. He didn't want to look stupid.

'I'll get dressed,' he said.

He went into the bedroom and found his best shirt, picking up the jacket that hung from a nail on the back of his bedroom door and dusting it down for a moment before giving up with a sigh and pulling it on.

Umm Ali trailed alongside them up the path that led from the *awama* to the road, still clutching her aubergines in her skirts.

'Everything is all right, I hope, *ya bash-muhandis*?'

'Everything is fine, thank you.'

'*Al-hamdoulilah*, thank God.' She was talking to Makana but her eyes never left the other man, whom she clearly suspected of all kinds of deviousness.

'May the Lord preserve you.'

'And may He watch over you and yours, Umm Ali.'

It wasn't hard to spot the visitors' car. When they came up on to the road there was a queue of battered vehicles stacking up, trying to get a good look at it. A steady stream of earthy comments was being flung at it. The big man in the cheap suit climbed impassively behind the wheel. Makana thought it was one of those Mercedes they used to call a 'ghost' because they are so silent and had no number to identify the model, but his knowledge of cars was probably as outdated as the pyramids. When they got inside the big white car the locks on the doors clicked shut and Makana discovered another possible reason for the nickname. Once inside the dark interior, the air conditioning and the tinted windows cut off the outside world. It was like entering another dimension – a spirit world where nothing could touch you, physically or otherwise. This is how the rich live, he thought as he settled himself into the plush seat. Out of sight of the rest of us.

Chapter Two

As they drove, Makana tried to recall what he knew about the man he was being summoned to meet. The name Saad Hanafi was not unfamiliar to him, just as it was not unfamiliar to anyone in the country who had eyes and ears. Umm Ali would have passed out in a dead faint if she had heard that name uttered on her *awama*. Saad Hanafi was one of the richest men in Egypt. He was also one of the most influential. His interests ranged from substantial stakes in a handful of foreign automobile franchises, to include frozen-food lines, insurance companies, a good deal of real estate . . . and, most important of all, a football team.

In this world, it seemed, if you wanted to assure yourself of a seat in the temple among the great and godly, owning your own football team greatly improved your chances. And whereas most teams were associated with one particular part of the city or another, the Hanafi DreemTeem represented the aspirations of millions. This was what he really offered: a dream that everyone could share. In a draw held once a month, he gave away an apartment to some fortunate person. On television you could watch them screaming and fainting as they were given the news. They wailed and howled and fell to the ground. They tore at their hair and jumped up and down. People supported Hanafi's team because they wanted something to believe in.

From what they printed in the papers, his own life story was itself something of a fairy tale. It was referred to over and over again, despite the detractors who claimed that, like so many tales swirling through the air like the dust in this country, it was more myth than fact. The papers printed the story because it was a fable people wanted to believe in – needed to even, in these hard times.

According to legend, the man who now dined with kings and presidents, who ate off silver platters, whose water flowed out of gold taps, had started out in life plucking bricks from a hot oven in a small muddy village in the Delta. Children are used for this task because they have small hands and because they are nimble and quick. An older person would get burned. By the age of thirteen he was trawling the streets of Cairo collecting scrap metal. Eventually, through hard work and good fortune, so the story went, he began acquiring apartments, running his own construction company.

There was a darker version of this fairy tale, in which Hanafi figured as a common *bultagi*, a thug, but even this legend had been bent out of shape, smoothed over by countless reiterations. He stole from the rich and gave to the poor, they said. As a teenager he ran a small gang of hoodlums. They robbed merchants and broke into warehouses. If you wanted someone roughed up, or even killed, they would take care of it for a price. Hanafi, they said, was never caught because he kept people loyal to him. He redistributed his ill-gotten wealth among the less well off, and in return the inhabitants of those neighbourhoods saw him as a hero, defending him to the death. Families who could not afford to pay the rent were allowed to stay on and pay when they could. Children never went hungry to bed. If you went to him for a favour, he would always help. If you had a sick child in need of medicine or the services of a doctor, he would take care of that for you as well. Everyone was in debt to Saad Hanafi, even the authorities. Police inspectors would arrive home to find a fat sheep tethered to their front door for the Eid el-Adha sacrifice. And since police inspectors never made enough money anyway, it was natural that soon he had many loyal friends on that side of the law too. By the time he was in his twenties he was running a protection racket, using muscle to buy any property he was interested in. There were nasty stories about how he'd dealt with those who refused to sell at the price he offered. Tales of stubborn tenants falling off rooftops, or under the wheels of trains.

In the 1970s when Sadat was in power and busy liberalising the economy, making his friends rich in the process, Hanafi was getting into his stride as a semi-respectable businessman. Pretty soon he owned large chunks of the city, knocking down ageing villas and throwing up apartment blocks with alarming rapidity. Most of Heliopolis was his, if you believed the stories. He used the same hard-headed tactics as in his early days. Newly acquired political leverage allowed him to bulldoze through any laws that got in his way.

Hanafi had worked hard to distance himself from his shady beginnings, but those old rumours still lingered like the early-morning *shabour* that hung over the city. The DreemTeem was part of his PR makeover. His face was everywhere, smiling down from billboards like a venerable old patriarch, offering up bowls of steaming *ful medamas* and *taamiya* as an offering. The father of the nation, as he liked to see himself, putting food on the tables of the people. Hanafi was an institution, as much a part of the national panorama as the pyramids – as one sycophantic journalist after another kept repeating, thinking flattery would get

14

them everywhere, which it often did. Hanafi had the newspapers in his pocket; without his sponsorship entire television programmes would disappear. If he decided to run for president tomorrow, people said, he would win hands down . . . assuming the current President approved, of course. Saad Hanafi sold dreams, or rather one dream in particular: the dream that anyone could wake up one morning and find themself living on top of the world in a fine palace . . . even though there was as much chance of that actually happening as there was of the sun sailing across the sky in a boat.

'You are rather an unconventional man, Mr Makana.'

He turned his attention to the upright figure sitting beside him. The man in the fancy suit carried himself with style. He wore expensive cologne that made Makana wonder if he himself should have devoted a little more time to his preparations for this meeting.

'How exactly did you come by my name?'

'Oh, you come highly recommended, by an old acquaintance.' The slim man smiled reassuringly in a way that made Makana dislike him all over again.

They drove quickly south alongside the river, the gorilla using the horn the way he might have cracked a whip, sending other road users scattering to left and right. The centre of Hanafi's empire overlooked the Orman botanical gardens – fittingly, perhaps, as they had once been part of the Khedive Ismail's private grounds. The building itself was a blunt pinnacle of concrete and glass that seemed to hang in the air in defiance of gravity. Vines and fronds draped the many tiered balconies, stacked up like verdant steps leading to the sky. They called to mind the Hanging Gardens of Babylon or some other such ancient wonder. It wasn't hard to believe that the people living in a place like this eventually started to think of themselves as gods. The other apartments in the building were occupied by ageing divas and film stars, directors and magnates of one kind or another, plus the odd African dictator hiding from justice. Lesser beings, one and all, content to perch their tents on a ledge beneath the enigma that was Saad Hanafi. The upper floors were reserved for the man himself. A tower of shimmering luxury rising out of a city flooded with poverty. A fairy-tale castle in the clouds. Makana knew the building. He'd passed by it enough times and had looked up and wondered like everyone else what life would look like from up there. He had never imagined he would one day find out.

As they approached alongside the river, Makana noted how the building resembled a medieval fortress. A *burj* from the days of the Mamluks. Only it wasn't an invading army they were worried about these days, but the millions of hungry people who might one day grow tired of filing dutifully past the front door every day. It was anonymous and complete unto itself. The neighbours were several four-star hotels and a handful of despondent animals in the khedive's old zoo across the street – a dusty and dilapidated reminder of that other empire which had pitched camp on this same river bank some two centuries before.

The silent car didn't pause in the street but instead swooped straight down a ramp, like a big white bird, past a barrier and a vigilant security guard and into a subterranean parking area. Rows of cars were lined up on either side along the walls. Straight ahead was an extra-wide lift. As they approached, the driver pressed a button.

'Open sesame,' muttered Makana, as the doors slid aside and the long white car slipped into the waiting lift. Without anyone moving a muscle, they began to rise silently through the building. When they came to a halt Makana climbed out and followed the slim man through a door which led straight into a wide living area. The sensation was rather like stepping on to a cloud. Milky-white sheets of marble stretched away in every direction. You could have ridden a camel through the place without needing to lower your head. Two giant glazed ceramic leopards stood guard by the entrance. A reminder that when you had all the money in the world, you didn't need taste.

'This way.'

Makana followed obediently, noticing as he walked how dusty and scuffed his shoes looked against all that polished stone. The penthouse was roughly horseshoe-shaped, with windows on one side that curved around a large terrace. In the middle of the room the ceiling bulged into a high cupola below which hung an enormous glass chandelier. Through the sliding glass doors beyond was an oval of clear blue water. The pool area was crowded with mock-Roman pillars and Greek sculptures, marshalled by parallel rows of sphinxes in red marble.

They trekked across a wide salon divided into various levels, and all cluttered with more of the same – ceramic creatures, wooden Nubian attendants in pharaonic costume, stone statues of Isis and Osiris that looked as though they ought to be under lock and key in the National Museum, along with accompanying sets of sofas, chairs, television sets, bars, dining tables and even a roulette wheel. The furniture alone would have been enough to sink Makana's humble home.

At the far end they reached a wide arch with mahogany double doors set into it. A statue of an Arab swordsman wielding a scimitar stood guard to either side, looking suitably ferocious. The doors opened as they approached and Makana found himself ushered into an enormous study. There were shelves along the walls, lined with more items that probably should have been in glass cases with labels on them, and cabinets full of books, all looking fresh and clean, as if no human hand had ever touched them except to dust them down once in a while. A complete lionskin was nailed to the panelled wall between the shelves and a niche which contained a series of framed photographs. Makana paused to examine these. They revealed a small, ugly, fat man with a mottled face, in the company of several of the world's best-known presidents, prime ministers, royal personages, Arab sheikhs, with a few stars of stage and screen thrown in for good measure. The same man could be seen in the company of a group of football players, holding up a shirt featuring the DreemTeem logo and lettering in English and Arabic. A long beige leather sofa took up the left-hand side of the room while at the far end stood a huge desk made of ebony, supported by two pairs of enormous gold pedestals embellished with elephant tusks. Upon the desk stood several frames containing more family portraits. In one black-and-white photo a much younger and slimmer Hanafi appeared, wearing a toothbrush moustache, accompanied by a stout woman and three girls of varying ages. The next, taken some years later, showed him wearing a pair of outsized sunglasses and a plaid jacket, in the company of a slim woman holding a boy by the hand. A third picture showed him surrounded by his four daughters, now grown up.

'All of these pictures look somewhat dated.'

An expression of irritation passed over the slim man's face.

'Mr Hanafi's two marriages ended, sadly. The first Mrs Hanafi passed away many years ago, although he enjoys an excellent relationship with his daughters.' He indicated the black-and-white picture of the stout woman with the three girls.

Makana leaned forward to examine the four girls in the last

picture. There seemed to be quite an age difference between them. He turned his attention to the photograph next to it, of the woman holding a little boy by the hand.

'And this one?'

'His second wife and his only son. They were tragically killed in a car accident.'

'He doesn't seem to have had much luck in that department.'

'If you don't mind . . .'

The slim man gestured and Makana followed him out through some open glass doors that gave on to a raised deck covered with bright green artificial grass.

Good living had taken its toll on Saad Hanafi. The same small, ugly man who featured in the photographs was clumsily wielding a golf club. It swung back and forth a few times, like the wayward hand of an errant clock, and then struck the tiny white ball with a hard, powerful clip that sent it arching up into the air. It vanished over the end of the terrace in the direction of the river. Saad Hanafi clearly didn't bother retrieving them and Makana wondered how much damage you could do with a golf ball dropping from a great height. The slim man motioned for Makana to remain silent while Hanafi teed up again for his next shot. A servant wearing white gloves bent down to place another ball. Hanafi made a few tentative swings, then wound himself back and swung the club. This time his aim was off and the ball flew up at an angle, causing the attendant to duck, before clipping one of the Greek statues and finally smashing into the glass screen at the far end with a splintering crash. Disgusted with his own performance, Hanafi tossed the club aside.

'I'll never understand this game,' he spat, turning to look Makana up and down with a look of undisguised contempt. 'Is this him?'

'This is Mr Makana,' the slim man confirmed with a barely perceptible nod.

No time was wasted on further introductions. Hanafi led the way back inside his office. Taking a towel proffered by his assistant, he wiped his brow. Saad Hanafi's face was lumpy and disgruntled-looking. The wispy moustache and the few remaining strands of hair on his head were dyed an inky blue-black. His skin had a greyish tint to it, as though he had been soaking in muddy water for a long time. A tray of cold drinks had been set on the table and he helped himself, draining a glass of fruit juice in one long draught and smacking his fleshy lips together.

'Do you have a family, Mr Makana?' When there was no immediate reply, Hanafi glanced up. He slowly set down the glass and began to remove his golfing gloves. 'Tell me something about yourself.'

'What would you like to know?'

'Gaber here says you were a policeman . . . that you came to this country for political reasons. Is that correct?' His voice was like gravel churning steadily in a cement mixer.

'I didn't have much choice in the matter.'

'Would you describe yourself as an idealistic man, Mr Makana?' There was no warmth in the rigid smile on Hanafi's face.

'I'm not sure I follow,' he said, meeting the other man's gaze without flinching.

'Sudan and Egypt are brothers, of course, so you will always be welcome in this country, but anyone working for me leaves his political ideas at the door. Do you have a problem with that?'

'Not yet,' said Makana.

The sneer on Hanafi's face suggested a man who relished confrontation. He took another moment to size Makana up again and then flipped a finger in the direction of a low seat as he went round to the other side of the desk and settled back into a high winged chair. Makana sat down.

'I have a problem with one of my players . . .'

Makana was not particularly interested in football. To his mind, one person kicking a ball was pretty much as good as another, though he knew that wasn't how a lot of people saw it. The idea that a player could be a cause for concern was news to him.

'What's the problem?'

'He has disappeared. Gone missing.'

Makana waited. Hanafi glared at him. He seemed annoyed that his words weren't producing more of a response.

'I'm not talking about just any player. This is Adil Romario.'

Even Makana had heard of Adil Romario. The DreemTeem star player's face was everywhere, even more prominent than that of old man Hanafi himself. There was nothing under the sun Adil Romario did not appear to endorse with a bright smile that was far whiter than Allah had ever intended any man's teeth to be. Cars, soft drinks, telephones, clothes . . . along with all kinds of strange snacks that kids got fat spending their parents' money on.

'He has one of the most well-known faces in the country. How could he disappear?'

'If I knew that I wouldn't need your help,' grunted Hanafi.

'How long has he been gone?'

Gaber stepped in then. 'Ten days ago Adil was due to come here for dinner. He never turned up. Since then he has missed every practice session and does not appear to have slept in his home.'

'Ten days is a long time. He could be anywhere in the world.'

'He didn't take his passport with him,' said Gaber. 'And his car is gone too.'

'So you think he's still in the country. Why did you wait so long to start looking?'

'There is the small matter of the press.' Gaber wrung his hands. 'Our reputation is at stake. We don't want the whole country to start speculating about this.'

Makana's gaze wandered back and forth between the two men for some hint of what they were not telling him.

'Presumably you want to get him back?'

'What kind of a question is that?' snarled Hanafi. 'Of course I want him back.'

'Then I don't understand . . .'

Hanafi heaved in a deep breath. He was clearly making a conscious effort to control himself. Gaber opened his mouth to speak, but the old man silenced him with a jerk of his hand. He leaned forward and spread his stubby hands on top of the desk.

'As I am sure you can appreciate, Mr Makana, no man gets where I am today without making a few enemies. I can trust no one. The moment I am seen to display any weakness, they will be on me like a pack of hyenas.'

'I take it this is not the first time he's gone missing then?'

A wave of exhaustion passed over Hanafi's face. Gaber was staring at the floor. He shook his head.

'But never for this long.'

'Where does he usually go, when he disappears like this?'

Again it was Gaber who answered. Hanafi seemed unable to muster the energy.

'A player like Adil is under a lot of pressure. It's easy to understand. Sometimes he just needs to get away. He goes to the beach, to Sharm el-Sheikh to dive, or else to Africa . . . Mombasa maybe. Places where he can relax and nobody knows him. But he always leaves word, or gets in touch.' Gaber held Makana's gaze. 'It's never been this long with no contact.'

'That still doesn't explain the delay.' Makana openly studied the coarse features of the powerful man sitting behind the desk. 'Did something happen? An argument . . . a disagreement about money?'

'No, nothing like that,' growled Hanafi.

'Okay, then why don't you tell me why you *think* he disappeared?'

'I don't know.'

Makana got slowly to his feet. The two men stared at him.

'I'm not sure I'm the right man for this job.'

'Sit down!' growled Hanafi. 'Don't you know who I am?'

'Me and about seventy million people outside that window.'

'You should think very carefully before you turn me down.'

'Is that a threat?'

Behind him Gaber said quietly, 'I wouldn't have thought a man in your position could afford to turn down an offer such as this.'

Makana turned to look at him. He hadn't thought it possible to like this man any less, but he realised now that he had been wrong. This whole set-up didn't ring true. All his instincts told him just to walk away, but instead he said, 'I can't help you if you are not going to tell me everything.'

Hanafi chewed his lip for a moment and then relented, waving Makana back down into his chair.

'Okay, all right. *Maalish*. Sit down.' He took a deep breath. 'We argued.'

Makana sat down again. 'What about?'

'It's stupid . . . it really makes no sense at all.' Hanafi examined his outspread hands. 'We argued about my health.'

'Your health?'

'The boy worries about me . . . about my health. Adil felt I should be taking it easy, not working so hard. The fact is that I hardly do any work nowadays. Gaber takes care of most personal things for me, and the company runs itself. Adil wanted me to take a holiday, go away on safari to Kenya, you know? Hunting animals. Me!' Hanafi laughed, suddenly a sentimental old man. 'I never took a holiday in my life. I wouldn't know myself, shooting animals and chasing whores . . .' He shrugged. 'Anyway, that was it. We argued. He went home and the next day he was gone. I haven't seen or heard from him since. It was my fault, I know that. I am used to people always doing what I tell them.'

Humility was the last thing Makana had been expecting from this man.

'I understand your need to keep this quiet, but why don't you just call one of your friends in the police? You must have enough of them in your pocket, people who can be discreet.'

Hanafi gave Makana a beady look. Then he got to his feet and paced over to the open doors, looking out at his little practice range, his terrace, and the city beyond – a good chunk of which was also his. A lot of people worked their whole lives and died without ever having a view like that, but perhaps from where Hanafi was standing it looked less like heaven and more like a prison.

'You would be surprised how few people I can trust, Mr Makana.'

There followed a long silence. Makana glanced at Gaber, who appeared to be waiting for his boss to carry on.

'Adil was just a boy when I found him. I don't know what it was about him . . .' The broad face split into something resembling a smile. 'He made me laugh. Just like that. A little boy. He

24

reminded me so much of myself. He wasn't afraid of anything. A natural talent. Wild. The word "discipline" was lost on him. My mind told me he would be trouble, but my heart told me otherwise. I have always acted on instinct and I was not wrong in Adil's case. He has turned out to be the star of our team.'

The way he spoke, it sounded as if Hanafi was talking about a favourite son. Gaber shifted his feet before breaking into the conversation.

'The Hanafi DreemTeem is one of the most popular commercial football teams in the region, and also one of the most successful. The fan base is not limited to this country. We have sponsors all over the Middle East.'

'So, losing Adil would damage your image?'

'Not just our image. Our business depends on investors. Of course,' Gaber cleared his throat, 'that's not the main reason we are concerned about Adil's welfare.'

'Of course not,' said Makana. 'I take it there has been no indication of kidnapping, no ransom demand?'

'Nothing of the kind.'

'No threats?'

'Not that we know of.' Gaber was adamant.

'Will you find my boy for me?'

Makana's attention was drawn back towards the window where Hanafi stood, his face crumpled as if he was in great pain.

'We haven't talked about a fee.'

'A lot of people would help me for nothing,' grunted Hanafi, returning to his usual self as he approached the desk. Those malevolent little eyes fixed themselves on Makana as he settled himself down again, reaching into a drawer for a pen and paper. It was a plump, gold-plated fountain pen. The kind you might write big cheques with.

'I am going to write a number on this piece of paper. For every week that it takes you to find Adil, I shall cut it in half.' He handed over the paper and Makana looked at the number.

'People must love working for you.'

'Motivation is easy to buy, Mr Makana, loyalty is another matter.'

Makana got to his feet. 'Excuse me, I'm getting poorer by the minute.'

As he seized his hand in a firm grip, Hanafi reached out for Makana's shoulder and pulled him in towards him. He had surprising strength for a man of his age. Makana found himself unable to ease away. The scent of Hanafi's hair oil was filling his nostrils; he could see the swollen blood vessels in his eyes, and then, as the grip relented, Makana saw the shadow of something else cross the older man's face. He struggled to work out what it was.

'Someone is trying to get to me through the boy,' Hanafi whispered, staring off into the distance. 'But the man hasn't been born yet who can scare Saad Hanafi. I will find them and I will crush them like insects.' Letting go of Makana's hand abruptly, he turned back towards the window again.

'Gaber will give you everything you need.' He held up a stubby finger. 'Do right by me, Makana, and your life will change for ever . . . for the better.'

As they walked back across the white marble clouds Gaber handed Makana a large brown envelope.

'This contains all the necessary details you will need. Addresses, telephone numbers, etcetera. There is also a letter of introduction, signed by me, which gives you access to any level of the company's operations. It suggests that you have been hired to write a biography of Adil. If anyone gives you any trouble, ask them to call me.'

'A biography? Who came up with that idea?'

'I did.'

Just then Makana's eye was caught by the reflection of light on the ceiling. It drew his attention to the pool in the centre of the terrace. A girl in her twenties, whom he guessed to be one of Hanafi's daughters, was swimming lengths. She was a good strong swimmer. He watched her climb out of the water on the other side and disappear between the rows of sphinxes. He turned back to find Gaber waiting for him by another lift.

'Is that one of the daughters or the latest wife?'

'That is Soraya, Mr Hanafi's only daughter from his second wife.' Gaber sighed. 'Do not allow yourself to become distracted, Makana. Mr Hanafi was not joking when he said that your life could change. If you are successful then it is quite possible we could find you a permanent position in the security department of Hanafi Enterprises. He believes in rewarding people who are dedicated and hard-working. You would never have to worry about money again.'

'How long have you been with him?' asked Makana.

'A very long time,' said Gaber.

'He must be a difficult man to work for.'

'Mr Hanafi has his own particularities but he is a fair man, as I am sure you will discover.'

This lift was smaller than the one they had come up in but the doors opened to reveal a space big enough to park a small car in. He looked at Gaber steadily.

'That is a very generous offer, of course, but I'm going to need a little money for expenses to start with.'

Without blinking an eye, Gaber reached into his jacket pocket and produced another, smaller envelope. Makana peered inside to find a thick bundle of banknotes.

'When that is finished, come back to me.' He held out his hand to shake Makana's. 'We are counting on you to resolve this issue as quickly as possible. This matter is weighing heavily on Mr Hanafi's health. Every day counts.'

The lift whisked Makana down to the ground floor, smoothly and swiftly. He felt something like disappointment when the doors opened and he found himself in a lobby with a security guard in uniform, a tall man with a belly which betrayed his fondness for eating.

'Tell me,' Makana said as the guard walked him to the door, 'how much does an apartment in this place cost?'

The guard eyed him warily. 'I don't think you want to know the answer to that, sir.'

'No.' Makana nodded. 'On second thoughts, maybe I don't.'

As he came out into the street he bumped into someone hurrying along the pavement: a young man wearing spectacles. He pulled up abruptly and stared at Makana intently for a long moment before finally muttering an apology and moving on. People even look at you differently when you come out of a place like that, thought Makana. The street seemed hotter, more noisy and dusty than he remembered. It made everything he had just seen feel all the more unreal, as if he had dreamed the whole episode.

It took him a dozen steps before he remembered that he could now afford a taxi, so he stepped over to the roadside and waved. As he climbed into the rickety car, that moment when Hanafi had grasped his hand and held it tightly came back to him. He knew now what he had seen in the tycoon's face: fear.

Chapter Three

Despite the sudden improvement in his fortunes, Makana still had a few lingering doubts about working for such an illustrious client. He knew of Hanafi's reputation and was in no doubt that the great man could be ruthless and dangerous. On the other hand, it didn't seem that he himself had much choice but to take the case. Besides that, Makana was intrigued by the fact that they should ask him to find Adil Romario. Hanafi's response to that question had not been satisfactory. Undoubtedly, he had enemies and would not be keen on exposing any sign of vulnerability, but still a man like that had not survived for so long by bowing to his fears. It was also difficult to imagine anyone mad enough to try and make an enemy of him, particularly now that he was such a public figure. He had the ear of politicians. It was said that even the Pharaoh himself, as the President was often referred to, consulted him on matters of state. Flattering though it was to think that his reputation as a man of integrity might have spread to such lofty heights, Makana was inclined to believe there was more to it than that. Hanafi was afraid of something, something so big and dark that he couldn't trust any of his usual contacts inside the police.

Makana stopped off at a place he sometimes used in Ezbekia Square. To all appearances it was simply a tiny booth under the flyover, run by a one-eyed man and his numerous family. It was open twenty-four hours a day and was no wider than a doorway. Someone was always there. On the shelves that extended themselves deep into the bowels of the crumbling building, however, there was everything you could possibly need, from candles to matches and batteries, to light bulbs and hosepipes, electric cables and plungers for blocked drains. There was every manner of tool and implement imaginable. A bottomless emporium with no end to it. The shopkeeper or one of his sons would disappear into the shadows and remain out of sight for several minutes before emerging with the heating element or the set of dental forceps requested by a customer.

Makana wanted nothing so complicated, although he had spent many an hour observing as they extracted more and more bizarre instruments from that tiny crack in the rock. Now he leaned against the high counter and reached for the telephone. The circular dial was fixed with a padlock which Goumri kindly removed. As he did so, Makana spotted a poster of Adil Romario stuck on the grubby wall behind him. He wondered why he had never noticed it before. It was an advertisement for some kind of green-coloured drink. Adil Romario smiled his beaming smile and held up his thumb while a girl in tight jeans sprayed water over him from a hosepipe.

'People say he will lend his name to anything,' Goumri muttered, following Makana's gaze. 'If I were in his shoes and they wanted to pay me to stand next to that donkey of a President, I wouldn't hesitate for a moment.'

Makana spent an hour calling anyone and everyone who might be able to shed some light on the matter of Hanafi's current situation. Firstly there was Nabil, a contact at *Al Ahram* newspaper. 'I want you to dig up what you can about Saad Hanafi and Adil Romario.'

'You're moving up in the world.'

'Keep it to yourself.'

'Does that mean I get paid this time?'

'What's happened to your sense of civic responsibility?'

'It's like everything else with today's inflation – it has shrunk.'

Amir Medani, a human rights lawyer he knew, talked at length of Hanafi's political connections: 'He practically has the government in his back pocket. If he needs a law changed for one of his building projects, all he needs to do is make one phone call.'

Others said Hanafi was good at making enemies. If a journalist wrote something bad about him, he could expect to find himself out of work in a matter of days, sometimes hours. A contact in Bank Misr said Hanafi Enterprises was one of the strongest names on the Egyptian Stock Exchange. 'If you want some shares . . .' Makana declined the offer.

After that he felt hungry and decided that the sudden improvement in his financial situation, along with the comforting bundle of ready cash tucked into his pocket, ought to be celebrated in style. He had a few debts to settle, but his first priority was to treat himself to a decent meal. It took him ten minutes to walk to Aswani's restaurant.

As usual, an air of weary desolation hung over the place. A fan turned lazily over the deserted metal tables, and the buzz of white strip lighting competed with the urgent frenzy of flies trying to get into or out of the cooling cabinets where all manner of raw meat rested on steel trays. A small fat man waddled across the floor towards him. Ali Aswani bore a distinct resemblance to an oversized duck, apart from his big Turkish moustache whose bushy handlebars stood out stiffly to left and right like rabbit's ears. Makana chose a table in a corner at the back, where he could be undisturbed and keep an eye on the door at the same time.

As he went he swept up a well-creased copy of the day's newspaper. Ignoring the usual front-page stories glorifying the actions of various government ministers, the President's wife, etcetera, he turned to the sports pages. There he read that the DreemTeem was currently slipping down the league table. A columnist speculated on the reasons behind this; were the rumours of discontent within the team true? And where was their most famous player in this hour of need? After that Makana settled down to read carefully through the folder Gaber had given him. It contained photographs of Adil taken in a studio. They were the kind of official pictures you might see on a club wall. Makana had looked for missing people before, but never one as well known as this. Usually you were given a blurred snapshot, or an out-of-date passport picture, but here he had dozens of promotional shots. There was also a thick stack of newspaper clippings charting Adil Romario's rise to fame, from skinny teenager to muscular athlete. The early articles praised his skills, calling him a natural genius. Alongside many such articles were sheafs of adverts featuring endorsements by Adil Romario. It made Makana wonder just how much Hanafi Enterprises depended on him.

Soon Aswani began arriving bearing plates of sliced flat bread and tahini dip, along with a salad of fat green *girgir* leaves. Skewers of kofta were already sizzling on the grill. It was a while since Makana had allowed himself the luxury of coming here. Over the last few months he had simply been unable to afford it; though he knew Aswani was always happy to put it on his tab, Makana was wary of running up debts. Today was different and even Aswani noticed that, holding back as he approached, plates in hand, and cocking his head to scrutinise his customer.

'Are you working again?'

'I might even be able to pay you some of what I owe you.'

'I'll call the radio and television stations,' said Aswani with a weary sigh, setting down the dishes. 'They might be interested in the news.'

'You know I always settle up when I have money.'

'Maybe you're right,' said the other man, leaning back with his hands on his broad hips and staring up at the ceiling for a moment before shaking his head. 'No. It's been so long, I can't remember.'

'Just fetch your accounts book and we'll take care of it.'

'I swear I'll say the Mahgrib prayer twice today in your honour,' muttered Aswani as he turned to waddle away. Makana continued reading as he ate. The food here was simple but good. The place didn't look like much but the cook claimed he never served anything that he wouldn't be happy to eat himself. His broad girth was his best advertisement. 'I only eat here to keep up appearances,' he would say, whenever he was caught with his mouth full, which was often. 'Who would trust a cook as thin as a stick anyway?'

Makana turned back to the matter of Hanafi. A number of things had struck him as odd about this morning's meeting. First, there was the question of how they had managed to find him. Makana was under no illusions that his reputation was so good that he had been the obvious choice. Gaber had mentioned that Makana had been recommended. He hadn't said by whom. Then there was the fear he had seen in Hanafi's eyes. Did that have more to do with protecting himself than any concern about Adil, no matter how much he professed to care for him? Hanafi had hinted that he could trust no one in his inner circle. This implied that he suspected there was more to Adil's disappearance than a young man simply wanting to get away from it all. Had Adil become involved with someone, or rather the wife of someone? A business rival, say, or the wife of a diplomat or politician? Then there was the matter of their argument. Hanafi said that Adil had wanted him to take a holiday. Was that significant?

Makana looked up as Aswani returned, dismayed to see that he wasn't carrying any delicious skewers of kebab, and no sign either of the grubby piece of string threaded through countless strips of paper which he called his accounts book.

'Do you mind if I sit for a moment?' Aswani asked, gesturing at the chair opposite and then sitting down before waiting for an answer. Makana sat back and waited. Ali pushed the little round skullcap back on his head. 'This is something that has been troubling me.' His fat fingers twirled the ends of his moustache. He resembled a Turkish general mulling over which strategy to apply on the battlefield. 'You see the *afranji* woman who is sitting over there in the corner?'

Almost the only other customer in the place was a European woman who was sitting alone on the far side, virtually invisible against the brown-tiled wall. Thin and bony, in her forties, her appearance suggested someone who was down on her luck. Personal hygiene appeared not to be high on her list of priorities. Her hair was unkempt and her clothes dirty. She was chewing her nails and smoking a cigarette, all at the same time.

'What about her?' Makana dipped some bread into the sauce and chewed.

'Well, you know, it's a strange thing . . . I've seen her before. This is not the first time.'

'Maybe she likes your cooking. Is she always alone?'

'Always.'

Makana took another look. The woman appeared to be talking to herself. She stared into the air above her head, muttering, and then began scribbling in a notebook on the table in front of her. As he watched she suddenly began scratching out whatever was written there with furious slashes of her pen, grinding it back and forth across the page.

'A writer,' Makana concluded, 'she's including your establishment in a guide. You will be inundated with foreign customers in no time.'

'*Ya salam*, some detective you are!' Aswani leaned his elbows on the table. 'We get all sorts in here. Believe me, I've seen some of the craziest ones, but none ever disturbed me like this one does. I swear on my mother's grave.' He clutched Makana's arm. 'I'm afraid she's going to do something.'

'Something like what?' He widened his eyes dramatically.

'I can't say. It's just a feeling I have. She looks . . . lost. You know what will happen if a European woman gets herself into trouble? It will be bad for all of us.'

'I see.' Makana extricated his arm and reached for another piece of bread. 'What exactly do you want me to do?'

Aswani tilted his head. 'Perhaps you could just have a word with her.'

Makana chewed in silence as Aswani went on, 'Since you speak English and everything, you could just ask her what she is doing. If she's all right, then fine, no harm done. But if something happens to her it will be on my soul until Judgement Day.'

'Tell me, Ali, do you worry about all your customers like this?'

'You know I do,' he said, getting to his feet. 'Now let me go and see about your kofta, and eat what you want today. It's not going on the account.'

Makana sighed and pushed back his chair. It wasn't as if he needed a free meal at this point, or further distraction, but Ali had seen him through some dark times and if it would make him feel happier then Makana was obliged to make the effort.

'Excuse me,' he said, feeling rather foolish. The table was littered with tobacco and broken cigarettes. Ash was scattered over everything. There were several notebooks and sheafs of paper. The woman was lighting another cigarette as he spoke. She stiffened perceptibly. He smiled amiably. 'I couldn't help noticing that you seem worried about something . . .' Makana felt like a complete fool, realising as he spoke that this approach could easily be misconstrued. 'Is there some way I could help?'

The woman blew smoke away from her face. Her eyes fixed on him coldly. 'You speak very good English.'

'Well, thank you . . .' Makana gave a small bow.

'And so you will understand perfectly when I tell you to get lost, you creep?'

Makana's face was an awkward mask by now. Still, he managed to step back and dip his head gracefully. 'I understand perfectly. Sorry to bother you.' Then he spun on his heel and went back to his food. The woman could go to hell. At least he had done right by Ali . . . although, having seen her close up, he was convinced the cook had not been wrong. There was something the matter with that woman; she was clearly insane. Aswani arrived hotfoot from the grill, bearing Makana's reward, a huge mound of freshly grilled skewers of lamb.

'How did you get on?' He kept his voice low.

'You don't need to worry about her,' said Makana, reaching for the kofta which was always best when it came straight off the heat. 'I think she can take care of herself.'

The cook stood there fretting, completely forgetting what he was supposed to be doing. He started to wander back towards the kitchen.

'Ali?' Makana called him back and pointed.

'Sorry.' He set down the plate and disappeared, the fretful expression still fixed to his face. Makana returned to the folder as he continued to eat, only to have his concentration broken again a few minutes later.

'I'm sorry . . . about earlier.'

Without hesitation, the Englishwoman slid into the chair opposite Makana's.

'My behaviour was quite inexcusable. I'm sorry. I just don't . . .'

Her head was bowed. Makana shut the folder, silently cursing his luck.

'Are you hungry?'

'No, thank you,' she said. 'I just ate.'

'Would you like something to drink? Tea or coffee?' He pushed some plates aside and reached for his cigarettes.

'Tea would be fine.'

Makana signalled to Aswani. The woman sat with her hands clamped to the seat of her chair, staring down at the table. Makana had been convinced she was suffering from some form of mental illness, possibly depression of some kind. Now he saw that she was simply very unhappy.

'Are you writing a book?'

'A book?' She frowned deeply. 'Oh, that. No, I just keep a record of everything.'

Makana took a moment to study her more closely. She looked older than he had at first thought, although this might have been the result of her obvious distress. Skinny as a bird, with eyes that were red and swollen. Stress lines crimped the corners of her mouth. She smoked in quick nervous puffs. Makana imagined she was the type of hardy traveller who came to Egypt in search of authenticity. The kind who would never be satisfied with guided tours and pyramids, trips on a felucca and an evening of belly dancing. They came in pursuit of Flaubert, or some other romantic figure, in the spirit of the nineteenth-century European fascination with this part of the world. They wanted to see the real Egypt, to meet the people, to travel and eat among them. They wanted to maintain the illusion that the world was a state of mind, ruled by fluid borders, where everyone lived happily in freedom and equality. They neatly omitted to consider the privilege of free passage they carried in their back pocket like a magic charm, and the travellers' cheques and credit cards that went along with the passport. A real experience, hence the need to 'record' everything. She struck him as disillusioned and terribly sad at the same time.

The tea arrived. Aswani caught Makana's eye and gave him a brief nod of gratitude before moving away discreetly. Makana sighed. His entire life could be expended performing favours for friends and acquaintances. He would wind up a curiosity in a corner of the bazaar. Children would point him out and laugh. After what felt like a very long time, the woman began to speak. Her head was angled to one side so that she appeared to be addressing one corner of the table.

'Years ago, I came here with my little girl, Alice.'

She spoke in fits and starts. A shudder ran through her and one bony hand came up to her face as she sucked in another lungful of smoke. 'We were staying right across there, in a hotel overlooking the square.' She nodded over her shoulder. Makana sipped his tea. The woman's eyes looked up and met his. 'And then one day she disappeared.'

Makana set down his glass. 'How did it happen?'

'She was in the bedroom.' The woman was shaking her head repeatedly, as if the gesture might be enough to change the outcome of the story she was trying to tell. 'I don't know. One minute she was there, lying asleep, and the next . . .' The effort of speaking seemed to overcome her. She was silent for a long moment, staring at her hands clasped together on the table. 'They never found her.'

'How old was she?'

As she struggled to regain her composure, the woman's chin bobbed up and down.

'She was four at the time.'

'She couldn't have gone far.'

'No.' Her eyes came up to meet his. 'But she was gone. I never saw her again.'

Makana was silent for a long time. He told himself this was mere coincidence, that this woman he had never seen before in his life knew nothing about him or his past.

'When exactly did this happen?'

The woman began to speak and then stopped, pressing a hand to her mouth to stifle a cry and closing her eyes tightly. A tear squeezed out of her left eye and ran down to her chin where it hung for a moment before dropping to the table.

'Seventeen years ago this autumn.' She was fumbling for another cigarette. The packet was empty. 'It was when Sadat was killed. I remember that.' Makana pushed his Cleopatras across the table to her. 'I don't know why I'm telling you all this,' she went on. 'It's a little ridiculous to come back year after year expecting to find her. But that's the thing about having children – you can never give up.'

'I understand,' said Makana, unable to bring himself to say more.

'Do you, really?' The woman exhaled smoke into the air above her head, totally absorbed in her memory of that time. 'I was frantic. I ran round in circles. My head was spinning. Eventually the police came and . . . it was hopeless. Nothing helped. I kept thinking she would reappear, that I would look around and find her standing right behind me, with that same cheeky smile on her face. I never did.'

'What did you do then?'

'What could I do? In the end I went home. I went back to England and tried to carry on. It doesn't go away though, it never leaves you.' She pushed a hand through her unkempt hair. 'For some years I couldn't cope. It was so awful. Eventually, I got better. It took a long time, but I really believed that it was because of her, Alice, wishing me to recover so I could come and find her.'

'And that's what you did?'

'For the last few years I've been coming back regularly, going over the same old ground, hoping something will turn up.' She studied him closely for a moment. 'Do you have children?'

Makana paused. 'A daughter.'

She nodded as if she had expected this answer. Then she smiled. 'How is it that you speak such good English?'

'My wife,' said Makana, this time hesitating for only a brief moment. It got easier once you were over the initial hurdle. 'Muna. She did a postgraduate degree at London University. In botany.' He stopped speaking, suddenly uncomfortable. 'It was a long time ago.'

'People tell you there is nothing you can do, that it's best to leave it in the hands of the professionals. But it never is. Your child is just another name to them. The police . . . the embassy.' The woman glanced over her shoulder at the open doorway and the light in the square.

Makana took a deep breath and then started to gather up his things, putting the cuttings and photographs back in the folder, sliding the folder into the envelope.

'They all know me in the bazaar. I ask them the same questions every time and they nod and smile and ask me how I am doing, but they have nothing to tell me. I know that someone there knows something. I'm sure of it. I go round and round the streets, the stalls, the artisans. I can't shake off the feeling that I'm missing something, a secret door with Alice behind it.'

The woman fell silent. Makana reached for one of his own cigarettes and realised there were none left in the packet. He crumpled the paper quietly in his hand.

'Thank you for listening.' She gave a loud sniff and started to get to her feet. 'I'm sorry for taking up your time. Your food will be cold now.'

As she made to move away, some impulse caused Makana to reach into his pocket for one of his business cards. He held it out. 'If you need help with something, you can call me.'

She took the card absently without looking at it. 'Thanks. Sometimes I think that talking about her is the only way I can keep Alice alive. I suppose you'll understand that, being a father?'

Makana smiled but said nothing.

'And I'm sorry about the way I spoke to you earlier.'

'It really doesn't matter.'

'No. It was unforgivable.'

Makana watched the strange sad woman as she walked towards the door and disappeared from sight. He felt drained emotionally. All thoughts of Adil Romario had been driven from his head. He got to his feet and stumbled out into the open air.

Chapter Four

They were still with him. He would have liked to think they always would be, but he knew that wasn't true. Recently he had begun to feel almost as if they were taking leave of him, as their memory faded with time. But not today. Now he felt their presence more strongly than ever. They were here with him, in this crowd, their faces bobbing upon the sea of strangers around him, their voices in his ear.

Baba!

Turning instinctively, Makana stared down at the child, realising his mistake too late. It was always too late. The fleeting glimpse of a woman's back as she moved away from him, a little girl holding her hand, her face twisted back in his direction. For a brief moment the big round eyes, the thick hair falling in plaits around her ears, spoke to his heart, convincing him of the impossible, telling him this might have been Nasra. It was all he could do to stop himself from calling out.

Propelled by the need to get away from the Englishwoman and her loss, he felt himself being pulled in as he quickly crossed the square to plunge himself into the crowded narrow lanes of the bazaar, like a meteorite falling to earth, his heart pumping the old anger through his veins, through his muscles, until it burned itself out in the stifling air.

With all its noise and bluster, Cairo would always be alien to him. The gigantic bluffs of concrete, with their buttresses and pinnacles, were an unnatural landscape to a man who hailed from a small city of single-storey houses with open yards and dusty trees that blew green and lazy over the river at dusk. The trees here were stark, ashen silhouettes that belonged to a twilight world. The world he haunted now. Ghost trees to fit a ghost town. Makana was grateful to this metropolis for giving him shelter, for taking him in and giving him a chance to start again, but it would always be an uneasy relationship. This city whose whole history was an obsession with opposites. Night and day. The separation of the realm of the living from that of the dead, the Underworld. The flow of life from the river to the cosmos. It was an accumulation of burial mounds, *mastabas*, graves, pyramids . . . century upon century, dynasty upon dynasty.

For the last seven years Makana had been going through the slow process of learning to live again. In the manner of an invalid recovering after a bad accident, rediscovering the use of his limbs, learning the basics, one step at a time, coming back to life, adjusting to his new existence as a nonentity. A restless spirit in an unfamiliar world. Work, though it came in spasmodic, irregular bursts, and usually from unexpected directions, was a relief. He was doing the only thing he knew how to do. It allowed him to immerse himself in the land of the living; people's fears and hopes, their weaknesses and desires. Work he could deal with. It was the long lay-offs in between when he felt himself slipping back into the shadowlands. Interludes which occasionally stretched into extended droughts with no hint of rain for months. Interminable idleness that drove him almost to desperation. It was at those times the memories came crawling back into his mind; when the dead lay heavy on his chest, making it impossible some days to summon the energy to get out of bed.

In Makana's former life he had been a police officer. A good one. An inspector. It seemed to him now like another age, a previous incarnation. So remote and distant he sometimes wondered if he had dreamed the whole thing. It had not been a bad life. The cases that came his way were usually straightforward crimes of passion. Explosions of violence that in a brief instant transformed for ever the lives of victim and perpetrator alike. Most homicides were committed without forethought or planning. People killed those they were closest to: they killed their loved ones, their wives or husbands, brothers or neighbours. They killed them in the heat of the moment, with a kitchen knife snatched up in anger, with a brick, a hammer, or by cramming a pillow over their heads and holding it down until there was no more struggling. They doused them in kerosene while they were sleeping and struck a match, standing out in the yard to watch the flames darting through the wooden slats of the window shutters. People killed because they could no longer stand to go on. Abuse, hatred, suffering in silence, rage, jealousy . . . Makana would find the culprits. He would wear them down until they confessed. Often it didn't take much. They came running to the police station covered in blood, trying to rip out their own hearts in their anguish and pain. It made you wonder just what kind of creature man was.

All of this took place against a backdrop of violence on a larger scale: the civil war that was as interminable as it was absurd. There were no winners, only losers, hundreds of thousands of them. They lost their villages and homes, their land and livestock, their children and parents, husbands and wives.

Occasionally, it spilled over into the life of a police inspector. A soldier returned from the front to discover that his wife had remarried in his absence. He had lost an arm in the war, but that didn't stop him slaughtering his entire family with a bayonet. Makana had never seen so much blood, the house reeked of the stuff. A curtain of flies flew into his face as he ducked in through the doorway of the bedroom.

Flexibility and patience, these were the two key virtues required to do his job. There were robberies and smuggling gangs – contraband alcohol and tobacco brought in over the border from Eritrea or down from the Red Sea. Sometimes more serious items, such as weapons. The economy was bankrupt. The shops were empty, even basic goods hard to come by. There were demonstrations over the price of sugar and bread. The weekly salary of an ordinary policeman would buy you a kilo of tomatoes. Things were bad, and the politicians were worse than useless. They buried their heads in the sand and offered platitudes and pathos. People managed somehow. They battled on, they helped one another. Once a week you had to get up at four in the morning and line up at the petrol station to collect your fuel ration. They would all go, his daughter Nasra crawling into the back seat to doze while they waited. He and Muna would spend the night talking in the car until they opened the pumps. It reminded them of when they were courting. Nights in the petrol queue became their special time together.

Then one day the country awoke to find a new regime had arrived, announcing that the solution to all their problems lay in a more rigorous embrace of Islam. The self-styled Government of National Salvation promised to overturn the hierarchies of class and ethnicity to make all equal under the sun of religious faith. Salvation? wondered Makana. What kind of salvation?

'That's politics,' Mek Nimr, his then sergeant, had remarked. 'Never mix politics with police work.'

Everything was always so simple to Mek Nimr. In retrospect, perhaps Makana might have benefited from paying more attention to him back then. Mek Nimr saw what was going on more clearly than his superior officer. He was swift to take advantage of the opportunities. Makana never saw trouble coming until it was too late.

With the new regime everything changed, even the business of murder. Never mix politics with police work . . . only now everything was politics. Makana's department was placed under the command of Major Idris, a stiff-necked military man who not only knew nothing about police work, but didn't want to know. He didn't have time for it. To Major Idris, it was all a matter of filling out the right forms and keeping his nose clean. A party member, he was on his way up. Nothing else mattered. Catching criminals was certainly not a priority. Praying was a priority. Keeping his superiors happy was a priority. With Idris came a flood of similar types, Makana had no idea where from. He had never seen them before. They seemed more concerned with flushing out potential critics of the regime than pursuing law breakers.

It wasn't just the formalities which had changed, it was the very nature of crime itself. You picked up a victim by the side of the road with a bullet in his head, or a man with water in his lungs lying in the middle of the desert, and you asked yourself, how could this have happened? Nobody really wanted to know. As Major Idris reminded him more than once: 'You're a smart man, Makana. Smart enough to know that if I tell you these things are out of our hands then there is no need for you to worry yourself further.'

Muna tried to persuade him to see sense. They sat together at night in the yard and whispered in the dark, fearful of the neighbours overhearing their words across the wall. Everyone was afraid of informers. Another sign of the times.

'You rationalise everything,' she chided him gently. 'For you it always has to make sense.'

'Am I supposed to stop thinking about catching criminals and start protecting them?'

'It's a warning. Don't you see?'

'I can't just look away.'

'Why not?'

'Because I uphold the law. That's my job. They can't tell me that the law goes only so far and no further. Idris is an idiot.'

'Idris is trying to help you. If you looked at it like that, you might be better off.'

He still remembered her face at those times – arguing fiercely because she was convinced she could show him what he couldn't see, and often she was right. When she knew she was not getting through a kind of lost smile appeared on her face, as if she was seeing ahead to some time in the future when she was no longer around and he would be remembering her.

It was a good marriage. They complemented one another. Their life together ran a smooth, untroubled course. The only difficulty they had was in starting a family. It took five years for her to become pregnant. And when Nasra finally came, she nearly cost Muna her life. They promised one another they would never go through that again. It wasn't worth it. They called her their little victory – Nasra. Only one? people asked. And they smiled and said, in this case, one is enough.

Makana told himself that he didn't believe in fate, or even God, if truth be told. But how could you explain the sequence of events if it was not pre-ordained in some way? He didn't know where it began, but he could certainly recall the moment when he began to see that things around him were changing, evolving, slipping out of his grasp.

He walked on through the old bazaar, looking for the face of a child he knew he would never find.

Chapter Five

According to the gossip pages, Adil Romario was romantically involved with an actress in her thirties named Lulu Hamra. Perched on the Louis XIV-style sofa in her apartment, she snatched tissues from a gilt box studded with coloured stones as if plucking feathers from a hen. She was surprised, she said, that Makana had come to her. Secretly, however, she seemed flattered. Lulu Hamra's star had long since faded to a dim glow.

'They are always finding new actresses, young girls who will do anything to get a part.' She fixed Makana with a direct stare to ensure he was in no doubt as to what she was implying. As for Adil Romario, she still loved him, of course. 'But he broke my heart,' she sniffed, dabbing deftly at the corners of her eyes to stem the flow of running mascara. 'Adil may be many things, but artistic he is not. He thinks his destiny lies in the movies. Who doesn't these days? I told him, you need an artistic soul. It was the truth, but my honesty cost me his affections.' Her substantial bosom heaved with torment. 'Look at me, my heart is torn in two.' It seemed that Makana was a little behind the times. As far as she knew, Adil had lost interest in her. She kept breaking off her sobs to ask for assurances that details of this relationship would not be released to the press: 'A woman in my position has her reputation to think about.'

'I'm sure your reputation is unblemished.' Makana tried to summon up conviction and failed miserably. 'Did your relationship end when you told him he had no future in film?'

'Did it end? How can anyone think these tears are not real?' She looked genuinely offended and Makana struggled to make amends.

'I was only curious to know what had happened with his film career.'

'Who knows what he did? I can't keep track of all of his sorrows.' Lulu Hamra snorted and buried her nose in a fresh tissue. 'I told him what he didn't want to hear, and he abandoned me.' Her eyes, heavily made up with rings of turquoise and black, narrowed to slits. 'I don't take betrayal lying down. Ask anyone. Any man who turns on me will regret it.'

'It's entirely understandable. You were upset.'

'Who knows?' she sniffed. 'Perhaps I went too far.'

'Might I ask what exactly you did?'

She paused, plucking out five tissues in quick succession. 'I have a lot of influence in this town. Ask anyone. Lulu Hamra does not allow herself to be used. I made sure no one would speak to him.' She threw back her head, tossing her hair over her shoulders, and then clapped her hands. A tiny maid appeared instantly.

'We will take coffee now, please.' When Lulu fluttered her eyelashes at him, Makana had the distinct feeling he was being considered for lunch.

'I am sorry,' he said, rising to his feet. 'But I should be going.'

'Won't you even stay for coffee?' Lulu Hamra purred coquettishly. 'What paper did you say you worked for?'

Makana ignored the question, fiddling instead with his notebook.

'Do you know of anyone else in the business who may have had dealings with him?'

'Nobody that I know, or who treasures my acquaintance. A woman has her pride, you see.'

Safely back down in the street, Makana stretched and filled his lungs with air, tapping his pockets in search of his lighter and not finding it. He stopped and turned instinctively, convinced for a moment he had left it behind in Lulu Hamra's flat and might go back for it. The thought was rejected almost as soon as it came into his head, but as he turned he noticed something odd. A slim man, about fifty metres back, ducked hastily into an alleyway. It was an awkward movement. The kind of mistake that someone not too skilled at following people might make. Resuming his walk, Makana made a mental note. In his late twenties. Dark-skinned for an Egyptian. He wore a long-sleeved chequered beige and white shirt, buttoned to the neck and down to the cuffs. After buying a new lighter from a blind boy sitting on the kerb, Makana hailed a cab. He watched through the rear window but saw no sign of the beige shirt. Perhaps he was beginning to imagine things.

Adil Romario's penthouse flat was located in a glassy tower in Garden City. A stiff-necked housekeeper dressed in black was at first reluctant to let Makana in. She gave him the swift up-and-down appraisal of someone who knows instinctively where to place strangers on the social scale, and Makana clearly didn't rate very highly.

'Are you the one Mr Gaber sent?' she asked in a tone of disbelief.

'He called you?'

'He said I was to help you in any way possible.' She clasped her hands together and clucked disapprovingly. 'But don't expect I'm going to let you out of my sight.'

Makana would have preferred to have arrived unannounced. As he wandered through the rooms with her trailing a few paces behind, putting everything he touched back in place as if she expected him to slip a few items into his pocket, he realised that the flat had been thoroughly cleaned in preparation for his inspection, which was what she obviously took this to be.

'Have you been working for Adil for long?'

'Almost three months. Mr Adil has never had any cause to complain. He trusts me with anything. I have always been a hard worker. You can ask anybody.'

Quite who he was meant to ask, Makana did not know. Adil Romario wasn't his real name, of course, his real name was Adil Mohammed Adly, but throw a stone on any street in Cairo and you were bound to hit someone called Mohammed. There was a certain tradition in Egypt of players adopting the names of famous international footballers. They began as nicknames, among their friends, based perhaps on a favourite player. Then journalists would pick up on them and it added a touch of familiarity, not to mention glamour, to the Egyptian players and their game. There was a Maradona, a Pele, a Zidane, and so forth. There was even a goalkeeper called Beckenbauer for some reason nobody had ever managed to explain fully to Makana.

The large black-and-white framed fashion photographs that hung on the wall suggested Adil Romario was a rather vain young man, with a lot of very white teeth, who stared at the camera with a mixture of arrogance and resentment. Why would anyone want to be surrounded by pictures of themselves? Makana, who couldn't remember the last time he had visited a dentist, wondered if people's teeth really glowed like that, or whether there was some photographic trick involved.

Adil was central to the Hanafi fable. A young boy kicking a ball around a dusty street one day catches the eye of a wealthy philanthropist. It was every boy's dream. Hanafi set up a school to rear local talent. It gave disadvantaged kids a home. He brought in expert trainers to coach them. The television channels loved that kind of thing. If the boys were lucky and worked hard they were given a place in the DreemTeem. But Adil Romario was the only one anyone really remembered.

In the hallway a more recent picture showed Adil at some kind of gala evening, in formal evening dress and bow tie. Perhaps it was the clothes, or the quality of the picture, but his face looked puffy and his eyes dilated, as if he had been drinking. Hanafi stood next to him, one arm around Adil's shoulders, smiling like a fat cat who had secured himself a fish.

The apartment itself said little about Adil as a person. He seemed to have few interests outside football and movies. There were several shelves of DVDs, the films mostly featuring tall dark leading men in action-packed roles, waving guns and looking menacing. Was Adil studying for another career in films as Lulu Hamra had said? In the bathroom, Makana discovered a vast array of colognes and after-shave lotions. He sprayed a couple of these in the air for good measure, inviting a dark look from the housekeeper who appeared as if summoned from one of the bottles.

'You reported him missing on Thursday. When was the last time you saw him?'

'Oh, about a week before that. Maybe longer.'

'A week? I understood you come here every day.'

'Oh, yes. Every day. Mr Adil insists, even though most of the time there is nothing for me to do. I take care of everything. When it needs cleaning I do that. I take care of the laundry. Sometimes I cook for him, but he usually eats out.' She sounded more like a disappointed wife than a housekeeper.

'Why did it take you so long to realise he was missing?'

She straightened her back haughtily. 'I am not employed to keep an eye on Mr Adil. Often, I won't see him for days. He comes and goes as he pleases and it is not my place to ask him where he spends the night.'

'Then what made you call Mr Gaber?'

'That,' she said, pointing to a large glass bowl by the door. It was another one of those curious objects which seemed to strike people with too much money on their hands as a good opportunity to unload some more of it. Adil Romario probably paid somebody to clutter up the place with things like this.

'What is it?'

'Well, Mr Adil always leaves his car keys in it. If he is home I have to be careful not to make too much noise, in case he is sleeping.'

Makana recalled from Gaber's file that Adil drove a silver SUV, a Cherokee Jeep.

'So sometimes he is here but you don't actually see him, is that right?' The woman nodded. Makana went on, 'You noticed the keys were missing on Thursday. When was the last time you actually saw him?'

'Oh, I don't know, maybe a week before that.'

'A week? How about the last time you saw the keys in that bowl?'

'Two or three days before that.'

Which meant that Adil Romario could have been missing for nearly two weeks now.

'Tell me about his friends.'

'Oh, I have nothing to do with that side of his life.'

Makana stared at her. 'I am here to try and help him.'

'That's fine, but I am not paid to see things.' Then she touched a hand to the knot that held the scarf tied at the back of her head and nodded towards something in the next room. 'I think he keeps their names in a book over there.'

The slim black address book rested on the desk in the study as if it had been placed there for him to find.

'Did Mr Gaber telephone to tell you I would be visiting?'

'No . . . Mr Gaber came by.'

So Gaber had set the stage for him. The apartment, even this book carefully placed on the desk for the detective to find. Makana sat down. He felt like an actor following directions. When he glanced up he saw the housekeeper still hovering in the doorway, obviously worried he might steal one of the carpets or something.

'Could you get me some coffee?' He didn't really want coffee, but he needed some breathing space. Reluctantly, she turned away and clumped noisily down the hall, every step a thump of protest. Makana flipped through the address book and dropped it on the desk. It could take him a week to follow up on every contact. Next he tried the drawers. Three of them down the right side of the desk. The top one was locked. He reached into his jacket and produced a slim, sturdy knife which had served him well on occasion. Opening it, he eased the blade into place and slid the tip under the lock mechanism on the drawer. He levered it up far enough for the lock to free itself. It was a disappointing haul. The drawer slid open to reveal nothing inside but a heap of old bills. Water. Electricity. A new television. Under these sat a leather-bound Quran. Putting this to one side, he scrabbled about at the back of the drawer where something was rattling about. His fingers found a handful of small shells. As he turned them over a few grains of sand fell out into his palm. Seashells with soft, fading whorls on their smooth surfaces. He slipped one of these into his pocket and was about to close the drawer when his eye fell on the Quran. He flicked through its pages, only to discover that half of them were glued together. The sacred book fell open to reveal that the centre had been hollowed out. It contained a thick bundle of banknotes. Adil Romario obviously didn't trust his housekeeper entirely. When she came back, she saw the heap of money. She set the cup down with such a thump that the coffee spilled over the side and stained the saucer. Her eyes went to the drawer.

'How did that happen?'

'I used a little too much force,' he smiled. 'I thought it was jammed.'

'You can't just break people's furniture.'

The coffee looked surprisingly good, though he wouldn't have been surprised if she had poured in a dose of rat poison as well. He took a sip and then lit a cigarette.

'You can't smoke in here.'

'Open a window, or call Mr Gaber, I'm sure he'd like to know why it took you so long to report Adil missing.'

She turned and left the room without another word. Adil didn't trust her and neither did Makana.

He turned his attention to the telephone on the desk. It had a built-in answerphone system which was activated. The counter showed it had registered twenty-one messages. He rewound the tape and went through all of them. Six were from someone at the club, a man Makana guessed was the assistant coach. Five were from Gaber and another four from someone called Soraya, Hanafi's youngest daughter. She sounded worried. 'Adil, where are you? Please, it's never been this long.' None were from Hanafi himself. Several callers mentioned that they had tried his mobile telephone and got no answer. Three were from a woman who identified herself as Mimi. Her tone was frantic. She wanted to see him. In the final one she didn't give her name, but Makana recognised her voice. 'Please, tell me why you are doing this to me?' she begged. 'What have I done?' Then there was a long pause and a sob, before finally the line clicked and went dead with a resigned tone.

The remaining message was not a real one at all. There was no sense of urgency to it. Instead, in response to the beep, there was a long silence. It was so long that Makana thought for a moment there was no one there. Then he heard the breathing, slow and even. Finally, a voice enquired, 'Adil?' once and then fell silent. No name, no identification, no message. Still, the caller waited, as if he thought Adil might be avoiding him, refusing to pick up because he knew who was calling.

Makana picked up the address book again and went through it. The name Mimi was circled and underscored. A series of numbers was scribbled alongside it. He tried them one after the other but they were all disconnected. No address was given.

He spent some time going through all the names in the address book, ticking each of them off after he had made the call. Nobody had seen or heard from Adil in weeks; in some cases it was months. Despite his success, it seemed that Adil Romario had few regular or close friends. The ones Makana spoke to tended to be on the frivolous side in general. Happy-go-lucky, playboy types, media darlings, movie celebrities and television journalists with shrill voices, male or female. They told him nothing. With friends like these your absence would be noticed for about as long as it took for someone else to call.

Makana slipped out of the flat without seeing the housekeeper again. In the front lobby he cornered the doorman, a sophisticated version of the usual *bawab*, wearing a uniform the colour of boiled spinach. He was reluctant to talk until Makana produced the envelope of expenses. 'He keeps himself to himself, always polite, but you know how it is with people like that. They live in another world from the rest of us.' The delivery boys in a take-away place next door wore red uniforms with a logo of a monkey on roller skates holding a pizza box. A bland electronic storm of syrupy music gushed from the overhead speakers, loud enough to make conversation all but impossible.

'We know who he is, sure.'

'He's a regular customer.'

'Is this for a magazine? I have a friend who works in television. Maybe you know him?'

'It's fine being a big star and everything but you'd think a guy like that could manage to smile once in a while,' offered one of them as Makana made to leave.

Chapter Six

The DreemTeem Football Club looked like a bomb had hit it. Over the old stadium an enormous new edifice was being constructed. Cranes swung through the air and jackhammers pounded. Scaffolding clattered and heavy lorries rumbled in and out of a deep pit in the ground, churning clouds of grey dust like hot pepper into the air. Alongside this a semi-circular building housed the main offices of Hanafi Enterprises.

Makana was hoping to interview some of Adil's team mates. Gaber had made an appointment for him with the team's manager, Guido Clemenza. Makana arrived ten minutes early. Still, Clemenza kept him waiting another forty, and when he did finally appear he seemed reluctant to talk.

'I should warn you,' he began, 'you won't get much cooperation from the players.'

Clemenza was Italian, a heavily built man with a tanned face and grey spiky hair that stuck up like bristles on a wire brush. He wasn't exactly an examplar of healthy living, considering he was the manager of a football team. He smoked incessantly while they spoke.

'Why is that?'

'Don't you read the papers? They all think they deserve the same attention as he gets.'

Makana recalled the piece he had read in the newspaper about conflict within the team.

Clemenza sucked his teeth. 'Gaber said he had hired you to find Romario. Personally, I don't see the point. If he doesn't want to play, why not let him go?'

'I thought you would be keen to get him back.'

'Think again. He's overrated. Give me a player with less talent and more motivation any day of the week.' His flinty gaze was sharp as a hawk's and gave little away.

'Hanafi seems to think differently.'

Clemenza smiled conspiratorially. 'It's his club, Hanafi can think what he likes.'

'The team isn't doing so well without Adil Romario.'

'It's motivation we're lacking, not Romario. You promise people the world and then one man gets all the glory. The players feel that no matter how hard they work, they are never recognised for it. Win or lose, it makes no difference to them.' Clemenza smoked for a time. He seemed to be trying to decide something. 'What exactly made Hanafi hire you?'

'You'd have to ask him that. Why do I get the feeling you don't much care for Adil?'

'There's no love lost between us,' the Italian grunted. 'It's no secret. Everybody knows.'

'You argued?'

'Don't get your hopes up. Players are like racehorses. You have to treat them with care or they break a leg. He's an arrogant prick who thinks he walks on water.'

'Because Hanafi looks out for him?'

'He's the public image of the DreemTeem. The kid who came from nowhere and reached the stars.'

'And in terms of the team?'

A brusque shake of the head. 'Adil's heart is no longer in it. He's a hindrance, a prima donna. He can put the ball into the net, sure, but you have to serve it up to him on a platter, and even then, nine times out of ten, he screws up. Raw talent only takes you so far.'

'His heart isn't in the game then?'

'You got that right. And now I am going to have to leave you.' Clemenza got to his feet. A woman had appeared in the doorway and was signalling to him like an extra in a television melodrama.

'One last question. Can you think of any reason Adil might want to disappear?'

'As many reasons as there are days in the month. I tell you, when I walk out on to that training pitch it never fails to surprise me that there are players out there. No one wants to work any more in this country. They want it all for free.'

With that he was gone. Makana stretched and went over to the window. He was in the conference room of a large modern building set right on the river's edge in Giza. This was the seat of the Hanafi empire and from it Makana had a panoramic view of the pyramids and the Great Sphinx in one direction, and the city skyline in the other. Between where he stood and the river lay the vast construction site of what would one day become Hanafi's flagship – the new stadium.

The foundations had been laid and a ring of columns was being built circling the inner oval. A number of these appeared to have massive stone figures on top of them. These resembled the statues of ancient kings, Ramses and Thutmose and all the rest of them. There was something about the faces of the statues that struck Makana as being wrong and yet oddly familiar.

Outside, by the lifts, a girl was sitting behind a reception desk. 'Who would you like me to call next?' she asked as he approached.

'Oh, let me think . . .' He waved one hand vaguely. 'Is there a bathroom I could use first?'

The girl looked at him as if uncertain if his access qualified him for the privilege before finally consenting. She pointed him down the hall. 'Go to the end and turn right.'

Makana smiled his thanks and walked in the direction she had indicated. When he reached the bathroom door he went straight by. At the end of the corridor a door led to a staircase. He went down it and emerged into the old training area of the club. A sign pointed down a ramp to the players' area.

A small fortune had been ploughed into the recruitment of the Hanafi team. With his backing they could afford to purchase established players just as they were falling off the European circuit, which gave them a fairly international line-up. They had Dutch and British players, several Spanish and Italian. Most of them were past their prime, of course. Some were well on their way down, but they were still professional enough to take on most teams in this country and their names were familiar to the fans. There were also a number of African players: from Senegal, Nigeria, Cameroon. The majority of the team was Egyptian, of course. Some of these players were familiar to Makana, men who had played for well-known clubs like Zamalek and Al Ahly. A couple had been on the national team. They helped consolidate the local fan base. It was one of these he spotted coming out of the changing rooms with a sports bag slung over his shoulder, Ahmad Essam, a tall, taciturn man Makana remembered from years back.

'Essam?' He held out his hand. 'I watched you score in the Africa Cup. What a goal!'

'Thanks.' The player took Makana's hand and shook it. They walked out together through the tunnel and into the sunlight. 'Not many people remember that.' Essam looked weary, as if the occasional brief moments of glory had gradually been obliterated for him by decades of steady defeat.

'You scored against Zambia.'

'Those were the days. People really cared about the game. Now it's every man for himself.'

'You haven't done so badly.' Makana nodded at the new stadium going up.

'Sure, it's all change now.' Essam's face remained unsmiling. 'Are you looking for someone?'

'I came to talk to you about Adil Romario.'

'To me?' Essam hefted the weight of his bag higher on his shoulder and looked Makana over. 'You're not even supposed to be in here, are you?' He started walking again.

'Look, I wouldn't be in here if I didn't have permission, right?'

Essam paused and eyed him again. 'So what are you doing?'

'I'm writing a book on the team. Hanafi hired me.'

'What, the whole team?'

'The whole team.'

'Really?'

'Sure. Actually, the old man thinks the team needs more motivation. You can't achieve greatness if everything is centred on a couple of big names.'

'Or one.'

'Or one.' Makana nodded, pulling out his notebook and pen. The tall player gestured towards a beaten-up red Mazda parked against the wall. They walked over and leaned against the side.

'So what do you want to know?'

'Well, this is all just background material right now. I need to get a feel for the dynamics between the players. What it's like to be part of such a high-profile team.'

'The dynamics?'

'Take yourself, for example. You are probably the most experienced player on the team. The others look to you for direction, I imagine.'

'Sometimes.'

'I guess it's not that easy?'

'It's not,' Essam conceded with a shrug. Then went on, 'My legs are going. I have to work twice as hard these days just to keep up with the younger players.'

'So, tell me about Adil Romario.'

'The truth?'

'The truth.'

'You know what the problem is? Nobody sees the rest of us. I mean, take me. I worked my way up the hard way, just like him. My father was a *fellah*. I played for the national team. Then this kid comes along from nowhere and suddenly he's the star of the team.'

'Who decided that . . . Clemenza?'

'He changes the line-up for almost every match, and never seems to get it right. The result is, we are losing. Other teams are beating us though we have better players.'

'So how come Adil gets all the attention?'

'Because it's not about the game any more. It's about all the other stuff. You know, he has to be seen with this actress and that singer, and they want him advertising perfume and potato chips.'

'I hear he doesn't even turn up for practice these days.'

A wry smile appeared on the other man's face. 'He does that

from time to time. Just takes off. No explanations given or asked for. Clemenza doesn't dare take it out on him.'

'Where does he go when he disappears?'

'I don't know. He takes that big fancy car of his and drives off somewhere.'

'The silver Cherokee?'

'That's it.' Essam gave his own Mazda a dirty look. Makana recalled the shells he had found in the desk at Adil's apartment.

'Does he have a place somewhere by the sea that he likes to go?'

'Not that I've ever heard of.' Essam looked off into the distance. 'Between you and me, he enjoys himself too much. The parties, the girls . . . He's not serious about the game, not any more.'

'You think he doesn't care about the team?'

'The team?' Essam choked on a bitter laugh. 'If you want my opinion he's probably in Europe right now, signing with one of the big clubs.'

'What would Hanafi say to that?'

'From what I hear, Adil has the old man wrapped around his finger.'

'Why Europe?'

Essam stared at Makana as if he was mad. 'There isn't a player in the world who doesn't dream of playing for one of the big European clubs. It's not just the money. In a few years you can get a passport and then you're free.'

'Mr Makana?'

The two men looked up to find a tall woman in her twenties standing before them, hands on her slim hips. Sharply dressed in a neat charcoal grey suit, she had long brown hair that hung to her shoulders.

'I am Soraya Hanafi.' Makana felt his hand seized in a firm

grip. She was looking at him in a puzzled way, as if uncertain what to make of him. 'I see you have already met some of our players. How are you, Ahmad?'

Mumbling a greeting, Essam began fumbling for his car keys. Soraya turned back to Makana.

'We thought we had lost you.'

'I thought I would take a look around.'

The Mazda coughed black smoke and began to back away, rattling noisily. Makana followed Soraya back towards the main building.

'We nearly met yesterday. Was that you swimming at your father's flat?'

Her expression was a mixture of distrust and curiosity, as if she couldn't work out whether or not to trust him.

'I try to swim every day.'

Soraya Hanafi had an air of confidence about her you might expect in a woman twice her age. She was striking rather than beautiful and her direct gaze only compounded the unsettling effect she had on Makana. They took the lift back up to the conference room in silence.

She asked him to sit down and gave him a brief introduction to the company. It was, he discovered, far more extensive than he had realised. Hanafi Foods grew beans and okra, and froze them or tinned them for export all over the world. They imported wheat from the United States and turned it into pasta. Hanafi Autos assembled cars and minivans made in Korea. There was an insurance company as well. The biggest section of all, however, was their construction company. Hanafi Developments was busy building everything, from tower blocks in the city and villa complexes in the Emirates to luxury hotels on the Red Sea and in Upper Egypt.

When Soraya had finished talking she sat back and appraised him.

'You are not comfortable in the presence of women, I see.'

'I'm not that old-fashioned,' he protested, reaching for his cigarettes. The look on her face told him to put them away again, which he did.

'I'll be honest with you, Mr Makana, I have no idea why my father hired you. There are plenty of good investigators in this town. Many of them come with a long record of service in our police force. These are people we know. People who know their way around the city. They have contacts. You, on the other hand, are a complete outsider.'

Makana wondered just how much Soraya Hanafi knew about her father's former life. As the daughter of his second wife, by the time she was old enough to understand fully, doubtless all of the questionable side of it would have been conveniently swept away out of existence. Gangsters replaced by bankers. Thugs by police chiefs. She would have grown up thinking she had a wealthy businessman for a father. A sheltered life where the occasional hint of untoward dealings could be dismissed as malicious rumour stirred up by her father's rivals.

'I can't tell you why your father decided to seek my assistance. You'd have to ask him that, but I believe he has his reasons.'

Her pointed chin lifted for a moment, and then Soraya gave the briefest of nods, as if to herself, saying this would have to be good enough for the moment.

'My father never does anything without good reason. I don't know what those reasons are, but I am willing to cooperate with you in any way, if it will help.'

Makana stretched his legs out under the table. 'Then tell me about him . . . about Adil.'

'What would you like to know?'

'Everything. Interests, friends, habits. At this stage anything could be useful.'

'Well,' began Soraya Hanafi, gazing down at her lap, 'I've known Adil for as long as I can remember. I was alone from an early age. My mother and brother died in a car accident. My sisters from my father's first marriage are much older. I was a lonely child. Adil was one of the first boys taken into the Hanafi Sports Academy. We spent a lot of time together when we were young.' Her tone softened as she spoke about him.

'I understand,' Makana said. 'This must be very difficult for you.'

'It's difficult for all of us.' She wrapped her arms around herself, as if she was cold.

'Your father must have taken a real liking to him, to bring him into the family like that.'

'My father comes from a similar background. I imagine he saw something of himself in Adil. When there is something he wants, he goes after it.'

'And you, are you similar in character?'

The question surprised her. 'Is that relevant to your enquiries?'

'At the moment everything is relevant.'

'Very well.' Soraya Hanafi crossed her arms in front of her, and looked him in the eye. 'Yes, some people would say that I have inherited that side of his temperament.'

'And what position exactly do you hold in your father's business enterprises?'

A faint twitch of irritation passed across her face and vanished.

'My father is not getting any younger, Mr Makana. I am gradually taking on more responsibility. In the end, I expect to take over the company.'

'Wouldn't that make you something of an exception in this country?'

Her head tilted to one side and her eyes narrowed. 'I sense disapproval.'

'Not at all.' Makana tried to make amends. 'But I imagine there are some circles where the idea of a woman your age running a company this size would be frowned upon.'

'We're behind the times in this country, especially now, with all this religious nonsense. If some people want to live in the Middle Ages, let them. It's not something I worry about.'

'What about Adil's family, his parents? Does he have any contact with them?'

'They passed away, but he more or less cut all ties to them before that. Adil had a difficult childhood. His parents were very poor. He often says that my father saved his life.'

'What does he mean by that?'

'I suppose he means that his circumstances did not provide him with many opportunities at birth. In all probability, he would have ended up in a life of crime or deep poverty at best if he had not been given a chance by my father.'

'You're saying he broke all contact with his family?'

Soraya Hanafi paused, locking her fingers together on the table. 'I think he despised them.'

'Despised?' Makana said. 'Isn't that pretty harsh?'

'I don't believe it's an exaggeration. He's never forgiven them for not putting him in school . . . for making him work in the fields from a very young age. He couldn't read or write when he first came to the academy. He was determined to make himself free, never to go back to that world. I've always admired him for that. A world of darkness, he calls it.'

Makana had the feeling he was dealing with an enigma. A

man who had everything. Life had taken Adil from humble beginnings to fame and fortune. He lived under the protection of one of the most powerful men in the country. Yet who was Adil Romario, beyond the smiling figure on the billboards and advertising spots? It was as if he had disappeared back into the same obscurity he had come from. Makana reached absently for his cigarettes. This time he managed to get one almost to his mouth before he noticed Soraya's look of disapproval. He set the packet back on the table.

'Is any of this really useful?' Her tone implying that she clearly didn't think so.

'Tell me more about these disappearances of his. Where does he go?'

'It's not that hard to understand.' She shrugged. 'He's under a lot of pressure. Matches . . . publicity shoots. Sometimes it gets too much. He needs to let off steam.'

'Your father said that they had argued – that Adil had wanted him to go away with him on holiday, a safari or something.'

'It's possible.' Her shoulders lifted and fell again, more slackly this time.

'This might sound a little strange, but do you think it's credible Adil was trying to get your father away from here for a reason?'

'What kind of reason?'

'Adil might have been trying to protect him.'

'Protect him from what? You think my father might be in danger?'

'It's a possibility. He said he came to me because he doesn't want word to get out. But maybe there's another reason. Maybe he doesn't trust the people around him.'

He half expected her to laugh, to dismiss the suggestion as

ridiculous, but instead Soraya seemed to draw herself inward, lowering her head to examine the grain in the polished wood of the table.

'You don't build a company like this without stepping on other people's toes. My father has a lot of rivals.' She spoke gently, with no trace of emotion. 'But the idea that someone around him, as you put it, someone inside this company, might be working against him, is absurd.'

They walked back out to the reception area where models of construction projects in progress or recently completed, including the new stadium, were displayed.

'Is that what it's going to look like?'

'Yes,' Soraya said, pointing out various features. It didn't end with the club, or the Hanafi Sports Academy as it would become, promoting excellence among the country's youth. There would also be apartments and a hotel, a residential complex with a riverside promenade, shops and restaurants. It would be vast when it was finished. The pitch itself was set inside a huge oval-shaped space, with curved walls rising up around it. There were little model figures walking across the big concourse, and off in one corner was a wedge of high-rise buildings. The perimeter was marked by a framework of pillars, the row of twelve pharaonic figures, giant statues of Ramses that Makana had noticed earlier. Again, he was struck by the fact that they all had a certain familiarity. Leaning down, he peered at them more closely.

'They all have your father's face.'

'Yes,' she laughed. 'That's how he wants them.'

'And what is this?' Makana pointed at another model, this time showing a complex of villas embedded in a gently sculpted landscape of hills, trees and artificial ponds.

'That is the Hanafi Heavens,' she said. 'It is a pilot project . . .

the first of many, we hope. Probably the most modern residential community of its kind.'

'Really?' Makana leaned over for a closer look.

'Oh, yes,' she went on. 'It will be quite luxurious, and completely self-contained. An oasis of calm, far from the noise and pollution of the city. People have a right to clean air and some peace and quiet, don't you think?'

'If they can afford it,' he said.

She smiled at him, as if that had been the kind of quaint irrelevancy she'd expected from him.

'And these little patches of desert add a romantic touch, I suppose?'

'That's part of the golf course.'

'Of course,' nodded Makana, wondering why he hadn't known that.

When he finally emerged from the meeting, he gratefully lit a cigarette. The sky was growing dim, the colour of amber, streaked with dark angry threads of blue and red. Dots of artificial white light were strung against it like necklaces of cheap pearls. His first day was almost over and he felt that he had achieved little. If someone was using Adil Romario to get at Hanafi, the range of possible suspects could run into the hundreds if not thousands. A disgruntled team mate or a family member . . . Makana wondered who was more dangerous to Hanafi? His own encounter with Soraya still occupied his mind. She intrigued him, but he couldn't decide if this was good or bad.

Chapter Seven

Amir Medani's office was hemmed in by concrete flyovers. They criss-crossed through the air like enormous tentacles that sprouted from the ground and wrapped themselves tightly around the crumbling old buildings downtown. Along these endless grey funnels rattled an unbroken stream of scrap metal on uneven wheels. The window that Makana stared through was so grubby you could barely see anything beyond it. On the other side of the highway a light came on and he saw a young woman appear, brushing her hair, her face illuminated by the headlights of the vehicles flying between them.

'I wasn't expecting you to pay me back, you know,' protested Amir Medani.

Sitting behind his desk, he rubbed one hand over his slack features. He had the perpetual look of a man who has just been woken up in the middle of the night and is wondering where he is.

'You should take it while I still have it,' Makana said. 'I have no idea when I'll see any more of that.'

Tapping the notes on the desk in front of him, Amir Medani opened a drawer and dropped them inside. Despite his generosity,

Makana knew that the lawyer's funds were as tightly stretched as Makana's own. The only money he had coming in came from human rights organisations around the world, the occasional assistance from a United Nations body, and that was about it. In exchange he carried out a one-man battle to denounce torture and other abuse as well as the plight of the millions of Sudanese trapped in Cairo, many of them living in misery. He was well connected in the political system and was forever jetting off to conferences in Helsinki or Stockholm, trying to convince the world to take an interest, although looking at the clutter of papers in this office it was a wonder he ever managed to find the door.

'Actually, I was thinking about calling you.'

Makana turned away from the window as Amir lit a cigarette and immediately disappeared in a cloud of smoke and began coughing. He fanned the air and thumped his chest. When he got his breath back, he pushed his spectacles back on top of his head and peered at Makana.

'Has anyone tried to contact you?'

'Like who?'

'Someone from the old days?' The lawyer gestured. 'Anyone.'

'What have you heard?'

'It may be nothing.'

Which told Makana there definitely was something. Amir Medani was secretive to the point of paranoia. He wouldn't tell you something unless he was pretty sure he needed to.

'You heard about Sanhouri?' Amir put down his cigarette and leaned back, hands folded behind his head, the chair creaking under the strain.

'What about him?'

'He fell from the balcony of his apartment. You didn't know?'

'I haven't really been in touch with a lot of people recently.' Makana idly turned the handle of the pencil sharpener on the desk. 'You're saying it wasn't suicide?'

'That's just it, nobody knows. His family is distraught, as you can imagine.'

Makana recalled that he had never known Sanhouri well; that he belonged more to Amir Medani's political circle. Its members spent all their time talking about returning home, about forcing the current regime to yield power, but nothing ever seemed to come of all their talk, and Makana preferred to stay away from it. He would go home when the time came. Until then, all he cared about was surviving here and now.

'Didn't he have police protection?'

'That's just the thing.' Amir sat forward suddenly, the chair protesting so vigorously it threatened to disintegrate into matchwood. 'The Egyptians cancelled his protection.'

'They cancelled it? Why?'

'You know how it is. Every time they have a crisis, the Egyptians blame us.'

When it was discovered that Sudanese Islamist radicals were behind an attempt on President Mubarak's life in the Ethiopian capital three years before, he'd turned against them. The open border agreement between the two countries was ended and Sudanese were reduced to the status of any other foreigner.

'Is it possible they let Sanhouri be killed?'

Amir Medani's eyes swivelled towards the walls, as if expecting to see the answer to the question written there.

'The thing I like about you, is your devious mind. It almost matches mine. Officially, the Egyptians are against the regime in Khartoum, especially since Addis, but there are elements within the SSI who are friendly to the Islamist cause.'

'I take it there were no witnesses?'

'No witnesses. Eight floors down.' Amir gave a single nod of the head as if seeing it happen right in front of him. 'He landed under a passing minibus. It was a terrible mess.'

'So I should stay away from balconies?'

Amir sighed. 'It is possible that you may be in danger.'

Makana had been fiddling with the paper clips that clung to a magnetic Eiffel Tower – a reminder that Amir had spent a number of years living in Europe after getting out of prison back home. There had been a woman involved, Makana recalled, even a couple of children.

'But I'm not a politician like Sanhouri. I have nothing to do with any of that. You know I keep away from politics.'

'You have enemies. People who might want to see you dead.'

'You mean Mek Nimr?'

'He's a big man nowadays, or so I hear.'

Makana reached for the cigarettes in his shirt pocket. A memory from the street outside Lulu Hamra's building came back to him. The man in the beige chequered shirt he had been convinced was following him. Had he been sent by Mek Nimr?

Outside in the hallway an argument was starting up between a woman with a strident voice and a meek-sounding fellow who was doing a bad job of defending himself.

'You think the Egyptians allowed Sanhouri to be killed?'

'All I am saying is, you should be careful.' Amir studied the tip of his cigarette. 'State Security were supposed to be protecting him. They didn't do a very good job, did they?'

'I'll stay away from high places,' said Makana as he turned to leave.

'Just remember what I said, and be careful.'

Out in the hallway, Makana eased his way round the large

woman still berating the timid man, who was obviously her husband. He threw Makana a pleading look as he went by. Her voice followed him down into the street. It was clogged with night-time traffic that bumped and hooted its way through the downtown snarl-ups. Couples walked along examining the bright displays of clothes and shiny shoes; the mannequins that displayed them were stick-thin and pale as milk. European models. Bizzare to try and imagine any of the passers-by in those outfits, and yet they took comfort from these boulevards of opulent dreams.

Nabil was waiting for him at Felfela's. His contact at the largest state newspaper, *Al Ahram*, was a short man with a large paunch and a receding hairline. He stood at the counter with a stack of sandwiches in front of him, putting them away as if a law might be passed at any minute, forbidding the consumption of food by overweight men. Makana indicated a quieter spot in a corner and waited for Nabil to transfer his snack. He passed over a thick envelope between bites.

'That's basically a selection,' Nabil said, managing to stop chewing for long enough to get the words out. 'I could have brought you twice as much. The papers adore him.'

Makana pulled out the photocopies and began leafing through them. Most of it he already knew. Adil Romario had come out of nowhere. He had no former track record, had never played for another team before. There was a description of life at the Hanafi Sports Academy. They had selection days and anyone good enough to impress the scouts would be offered a place. It meant somewhere to live, an education and regular meals. If you worked hard enough you got into the DreemTeem. Adil appar-ently devoted a lot of time to charity work for the Academy, touring the city, the country, showing little boys what they could achieve if they set their minds to it.

'This is the one that caused all the trouble,' Nabil interrupted, leaving a greasy mark on the page he tapped.

'The trouble?'

'You know, all the rumours about the other players hating Adil.'

Makana cast an eye quickly over the copy in front of him. He realised that the shorter piece he had already seen was referring to this article. It was by a journalist named Sami Barakat who promised an exclusive insight into the conflict that was tearing the DreemTeem apart from within. Rivalry there had apparently reached unprecedented heights. His team mates were furious about Adil Romario's poor performance. 'The team is being sacrificed for the boss's favourite boy,' he summarised.

'Who is this Sami Barakat?'

'I don't know him, but he obviously isn't planning a long career in journalism,' judged Nabil. 'Hanafi will have him thrown out on his ear before too long, mark my words.'

Makana paused in his reading to look round the brightly lit snack bar. There was a constant stream of people coming and going. Groups of students,young and old. Solitary men stood and munched quickly, eyes fixed on their food. He realised that since his conversation with Amir Medani he was automatically being more cautious.

'What's this all about anyway?'

'It's about discretion.'

'I'm just asking.' Nabil wiped his mouth with a napkin and swallowed half a can of some kind of pink drink with a picture of Adil Romario on the label.

'What is that stuff?'

Nabil frowned at the bottle. 'Pineapple and watermelon.' He held it out. 'You want some?'

Makana ignored him. 'I've seen most of this material before,' he said. 'Did you find anything about his interest in films?'

His mouth once again full, Nabil reached across and rifled through the heap of papers, managing to distribute oily crumbs and a slice of onion before he found what he was looking for. It was a brief, highlighted note, tacked on to the side of another in-depth article on the player. Most of it was unashamed speculation:

Egypt's heartthrob Adil Romario is set for movie fame, our sources tell us. He has set up a production company of his own, Faraga Films, with veteran director and producer Salim Farag. Watch this space, movie lovers!

'This is better,' said Makana, tucking the sheets away. 'But I need more, and I want you to find out about his family. Who they are and where they lived.' He extracted a few notes from the envelope Gaber had given him. When Nabil pulled a face at the amount, he said sternly, 'I don't pay you to get me what I already know. Get me something I haven't seen.'

On his way home, rattling along in yet another taxi that appeared to be on its last journey in this world, Makana decided he could no longer put off sharing some of his newly acquired wealth with Umm Ali. Benevolence was not his only motive. His landlady had applied her tried and tested technique of disconnecting the cable that delivered electricity to Makana's sinking palace. The supply line looped down from the main road and dropped to a distribution box high on a pole set conveniently close to the plywood shack tacked on to the river bank. The youngest of her lovable little urchins could scramble on to the precarious roof and disconnect the cable. She only ever took this measure when the rent was too long overdue. Of course, Umm Ali would never admit to such retaliation. It was merely an unspoken understanding between them that when his finances were at a low ebb, the power might begin to fail. The first time it happened Makana had wasted a morning at the central exchange being told there was nothing wrong with the line. When he approached his landlady with the required money the power would be miraculously restored, sometimes within seconds.

Umm Ali was overjoyed to see him counting banknotes off into her hand, though she had no doubt been anticipating such an event since she had first set eyes on Hanafi's big car pulling up outside. She could barely contain her joy.

'I will bring you another bag of pickles this evening,' she promised with a warm smile. Umm Ali was proud of her pickles. There were months when Makana felt as though he practically lived on her pickles.

'Perhaps you might check the electricity again?'

'Right away, *ya bash-muhandis*, you don't even have to mention it.'

She turned and let out a blood-curdling shriek, and a boy who had been dozing on the ground outside the hut like a cat, leaped up and scuttled on to the roof.

'An important man like yourself cannot afford to live without any light in his house. How are people supposed to find you?' Chuckling to herself, she tucked the money into her bosom and went off a happy woman.

On the upper deck Makana sat in the watery restored glow of his reading lamp and went back through all his material, Gaber's file and Nabil's envelope, looking for something he had missed.

Adil Romario became star material early on. At the age of twenty-one he was declared the most eligible bachelor in the country. There were plenty of photographs of him in the company of the glamorous set: actors, movie directors and producers from Egypt's thriving film world. Women in flashy gowns smiling like their life depended on it. Fat old men and handsome younger ones. The glitzy life of stardom. Adil Romario appeared to have had his picture taken with all of them.

One picture caught Makana's eye. He studied it for a moment. Adil stood in the centre of a group of smiling people. In this case several older men who appeared to be overjoyed to be snapped next to the famous player. To one side stood Gaber, looking exactly the same as always. Next to him was a slight, unremarkable man in a navy blue suit. He looked uncomfortable. The kind of man who did not like having his photograph taken. Makana remembered him. A face from the past, though his name was unknown. Carefully, he folded the clipping and tucked it into his jacket pocket.

At some point, Makana must have dozed off. He remembered staring at the sky, trying to pick out the stars above the carnival blaze of the city, then his eyes must have closed. When he opened them again he felt the cold night breeze blowing in from the water. He remained where he was for a long time, listening to the world around him.

Makana sat up slowly. He knew something was wrong. Someone was moving around down below. As quietly as he could, he picked up the handy length of piping he kept by his chair. At the head of the stairs he looked out at the embankment. There were no lights showing from Umm Ali's shack. Nothing was moving and at this hour there was little traffic up on the road. A solitary car went by, trailing a snatch of a popular song, before being swallowed by the silence.

Moving down the stairs, stepping cautiously, Makana reached the lower deck and paused to listen. A cool breeze blew in from the river. He heard the water lapping gently against the sides of the hull. He edged along the outside, feeling his way carefully with each foot. Then he froze. A ray of light had just brushed the slats of the window shutters in front of him. Someone was moving about inside with a flashlight. For a long time Makana stood waiting. Then the *awama* stretched itself in one of those long, weary movements that he had become used to. A creaking that started somewhere down inside the hull and transmitted itself through the entire frame with a shudder.

The intruder was not prepared. The light went off with an audible click. Makana opened the door with his left hand, grasping the heavy piping in his right. He sensed rather than saw the figure coming towards him. He swung the pipe and felt it connect. There was a groan and then the full weight of the man crashed into him, sending Makana backwards against the wall. He heard the wood crack in protest. Struggling to his feet, Makana pushed himself up and out. The other man was moving quickly. He dropped over the side of the railings and on to the river bank, his shadow dissolving into the tall reeds and grass that lined the water's edge. By the time Makana reached the rear of the *awama* there was nothing to see. There was no moon, only the glow of the lights on the road above, which threw more shadows than light on the matter. After a time he heard the sound of an engine in the distance.

Back inside, Makana surveyed his quarters. There was little to show that they had been visited. The intruder had been looking for something, but quietly. A simple burglar? It wouldn't be the first time. But Makana couldn't shake off the feeling that it was something more than that. As he switched off the lights and

82

began to climb the stairs he heard the telephone ringing, which in itself was something of a miracle as it hadn't worked for weeks. Umm Ali again? he wondered as he lifted the receiver. Before he could speak his name a voice began screaming in his ear.

'What took you so long? Don't tell me you were asleep. Get dressed. I'm sending a car over for you right now.'

Within a few minutes he heard the sound of an approaching siren. When he looked up he saw the flashing lights coming across the bridge for him. With a sigh, he got to his feet and pulled on his jacket again. By the time he got up to the road the police car was already in sight.

Chapter Eight

With lights and siren going it took them under ten minutes to get downtown to the Al Hassanain Hotel in the Khan al-Khalili. Makana still had no idea what this was all about, but he supposed that Okasha would not send for him in such dramatic fashion unless it was called for. At this hour the streets were deserted, but still, the flashing lights had managed to draw a small crowd and the uniformed officer who accompanied Makana to the door seemed to relish the opportunity to shove people out of the way, yelling in a manner that seemed both alarming and ineffective.

The hotel had seen better days. The stairwell gave off a fetid air of decay as Makana climbed it, deciding not to take his chances in the lift. A familiar figure awaited him on the landing of the third floor. Inspector Wasim Okasha of the Department of Criminal Investigations was a tall, big-shouldered man with a wave of jet black hair combed stiffly back from his broad forehead, and a thick moustache. His dark face seemed to be made up of flat planes and knobbly bones. A stubbly, hard nut of a man, he wore a grey woollen shirt underneath a heavy police overcoat against the January cold. In his hand he held a mobile telephone. When he had finished talking he waved it in Makana's face.

'When are you going to get one of these and save us all a lot of trouble?'

'I told you, they'll be out of fashion before I get round to it.'

Makana surveyed the small hotel room from the open doorway. Inside, several men in blue jumpsuits were moving around. There was a chemical smell in the air, and another odour that brought back all the bad memories. He glanced at Okasha, who snapped his fingers for the others to make room for them and then indicated for Makana to follow him inside. The lab technicians, their faces covered with white masks, stood to one side with an air of irritation.

The chair was lying on its side. The woman strapped to it was in a seated position. Her hands were twisted behind her back and bound together with a strip of bloody towelling. Other strips had been used to tie each of her ankles to the chair legs. That was what he saw first. He could not as yet see her face. A European, he thought. Her body was a mottled blue colour, with heavy bruising to her face and arms as well as along the thighs. She was wearing a yellow T-shirt, the front of which was stained with blood, and white underwear. Nothing more. A necklace of blue marks ringed her throat. As he moved around he saw that her eyes were open and her tongue protruded into the air, like a rigid purple beak. Flies buzzed around her nose and mouth. Makana crouched down for a better look at her face. In death, the woman was barely recognisable as the one he had spoken to in Aswani's restaurant less than twenty-four hours ago. The light had faded from her eyes, which were now as lifeless as glass. They stared blindly at the window as if seeking the stars beyond.

'Our brothers are becoming more inventive in dealing with the tourist trade,' Makana commented.

'Torture is new. We can't rule out any sexual motive until the pathologists do their work.'

'What else, then?' Makana looked round the room. 'Robbery?'

'It looks like she was asleep. Someone broke in.'

'Cause of death?'

'I would say a broken neck. It looks like someone was strangling her and then she struggled and went over. Bang.' Okasha clapped his hands together.

'An accident? Why torture her?'

Okasha shrugged and nodded at the bedside table. 'Money and passport are still over there. And we found this.' He held up a plastic bag in front of Makana's face. It contained his business card. Makana looked down at the dead woman and recalled their conversation.

'She came here to find her daughter.'

Okasha held up a hand to stop him. 'Hold on, I can't breathe in this stench. Let's go downstairs and have some tea.' He turned to address the others in the room. 'Make sure you don't miss anything, because if you do, I will personally make sure that you spend the rest of your life standing in Tahrir Square directing traffic, is that clear?'

'*Hadir, ya bash-muhandis*,' they all muttered obediently.

Makana was examining the door. He flipped the lock back and forth and noted the splintered wood of the door frame. It had been forced so many times you could have blown on it and it would have opened. Okasha shouldered his way past.

'I didn't ask you here to give us a lesson in detective work. A child could have opened that door by pissing on it. Come on.'

He was already on his way out, pushing his way through the

crowd thronging the small reception area downstairs. There were a number of journalists and photographers among them.

'*Yallah!* Clear these people out of here. I don't want civilians dirtying up my crime scene.'

'When are they going to let us up?'

'Who did it, *ya Kaptin*?'

'Who did it?' Okasha turned on them, causing several to take an involuntary step backward. 'I tell you, I wouldn't be surprised if it was one of you jackals. And you can take your pictures right here, because this is the closest you are going to get. A statement will be released in the morning, in the usual way. Now, my men are busy doing their work, and if I hear any one of you has been bothering them, you will have to read about this case in another paper from now on. Is that clear?' He threw up one hand and, like Moses, a passage cleared for him as he made his way through the crowd with Makana in tow.

When he had first landed here, seven years ago, it was Okasha who had put him in touch with his first clients, people whose cases had been dropped by the police, cases on which he couldn't justify more time or expense. They'd met soon after Makana's arrival. In his usual forthright manner, Okasha had come directly to the hotel where he was staying. It had not been very different from this one. He'd stated his case bluntly so there would be 'no confusion', as he put it.

'We've been asked to keep an eye on you,' he said as he paced round Makana's room, peering into every corner. 'Because you have a political history, and because, despite all this talk of our countries being brothers, actually we don't trust you one little bit. But the fact of the matter is that I don't much like what those people are doing to your country. I mean, what is it that makes them think we need reminding that we are all Muslims? Don't we say our prayers, go to the mosque on Fridays and fast during Ramadan? That's not good enough for them? Show me where it says that one Muslim is better than another and I will sign up. The fact is we have no right to stand in judgement on one another, and so I refuse to stand in judgement on you.'

Makana had observed the performance in silence, not quite sure what he was dealing with.

'Since you decided to come back to the modern world from whatever century you think you are living in down there, I take that as a sign of your good sense, which means I will help you with whatever you need.' He'd leaned closer to Makana and given him a wide, wolfish smile. 'It's all about trust.'

From that day on Okasha would look in on Makana from time to time. In those early days he was just a detective sergeant, but he had risen quickly. His methods, brash and at times ethically dubious, were nevertheless effective. Over the years Makana had tried his best to strike a balance between keeping Okasha happy and protecting his own interests. Sometimes it worked, other times not.

Fishawy's was closed at that hour, but that didn't stop Okasha. He kicked a bench on which a figure bundled in a blanket was trying to sleep.

'Get up and make some tea for those of us who have to work.'

The figure, which turned out to be both a young boy and an old man, came awake and began rattling open gates and lighting stoves. Okasha settled himself down with his back to the wall.

'Everyone tells me this Englishwoman was crazy. She's here alone, she gets herself killed. So far, so simple. Then I find your card and somehow I'm sure this is going to be more complicated than I thought. How do you know her?'

'I met her by chance in a restaurant. She was down on her

luck. Told me she was here trying to find her daughter, who disappeared years ago.'

'How long ago was this?'

'Seventeen years, I think she said.' Makana tried to recall as much as he could of their conversation. 'She'd been coming back over the years, to look for her child.'

'What for? The girl is either dead or so far away she will never come back.'

'It was her daughter,' said Makana quietly. 'Maybe you'd understand if you had children.'

Okasha took a deep breath and exhaled slowly. Makana was one of the few people who could talk to him that way, and he still wasn't altogether sure why that was. In this case, however, he knew.

'All right.' He brushed a hand through the air in lieu of an apology. 'So she was looking for her daughter. Now tell me why anyone would want to torture and kill her.'

'She seemed alone. Completely. As if she didn't really know anyone in the world.'

'So again, why? The medics will tell us if she was interfered with, but it doesn't look like a sexual attack. And not robbery either. So why?'

The tea finally arrived, carried by the old man who was yawning as he set down the glasses.

'About time,' said Okasha. He started tipping spoons of sugar in until there was a thick layer in the bottom of the glass. Then he began stirring.

'I don't care what you say, a woman travelling alone will always end up in trouble. But this . . . We're going to have diffi-culties with this one, I can tell.'

Chapter Nine

It was late the next morning when Makana stepped in through the scruffy front entrance of a building on a gloomy arcade near Midan Mustapha Kamel in the Tewfikiya area downtown. It wasn't exactly the kind of address he'd expect to be associated with the cinema business. Instead of glamorous, it felt distinctly derelict and forgotten. A listless *bawab* shuffled into sight before disappearing again without a word, sucked back into the shadows of his hidden nook off the front lobby. Makana took one look at the lift and chose to climb the stairs in almost complete darkness, running a hand along the wall to guide himself. It was black as a tomb in here. Emerging on the third floor, he struck a match and held it up to a faded sign which looked as if it hadn't been cleaned for years. He pressed the bell beneath and waited. After a long delay the door swung open to reveal a small woman in her forties. A round, puffy face buried under a thick dusting of powder and make-up peered inquisitively at him. A powerful reek of stale clothes and cheap scent assailed Makana as her eyes ran over him impatiently and her face set in a look of disdain. Here was trouble, she seemed to be thinking.

'Yes?'

'I'm here to see Mr Farag,' said Makana.

'Do you have an appointment?'

'Do I need one? Saad Hanafi sent me.'

The name apparently didn't mean much to the woman. She blinked heavily lined eyelashes at him for a moment before returning inside her office and lifting the telephone receiver, only to drop it instantly back into its cradle. Then she waddled away down a long corridor. Makana watched her disappear through a door at the far end. A moment later she emerged and walked all the way back, not saying a word until she was seated behind her desk again.

'He will see you now,' she said, extending a hand in the direction from which she had just come.

The office at the end of the corridor was dark and dusty. The air was thick with cigar smoke and the moist, fetid stench of decay. The window shutters, which had probably not been opened for decades, admitted only thin slivers of light. Makana could make out heaps of paper scattered about the desk behind which sat a large man with slack, flabby jowls and a scraggly grey beard. As Makana entered he heaved himself up and came round the desk, breathing hard. His hand when he offered it was as soft and clammy as a fish.

'Salim Farag. Come in, come in. So, you work for Hanafi, eh?'

His manner was breezy and over-familiar. He stood so close there was nowhere for Makana to move. The furniture in this office was crammed together and strewn with all manner of items. Farag reared back abruptly, his thick eyebrows clamping together like a vice.

'You're not a lawyer are you?' When Makana shook his head, the jelly-like face relaxed again. 'No, you don't look like a lawyer.

I'm generally an excellent judge of people. Please, sit. Tell me what I can do for you.'

Makana looked around. Farag lifted a heap of paper from a chair and then lost his grip and the whole pile toppled over on to the already overloaded sofa by the wall.

'It's about Adil Romario.'

'Why didn't you say so?' Farag chuckled heartily. 'What kind of trouble has my friend got himself into this time?'

'I was hoping you might be able to tell me,' said Makana.

The man's hand froze in mid-air, halfway towards the cigar that lay smouldering in an empty film can which stood in for an ashtray on his desk.

'Not a lawyer, eh?' His tone changed as he retrieved the cheap cigar, scrutinising Makana through quick, nervous puffs of smoke. 'So, you're one of Hanafi's dogs come to scare me off?'

'You sound as if you were expecting him to send someone.'

'Don't play games with me.' Farag leaned forward and pointed a finger at him. 'Let me tell you, I don't scare easily.'

'I'm not playing games, so why don't you cut out the melodrama?'

'Who exactly are you?' Farag's sagging lower lip quivered like a dog's.

'I told you, I'm working for Hanafi.'

'Anyone can claim to be working for Hanafi.'

'All you have to do is pick up that phone and call him.'

Farag stared at the phone as if it was a venomous snake coiled to strike. He made no attempt to touch it. Makana looked around him. It was hard to believe anything creative came out of this place, much less any films.

'I'm curious, what exactly is going on between you and Adil?'

'I don't see how that's any of your business, but it's no mystery. We're business partners.'

'Why would someone like Adil Romario go into partnership with you?'

If he took offence, Farag didn't show it. Maybe he was used to such remarks.

'Adil wants to get out of the game. Every player has to eventually. He's twenty-eight. In a couple of years his knees will start to go. Adil has been playing since he was a kid. And besides, there's no money in football, not real money.'

'His face is plastered everywhere. He must be doing all right.'

'All of that is peanuts.' Farag gave a nonchalant wave of a hefty hand bearing a fake Rolex whose gold effect was tarnished. 'The real money is in movies.'

Makana looked around him for something he might have overlooked. The gloomy, cluttered room, the worn furniture, the dusty piles of paper . . . Whatever Farag's game was, it didn't look as though finding money, real or otherwise, was exactly one of his strong points.

'Try to see it from my point of view. Hanafi is concerned. I need to give him something.'

This reminder caused Farag to reconsider. He swallowed with difficulty, took the cigar from his mouth and examined it.

'This isn't like growing okra and sticking it in bags, *enta fahim*?'

'I understand, but I need to know if you have any idea where Adil might be right now.'

'Look, I'm not his mother. Adil is a grown boy. He can take care of himself.'

Makana tried another tack. He nodded up at the grubby posters on the walls, none of which looked a day under thirty years old.

'You really think Adil could make it?'

'Sure.' Farag grinned, cheering up. 'Why not? He's a good-looking man, and there are girls out there who would do anything for a film star, you understand?'

'I get the picture. So, tell me, were you actually working on something, or is this just more cigar smoke?'

'Oh, yes, indeed.' Farag sat up, as if he had hooked a live one. 'We have a script. We even shot a few scenes. Want to see?' Perhaps he thought Hanafi might invest in his hopeless project. He began rummaging about until he came up with a remote control. A screen to Makana's right hummed into life. There was a whirring sound and a series of clicks. Unsteady lines chased each other vertically until they eventually settled into something like an image. Makana could make out two girls who appeared to be fondling one another on a bed. There was a muttered curse, followed by the whirr of the tape fast forwarding. Then more clicks and clunks.

'Ah, yes, here we are.'

This time the image was of a room in a brightly lit house. Sunlight flashed in the distance off something shiny. The camera panned rather inexpertly around the room.

'Is that Adil's house?'

'No, it belongs to Vronsky . . . one of my production partners. Ah, here it is.'

Makana turned his attention back to the screen as a door opened and Adil Romario entered. He was tall and slim and dressed in a crisp white shirt and jeans. He wasn't striking, but probably good-looking enough to be considered handsome. But as far as his thespian skills were concerned, he left a lot to be desired. Removing his sunglasses, he moved around the room in an awkward, self-conscious fashion. He seemed to be going through the motions like a man in a trance. He appeared to be looking for something – opening drawers, etcetera. There was a sound behind him and he spun around, eyes wide in theatrical alarm. The bad acting was distorted by the shaky image, as if filmed by someone with a bad case of delirium tremens. Makana had a feeling he knew who the cameraman was and a brief sweep past a mirror confirmed that it was indeed Farag himself. The woman who had just appeared in shot was slight and young and quite beautiful. She was holding a pistol like it might bite her.

'What are you doing here?' she demanded, rather uncertainly.

'I've come for what is owed to me.' Adil Romario delivered his lines with all the energy of a tired man ordering a sandwich in a snack bar. He moved into a lengthy monologue, most of which he got straight. It wasn't much of a monologue to begin with, but it was delivered in the wooden staccato of a man who has difficulty reading from a sheet of paper.

'Who's the girl?' Makana asked.

'Mimi Maliki. She's new. Hasn't really made it yet. She will, though. Look at that face!'

Farag was enthralled by his own work, staring at the screen with rapt attention, the slack mouth hanging open, cigar forgotten.

Makana found himself drawn in by this fleeting glimpse of his quarry. He scoured every movement, every gesture, in Romario's underwhelming performance, in search of some clue as to what was going on inside his head. He saw an angry young man determined to turn himself into a god of the screen. Having no natural talent might not be much of a hindrance to someone who was already a big star. Adil Romario had his face impressed on the hearts of his adoring public already, which made Makana wonder why he wanted to go to all this trouble? He clearly didn't enjoy acting. So why do it? Was it just the money? And why here of all places?

'How do I get in touch with this Mimi?'

'Oh, I'm sorry. I can't help you there. A professional matter.'

'I could make it worth your while.' Makana reached for the envelope.

'It's not a matter of money. It's simply the principle of it.'

Farag didn't strike Makana as someone to whom principles meant a great deal. His attention was drawn back to the screen as a voice shouted 'Cut'. The tape ran on a little further as the camera continued to roll, apparently forgotten. It panned around the room dizzily, obviously dangling in the hand of the director, affording a fleeting glimpse of the sea in the distance. As it vanished, Makana caught a brief glimpse of another woman. She was standing back in a doorway as if trying not to intrude. It wasn't clear if she was part of the set-up. She was dressed in a dark skirt and white blouse that resembled a maid's uniform. Then the screen went dark.

'Not bad, eh? You see what I mean?'

'I'm not really an expert.' Makana got to his feet and handed one of his cards across the desk. 'I'd like you to call me if you hear from Adil.'

Farag grinned, revealing teeth stained the colour of corn. 'Anything for Mr Hanafi,' he said thickly.

'Oh, and do you think I could borrow that tape for a few days?'

'Please, be my guest.' Farag rattled it out of the machine. 'I have plenty of copies.'

Makana glanced at the receptionist as they went by. She looked away quickly.

Chapter Ten

A cross the street from Farag's office was a news stand where a man was serving tea and coffee through a narrow, blackened hole chipped in the wall. He had a telephone that worked, perched on the ledge. The plaster round the aperture was stained black from being continually rubbed by human hands, and from the countless cups of coffee and tea that had been passed through it. Makana dialled his home number and accessed his telephone messages. There was one from Soraya Hanafi asking if they could meet. Another from Okasha, who wanted him to call as soon as he got the message. When Makana finally got through it sounded as though he was inside a speeding squad car.

'You took your time,' yelled Okasha above the siren.

'What's the problem?'

'I am going to ask you a favour which you cannot refuse me.'

'You haven't told me what it is yet.'

'It doesn't matter. You still can't refuse me . . . this is about your girlfriend from Aswani's. Two detectives are arriving from Scotland Yard in London.'

'I don't understand,' said Makana. 'She was in the police?'

'No, but her father is a lord or something. Now, listen to me

– one dead Englishwoman is enough of a headache without adding in politics. Anyway, the point is, you have to be there.'

'You don't need me.'

'Already you have saved my face by telling me about the disappearance of her child. And besides, you speak English better than any of my fool assistants. It's nothing, just a formality. They will fly in, look down their noses at us for a while, and then write their predictable reports saying our methods are as ancient as the pyramids.'

'I still don't see . . .'

'You don't have to see, you just have to be there. The point is to make a good impression.'

The area around the Hilton Hotel in Tahrir Square was strangely quiet, considering it was midday and that this ought to have been the high season for tourists. Across the street a single bus pulled up to the National Museum and disgorged a handful of intrepid figures. As he got out of his taxi Makana saw Okasha coming towards him, one finger raised. 'So, tell me this, if her father is a lord and whatnot, why stay in a cheap hotel and not here? These things don't happen in the Hilton.'

'Maybe she wanted to be closer to the Egyptian people.'

'Look at that.' Okasha nodded at a pack of small boys rushing up to surround a solitary Westerner who had emerged from the hotel. They were all yapping and waving sheets of papyrus at him. 'A year ago they would have charged you ten pounds a picture. Nowadays you can get ten for one pound.' The besieged man tried to flee, first one way and then the other, panic replacing his confidence as he gave up and hastily retreated into the hotel.

The lobby was deserted. A couple of Chinese in padded jackets were smoking and smiling, taking photographs of one another against the backdrop of the river, while a French group were drinking coffee and gesticulating wildly. Other than that the atmosphere was strangely muted, as if everyone was waiting for something to happen. The waiters stood around in listless pairs, having given up trying to look busy.

'It's ironic.' Okasha swept imperiously past the metal detector with a perfunctory salute. 'It couldn't be safer in this country right now, but people are still too scared to come.'

'You can't really blame them.'

Barely two months had elapsed since the worst terrorist attack on record had taken place in Luxor in Upper Egypt. A group of armed men ran into the Temple of Hatshepsut and massacred sixty-two people, most of them tourists. They gunned them down, eviscerating and decapitating a couple of them for good measure, before running for the hills. Security forces managed to gun down as many people as were killed by the attackers. The radicals were later discovered in a cave nearby. They were seated in a circle after apparently having carried out some kind of suicide ritual. The number of foreign visitors to Egypt had plummeted since then, causing a severe slump in the tourism sector.

'In a way they made our job easier,' said Okasha. 'Everyone hates the Islamists now.'

Take the food from people's tables and they will turn on you pretty quickly. If the Nile was the lifeblood of the country, the ancient temples which dotted its banks put bread on the table for some eight million of its citizens. The upside was that the Luxor attacks appeared to be a last-ditch attempt by a group which already felt their cause had been marginalised. The previous year the government had offered an amnesty to some of the twenty thousand Islamists being held in prison, in an attempt to alleviate the problem. Too little, too late, some warned. But nobody was planning to let their guard down, least of all Okasha who took the task of hunting down militants as his own personal mission in life.

'By the way . . .' he grasped Makana's arm as they surveyed the lobby, 'I looked up the investigation into the English girl's disappearance.' Okasha heaved in a lungful of air. 'Elizabeth Markham, the mother, was uncooperative, to say the least. They discovered drugs in her room. And she refused to explain what she was doing in this country. Her story was full of holes. As you can imagine, that didn't go down well. They dismissed her as crazy . . . paranoid. They even considered the possibility that she might have sold the child herself, to make some money.'

Makana tried to square this with the image he had of Liz Markham searching desperately for her lost daughter. Could it have been remorse for her own actions that had brought her back here, year after year?

'She told me she'd had problems. That's why she couldn't come back right away.'

'Maybe they locked her up.' Okasha glanced around. 'Okay, so which ones are they?'

Turning his attention back to the lobby, Makana picked out a couple sitting on a sofa in the far corner as the most likely candidates. A man and a woman, both in their thirties. The woman looked to be slightly older than her companion. Slim and with short dark hair, she was wearing black slacks and jacket. The man beside her was large and red-faced, heavily built, with thinning sandy hair.

'There.'

Okasha followed Makana's gaze. As he did so the woman got to her feet and turned to face them. 'You've done it again,' he murmured, as he led the way across the room. The formalities were dispensed with as briefly as possible. The British detectives introduced themselves as Bailey and Hayden. They weren't from Scotland Yard, as Okasha had thought, but from something called Special Branch. The woman was the senior of the two, something which it took Okasha a while to grasp. He insisted on addressing Bailey alone and ignoring the woman until Hayden cleared her throat noisily.

'Just to make it clear, Inspector, this is a formality. We are not here to take any part in the investigation, or to pass judgement on you.'

'You are looking for a connection to her father?' Makana asked.

'Lord Markham is a member of our House of Lords.' Bailey spoke as if lecturing a couple of schoolboys. Okasha sniffed and threw him a wary look. The intricacies of the English peerage escaped both the inspector and Makana. They had little bearing on a murder investigation in Cairo. If the British felt it necessary to go to all the expense of sending people around the world to please one of their titled subjects, then that was their business.

'On the telephone, you mentioned that you believe she was tortured before she was killed?' Hayden enquired.

'That is correct.' Okasha nodded briskly. 'Look, if you have information suggesting this was a political murder then you must share it.'

'I'm afraid we're not allowed to do that,' said Bailey, with a poker-faced expression.

'They're playing games with us,' muttered Okasha to Makana as they descended the steps to the waiting cars. 'They want to connect this to our terrorist problem.'

'Why would they do that?'

'Politics. It gives them a big stick to beat us with.'

It seemed unlikely, but while Okasha gave the orders, doors

slammed and the convoy raced away, Makana couldn't help wondering if there might be something he had failed to spot in all this. Could there be a connection between Liz Markham's death and the recent terrorist outrage?

Okasha had obviously decided to impress the visitors with his security measures. Motorcycle outriders wailed past them with sirens blaring and lights blazing. The circus was coming to town.

'Is this really necessary?' asked Hayden.

'You are our guests. We give you a welcome like a president.' Okasha was grinning like an idiot. Makana noticed the other officer, Bailey, shaking his head to himself. Clearly, the spectacle served merely to confirm his perception that the police in this country were a bunch of clowns.

When they reached the square outside the Al Hassanain Hotel they were met by a crowd of onlookers and a heavy police presence. Okasha leaped out and started issuing more orders left and right in his usual muscular fashion, making his men jump. It was quite a performance. The entourage jogged up the stairs into the lobby of the hotel. Hayden looked around, taking in the general air of decay. This clearly wasn't the Hilton.

The manager was a podgy, unhappy-looking man in a *gellabia*. He wore round spectacles and an expression like a sheep being led to the slaughter as he scurried along behind, asking when he would be able to have the room back. Okasha batted him away like a pesky fly.

The blood on the floor had congealed into a rigid brown map stretched out across the tiles. The chair and the bloody strips of towelling had been removed by the forensics team. Hayden and Bailey paced about the room, clearly hoping to find something that had been overlooked. There wasn't much to see. Okasha had made sure of that. Makana remained in the doorway. He stared at the brown mark and wondered about the woman whose life had ended there.

'We would like to see the body,' said Hayden.

'Of course.' Okasha nodded. 'Unfortunately, it cannot be arranged before tomorrow. Today is Friday and the medical officers do not work today.'

'Don't work?' echoed Bailey.

Okasha stood his ground. 'That is correct.' He smiled. 'You should take advantage of the fact – do some sightseeing and shopping. We have the most historic bazaar in the world. Or have you seen the pyramids? I can arrange for a car to take you there.'

'We're not here on holiday,' said Bailey as he pushed by into the hallway. He lit a cigarette and stood glaring into space, pointedly ignoring Makana.

'That's most kind of you, Inspector, we'd be happy to accept,' said Hayden with a conciliatory smile.

'Very well. A car will remain here to take you wherever you like.'

With that, Okasha stepped out and jerked his head for Makana to follow. They took the stairs down to the lobby and went to a café in a square nearby. Okasha studied his surroundings carefully before choosing a table and sitting down at it with a heavy sigh. He spread his legs and pushed back his coat so that the large pistol in the leather holster at his waist protruded visibly. He eyed everyone in sight warily, like a cowboy in a film, until satisfied there was no immediate threat in the vicinity. He never let his guard down. He couldn't afford to.

'We're wasting our time, playing tour guides for the interfering British.'

Okasha grunted and snapped his fingers in the air for tea,

which came faster than Makana had ever seen. He leaned over the table, his big hand plucking a couple of leaves off the sprig of fresh mint set in the middle. He dropped them into his glass where they floated limply, lost tropical islands in an amber sea.

'Thanks for coming,' he said. 'I think I would have lost my temper if I had been alone. Such insolence!'

'He was just doing his job.'

'You're being too generous. Perhaps it is your nature, or maybe the years you spent in their country with your wife left you with happy memories.'

Makana reached into his jacket and produced the newspaper photograph showing Adil Romario standing with Gaber and the group of men. Next to Gaber was the slight man Makana had failed to identify.

'Can you tell me who that is?' he asked, holding out the clipping. Okasha's eyes dropped and he stared at it for a moment before looking up.

'How do you know him?'

'I don't,' said Makana. 'He interviewed me when I first came here. He never gave me his name. That's why I remember him.'

Okasha gave him a long look, and then he nodded. 'It's Colonel Serrag of Intelligence. A very important man.' He handed back the clipping. 'You want to stay away from him.' Then he got up and stamped his feet. 'The British, eh? They still believe they rule this country, like the old days, or maybe they think it's the whole world now. *Yakhrib beitum.* Can I give you a lift?'

'No,' said Makana. 'I think I'll stay around here for a while.'

'Don't go catching any murderers.' Okasha wagged a finger at him. 'At least, not before I do.'

Chapter Eleven

In Arabic the city is known as *al-Qahira*, after the planet Mars – 'the vanquisher'. In the latter part of the tenth century the Fatimids built an imperial enclave here with high walls to keep the exquisite palaces and their occupants from prying eyes. It soon became the most illustrious city in the Muslim world. The astrologers predicted that the name would bring good fortune. A city named after a distant planet. As if this would keep them safe.

History of another kind was on Makana's mind. His own personal history. The reasons that had led him to this city. He still found it hard to shrug off certain traits or superstitions, delusions . . . call them what you would. He didn't believe in coincidence, but couldn't help thinking that things were often linked together according to some strange predestined plan. In the days of the Fatimids he would probably have been strung up from the very gates of this city, hung, drawn and quartered.

There was more connecting him to Liz Markham's death than mere happenstance. It wasn't anything he could prove, more like a nagging premonition. The old bazaar . . . The answer had to lie here. Had her enquiries about her daughter sparked off the events that had led to her death?

People rushed by, calling out their wares, services, greetings, jokes, curses. Life. It was all here. The Khan al-Khalili was said to comprise some of the most valuable real estate in the world; more expensive, metre for metre, than London, Paris or New York. It was subdivided into fractions. The artisans sat cramped in their minuscule workshops, tapping away all day like blind men feeling their way along the lines of their engravings. In the old days the narrow lanes would have been teeming with visitors from all over the world, all eager to strike a bargain; today it was virtually deserted. This was the world he belonged to now. To Liz Markham, searching for her little girl, it would have been a crazy labyrinth. His brief impression of her had been of a determined woman, wounded, angry at herself, at the world. Not the kind of person who takes no for an answer. To keep coming back here all this time testified to her determination. It had taken courage and conviction.

Makana knew he ought not to be wasting time. Hanafi's generous reward was slipping through his fingers like sand through an hourglass.

There were familiar faces here, people Makana had spoken to over the years: men hanging about in their doorways, chatting across the narrow passageways with their neighbours over the heads of the passers-by. They talked about food and football and the price of gold. They broke off to murmur a greeting whenever a visitor wandered by. Good morning, madam, please step inside, sir. No charge for looking. They could express themselves in every European language along with a phrase or two in Japanese. They had heard about the murder, of course, and muttered darkly about how it was going to be bad for business. The last thing they needed. Many recalled the *magnoona* Englishwoman, who came back year after year, passing out photos of her child. 'Everyone knew she was crazy,' said Helmi, an old acquaintance, perched behind the counter of his jeweller's shop which was no bigger than a large telephone booth and draped with strings of golden scarabs. He had one eye pressed against the lens clipped to his glasses. 'People said she had been mixed up in something bad, long ago. Many kept away from her, turned their backs. Maybe if they hadn't, she would still be alive.'

Beside a dusty arch of medieval stone leading to a narrow passageway that threaded its way along the back of the bazaar, close to the old city wall, Makana came across a curious shop he hadn't noticed before. Away from the bright lights and shiny displays, this corner looked rundown and dull. Few tourists ventured this far. A few battered stalls sold old junk, rusty tools and artefacts. Instruments that a dentist or a vet might have used a century ago. There were carpenter's planes and horseshoes, heavy old brass keys and iron door knockers. It was the only shop in sight, set back in a dogleg just beyond the stone arch. Perched on a rickety chair outside sat an old man wearing a pair of dark glasses held together with Sellotape over the bridge of his nose. Even the tape was cracked and yellowed. He was wearing a dirty brown *gellabia* and smoking a cigarette. When he spotted him, Makana had the feeling the man had been watching him for some time.

Still, he made no effort to rise as Makana peered through the window next to him. The layers of dust visible spoke of the unlikely collection of objects inside as not having been stirred for decades. Makana spotted little rectangles of wood about the size of a small page with metal plates and edges to them.

'What are those things?' he enquired.

'Printer's blocks.' The man tilted his face to stare at Makana.

'I've seen you before,' he said. His cheeks were hollow and he sucked them in further as he inhaled the blue smoke deep into his lungs. 'I never forget a face. What are you looking for this time?'

'A little girl.' Makana considered him for a moment. 'She disappeared. An English girl.'

'A long time ago. Was it something to do with the woman they killed?'

'It was her daughter.'

'A bad business.' The man sucked his few remaining teeth. 'But why are so you interested? That was more than ten years ago.'

'Almost seventeen.'

'And you come looking for her now?'

'You know how it is.' Makana shrugged. 'Sometimes one story is connected to another.'

'You are trying to connect the stories, is that it?'

'You must have been around in those days, do you remember it?'

'When the girl disappeared? Of course, we all do. It brought shame on us. We don't steal little girls around here, it's not our way.'

'How about the police? I suppose they made your life difficult.'

'The police? They didn't do anything. They knew better than to get involved.'

'Oh, why is that?'

'Anybody ever tell you that you ask a lot of questions?' The old man got to his feet as a woman covered in black from head to toe, curious to see what Makana had been looking at, tugged her ragged child over to the window to peer through the grimy glass.

'What have you got in there?' she asked.

'Nothing of interest to you,' the old man snapped, so harshly that the woman was lost for words. Her jaw dropped and she stared at him blankly. 'Go away and take your filthy child with you.' He got to his feet and waved them off. The woman snatched the little boy's hand and hurried off, glancing over her shoulder at the madman.

'You don't need any customers, then?'

'I don't like my thoughts being disturbed.' It seemed a strange attitude for a shopkeeper. Before turning away he paused to deliver one parting comment. 'I say now what I said back then. If they never found that poor girl, it was because they didn't want to find her.'

With that he tossed his cigarette butt aside and ducked inside his shop. Makana considered following him in, but he had the idea that it wouldn't do much good. With some people, the more you pressed them, the further into the wood they would burrow.

When he arrived back at the main square Makana spotted the female English officer, Hayden, sitting alone. He would have avoided her if he had seen her in time, but she had already spotted him and was gesturing at the chair beside her.

'Where is your colleague?'

'Bailey? Oh, he's in there somewhere.' Her thumb jerked vaguely in the direction of the bazaar. 'Said he wanted to buy a waterpipe.'

'Ah, yes.' Makana nodded. He sat down and studied her for a moment. At close hand he could see that she was younger than he had first thought. She dressed like an older woman, perhaps to draw less attention to herself or to assert her authority.

'Your first visit to Cairo?'

'Well, I was here years ago, when I was a student.'

'Tell me, please. I am curious. Lord Markham, is he very important?'

Hayden smiled. 'Not really, but the family name still wields some influence. We have to be seen to be doing our bit.'

'Do you believe Elizabeth Markham's death may have been politically motivated?'

'You tell me?' Hayden tilted her head to one side, waiting.

'I doubt anyone here knew who she was. There's no political gain to be had from killing unknowns.'

'You think we are overestimating our own importance, don't you?'

'You are following your protocol, and . . .' he hesitated, 'if you'll permit me to say, I think you misunderstand the primary motive of our Islamists. Their aim is to bring down the government, not to attack Westerners.'

'They seem to do a good job of it if that's not what they're after!'

'It's a way of attracting attention . . . creating panic, damaging tourism.'

'Well, they've been very effective in that, wouldn't you say?'

Makana conceded the point with a smile. 'It would be useful to know something of Elizabeth Markham's background. She told me she had been coming here for several years.'

'You met her?' Hayden looked taken aback.

'We met purely by coincidence,' Makana explained, waving to attract the attention of a waiter who was busy polishing his shoes with a paper napkin and clearly had no time for distractions.

'She's the one who told you about her daughter?'

'That's right.'

'I admit we were pretty impressed that you managed to find out about the girl so quickly.'

'It was many years ago, it's true.'

'And you think that Elizabeth's death might be connected to the child's abduction?'

'It's a distinct possibility, don't you think?' Makana waited. Hayden seemed to be considering something. The waiter had finished with his shoes and had now turned his attention to the creases in his trousers.

'There's something you should perhaps know,' Hayden began. 'Liz Markham had a nervous breakdown after she lost her daughter. She was in a mental institution for several years.' Over Makana's shoulder she managed to attract the waiter's attention just by smiling at him. 'Tea?'

Makana nodded. 'That's why she couldn't come here? She was in hospital.'

'Exactly. Liz Markham's drug problems began when she was still a teenager at boarding school. Lord Markham had practically no relationship with his daughter for many years. When Alice went missing, he had Liz put away.'

'I didn't know you could do that in England.'

'You can if you're powerful enough. Markham has a lot of friends in high places.'

'And when she came out, the first thing she did was to come here and look for Alice.'

'There has never been any sign of the girl since, right?'

'Not so far as I know.'

'But you intend to look into it?' Hayden was watching him carefully. Makana nodded.

The tea arrived. Hayden watched him select a couple of mint leaves and drop them into his glass, and followed suit.

'Is that a mosque?'

Makana followed the direction of her gaze across the square.

'One of the holiest sites in Islam. The shrine where the head of Imam Hussein is said to lie.'

'Only his head?'

'It's questionable whether even that is actually there.'

'What happened to the rest of him?'

'They were separated on a battlefield in Karbala.'

'Ah,' said Hayden, sitting up. 'The most famous battle in Islamic history. It marks the division between orthodox Sunni and Shi'a Islam. The death of Hussein marked the end of the line of Rightly Guided Caliphs, who were directly descended from the Prophet Muhammed.'

'You prepared for the trip.' Makana was impressed.

'I read a couple of guidebooks on the plane.' Hayden shrugged dismissively. 'You seem to have given all of this a lot of thought.'

'I know what it's like to lose a daughter.'

He regretted saying it as soon as the words were spoken. Hayden set down her glass.

'I'm sorry to hear that.' She looked away for a moment, acknowledging his loss, then she turned back to him. 'Do you mind if I ask you what exactly the relationship is between you and Inspector Okasha?'

'We're friends.' It would have been easy to lie, but somehow he couldn't, not now. They had crossed a boundary of trust. And besides, he had a feeling she would see right through him.

'But you are a police officer?'

'Not any longer.'

Hayden's tea was forgotten. She studied him for a long time and then nodded to herself slowly, as if she understood or accepted the explanation as it was.

'He must have great trust in you.'

'He has his moments.' Makana lit a cigarette.

'Why do you think Liz Markham was tortured?'

'My feeling is that her death is related to her past here, to the disappearance of her daughter.'

'But the investigation into that turned up nothing.'

'The police were convinced they were dealing with a person of dubious moral character. Liz had a drug problem. Here that is looked on very gravely.' Makana took a deep breath. 'Usually, if a little English girl goes missing, they would move heaven and earth to find her. It's bad publicity otherwise. No one wants to visit a country that preys on little girls. So why didn't they in this case?'

They both fell silent, reflecting on this.

'Do you have any idea why she came here to Cairo with a small child, all those years ago?' he asked.

'None at all,' said Hayden. 'I assumed it was for a holiday.'

'And the identity of the girl's father. Do you have any information about that?'

'To be honest, we didn't consider the child relevant to our investigation. It was a long time ago,' said Hayden apologetically. 'I do know that when Alice went missing, Lord Markham hired a detective to help find his granddaughter.'

'I would be interested to hear what he discovered.'

'Of course.'

Makana was feeling as if they had reached some kind of understanding when a shadow fell between them. It was Bailey, carrying a waterpipe under each arm. A wide grin split his broad face.

'You found one then?' Hayden looked up brightly.

'Cheeky buggers try to charge you a fortune. Managed to knock them down, though.'

'I should be going,' Makana said.

'Oh, please, not on my account,' said Bailey, sitting down. 'How can you drink tea in this weather? I need something long and cold, like a beer, say.'

The waiter rushed off to oblige. Hayden got up to shake Makana's hand as he made to leave.

'Thank you for being so candid.'

'Please, enjoy your stay.'

She watched him walk away across the square.

'What was all that about?' Bailey demanded.

'Oh, nothing,' she said with a smile. 'So, go on, show me what you found.'

Chapter Twelve

It was late afternoon and the steady flow of commuters making their way home had begun. Car horns jabbered at one another and the air swelled with the thick heat of shuddering engines and choking clouds of black exhaust. Crossing the street, Makana bought a newspaper and stood and waited. Twenty minutes later Farag emerged from the grubby entrance. He was wearing a dirty brown leather jacket and sunglasses that looked flashy and out of date. Looking neither left nor right, he walked in the direction of the main road. Again, it struck Makana what an unlikely pair they made, Farag and Adil Romario.

Five minutes later, Farag's secretary appeared. She moved slowly, as if her legs were giving her pain, dragging a heavy handbag like a shapeless black dog. When she turned the corner Makana followed. She walked in the direction of Tahrir Square and down into the metro at Sadat station. He kept far enough behind to ensure he wasn't seen, pausing to drop a note in the window and getting a ticket flung back at him in return. Passing the mural of the great leader as peacemaker, he arrived at the platform in time to see the squat figure shuffling down to the far end, where the women-only carriages at the front of the train would stop.

When the train arrived it was crowded. Passengers patiently stepped aboard, with Makana staying as close to the front as possible. He watched her through the connecting doors. She appeared to be sleeping, the black bag on her lap now, her head nodding slightly as the train rushed under the river in the direction of Dokki. She looked so tired he could probably have stood right in front of her and she wouldn't have recognised him, but still he took his time, allowing her to get ahead of him before he slipped into the crowd making its way up to ground level.

She walked south for a couple of blocks before turning into a narrow, uneven street cluttered with dusty, immobile cars that looked as if they had been petrified in volcanic ash. Her destination was a modest apartment block. The door of the lift clanged shut as Makana came into the lobby, climbing the stairs, listening all the time for the lift to stop. On the fifth floor, he heard the door creak open and then swing shut. There was more heavy breathing and the dragging of footsteps across the narrow hall, followed by a key being inserted into a lock. Makana stepped neatly up in time to see a door close. He waited a moment or two before leaning on the buzzer, hearing the corresponding noise from within. There were more laboured footsteps and finally the door opened and the woman stood before him. She stared at him blankly for several moments before realisation slowly dawned. The blood drained from her face. When it seemed to occur to her to close the door, Makana put his foot forward quickly to block it.

'I don't want to do you any harm, but I think there is something you want to tell me.'

'Are you mad? How did you find me? You must go, now. My husband . . . He will be back any moment.'

'I see,' said Makana. 'And does he know?'

'Does who know what?' Her face flushed as if she had been slapped.

'Does he know what kind of work you do for Farag?'

'Go! My husband is coming now.'

The emotion in her voice betrayed a fear greater than anything Makana presented. She seemed to lose her balance and stumble backwards, letting the door swing open. Makana stepped inside. There was no resistance. The woman sank back on to a conveniently placed chair, clasping her hands together.

'I knew this day would come,' she whimpered. '*Ya rabbi*, what is going to happen now?'

'I'm not here to hurt you,' Makana said gently.

'I have done nothing.' She bit her index finger. 'I knew you were police the moment I saw you.'

'A woman in your position can't afford to do nothing.'

'I knew it would come to this,' she repeated. 'My husband will kill me if he finds out anything. Please, you have to go right now! I'm begging you.'

'Maybe I should wait to talk to him.' Makana folded his arms.

'No, please! I swear, he'll kill me.' Pressing her hands to her face she began to sob, rubbing her fists into her eyes until the kohl ran, making her resemble a panda.

'I swear I thought at first Farag was a decent man. I mean, I never liked him, but it's a job. At the end of the day there's no difference between one man and another. You're all animals.'

'Is Farag blackmailing Adil Romario?'

The woman stiffened and Makana realised he had made a mistake. Now her eyes narrowed.

'You don't know.' She had one hand pressed to her heaving chest. 'You have no idea. *Ya satir*, and I almost told you everything . . . I'll bet you're not even with the police.'

'Tell me about the girl, the one in the movie with Adil . . . Mimi Maliki?'

'That's all you want?' The woman pawed hopelessly at her tears with a handkerchief taken from her sleeve, smearing her face. 'You men are all the same.' Somehow she had found the strength of purpose to stand up to him. 'I'm telling you to get out!'

There no longer seemed to be much point in fighting her. As he descended the stairs, Makana had to step aside to make room for a large man, who was huffing and puffing as he climbed. He didn't raise his head as he went by.

Chapter Thirteen

This time Makana spotted the young man almost as soon as he left the building. Standing off to one side, back against the wall, folding away a newspaper, the man pretended to ignore him, but Makana knew immediately that he had seen him somewhere before. It wasn't until he had almost reached the end of the street that he remembered where. Increasing his pace, Makana turned the corner and spun round on his heel, pulling up sharply. In his haste, the young man rushed round after him – and bumped straight into him.

'Excuse me,' he said, narrowly avoiding collision and moving aside quickly. As he made to move off, Makana stepped sideways to block his escape.

'What's the rush, brother?'

'I beg your pardon?' The man rocked back, head bobbing in wordless enquiry as he tried to find his way round.

'Why are you following me?' Makana again moved to stop him escaping. 'The first time we met was near the zoological gardens, remember?'

The man's eyes darted to left and right, seeking any avenue of escape. He was in his late twenties, a small man with unruly curly hair and an unshaven face. He wore jeans and a grey sweater and carried a large bag over one shoulder.

'All right,' he said, finally, giving up his evasion tactics. 'Let's discuss the matter.' His keen, perceptive gaze surveyed Makana as he stabbed at the thick frame of his spectacles, bumping them higher on his nose. 'Which paper do you work for?'

'Who said I work for a paper?'

'Okay, I get it, you're freelance.'

Makana stepped towards him. The man backed off. 'We're getting away from the question I asked. Why are you following me?'

'Following you?' The young man attempted a laugh. 'I want the same thing you want.'

'Which is what?'

'The story . . . Adil Romario, of course.'

'What makes you think I'm interested in Adil Romario?'

'Come on.' The twitching of the journalist's face betrayed his keenness. He was sure he had Makana now. 'You were coming out of Hanafi's building, then you were at the club. You were asking about Adil Romario.'

'You seem to know a lot.'

'I've been covering this story for a while. Nobody knows this team better than I do.'

The faint shadow of doubt in his eyes, however, suggested that he was wondering if perhaps he had met his match. Makana reached into his shirt pocket for his cigarettes and lit one. As a rule he didn't like journalists. Most of them were lazy crooks, ready to beg, steal or lie their way to a good story, not caring who or what got trampled on in the process, least of all the truth.

'Why don't we sit down for a minute and compare notes?' suggested the man. He gestured to a café nearby. 'Maybe we can make a deal? A trade between professionals?'

'A deal?' Makana mused. 'What kind of deal?'

'We're both in the dark. We pool our information and both of us gain.'

Makana was unconvinced, but he needed to find out how much the other man knew.

'Okay, let's talk.'

'Not so fast,' replied the journalist. 'I need a coffee.'

They managed to make it across the wide boulevard of Al Tahrir Street without being run over. The café was a simple place with blue tiles on the walls. There were four metal tables with low wooden stools set around them. The place was crowded and appeared to be run by a gangly kid of about thirteen who was taking orders and juggling coffee pots on the stove with a dexterity that belied his age. The journalist held out his hand.

'If we're going to work together, we may as well introduce ourselves. I'm Sami Barakat.'

Makana ignored his hand. He remembered the name. This was the author of the article about unrest in the team.

'Okay, Sami, let's begin by you telling me what you are bringing to this little partnership?'

The hand wavered in the air and then sank slowly. 'How do you mean?'

'Well, I get the feeling I've been leading you around this story like a child guiding a blind man. What's your angle?'

The other man squinted at him through the smoke. 'It's funny. You know, when I was following you, there were times I wasn't even sure you were a reporter at all.'

Makana met his gaze evenly. 'What else would I be?'

'The usual. Maybe police, maybe security.' Sami Barakat adjusted his spectacles.

'Look, you're the one who wanted to make a deal. I think

you're the one who needs to explain himself. How did you pick up on this story?'

'Well, it's simple, really. I've been covering football for some years now.' Sami Barakat dropped his cigarette butt on the floor amid a muddy paste of coffee grounds and tobacco flakes, and lit another one. 'You know how it is, nobody gives you a chance. You have to keep your eyes open for a big story that you can get clean away with. Well, this is my lucky break.'

Makana observed as the boy sauntered between the busy tables with all the flair of a dancer, sliding two cups of coffee and glasses of water between them before pirouetting away.

'Okay, so what's your take on Romario?'

'The difference between a reasonably good player and an exceptional one is their ability to be in the right place at exactly the right moment.' The journalist touched a hand to his forehead in a gesture of despair. 'But recently this guy is never in the right place at the right time. I mean, if he's standing there and the ball rolls up and shakes his hand, he might just be able to put it in the net, but don't ask him to go and fetch it.'

'He's overrated, then, in your opinion?'

'He's inconsistent.'

'How do you explain that?'

'I think he's lost it. Love of the game, I mean. He wants out but he doesn't know how.'

Sami Barakat sipped his coffee and lit another cigarette. It made sense. Adil had been brought up to be the star of Hanafi's team. But he'd lost interest in the game. He was tired of being a hired monkey. He wanted to be respected in his own right. Was it possible that he felt resentment towards the very man who had picked him out of obscurity and set him on a pedestal?

'It's like everything else in this country,' Sami Barakat

continued. 'We sold ourselves to the *shaitan*. Everyone wants to be nice to Hanafi so that he will be nice to them in turn. Nobody dares write the truth. Well, I did and I shall probably lose my job for it. It's all rotten. It begins with politics, never wanting to print anything that might offend someone . . . the Muslim Brotherhood, the Ministers, even the President. We'll forgive them all because the only thing for sure in this country is that sooner or later we all need a favour, and who better than Hanafi to do us one? He's everyone's generous uncle.'

'And the rumours of Romario being picked up by a big European club?'

'You surely don't buy that?' Barakat looked pained. 'Who would take him?'

'Hanafi has contacts, he might be able to swing it.'

'Even Hanafi can't pull off that miracle.'

Makana stirred sugar into his cup. 'What about Clemenza? Could he set it up?'

'The only thing Clemenza could set up is a card game.'

'He must still have influence in Europe.'

'I see where you are going with this.' The reporter nodded. 'Clemenza is as crooked as they come and he hates Hanafi enough to try something like that. But I just don't believe it's possible. Besides, Clemenza's on the way out. He hasn't won anything for ages and the players aren't fond of him. And I hear his gambling debts are sizeable. He spends most nights losing at the tables in the Semiramis Casino. He could do with a little commission but he knows better than to try and promote Adil.' Sami Barakat sat back and grinned. 'So you're not a sportswriter, eh?'

'I never said I was.'

Barakat thought about this and commented, 'I can't say that I really understand what you are up to.' Makana clicked his tongue but otherwise remained silent. Barakat took this as an invitation to continue speaking.

'I've read your work, right? I just don't know the face. I mean, that is exactly what is wrong with most journalists today. All too busy turning themselves into celebrities. They want to *be* the news, rather than report it. And here you are. Anonymous. Nobody knows your face. Now that's something I can respect.' He took another sip of coffee and lit a fresh cigarette. 'The papers are only interested in scandal nowadays, not what they get up to on the football field, right?'

'Millions of people would disagree with you there.'

'Where are you going?'

As he paid for the coffee Makana told the boy to keep the change. In return he received a mock salute: '*Shukran ya reis!*' Everyone was an actor in this town. Makana got to his feet.

'Hey, hold on a minute!' Barakat grabbed his satchel and followed Makana out into the street. 'I thought we were going to work together on this?'

'Then you thought wrong . . . and if you ever try following me again, you'd better hope I don't catch you. Understood?'

Chapter Fourteen

Like Makana's *awama*, most vehicles in this city resembled artefacts hijacked from a museum rather than any modern means of transport. Taxis sputtered, minivans squealed and heavy old buses lumbered by like ageing elephants heading for the graveyard. Trailing billowing tempests of acrid black smoke, the herds migrated daily, back and forth across the metropolis, packed with people on their way into town or out, on their way to work or home to their families, to sleep, to make money, to dream. The things that keep the world turning.

If Umm Ali had any dreams it was difficult to guess what they might be. The way she talked about her late husband one might have surmised that his death was the answer to a fervent prayer. Her problems had ended ten years ago when Allah decided to take him from her. Alive, he was nothing but a headache: 'Men! With their needs and their urges! When Allah says let every man till his field as he sees fit, that doesn't mean every night!' It was a favourite subject with her, the departure of her beloved from this world. He had managed to give her four children and, as she never failed to remind her tenant, 'Our Lord knows he was trying his best to give me another when his moment came.'

Makana always felt a pang of sympathy for the departed husband, particularly when she came to this final detail. Umm Ali never seemed to tire of reminding him that she had once been the object of one man's passionate affections, wafting before him like a diaphanous veil the possibility that there was no reason why this should not happen again, if Allah chose that path for her.

Umm Ali's eldest boy was away in the army. Her pride and joy, she would parade him endlessly around for the first day or two whenever he came home, waiting on him hand and foot, until she got tired of seeing him lounging about doing nothing all day but smoking cigarettes and sleeping. Then she would put him to work. For a few days he would hoe the fields reluctantly and fix everything and anything that had broken down in his absence, with a resigned but content smile. But by the end of the week he too had grown tired of the close family embrace and would be packed up and ready to return to his barracks. 'Only two more days to go,' he would confide to Makana, cadging a cigarette before his mother's strident voice sought him out once more. His eyes were already shining with anticipation, seeing himself leaping on to the back of an army lorry, bumping along a road towards a lonely outpost, to stand guard over who knows what useless strategic target.

Next in line were two girls who couldn't have been more different. One was trapped in the midst of plump adolescence, wiggling her broadening hips at the slightest glimmer of attention, while the younger one was skinny as a cane and cross-eyed, which people often assumed meant she was retarded when actually she was probably smarter than the lot of them put together. She helped her mother with the garden, which was their main source of food and regular income, and carried the vegetables with her to the stall they set up on a mat under the eucalyptus tree by the road. The last child was the little delinquent whom Makana would regularly catch going through his things, looking for something of value. He was the one who was handy with the pliers.

'Oh, I almost forgot,' Umm Ali, helpful as always, called out, as he reached the narrow plank that led on board. 'The telephone has been ringing.'

The sun was setting as Makana climbed the stairs to the rear deck. He often sat up there late into the evenings to read, when the insects were not too bad and there was kerosene in the old lamp on those occasions when the power was cut. Most of the time you didn't need lights; the glow from the city provided more than enough illumination for most things, with or without the electricity connected. Late at night a surprising serenity fell over the city, when the traffic started to die away and the moon appeared as a ghostly shadow hovering over the skyline. Everything seemed to be holding its breath. Then a sort of clarity would come over his mind. Now he reached for the telephone and dialled all the numbers for Mimi Maliki in Adil Romario's address book. Once again he had no luck and on the last attempt was about to hang up when, after about twenty rings, a hoarse voice answered: 'Who is it?'

'My name is Makana.'

'Do I know you?'

'I got this number from Adil Romario. I'm doing a story on him.'

'On Adil? And you want to talk to me?'

There followed a silence so long that Makana was convinced he had lost her, but then he heard her again, her voice floating in from far away.

'How much?'

'What?'

'How much will you pay me?'

'I don't know,' said Makana. 'What do you think is fair?'

'Two hundred US dollars,' she blurted out, as if the number had just come into her head.

'That's a lot of money.'

'*Ya salaam!* Did I call you? No. You want to talk to me or not?'

'Fine. It's a deal,' said Makana. 'Where do I find you?' She gave him an address in Heliopolis and before he had time to say anything more she hung up.

Makana sat back and watched the last traces of light draining from the sky. A band of amber ringed the western horizon. The river turned a deep shade of magenta. The memory of Liz Markham's battered body would not leave him. It was a distraction that kept nagging at him. Why would anyone torture her? He needed all his energies focused on Adil Romario, but he couldn't shake off the idea that there was a connection between Liz Markham and whatever malign forces were at work in Adil's case.

Or maybe it was just his own sense of guilt, taunting him for having been unable to save his own daughter seven years ago. Restlessly, he got to his feet and went over to the aft railings. Seven years ago he had looked down into this same river and watched his wife and daughter disappear before his very eyes.

No matter how many times he told himself there was nothing he could have done to avoid what happened, Makana still returned to it in his mind over and over, running through the course of events, trying to understand if there was something he might have done differently, if this might have affected the final outcome. The memory was like a physical wound that wouldn't heal. He carried it with him constantly, could not leave behind the pain and regret. He could still recall the swaying of the battered blue police pick-up as it juddered down the rocky slope that first day, when it all began to go wrong.

Ahead of him on the river bank he had spotted a small group of people gathered at a spot under the bridge. The pick-up's big wheels churned clumps of dried earth into a fine powder that swept in through the open windows, filling the cab with clouds of dust that stuck to the film of sweat already coating his face. It was just gone eight in the morning but already the heat made his shirt cling to his back.

The victim was lying face down in the shallows. Around her the water was fronded with green algae over the rocky bed of the stream. A long, diaphanous strip of cloth had wrapped itself around the otherwise naked body, floating around her like some strange plant. Tresses of hair ebbed back and forth as if alive. His sergeant Mek Nimr was there ahead of him, waving Makana down.

'Who are they?' Makana nodded at the five militia men standing around the body. They were all armed, Kalashnikov rifles slung over their shoulders, dressed in baggy peasant cotton.

'People's Defence Force. They are the ones who alerted us. They were driving by when a fisherman waved them down from the road up there.' Makana's sergeant pointed.

'And where is he, this fisherman?'

'We let him go.'

Makana turned on the man. '*You let him go?* Why?'

'He didn't have much to say,' Mek Nimr said quietly. He lifted his hand and pointed. 'He was rowing along here when he saw something in the water. That's it.'

'Find him.'

Mek Nimr tilted his head. 'I don't have any extra men.'

'I don't care if you have to swim up and down this river yourself, find that fisherman and bring him to me.'

The resentment in Mek Nimr's stare was unmistakable.

'I think you're making a fuss about nothing.'

'When you are made inspector you can do what you like. Until then, you'll do what I tell you.'

With an impatient click of his tongue, Mek Nimr turned and moved away. Makana watched him go, wondering why he didn't just file charges against him.

'Hey!' called one of the militia men, a wiry individual with a furrowed brow and thick beard. 'We have to cover this woman up.' He gestured at the naked body in the water. 'You can't leave her lying there like that. It's *haram*.'

All five of the militia men stared malevolently at Makana. Three of them were young; the one with the beard somewhat older. They carried themselves with the swagger of those who believed that blind, unquestioning zeal was the only qualification they needed. They were the embodiment of the new militia forces that were undermining the authority of the Criminal Investigation Department.

The woman's body still showed the early signs of bloating, which indicated that she had not been in the water long. The flesh on part of the right side of the face had been eaten away by fish. Makana saw puncture wounds, three at least, in the victim's side. The weapon used must have had a large blade. He turned to address the militia men.

'You have to stand back from here. You're trampling all over the evidence. This is a murder scene. Whatever you think you are, you're not policemen.'

'You can't talk to us like that.' The tall bearded man stepped forward. 'This is a clear case of moral corruption. You don't need to be a policeman to see that.'

Makana stepped up to him until their faces were almost touching. 'Get back or I'll have you arrested for obstructing police enquiries,' he said quietly.

The man stared contemptuously at him, then turned away, waving the others to follow him. When they had decamped to their pick-up truck further along the river bank, Makana kneeled down again beside the woman. Her head was tilted to one side. Despite the damage done by the fish he could see there was something familiar about her. Yes, he recognised her. She was a teacher in the nearby school across the river. Mek Nimr came back, ambling along the river bank, to report that there was no sign anywhere of the fisherman who had found the body.

'I think I've seen her before,' Makana told him. 'I think she's a teacher.'

Mek Nimr's lip curled in a sneer. 'I never liked teachers.'

'She was a good woman.'

'She can't have been all good, otherwise what is she doing here, without her clothes on?'

Makana stood up and looked around him. 'We don't know that she died here. She might have been brought here after she was killed, sometime early this morning.'

Mek Nimr gave a laugh of incredulity. 'How would they get round the curfew?'

Makana looked at him. He was right. The militia men huddled by their pick-up were involved in some kind of animated discussion. They fell silent as Makana approached.

'You say a fisherman called you down from the road?'

'It's what happened.' A small man with sharp, pointed teeth

answered for them. He had the wild, feverish look of a man with a taste for violence.

'Haven't I seen you before somewhere?'

The eyes darted sideways and the man was shoved out of the way as another one pushed in.

'Who do you think you are? You have to treat us with a bit more respect.'

Makana reached into his shirt pocket for a cigarette, noting their looks of pious disapproval. The bearded man was taking a back seat now, climbing back into the car.

'Until I get confirmation of your story, that's all it is . . . a story.'

They were crowding round him, like football players protesting against a penalty.

'There are five of us. You think we are all lying? We took an oath to defend this country and the believers in it.'

'My job is to look at the facts, not to listen to what people profess to believe.'

This provoked more scuffling. The more Makana saw of them, the less he trusted them.

'Why do you need this fisherman? Are our words not good enough for you?'

'He's the only other witness,' Makana sighed. 'For all I know you could have killed her yourselves and dumped her here.'

That was too much for them. They lurched forward, guns raised. Threatening a uniformed police officer didn't seem to be a problem for them. Mek Nimr finally stepped in. He was smiling, that thin, contemptuous smile Makana had come to know.

'You stand with your back to them,' Makana said. 'Does that mean you are more afraid of me than of five armed men?'

Mek Nimr lowered his hands and stepped back. The picture of humility. 'I was only trying to do my duty, sir.'

'Then get these *awaleeg* out of here. I want all their names and I want them checked for criminal records. That one I have seen before.' He pointed at the man with the sharp teeth. Makana was sure he had arrested him five or six years back for something. Aggravated burglary?

'They are People's Defence Force. You can't treat them like suspects,' protested Mek Nimr.

'No one is above the law, or has that changed too?'

The militia men were protesting loudly, calling on the Almighty to verify that they were speaking the truth, as if that was all the proof of their innocence that was necessary. Makana knew there was something wrong here. These men had not simply found this woman in the water, he was sure of it. There might have been a fisherman, but Makana knew they would never find him, not alive at least. Had he come across them dumping the woman's body, or worse?

He watched Mek Nimr lead them away. He seemed to have their ear. Why was that? Makana had the sense that something dangerous was being played out right before his eyes, though he still couldn't make it out clearly. It was pointless going to Major Idris about the run-in with the militia. Idris was too busy seeking out technological wonders of the modern age that had been foreseen in the abstractions of the Quran. It was a hobby of sorts. He published articles about it in the police gazette. He didn't want to hear about these incidents. The major already considered him a maverick. He was young and zealous and probably the worst policeman Makana had ever met. He'd once asked Makana why he never went to prayers during the day.

'I wasn't aware it was obligatory,' Makana had replied.

'You're not an atheist or something are you?' Then, without waiting for a response, Idris burst into laughter. 'I was only joking. Of course you are not!'

But the cold smile, the evasive eyes, told Makana that this was probably exactly what his superior was thinking. For him it wasn't about religion, it was about conforming. Idris had revealed his scorn for someone who did not know how to join in. An atheist heathen. Might he have been able to save them at that point? Makana wondered afterwards. If he had been smarter, if he hadn't been so stubborn, would he have managed to keep his family alive?

Chapter Fifteen

Decades ago, in his native Italy, Guido Clemenza's career as a player was halted by a scandal involving match fixing. There were rumours of links to the Mafia. The case was eventually dropped and he managed to reinvent himself as a trainer by going into exile. After an unsuccessful stint in the Gulf he had been hired by Saad Hanafi. In Egypt he was built up into the archetypal European technocrat. A dictator of sorts, obsessed with punctuality and efficiency. Physically, he fitted the bill perfectly, with his chilly blue eyes and steel-coloured hair. A new Mussolini. Clemenza's brutish face made regular appearances in the gossip columns, beside one model or another. Apparently he enjoyed the high life. His once trim waistline had expanded and the sharp angles of his jaw were sunk now beneath the onset of jowls. Clemenza put Makana in mind of a Roman senator from the days of Hadrian or Marcus Aurelius. Perhaps football managers were the modern-day equivalent. Certainly he could be ruthless. By all accounts he was good at what he did. He worked the team hard and got results. Or, at least, he used to. More recently their record had been disappointing. And there clearly wasn't much affection for him as far as the players were concerned.

Watching him now, sitting at a card table in the casino of the Semiramis Hotel, Makana saw that Guido Clemenza certainly did not look like a happy man. He was losing. The croupier raked in the chips and prepared the shoe for another round. It was an odd crowd in the casino, mostly foreigners, guests at the hotel, outsiders. Makana imagined it was like that most nights. A few Westerners, and a lot of Arabs, Malays, Chinese. They stood chatting at the bar, or wandered around to see what was happening at the other tables. Getting in had not been easy for him. The door was guarded by a jackal of a man with the flat, emotionless gaze of a seasoned criminal. He was wearing a tuxedo so shiny with wear that it might have been painted with varnish. It made Makana feel a little better about his own clothes. He was wearing his best suit, which had clearly seen better days.

'No access for Egyptian nationals,' the man said, holding up a hand to bar his entrance.

'I'm not here to gamble,' said Makana, reaching into his jacket pocket to flash one of Okasha's visiting cards, of which he had assembled a small collection over the years. An involuntary twitch crossed the doorman's face at the sight of the police insignia. He stepped aside, tilting his head for Makana to pass.

There was something distinctly sleazy about the casino, despite the care that had gone into setting it up. Everything, from the fake pillars and plastic vines round the entrance arch, to the waiters circulating with trays of drinks and the croupiers spinning the roulette wheel or dealing out the cards on the green baize-covered tables, felt off-key. Underneath the façade of sophistication was a hard, ugly edge, and Makana felt an unusual sense of moral repugnance asserting itself inside him. Still, the name of the game was separating fools from their money. Anyone foolish enough to come in here deserved everything they got, or rather lost. It was all a charade, the fancy waiters and the obsequious manners, all infused with deceit. Over on one table a pair of loud Iraqi men and their respective women were throwing money down in a doomed bid to outdo one another. Their luck was about to end. A tall croupier wearing white gloves tapped his younger colleague on the shoulder and quietly relieved him. The Iraqis didn't pay much attention, oblivious to the fact that they were about to start losing.

Clemenza, perhaps sensing that his own chances were diminishing, decided to take a break. He got up from the table and went over to the bar where he ordered himself a drink. He was dressed in an expensive linen suit with a pink shirt and a wide blue silk tie. He perfectly fitted the role of a rather vulgar Italian playboy. As he raised his glass he caught sight of Makana in the mirror behind the bar. He even managed to raise a smile as he turned towards him, though there was about as much warmth in it as in the ice cubes in his glass.

'Not the kind of place I would have expected to find you.'

'No.' Makana glanced about him. 'Nor me.'

Clemenza chuckled to himself as he sipped his drink. 'Always it is *teatro* with you people. Why does everyone in this country play a game of masks?'

'I thought you were here out of love?'

The Italian snorted. 'I would leave tomorrow if I could.'

'What's stopping you?'

Clemenza's chilly eyes were tinged with red. 'What do you want from me this time?'

'I'm just curious. With hobbies like this, Hanafi must be paying you a good salary.'

'It's none of your business, but yes, he pays me well enough,' said Clemenza, turning to lean wearily against the bar. 'And besides, the idea is that you win.'

'From what I hear, you haven't been doing a lot of that lately.'

'Everyone goes through rough patches,' he said, casting an eye over Makana's worn suit. 'But then I expect a man like you knows all about that.'

'With your current run of luck you probably could do with a little bonus.' Makana gestured round the room. 'To fund your gambling habit.'

'What are you talking about?'

'How much commission would you make on a transfer deal for Adil?'

'That old nonsense! Anyone in this room will tell you he is not good enough for that.'

'For a man who could arrange the outcome of matches before they even took place, a transfer deal for someone like Adil Romario shouldn't present too much of a problem.'

Clemenza's nostrils flared. 'I was cleared of all charges.'

'You were suspended, which is why you went abroad, which is how you ended up here.'

Setting down his glass, Clemenza snapped his fingers impatiently at the bartender for another. When it came, he lifted the glass and took a long, deep draught, then wiped his mouth with the back of his hand.

'Just where did Hanafi find you? Ask yourself why he went to all that trouble when he could pick up a phone and have any of the top men in the country at his service. Why did he pick you?'

'Maybe because he knew I couldn't be bought off.'

Clemenza chuckled, shaking his head as he raised his glass again. Across the room the tall croupier turned away from the card table, handing it back to the younger man who had been managing it before him. The Iraqis were rather more subdued now, having lost most of their chips. They gathered up their things and moved off towards the roulette table, looking sombre. Clemenza caught the eye of the older croupier, who removed his white gloves and ran the tip of his index finger over his moustache, watching Makana, his face impassive. Whispering a word of advice to his relief, he approached them.

'Is everything all right, sir?' he asked Clemenza, his eyes not straying from Makana.

'It's fine, but I'm afraid my friend here is feeling unwell. He is about to leave.'

The tall man straightened up, taking a deep slow breath. 'I understand.' He nodded, raising a hand. Two men in shiny tuxedos appeared.

'This is really not necessary,' protested Makana. 'I can find my own way out.'

'It's a big hotel. You might get lost.' The tall croupier smiled coldly.

Clemenza leaned closer. 'Don't come poking your nose in again. Is that clear?'

'I think Hanafi might have something to say about that.'

'I don't care what Hanafi says,' hissed Clemenza. 'He's finished anyway.'

The Italian turned his back as the two men took hold of Makana's arms and steered him out of the casino. People glanced in his direction but nobody said anything. The doorman studiously examined the guestbook as they went by.

Makana was bundled along a long hallway.

'I think the front exit is that way,' he said, as they passed the main staircase leading down to the hotel lobby. At the end of the wide curve of the mezzanine floor they turned into a narrower corridor. The two bouncers shouldered their way through a heavy fire door and descended a set of emergency stairs. Three flights down they came to another door which they kicked open, and suddenly they were outside. Makana was flung headlong against a wall. He put out his hands to protect himself and grazed the skin of his palms. The big men caught hold of him and jerked him back. The seams on his jacket gave as he was propelled forwards again to tumble head over heels and skid along the road. It all seemed to happen very slowly, but there was nothing he could do to prevent it. He was on the ground, trying to plan his next move, when he heard the door bang behind them as they went back inside.

Getting to his feet slowly, Makana dusted himself down and assessed the damage. Some of Hanafi's money would have to be invested in new clothes, he decided. The jacket had come apart down the back seam and his trousers were ripped. He touched a hand gently to one knee. It hurt to stand up straight. As he did so Makana became aware that he was being watched.

The alleyway ran downhill at both ends, arching upwards towards the middle. To Makana's left where the alley met the street there were lights from some kind of loading bay at the back of the hotel. Opposite this stood a row of parked cars. Makana stared for a long time before he made out the figure standing there. It might have been anyone: a homeless person looking for somewhere to sleep; a late-night reveller looking for a spot to relieve himself. But Makana knew it was neither of these. The figure stood motionless against the wall. Makana took a step backwards, out of the band of light coming from the windows high above. As he did so there was a cracking sound from the wall by his head and he felt brick and plaster shower down on him. It took him a second to realise that he had been shot at. The man had a gun with a silencer. When he looked again he saw that the shadow had moved. Makana felt a moment of panic. Where was he?

Ducking his head, he crouched down and began to run, hobble rather, in the opposite direction, down towards the exit on the river side. The pain in his knee made him grit his teeth. He was almost there when another man appeared, silhouetted against the light from the hotel's entry at the other end of the alley. Makana had no choice. To stop now would be to present himself as a sitting target. Instead, he threw himself forward, crashing into the man, sending both of them tumbling to the ground.

'Hey, what do you think you're doing?'

On his knees, Makana saw that the man underneath him, holding up his hands to protect himself, was none other than Sami Barakat. Makana lowered his fist.

'What are *you* doing here?'

'I was waiting for you, then I heard the noise.' Barakat sat up and dusted himself off. 'You could have hurt me.'

Makana winced as he put his weight on his injured knee and tried to stand. The journalist gave him a hand.

'What is going on here?'

'It's a long story,' said Makana, looking back into the darkness of the alleyway. 'I thought I warned you about following me around?'

Together they shuffled forward into the light from the hotel.

'I wanted to give you something.' Barakat reached into his bag and handed Makana an envelope.

'Couldn't it wait?'

'It's my story. It comes out tomorrow.'

Makana held the sheets of paper up to the light. '"Where is Adil Romario?"' he read.

'I'm not sure what your role in this is, but I thought I'd give you the chance to respond.' The younger man nodded at Makana's lamentable appearance. 'But I'm beginning to wonder if I understand anything about you at all.'

'I'm not doing your work for you,' Makana said, thrusting the pages back at him and turning away. He tried in vain to interest a taxi in picking him up. One slowed, saw the condition of his clothes and accelerated quickly away.

'I don't want to hurt anyone,' said Barakat. 'Nor, I suspect, do you.' As Makana carried on down the road, he followed. 'She's out of danger, by the way, in case you are interested.'

Makana lowered his hand. 'Who is out of danger?'

'Farag's secretary . . . didn't you know? She was taken to hospital.'

Makana was still staring at him when a taxi finally pulled up. Sami Barakat held out his story again, and this time Makana took it.

2

Old Enemies

Chapter Sixteen

That night he dreamed the *awama* had sunk, that it had foundered in dark water. All his furniture, his worthless possessions, his books of poetry and travel, his torn clothes, a pair of scuffed shoes, all of it turning slowly over in moonbeams. Eels twisted their way through the rooms, seeking him out, winding their long tails through his mind, dragging him back . . .

They had driven out together, Mek Nimr at the wheel of the dark blue police pick-up. The uniformed men up by the road waved them down with yellow beams from cheap Chinese flashlights, signalling the way through the fields. The body was lying on the ground where a farmer had come across it, half-buried in the soft loamy earth. Particles of dust swirled in the air over the dead man, like moths trapped in the headlights. They turned the body over and saw what had been done to his face. Makana fought the urge to throw up. It took him a while to understand what he was seeing. The lower jaw was shot away, both eyes gouged out. He bore little resemblance to the man Makana had once known. The feet were bare and tied at the ankles with wire that had cut deep into the skin. The soles were puffy and white.

Makana pressed the tip of a Biro to them and watched the skin come away in a thick layer. One of the younger officers gave a sound as if he was going to be sick and turned away.

'We're going to find out who did this.'

'Is that wise?' asked Mek Nimr.

Makana straightened up and turned to face him. 'It's our job.'

Mek Nimr stepped closer, lowering his voice so that the other officers could not hear his words. 'National security affairs are not our business.'

'Then perhaps they should be.'

'Maybe you're not seeing this clearly.' Mek Nimr shifted from one foot to the other. 'You know the victim. You shouldn't be on this case.'

'Who else is going to do it?' Makana stared at him until Mek Nimr sighed and turned away, but not before Makana saw the resentment in his eyes.

At first he had suspected that Mek Nimr was a simple informer, that he had been recruited by someone higher up to keep an eye on his fellow policemen. But by that point he was beginning to think otherwise. Mek Nimr was ambitious. Was he planning to sacrifice Makana in order to assure himself of a faster route to the top?

'How is it you know the victim, sir?' one of the other men asked hesitantly. The question gave Makana an excuse to turn his attention back to the body lying in the headlights.

'He was a colleague of my wife's . . . a friend.'

'Perhaps we should take a statement from her?' Mek Nimr suggested. It was meant as provocation. Makana didn't even look up.

'My wife is not to be involved in this,' he murmured, his eyes on the body.

'I don't follow. First you say you want to investigate and then you say you don't. It seems inconsistent to me.' Mek Nimr glanced casually around the assembled men, to see how many of them were with him.

'You say she was a friend of his,' he pressed his superior. 'This man was an infidel, an atheist.'

'An atheist?' Makana laughed. It was almost funny. 'He was a scientist . . . a biologist.'

'He taught that we are descended from monkeys.' Mek Nimr's voice rose excitedly.

'How is it you know so much about him?'

'I read the papers.' Again his eyes turned away, seeking darkness. Shelter.

Never in their four years of working together had Makana seen him show the slightest interest in any printed matter beyond the captions on the cartoon page. Getting him to write a report was a thankless task. It was easier to find one of the junior officers who could type to help him out. And now suddenly Mek Nimr was an authority on Darwin?

By then the course of events had been set. All Makana could do was stand back and watch his life disappear. Had Mek Nimr known what was to come, that day by the river? It was difficult to imagine that he had no clue. These were dangerous times. Even the Revolutionary Command Council for National Salvation, which had seized power less than two years ago, had become so paranoid that they met only with their weapons drawn and placed on the table in front of them. Within a few months some twenty officers were to face the firing squad. There was a purge of the entire system under way and Mek Nimr had read the writing on the wall early on.

A few weeks later it was official. Major Idris announced that

Mek Nimr was to command a new unit of the Revolutionary Security Force, an autonomous body which answered to nobody but the National Islamic Front. It seemed like the world had taken leave of its senses. Mek Nimr in charge of a group of armed thugs? It wasn't that he was incompetent, far from it. He had worked diligently at Makana's side. What Mek Nimr lacked was judgement, integrity. Left to his own devices there was no telling what he might do.

The new unit's duties were not exactly clear. All they seemed to do was tear around the streets in pick-ups, waving their guns in the air, scaring people. But it was all part of the new era. The regular police were sidelined. Religious piety was deemed the only significant qualification. Makana watched the justice system unravelling before him – people were arrested without cause, disappearing inside secret prisons or 'ghost houses', undergoing rape, torture and summary execution without trial. This was the order of the day.

It wasn't as if there weren't enough cases to attend to. Bodies turned up all the time, discarded on wasteland, by the roadside, in the river. More of them than ever. Cause of death varied: drowning, contusions, asphyxiation. Homicide, once largely a result of domestic strife, had entered the realm of the arbitrary. The victims were students, journalists, members of youth clubs, boy scouts. Usually, the cases would be taken out of Makana's hands before he had managed to type up an initial report. Still, he carried on, cataloguing all the deaths that came his way, meticulously, as if by sheer force of habit he might keep the world on its proper axis. The alternative was to flee. Afterwards there wasn't a day that didn't go by without him wishing he had done just that.

The cases kept coming. On a scale never before seen. Men

vanished from their homes. They failed to return from work. They were dragged off buses, or out of taxis. Their cars were found parked by the side of the road with no sign of where the occupant had gone, or why. No official record of them was made in the system. Makana went on doing his job, following the evidence, right up to the inevitable wall he came up against every time. What else could he do? Like a drowning man he struggled, even when he knew he was going down for the last time.

Chapter Seventeen

The sight of Umm Ali and her cross-eyed daughter tending the little vegetable patch that ran in an uneven strip parallel to the river added a touch of timelessness to the scene.

Makana sipped his coffee on the upper deck. He had not slept well, and had woken to discover his body was a mass of cuts and bruises. Getting out of bed was a painful struggle. His elbow and knee ached and when he tried to stand his right ankle protested. Closing his eyes against the glare of sunlight rippling across the water, he was vaguely pondering the matter of whether it was worth visiting a doctor when the telephone began to ring, the long insistent peals echoing out over the water.

A soft morning breeze lifted the pages of the newspaper which lay on the deck beside him, as if Iblis himself were flicking through it. Makana didn't have to look down to remind himself of the front-page article. He had read it twice already, once the previous night and then again this morning in its full printed glory. Sami Barakat had gone to town on the story that Adil Romario had disappeared. Nobody knew where he was, and, more to the point, nobody seemed too concerned about the fact. Why the big mystery? What was the club hiding?

The story would have shaken a few people out of their beds this morning, which Makana assumed explained the telephone calls. They had begun early and continued at regular intervals ever since. Out in the field, Umm Ali straightened up, one muddy hand to her aching back and the other shielding her eyes. She looked up at him but didn't say anything. Earlier she had called up to remind him that the telephone was actually ringing, but now she could see that he didn't want to answer it, and that was his business. After a time she went back to her tomatoes and cucumbers, and eventually the ringing stopped. With a sigh, Makana got to his feet and walked slowly over to the railings to stretch his aching joints.

Sami Barakat wrote in the kind of excitable language that reminded you of one of those hysterical melodramas on television, where people scream at each other endlessly and for no apparent reason. By his disappearance Adil Romario had managed to generate exactly the kind of excitement he had been hoping to achieve in the movies.

'Who has something to hide?' blazed the headline on the inside page. At the centre of a spider's web diagram was a picture of Adil Romario. Lines led outwards in every direction to connect with other photographs. There was Hanafi, of course, whose face the paper's editors had managed to flatten so that he resembled a bloated toad crouched at the top of the page. To the left was a picture of Lulu Hamra, the actress who had wanted to keep her name out of the papers. Makana had promised to do his best, which had clearly not been enough. He wouldn't be surprised if she was one of the people calling, although the context of the article was not unflattering. Lulu was described in glamorous terms as the secret love of Adil Romario's life, who had broken the heart of 'our hero'. Had the affair really ended, or had they eloped to Spain to be married in a secret ceremony in the 'ancient site of Muslim glory that is the magnificent city of Granada'? Barakat certainly knew how to pile it on. It read like a concession to those readers who really had no interest in football but might be drawn to a story of tragic romance.

The right-hand side of the page showed Clemenza, looking as despotic as Il Duce, his mouth open as he yelled at the players from the sidelines. This was the theory of most interest to football fans, namely that the Italian trainer was negotiating a lucrative deal for Adil Romario to play in Europe, the most likely buyers being Internazionale and Juventus. Clemenza still had old contacts in both clubs and was likely to make an incredible commission on any sale of the player. Why was he doing it? Because he was not happy with the way he was being treated by Saad Hanafi. More to the point, Sami Barakat noted, how would Mr Hanafi react to such treachery? It was reasonable to assume that he would not let his star player go that easily. How would he seek his revenge?

To complete the element of intrigue there was even a shadowy figure, whose image was blacked out with a question mark over his face. Who was the mystery man on the trail of Adil Romario? The reporter described how in the course of his investigation he had come across a second person hot on Adil's heels. A rival, had been our intrepid reporter's first thought, but after extensive checking he had ascertained that this was not the case. So who was he? A scout sent by another football club? Or was he connected to State Security Investigations, the *Mubaheth Amn al-Dawla*? And if so, did the involvement of the SSI mean there was some kind of government interest in the case of Adil Romario's disappearance? Or could there be some darker link – to the Jewish state, for example? Makana clucked his tongue impatiently. Sami Barakat left no string unplucked. Yet the populistic evocation of yet another Zionist conspiracy was really a foil to set up a more feasible, if less palatable, alternative explanation: was this mystery man linked with Hanafi's notorious connections to the criminal underworld? Was his past catching up with him? And if so, was it in the government's interests for this to emerge into the light of day? The possibility of a cover-up was further highlighted by the added detail that the mystery man had apparently threatened the reporter with violence if he continued to pursue the story. It wasn't hard for Makana to see that the menacing figure with a question mark for a face was intended to be him.

It was a lurid article, but he had to admire the deftness with which Sami Barakat had tied the pieces together into such a provocative tale. It was also courageous. There was a serious edge to the piece, which Makana liked. Barakat was not afraid of stirring things up. Nobody else had dared to speak out openly about Hanafi's past connections to organised crime. No wonder the telephone was ringing. Everyone knew Hanafi had protection in high places. To their credit, the paper's editorial staff lined up behind their star reporter, calling indignantly for a government commission to be charged immediately with investigating the matter. It was time to start raising questions about the links between investment in their country and illegal activities, they trumpeted. The piece would receive no real response from official circles, of course, but it implied that Hanafi was no longer as untouchable as he used to be. To Makana's mind it once again raised the possibility that Hanafi himself was the real target of all this. Could Adil be just a means of attacking him?

The telephone began to ring below once more. With a sigh, Makana realised that he was going to have to answer it. Then he felt, rather than heard, the big man step aboard. He looked down over the railings and saw the gorilla in a suit standing on the lower deck.

'Mr Hanafi would like to see you.'

'Yes.' Makana nodded. 'I thought he might.'

Descending to the main cabin, he walked straight past the ringing phone.

'Aren't you going to answer that?' The big man remained outside, looking through the doorway.

'If you leave it for long enough it usually stops by itself.'

The driver sniffed but said nothing. Makana lifted up the remains of his jacket and realised that it was in serious need of a good tailor.

'Hold on a minute.'

He retrieved another jacket which he pulled on before following the big man up the slope towards the road.

'You're pretty light on your feet. I'll bet you used to box.'

The man's grin was broad and his teeth dazzlingly bright. 'How did you guess? I was a light heavyweight. I nearly got an Olympic medal.'

'Nearly?'

The heavy shoulders heaved. 'I wasn't selected for the team in the end, but that was because there was money involved, you know how it is.'

'Sure,' said Makana. 'I know how it is.'

This time he chose to sit in the front, next to the driver. As they travelled at high speed along the riverside to Hanafi's apartment, the driver kept up a long monologue about his career as a boxer and how he once could have been as great as Muhammad Ali. He seemed like a totally different person from the driver Makana had first set eyes on.

'What did you say your name was?'

'Faisal, but I fought under the name of Sindbad.'

'Sindbad? I like that. How long have you been working for Hanafi?'

'About six years.'

'And they treat you pretty well?'

'Oh, yes. They pay well. I don't have to worry about anything.'

'I'll bet he's pretty strict about things, that Gaber.'

Sindbad tried to stifle a laugh and failed, giggling like a kid. 'Mr Gaber likes things to be exactly how he wants them. Otherwise he gets angry.'

'I'm sure. And how about the old man?'

'Oh . . .' Sindbad's tone changed. 'He's not as strong as he used to be. Sometimes you take him somewhere and he forgets what he's supposed to be doing, so you have to take him back again.'

As Makana climbed out in front of the building, the big man wished him luck.

The guards in the lobby were not talkative today. No smiles or cheery greetings. They led Makana over to the special lift without a word and slid home the security key that activated it. The sombre mood was palpable. As the doors slid open again Makana found Soraya Hanafi and Gaber waiting for him. As he stepped out on the penthouse floor there came a howl from the upper level of the suite and they all turned to look up. Hanafi, dressed in a navy blue dressing gown embroidered with gold crescents, was leaning over the balustrade waving a newspaper in the air.

'What is the meaning of this?' he yelled. 'I want answers and I want them now!' He came down the long sweeping staircase with great clumsy steps, threatening to trip over the hem of his gown, which was far too long for him. Gaber rushed forward to catch him as he stumbled to a halt. Hanafi pushed him roughly aside and pointed a finger at Makana. 'I hired you to be discreet, not to make a fool of me!' Waving the newspaper under Makana's nose, he shrieked, 'A gangster! That's what they are calling me. A common thug. A *bultagi*!' He rounded on Gaber. 'I want you to find the cockroach who wrote this. Find out where he lives, who his friends are. I am going to teach him a lesson he will never forget.'

'I don't think that's a good idea,' said Makana.

'Oh, you don't, do you?' Hanafi turned on him. 'Well, that's fine to hear, because it's not your face on the front page, is it?'

'It's what he is hoping for. An attack will only put wind in his sails.'

'Mr Makana has a point,' concurred Gaber quietly.

'Then call the lawyers. I want to sue the paper and the animals who work for it!'

'He's just a kid,' said Makana.

'You know him?' Soraya asked.

Makana turned to her. 'I caught him following me one day. I tried to warn him off.'

'Obviously, you were not successful,' said Gaber. 'This is not the first time this man has attacked us. He wrote a scandalous piece about the team only last month.'

'Most of the story is guesswork,' added Soraya. 'He doesn't really have anything. He blew it up as big as he could to please his editor and get more space for himself.'

Makana said nothing.

'You've talked to Clemenza?' Hanafi snapped.

Gaber nodded. 'I spoke to him first thing this morning.'

'What's all this talk about a transfer?'

'It's idle speculation. Clemenza assures me he has absolutely no plans to try and negotiate a deal for Adil in Europe.'

'I wouldn't put anything past that snake. I want him replaced . . . not right away, not in the middle of all this, but I want you to start looking for a replacement. And check with our people in Europe. See if there are any rumours to back up this transfer nonsense.'

'I have already made some calls,' Gaber said.

'Good.' Hanafi turned to Soraya next. 'I want you to get on to some of the people we have in television, on the radio, the newspapers. I've paid so much money out over the years, it's time for them to repay some of my generosity. I want to counter this with ten stories reminding people how much I have done for this country. And issue a statement countering all this nonsense.'

'I'll do it straight away.' She marched off.

'Gangsters, indeed!' Hanafi snorted, and stabbed a finger at Makana. '*You* I want to talk to.' With that he turned and stumbled up a few stairs into a long dining room that projected like the prow of an ocean liner over the terrace. Most of it was taken up by an enormous circular table. A glass wall curved round one side, affording diners a view of the pool below. As the door closed behind them Makana turned to face Hanafi, bracing himself for an assault. But the fight had gone out of the old man. He dropped the newspaper on the table, plunged his hands deep into his pockets and walked straight up to the window, to stare down as if his fate might be written in the faux-Roman mosaic on the bottom of the pool whose image swayed back and forth in the blue water.

'When I was a small boy I used to think that rich people were different. I imagined them living in a place where everything was always clean and new. They never got dirty. They didn't, you know, do their business like the rest of us. Now I am richer than most people in this country. I live in a palace, and the funny thing is, I still think the rich are different. Somewhere inside this old man there is still that little boy from Tanta with mud on his fingers. I shall never be one of them.'

The narrow eyes widened in sorrow. 'I did some bad things to get where I am today, I admit it. Some I regret, others I don't. I have tried to distance myself from them all, but I can't.' He stared down at his feet for a moment, hands clasped behind his back, then he raised his chin and stared Makana straight in the eye. 'There is something I must tell you. Perhaps I should have made it clear from the outset.' He paused to draw in a deep breath. 'Adil is my son.'

'Your son?' It took a moment for Makana to take it in. 'You mean . . .'

'I mean, my own flesh and blood,' Hanafi continued impatiently. 'The fruit of a . . . brief relationship I had with a woman a long time ago.'

'How many people know this?'

'Until today, nobody. Not even my closest family. Nobody except Gaber, of course. Gaber knows everything.'

'Who was his mother?'

'His mother?' Hanafi's face was a picture of puzzlement. 'His mother . . .' His voice took on the soft tone of an old man reminiscing. 'She was a young woman, a girl really, who worked for me. It would have been a scandal. There was no possibility of marriage between us.'

'I see,' said Makana slowly. 'Well, this changes things, of course.'

Hanafi blinked furiously. 'You understand why I have kept this a secret?'

'You're worried about your reputation.'

'It will be made public when the time is right.' Hanafi clasped his hands behind his back and bowed his big head, resembling a tired old elephant. 'I am ageing. When I am gone, I would like my name to continue.' He resembled nothing more than a benign and somewhat confused grandfather at that moment. Makana had to remind himself that this was a ruthless man with a very dubious past.

'It was wrong of me not to tell you right from the start. I can see that. Old habits die hard and I have kept this a secret for a long time. Pride is a terrible thing.'

'I think you mean vanity. Does Adil know?'

A slow shake of the head. 'I couldn't bring myself to tell him. I love that boy. He's the son I always wished for, but I couldn't bear to see the disappointment in his eyes when he heard that he was the product of such a . . . shameful affair.' Hanafi stared furiously at the floor.

'Eventually he will have to know.'

'Yes, of course.' Hanafi smiled foolishly. 'I suppose he will.'

'Tell me about his mother. What happened to her?'

'She was a simple girl. I took care of the family and later arranged for Adil to be taken into the academy.'

'You set it up just for him?'

'It was a way of allowing him to be close to me without telling the whole world.'

'Where is his mother now?'

'What does it matter?'

Makana straightened his shoulders. 'At the moment everything matters,' he said quietly.

Hanafi considered this for a moment and then sighed his acknowledgement.

'I believe she passed away some years ago.'

'You were married at the time?'

'My first wife was ill. She passed away and a year later I was married again and had a son on the way.' He blinked his eyes. 'But Allah saw fit to take him away from me.'

'Soraya's mother and your son died in the car accident. Soraya was the only survivor?'

Hanafi's gaze grew distant and returned to the pool.

'Only it wasn't a car accident, was it?'

Hanafi was losing patience. His eyes narrowed as they turned on Makana.

'All this is ancient history.'

'The pyramids are ancient history.'

Hanafi grunted, 'I tell people what they need to know. It wasn't necessary to explain what happened.'

'It wasn't a car accident.'

'No, you're right. It wasn't.' He turned back to the window, clasping his hands behind his back. 'They were trying to kill me. They might as well have slit my throat. They took the dearest thing I had, my only son.'

'Who was trying to kill you?'

'An old enemy of mine.'

Makana felt he was finally getting somewhere. 'Could he be behind Adil's disappearance?'

'He died,' said Hanafi quietly. 'A long, long time ago.'

'Okay, now listen to me. You didn't tell me Adil was your son. You lied about your wife's death. How much more of what you told me is untrue?'

Hanafi's tired eyes rose slowly to meet his. 'Do you believe in fate, Makana? Do you believe everything happens as it is written?' Makana found himself lost for words. 'Well, I do. I prayed for a son, and Allah gave me one – only to take him away from me in the cruellest fashion.' His eyes glinted. 'I was the cause of that boy's death as surely as if I had held the gun to his head.' Makana's impassivity seemed to provoke him. He emitted a low sob, wallowing in self-pity and despair. 'Do you know what it means to lose a son?'

Makana felt his throat tighten.

'All my first wife gave me was daughters, each more plump and empty-headed than the last. And then she died. I wanted a son and Allah gave me two, almost at the same time.'

'So when you lost the first boy, you went looking for the other,' Makana said. 'Does Soraya know the truth about Adil?'

'She does now,' Hanafi whispered. 'I told her before you arrived.'

'How did she take it?'

'She was shocked, of course. But I cannot bear to lose another son. I hoped you might be able to find him quickly, without knowing all the details, but now . . .' He sent the newspaper spinning across the table.

Gaber was pacing up and down outside, waiting. Without a word he led the way along a hallway to another room, his own office presumably. The window looked out over the road and the gardens opposite. Soraya was sitting stiffly in one of the chairs facing the desk. She didn't look up when they came in. Gaber closed the door and went behind the desk.

'Now, I need a full report on the progress you have made so far.'

'First things first.' Makana remained standing. He leaned one elbow on a teak filing cabinet beside the door. 'Why are you wasting time having me followed?'

Gaber twined his fingers together on the desk top. 'I wasn't aware that I was.'

Makana wondered if he could have been mistaken. He didn't trust Gaber but he also couldn't see the point of the man's having him followed. He glanced at Soraya, who was clutching the arms of the chair she sat in, staring at him. She was furious and probably with good reason, having just discovered she had a half-brother.

'Okay, so explain why I wasn't told that Adil was the old man's son?'

Makana turned as he heard Soraya's sharp intake of breath. She slammed back the chair and got to her feet.

'This is humiliating! Why must we discuss intimate family matters in front of a stranger?'

She was addressing Gaber, but staring at Makana. Gaber tried to calm her.

'Mr Makana is here to help us, Soraya. We have to trust him.'

'How can we be sure of him? For all we know he is working with that rat who calls himself a journalist, and probably earning a fat commission on top of it.'

'Your father hired me because he believed I could be of help,' Makana said calmly. 'If you don't agree then you should take it up with him.'

'Soraya, please,' Gaber urged. 'Sit down, let him tell us what he has learned.'

She wasn't happy but finally consented, sinking back into the chair without another word and staring fixedly at the desk in front of her.

'The fact is that I haven't uncovered a great deal,' Makana began. 'Perhaps if you had been frank with me from the start we might have avoided some of this unpleasantness.' He took his time over the last word, which he chose with the care of a diplomat. Soraya remained impassive.

'It was wrong, I agree. From now on, rest assured, nothing will be kept from you.'

Makana looked at Gaber and realised that he trusted him less than ever. He moved across the room and picked up a large porcelain figure. It was heavier than he had imagined and looked to be Chinese, depicting a bearded man with a protuberant belly and a stick held over one shoulder.

'Please,' Gaber implored. 'That is a priceless piece.'

Makana set the figure carefully back on the shelf.

'Adil is in business with a man named Salim Farag.'

'Never heard of him,' said Gaber. 'What kind of business?'

'Making movies. Does either of you know anything about that?' He looked at both of them.

'Well, he's expressed an interest in acting, but as far as I know that's all there is to it.' Gaber glanced over at Soraya who silently confirmed this assessment but said nothing more.

'Farag seems like a rather disreputable character. And there is a girl involved. An actress named Mimi Maliki.'

Makana noticed Soraya stiffen on hearing the name. He looked to Gaber for an explanation.

'There was some rather unpleasant business with her a few months ago.' Gaber reached for a sandalwood box on the desk and lit a cigarette. 'She claimed Adil had assaulted her. Wanted money to keep quiet. A woman of dubious moral character.'

'I never believed her story,' said Soraya, stamping her foot as she stood up again. 'All she was interested in was money. She was jealous and wanted to hurt him.'

Eventually, after much coaxing, Soraya consented to sit down again, but was clearly still seething with anger. Makana wondered how much of her father's past was known to her.

'This must be very distressing for you.'

She glanced in his direction briefly, then looked away again. 'There is a great responsibility that comes with running a company as big as Hanafi Enterprises. Whole families depend on us. We cannot afford to allow something like this to damage our business.'

'I can't control what they write in the papers.'

Her eyes were furious as she turned them on him.

'It's in your interest to protect our name.'

'I wasn't hired to protect your name. I was hired to find Adil.'

This caused her to waver. She gave a terse nod of agreement. 'What matters is that you find him.'

'I'll do my best.'

'I'm sure a man of your extraordinary abilities will find a way.' She stood up, calm now, and left the room. It had been, Makana was forced to concede, quite a performance. Gaber's voice brought him back to the present.

'Please don't take it personally. She is upset. We all are.'

Makana watched him smooth back the wavy white hair from his forehead. He preferred Soraya's sincerity, no matter how fiery, to this coldness.

'Hanafi told me about his wife and son . . . how they were killed.'

'He told you about that, did he?' Gaber's pale hands rested on the desk top as he sank down slowly into his chair.

'Does Soraya remember much about it?'

'She was a very small child at the time. Of course it affected her tremendously, as it did all of us.'

'But she only knows the official version, that it was a car accident?'

'She wasn't there when it happened.'

Makana nodded. 'The man who did it . . . the one who was trying to kill Hanafi . . . who was he?'

Gaber heaved a deep sigh and reached for the cigarette box.

This time he offered them to Makana – expensive English Dunhills. Makana held one under his nose to savour the smell of the tobacco.

'His name was Daud Bulatt. At one time he was very close to Hanafi.'

'What happened between them?'

'Who knows?' Gaber lifted a gold-plated lighter in the shape of the Sphinx and clicked the tail. He held out the flame to Makana. 'One day Bulatt decided to go his own way. He led a mutiny against Hanafi, wanted to take over everything. In the ensuing battle, Hanafi's wife and son were cut down in the street.' As Gaber fell silent there was only the sound of a lift humming somewhere in the building. Then he stirred and blinked, looking at Makana as if he had only just noticed him standing there.

'Is this relevant to your enquiry?'

'Everything is relevant.'

Irritated, Gaber shifted papers around his desk and straightened his tie.

'What else do you need to know?'

The cigarette tasted foreign and smooth. Yet another reminder that life at these altitudes was different. Makana told himself not to get too used to it.

'Tell me about the girl, Adil's mother.'

'Are you sure this is necessary?' Gaber's patience appeared to be running thin.

'We're wasting time,' sighed Makana. 'Let me tell you what I think happened. Hanafi would have been nearly fifty and she must have been young. How young?'

'Around sixteen,' said Gaber tersely.

'Sixteen. Unmarried. She caught Hanafi's eye and one day he

couldn't help himself. Nobody could ever refuse Hanafi, right? People were scared of him and he took what he wanted, but he also helped them. Enough to make them turn a blind eye to his bad behaviour. When she became pregnant you stepped in and smoothed everything over. Her parents brought up the child as their own.'

'That's more or less how it was.'

'What happened to the girl?'

'She killed herself.' Gaber's eyes never left Makana. 'It was all a long time ago.'

Through the glass behind the desk, Makana could see Hanafi and his daughter talking on the other side of the terrace. She seemed to be crying. Hanafi put his arms out to comfort her, but she pulled away and disappeared from sight, leaving the forlorn elderly figure alone with his sphinxes and his golf deck.

'Now tell me how all this is going to help you to find Adil?'

Makana glanced over at Gaber.

'That's the part I haven't worked out yet,' he said finally.

Chapter Eighteen

An hour later, Makana walked into Aswani's restaurant. It was early for lunch, but after spending the morning in Hanafi's world he needed to get back down to earth. It was strange, but nothing improved his mood like that place, gloomy as it invariably was. No customers anywhere to be seen today. The reddish-brown marble pillars that adorned the interior were streaked with white which made it look as though worms were crawling out of them, and there was a dull buzzing of flies over the meat counter which Ali Aswani was busy swabbing down with a rag and a bowl of soapy water.

'There's someone waiting for you,' he said, tipping his head towards the rear of the room.

Makana didn't spot Okasha until he was almost at the end of it. The inspector was seated discreetly out of sight behind one of the big square pillars. He folded his newspaper as Makana sat down.

'And they say your crimes never catch up with you,' he said, tapping the story about Hanafi on the front page.

'What do you think will happen?'

'With Hanafi?' Okasha shrugged. 'Who cares? He's nothing

but an old-time *bultagi*. There's a lot on his conscience. How he sleeps at night I'll never know.'

'How come he never came to trial?'

'Because his kind never do. He has people out there doing his dirty work for him, never got his own hands bloody.'

'And no doubt he pays well to keep his back clean.'

The theme of police corruption was not one that readily brought a smile to Okasha's lips. On this occasion he managed to limit himself to a blank stare and a shrug. He pushed a large envelope across the table to Makana.

'What's this?'

'Special delivery from London. I don't know what you did to that woman but she's worried about you, insisted I made sure you got to read this. So you see? Even I am at the service of the great detective. I am honoured.'

He gave a mock bow as Makana picked up the envelope and Ali came over to set two glasses of tea and a bunch of mint leaves down on the table.

'Are you eating today?' Aswani placed a bowl of pickles on the table and dried his big hands on the apron tied around his size-able girth.

The inspector yawned and rubbed his expanding belly. 'I have to watch what I eat. I'm getting out of shape. How about you?'

Makana shrugged.'The usual.'

Okasha clicked his tongue in annoyance. 'I give in. Bring me some of your kofta, Ali, but only half a kilo.'

Aswani twirled the ends of his moustache. 'You're a growing lad, you need your strength.'

'Okay, make it a kilo. You'll see me into the grave, I swear.' Okasha waved him away and leaned his elbows on the table. 'So, what does she say?'

Makana flipped the open seal on the envelope as he glanced at Okasha.

'You didn't even take a quick look?'

Okasha rubbed his broad chin. 'I can't read English to save my life.'

The envelope contained a sheaf of paper, which turned out to be a long letter from Hayden summing up the preliminary results of her investigation into Liz Markham's death. The letter was officially addressed to Okasha, but a yellow note stuck to the front page was for Makana:

The detective hired by Lord Markham to find his granddaughter is named Richard Strangeways. Unfortunately, I have been unable to locate a complete copy of his report. I spoke to him by telephone but he is getting on in years and his memory is not what it was. He cannot recall the name of Alice Markham's father, which unfortunately is not included in the pages I have photocopied for you. We are working on getting hold of a complete copy but this is complicated by the fact that the agency has moved several times over the intervening years and no one knows where everything is stored. Strangeways is pretty sure that the father of the child was Egyptian and that this was the reason for Liz Markham's visit to Cairo in 1981. I will get in touch again as soon as I manage to get hold of a full copy. I am sure that Inspector Okasha is grateful for all the help you can give him on the case, and of course I would greatly appreciate it if you could keep me informed of your findings.

Best wishes,

Janet Hayden

'You seem to enjoy better cooperation with Scotland Yard than I do,' sighed Okasha, leaning back to run a quick, wary glance around the room. Makana instinctively did the same, his eye catching a shadow flitting past the open doorway.

'It's not Scotland Yard. She's with Special Branch.'

'Forgive me.'

Makana's tea cooled as he skimmed quickly through Hayden's report of her interview with Strangeways before turning to the first photocopied page and beginning to read.

Richard Strangeways had arrived in Cairo on 18 January 1982, almost two months after Alice disappeared. He stayed in the Al Hassanain Hotel, the same place where Liz and Alice had stayed, and where, some seventeen years later, Liz had been murdered. Strangeways questioned the manager, the desk staff, cleaners, cooks and waiters . . . anyone he could lay his hands on. It was not a happy place, he decided. The staff were poorly paid and there was much resentment towards management, which suggested to him they might have been susceptible to bribes; certainly they'd had no trouble taking his money.

Makana wondered how many of them had been interviewed by the police at the time. From the report it was fairly plain that Strangeways did not enjoy being in Cairo. He didn't seem to like Egyptians much either, but that was perhaps understandable considering the lack of cooperation he received from the police, who hadn't taken to him. Easy to see why. An Englishman, not even a regular police officer, flies in to start poking around, claiming that he has the blessing of an English aristocrat on his enquiries. Makana could see how that would have gone down. Strangeways had drawn a similar conclusion: 'They still bear grudges against us. Over Suez, the bad old days when Britannia ruled the waves, and God knows what else.'

Hayden had noted against this on the report the fact that she suspected some personal conflict had arisen between Strangeways and the Cairo police. They seemed to have taken the disappearance of Alice Markham as a slur on their professional ability, something they preferred to cover up as quickly as possible rather than seriously try to solve. The man in charge of the investigation was particularly obstructive. He was named as Inspector Serrag. The same man Makana had picked out in the photograph with Gaber and Adil Romario.

'Did you know all this?' Makana asked. Okasha pursed his mouth as if he had just bitten into a lime. He nodded. 'I tried to raise it with him, but you know how it is. You don't just speak to someone like Colonel Serrag. You put word around and wait to see if he comes back to you.' Okasha bit into an olive and shrugged. 'He didn't come back.'

The food arrived and while Okasha immediately set to work on it, Makana hunched forward, completely absorbed in speculation. A faint nagging told him this was wrong, that he ought to be putting all his energy into Adil Romario's disappearance, but he couldn't shake off the conviction that there was a connection between that and Liz Markham's death.

Strangeways had once had a good, analytical mind. It came through in his work, in his descriptions of people and the possible links between them. But he'd clearly been out of his depth in Cairo. The language he used became more dense, abstract even, like a man caught up in an obsession. He was convinced that he'd found himself in the midst of a conspiracy, that the people who met him with smiles and polite apologies were hiding something. The area around the bazaar was ruled by ruffians, mobsters who ran protection rackets, all of whom were, in Strangeways's opinion, in league with the police. The Englishman did not hide his annoyance at the investigating officers' lack of cooperation. He went on at length about waiting in vain at division headquarters for a chance to speak to Inspector Serrag. The Egyptians were making him suffer because they were embarrassed by the case and resented being questioned about it by their former colonial rulers.

Besides the copy of the partial report, Hayden had also provided some more detail about Liz Markham's background. Born into a wealthy family, she had rebelled at an early age. Her father had inherited his title and the young Elizabeth apparently never came to terms with her privilege. The drug addiction began early on and led to her expulsion from a long list of expensive schools in England. She was then sent abroad, to France and Spain. She had run away on several occasions. It was on one of these excursions that she had landed up in Egypt and met the man who became Alice's father. When Liz arrived back in England, pregnant, her father disowned her and threw her out of the house. Strong-headed and determined, Liz Markham had decided to go ahead and have the child on her own. Again, probably in express defiance of her father's wishes.

Nevertheless, it was Lord Markham who had hired a detective to find Alice when the child went missing. Why? Makana remembered then what Janet Hayden had told him about Liz Markham having a nervous breakdown. Once back in England she was placed in a mental hospital and her father took over the search. That would explain the lack of input from Liz's side in the earlier days. In any case, Strangeways arrived in Cairo with little to go on. This might have explained why, right from the outset, he assumed that the disappearance of the little girl was driven by political motives. Makana knew what this meant: Strangeways had blindly followed his employer's assumption that someone had taken advantage of his gullible daughter going where she had no business going. It wasn't so different from Makana's own difficulties in taking instruction from Hanafi.

Besides that, Strangeways had arrived in Cairo at a difficult time. President Sadat, a friend of the West, had just been gunned down by his own soldiers. Egypt was lurching towards radical Islamism, fuelled by anti-Western feelings. This fed into the picture Strangeways painted of a country on the brink of anarchy. He saw bearded zealots everywhere, which only added to his sense of discomfort and personal insecurity. It also coloured his perception of the case. In his eyes Alice was the victim of some kind of jihad or holy war. He clearly believed that kidnapping the grandchild of an English lord would be a feather in the cap of any religious fanatic. Makana sighed as he read this. The Englishman had obviously concluded that the girl would never be found alive, although in the report he delivered to Alice's grandfather this was couched in more diplomatic terms.

Towards the end of the report, though, Strangeways began to hint at an alternative possibility. No ransom demand had been made and nobody had claimed responsibility for the girl vanishing. This led Strangeways to speculate that Alice's disappearance might have an explanation rooted in her background. He would have known about Liz's drug habit, and made the implied connection to the underworld. Was it possible, he wondered, that Alice Markham had been kidnapped by her own father?

At this point the photocopied pages ran out. Hayden had scribbled a note on the last page to explain that she would let Makana know as soon as she had something more. 'It seems entirely possible,' she went on, 'that Liz Markham might have crossed the line and made contact with people in the criminal world. Who did she know? Who was Alice Markham's father?' The last sentence was heavily underscored.

Makana paused to mull this over. Fair enough, Liz Markham was not the most reliable mother in the world. She had a serious drug problem and was in all likelihood incapable of taking care of herself, let alone a four-year-old child. What if she had simply found herself in deep water, dealing with characters she didn't really know, in a city she didn't understand? Had Liz made a mistake on that occasion, one she spent the rest of her life trying to put right? If she suspected who had taken her daughter, then her repeatedly coming back here made sense. But what if she hadn't come here looking for her daughter at all but for Alice's father instead?

It was entirely possible that the father, whoever he was, had not known that his brief relationship with the English girl had resulted in a child. Why had Liz Markham come to Cairo with her daughter in the first place? What had she hoped to gain? Makana tried to put himself in her shoes. She had a drug problem and an illegitimate child. Her father had disowned her and cut off her allowance. If she came here, it must have been to seek help. She'd brought the child along to persuade Alice's father to help her, which meant that he had money. She wouldn't have come here looking for a waiter or a pool attendant. Whoever Alice's father was, he would have to have been someone big . . .

'So where does this leave us?'

Okasha pushed aside the plates and burped quietly. Makana surveyed the havoc he had inflicted on them.

'It would really help if I could speak to Serrag.'

'I told you,' Okasha wiped his mouth with a paper napkin, 'Serrag is not going to speak to anyone . . . not me, and least of all you . . . about a case that took place so long ago. Why should the disappearance of a girl all those years before lead to the death of her mother now?' He raised his shoulders in a shrug. 'It makes no sense.'

'This is an ongoing investigation,' Makana reminded him. 'There are no certainties as yet.'

'No certainties?' Okasha queried. 'You see, that's the kind of comment you could only hear from a man with no one to answer to. You live outside the law, Makana, but some of us have to account for our actions. And besides, Serrag is no longer regular police. He's SSI.'

'There's something here that we are not seeing. Why would an Englishwoman be tortured and killed in her hotel room? The motive wasn't sexual, and no money was taken, so what was it about? The answer has to lie in her past.'

'Agreed, but all this stuff about the child and the father . . . do you really think that's relevant?'

Makana lit a cigarette and sat back, considering. 'I don't know.'

'You want to hear what I think?' Okasha picked his teeth with a matchstick. 'I think you are chasing straws in the wind.'

Then Makana remembered something Gaber had told him earlier.

'Does the name Daud Bulatt mean anything to you?'

Okasha shrugged his shoulders. 'I think he was one of the cheap thugs who used to operate around here, back in the old days.'

'Can you find out?'

'What for? Look, Makana, I'm going to find the person who murdered that woman, if only to show those arrogant English detectives that we can do our job. But don't forget that you're on our side, not theirs.'

Makana stared out through the open door. 'Alice would be a grown woman by now.'

Okasha's eyes hardened. 'She's dead,' he said quietly. 'Face the facts. Look, I know this is difficult for you. I'm telling you this . . . as a friend. You need to leave this case alone. You have to let it go. Sometimes it's better to let the past lie. You, more than anyone, ought to understand that.'

The two men stared at one another for a moment, then Makana got to his feet.

'Maybe you're right,' he said. 'Seven years is long enough to forget anyone.'

'Come on, don't do that! Hey, what am I going to do with all this food?' Okasha cried, as Aswani set down yet another plate piled high with freshly grilled kofta. But when he looked towards the door there was no longer any sign of Makana.

Chapter Nineteen

Makana knew Okasha was right. He was mixing things up in his head and was in danger of being swept away by his own theorising. Still, he could not help it. Thoughts of his own daughter and where she might have been now had she lived were never going to leave him. Was there really any purpose in going after Liz Markham's daughter? Was his intuition right? Could there be a connection between Liz Markham's death and Hanafi's past, or was that just wishful thinking on his part?

Having just read Strangeways's report, Makana looked at the bazaar around him in a different way. He imagined how it might have appeared to Liz Markham, scared and alone, with a little child in tow. The memory of Alice Markham was now written into these narrow streets, the cluttered shop windows, the glittering rows of gold and semi-precious stone, the tiny statuettes of goddesses and fiends, idols of another age. All around him was the intricate interplay of colour and inlay, angle and curve, shadow and light. Somewhere in the middle of all this a little girl had fallen through a hole in the world and vanished without trace. Who was he searching for among the stern faces of Horus and Osiris, all staring out at him from eternity? Was it Alice he hoped to find, or his own daughter Nasra?

Makana knew he needed someone who remembered the old days. Someone who had been around here back then. If Serrag was not going to cooperate, maybe he could find someone else who would. It took him only a few minutes to get back to the arch in the old city wall where the vendors had set out their collected piles of junk, their voices ringing back and forth across the narrow alley to the people brushing by. It was a relief to step out of the bustle and turn down the alley towards the dusty old antiquities shop. The area around it was deserted. Hardly anyone seemed to venture into that corner of the bazaar. The wizened old man in the dark glasses was exactly where Makana had left him. He sat, one leg crossed over the other, a cigarette smouldering between his skeletal fingers.

'Who are you looking for this time?'

'Do I have to be looking for someone?' asked Makana.

'Only you can answer that question,' said the man, getting slowly to his feet and motioning for Makana to follow.

The shop was even more cluttered than he had imagined the first time he'd peered in through the doorway. There were objects hanging from the beams and walls, as well as taking up every available surface. It was impossible to move in there without hitting something. Makana wondered why anyone would keep a shop full of useless, outdated objects. They seemed to have no possible value in today's world, and in such quantity served only to prevent anyone from actually getting into the place. And from what he recalled from his last visit, even if they tried the old man was liable to chase them out.

'Will you drink coffee?' The man's voice echoed faintly

from far inside the interior of the shop. He had disappeared from sight. Makana followed the sound to the far end of the room where he found a few steps leading down to a low doorway. Ducking through, he found another staircase with a workshop at the foot of it. The dust appeared to stop at the threshold. Inside it was dark and cool and spotlessly clean. Long and with a low vaulted ceiling, the room stretched ahead of him to wide doors at the far end, which opened on to a small, sunlit yard with a palm tree in the middle of it. The yard appeared to be dotted with wooden bird cages and the air was filled with song.

The wall on one side was lined with bookshelves. Opposite this a workbench ran the entire length of the room. There were strip lights suspended from the ceiling and an array of tools displayed on a rack on the wall. Makana saw pots of ink and stacks of various types of paper. He realised he was looking at a forger's workshop. There was a work light fixed above a huge magnifying glass on a stand. Over this, on the wall, was a papyrus painting – a copy of an illustration from the *Book of the Dead*. At the centre of the picture a large set of scales was depicted. Beside them a strange beast stood in attendance. It had the jaws of a crocodile and the body of a lion. Makana reached the yard as the old man placed a brass pot on a simple gas burner.

'This is from the Yemen, it's the best coffee there is. Bilquis, the Queen of Sheba, used to drink this.'

Marvelling at the way a tiny enclave of tranquillity had been created in the centre of the city, Makana moved around the yard, leaning closer to examine the birds in the cages. They were some kind of exotic species he had never seen before.

'How long have you been here?'

'In this place? Oh, longer than I can remember. I've seen people born, grow up to become fathers and die. Then I've seen their sons become fathers.'

'Then you must have heard most of what goes on around here.'

'There are things that I hear.' The old man's eyes glinted behind his dark glasses. 'And things that I don't.' He helped himself to one of Makana's cigarettes without asking. 'Why are you so concerned about this English girl who went missing?'

'Don't you think it strange? A woman loses her child and then seventeen years later is murdered in the same area?'

'I'm not sure strange is how I would describe it.' The old man stared into the brass pot as he gently stirred the bubbling black liquid. A rich, burned aroma filled the air.

'Then how would you describe it?'

The old man gestured for him to sit down at a small table set beneath the bird cages.

'I think things happen for a reason. We may not see it at the time. Indeed, it may be many years before the reasons become clear, but there is always a pattern into which these things fit.'

In another time and place, that might have sounded to Makana like the kind of spiritual nonsense in which people applaud themselves for finding comfort, but he found himself listening keenly to what the old man had to say.

'Something about this story has disturbed you,' the man observed. 'Is she related to you?'

'No.'

'Then perhaps you lost a child yourself . . . a girl?'

Makana reached over to take back his cigarettes. Silently, the old man watched him for a moment and then lifted his chin ever so slightly, as if he felt his opinion had been borne out.

Turning back to the little paraffin burner, he lifted the pot off the flame and poured the rich tar-like coffee into two small white porcelain cups.

'The path to oneness is full of suffering and pain,' he said as he placed a cup on the table in front of Makana.

'I don't know what that's supposed to mean,' he replied, mildly irritated.

'It means that I see what you yourself cannot.'

'And what might that be?'

The gaunt cheeks hollowed as the old man sucked smoke from the thin, poorly packed cigarette. 'To understand suffering and pain we must live in the present.' He exhaled. 'Between past and future. A Sufi lives in his words, which are secret paths through the world. His knowledge derives not from religious scripture but from the uniqueness of his experience . . . from the present.'

'I'm not really a very religious person.'

'Which of us truly is? People go through the motions.' The smile vanished from the man's bony face. He removed the dark glasses to reveal eyes like broken seashells, a strange blue-grey colour. 'Only the power of the spirit can make the past disappear, and your spirit is wounded. Displace the presence of the body and clarity will follow.'

'And how is that supposed to happen?' Makana couldn't keep the sarcasm out of his voice.

'Don't be so sceptical. The door to clarity can be opened by chance . . . A wanderer or invisible caller, whose spirit takes the place of the other and allows the "I" to disappear, so there is nothing to separate the Sufi from God.'

'So, a chance encounter with a stranger can be the key to unlocking our own spirits?'

'In your case, perhaps it is this English girl who is speaking to you, leading you away from yourself, to help you see.'

'To see what?' Makana found himself growing impatient.

'Only you can know that. The first step towards achieving harmony, the state of *shath*, is letting go of your memory.'

'You're saying I have to forget the past?'

The old man bared his few remaining front teeth in a grimace that Makana realised was a smile. 'You say you know nothing of these things, but I suspect you know more than you admit.'

Makana set down the little cup.

'You remember the time when she went missing?'

'I remember.' The old man nodded, replacing his glasses.

'The police investigation failed to find anything of use.'

'They had to tread carefully. The big sharks around here had them all in their pockets.' The old man chuckled to himself. 'Those were the bad old days, remember, when this whole area was ruled by gangsters. Those people had style. The kind of style you don't see any more.'

'You seem to know a lot about it.'

'I was here. I saw what happened. Most people struggle to make a living, and there aren't many ways of making a few pounds to feed your children without breaking the law.'

'Sounds like you miss it.'

'At least in those days you knew where you stood. Men had honour.' He clicked his tongue. 'Not like today. Now the thieves all wear big smiles and fancy suits. They sit in Parliament and tell us they have our best interests at heart.'

'So who was running this area in those days?'

'Who? Why, Saad Hanafi, of course.' The old man chuckled at the expression on Makana's face. 'Don't look so surprised. People nowadays only see the man who smiles down upon us from the sky, offering us *bamiya* and who knows what other nonsense. They have no idea what he was like in the old days. People were terrified of him then.'

'He was here when the girl disappeared? You're sure?'

'No, my mind is so ancient it plays tricks on me.' The old man screwed up his face so that all the lines drew together, like a net being drawn in. 'Of course I'm sure! Hanafi was a big man in those days. There was a war on, right about the time the girl went missing.'

'You mean the October War?' Makana, suddenly confused, doubted the accuracy of anything this man was telling him.

'No, that was 1973. I mean war in these streets. Between them, the dogs!'

'You mean a gang war?'

The wizened features grew motionless. 'I mean a war between Hanafi and his thugs. They wanted to get rid of him so they shot at him, right around the corner from here, in broad daylight.'

'One of his rivals tried to kill him?'

'The worst one of all.'

'Who was this rival?'

'Did you ever hear of a man named Daud Bulatt?'

Makana felt his pulse quicken. He leaned forward.

'This was when Hanafi's wife and son were killed?'

The old man gave a brief nod. 'Bulatt's men came after Hanafi and they made a mistake. He was supposed to be alone in the car that day, but for some reason, I don't know what, he wasn't.'

'Tell me about him.'

'Bulatt?' The old man raised a hand to run one warped finger-nail down the thin black scar slicing into the side of his neck, just below his left ear. 'He was the one who gave me this. Bulatt was a thug, a *bultagi*. He was young. He ran a protection racket, scaring people into giving him money. He dealt in contraband, too. He was well known in these parts.'

'What else can you remember about him?'

'He was a brute, not scared of anything. You were lucky to get away alive if you crossed him.' He gestured to his own face. 'I was one of the lucky ones. Hanafi used him to carry out his dirty work. Sent him round when the rent was slow in coming, or if he thought there was some kind of profitable business going on and he wasn't getting his share.'

'Then what happened?'

'Nobody really knows for certain. There was a fight between them. Some say that Bulatt became impatient and decided to take over Hanafi's businesses for himself. Some say it was over a woman.'

'What happened to Bulatt?'

'They carried on fighting and, in the end, Bulatt went to prison for something or other, and that was the end of it.'

'How so?'

'While he was inside Tora he had a change of heart. They say his life changed. Like many others before him, he found peace of mind in prison. He turned to Allah. From then on, he dedicated himself to living a pure life.'

'You mean he became religious?'

'He renounced everything. It was all over.'

'Was this before or after the girl went missing?'

The old man tilted his head to one side, trying to remember. 'I think it was around the same time. I'm not sure. It was all a long time ago.' He got to his feet stiffly and led the way back inside the workshop, signifying that the conversation was over. He paused in front of the papyrus.

Makana followed, his mind trying to digest this information. If

Bulatt had been in prison when Liz Markham came here it would have been impossible for her to find him, or for him to have taken her child . . . but could Bulatt have been Alice's father?

'You know what this is?'

Turning his attention to the illustration, Makana nodded.

'The Hall of Two Truths. Maat the goddess of justice weighs the heart of the dead man against an ostrich feather.'

'Very good. I sometimes think our pharaonic ancestors were more civilised than we are.'

Makana examined the burnished scales and the bizarre creature; Ammut the Devourer, its powerful jaws waiting to gobble up the heart and soul of the man if he was found to have anything weighing down his conscience. A man's soul against a feather. Makana cast an eye over the workbench and what appeared to be official documents of various sizes and qualities. Certificates of some kind . . . bank bonds.

'People have no imagination any more,' the old man said, coming up to stand beside him. 'They come to me for school leaving certificates, degrees in law, or to prove they are descendants of the Prophet.' He sighed. 'I dream of the day someone asks me for a copy of one of the great works of poetry or philosophy – Ibn Arabi, or Al Biruni's treatment of the heavenly bodies. Now *that* would be worthwhile.' For the first time his wizened face split into a gap-toothed grin.

Chapter Twenty

Mimi Maliki had the kind of looks that made grown men walk into walls, the kind that caused minor traffic accidents, that made them wonder if they had missed some wonderful opportunity in life which had now passed them by for ever. That kind of beauty.

Her apartment was in a row of empty plots and unfinished buildings in Masr al-Gedida. A graveyard of holes gouged into the earth and foundations rising like giant, half-built tombstones. Makana stood in the dust where the pavement ought to have been and peered up at the cement skeleton rising above him. Tenants impatient to get into their property had already moved in on a couple of floors. The walls had been filled in with breeze blocks, pasted roughly together with lumps of mortar oozing out of the cracks like hardened wax. Other floors remained empty platforms. A bird could fly straight through the building without hitting anything except possibly a pillar or two. Here and there occupants had brightened the raw, unsurfaced walls with coloured drapes. From the outside, in their present state, they looked no different from the makeshift housing in some of the poorer quarters of the city, only suspended high in the air.

Makana picked his way through an obstacle course of wheel-barrows and shovels, towers of bricks, heaps of cracked tiles, metal rods scattered like enormous burned matchsticks, ducking finally under a loop of electrical cable that strung together a couple of naked light bulbs which dangled from the flex like strange fruits on a vine. The lift was bright, shiny and absurdly pristine in the midst of this chaos. He edged around a fin of red marble jutting dangerously out of one wall, clearly put there in error. A cement mixer was grinding away noisily and labourers wandered back and forth, their arms and faces sprinkled with orange sand. Makana stepped inside the lift and pressed the button marked eight. To his surprise the doors slid smoothly shut and he began to rise. How long would that last? he wondered.

On the eighth floor a bouquet of coloured wires poked out of a hole in the wall at just the right height to take out an eye. Next to this was a heavy wooden door. The exposed wires were presumably where the bell ought to have been. He rapped on the door with his knuckles until eventually he could make out the sound of someone moving about inside. The door started to open then faltered as it jammed, grinding itself with a bump over the newly laid tiles on the uneven floor. Finally it opened, screeching in protest, to reveal a woman in her twenties.

'You'd think they'd be able to get the door straight, wouldn't you?'

This didn't seem to require an answer and Makana waited as she pushed her silky hair back from her face and frowned up at him.

'Who are you?'

'I'm Makana. We spoke on the phone? About Adil Romario?'

Mimi Maliki put a hand to her forehead as if about to swoon

and then spun on her bare heels without another word, one hand trailing gracefully behind her as she walked away.

'*Itfaddal.*'

To make a nation fall in love with you, you need more than just physical beauty. You also need presence, and Mimi Maliki had plenty of that. But still, some essential quality seemed to be lacking in her. Maybe along with all the other attributes required to become a star you also had to have luck, and somehow Mimi Maliki seemed to have missed out on that score. Makana recognised her from the movie clip he had seen in Farag's office where she had appeared quite beautiful, despite Farag's obvious lack of cinematic skills. In the flesh, she exuded an air of soft vulnerability that caused Makana to forget all the questions he had come to ask. He trailed behind her into an expansive living room with packing cases stacked along one wall. The sofas and armchairs, all white, were still covered in transparent plastic sheeting.

'You just moved in?'

'It's my uncle's place,' she said, by way of explanation as she dropped on to the sofa. 'He had to go abroad on business. I'm taking care of it till he gets back.'

'Nice for you.'

Something in his tone made her look up. 'You don't sound like a journalist,' she said as she lit a cigarette. There were grey lines under her eyes and her gaze was slightly unfocused. 'You sound like a cop.'

He smiled pleasantly. 'You'd be surprised how many people make that mistake.'

The room was spacious, with wide windows along two sides. Not that you could see much of the outside world, as the curtains were drawn, leaving just enough light for him to get around without thumping into the furniture.

'Did you bring the money?'

'I brought some.' Makana reached into his pocket and produced an envelope which he dropped on the long glass dining table. The girl bit her nails.

'That's not dollars. I asked for dollars.'

'The exchange rate is awful today.' Makana pushed his hands into the pockets of his jacket and tilted his head. 'I can take it back.'

Mimi considered this and decided to accept it anyway. As she leaned forward to pick it up Makana beat her to it, scooping the envelope back into his hand.

'Hey! If you don't give me that, I'll start screaming.'

He weighed the envelope in his hand as he walked over to the windows.

'You really want the police to come here and search the place?'

She slumped back. 'Who cares?'

It was an impasse of a kind. Makana dragged the curtains open, revealing the balcony which ran around two sides of the apartment.

'Hey,' she said, putting up a hand to shield her eyes from the light. 'Do you mind closing that again?'

The view was pretty good. Makana found he was looking down over the old part of Heliopolis. This quarter was rebuilt at the start of the twentieth century by Baron Empain, a wealthy Belgian, as a luxury enclave on the outskirts of the city, complete with a racecourse and Moorish villas, connected to Cairo by tram.

Mimi Maliki was still young enough to look good without making any effort, but that wouldn't be the case for much longer if she carried on the way she was now. He watched her lean forward to reach for an inlaid mahogany box and start rolling a joint. She moved as if in a kind of trance. After a moment she stopped and looked up as if she had just noticed him. He shook his head when she asked if he minded, but she had carried on anyway without waiting for an answer.

'You do look like a cop, you know.'

Makana turned back to the window. In the distance, the curious pinnacle of the Cambodian temple the Baron had built for himself was still visible. Once surrounded by grassy terraces and sensual statues, it was now a barren wasteland. At night it was a dark shell haunted by bats, a gloomy reminder of the days when the Europeans would dance there beneath mirrored ceilings and gilded fixtures. Long before that, of course, this was the site of the Temple of the Sun, said to be the place where the god Thoth had invented writing, an act so controversial that he was accused of undermining learning since writing would allow people to appear to know things of which they had no real understanding. Makana's thoughts reverted to the present.

'Tell me about Adil Romario.'

'What do you want to know?'

'How did you meet him?'

'How . . . ?' Mimi shrugged and stared blankly at the wall in front of her as if expecting the answer to appear there by some feat of magic. '*Wallahi*, I don't know. I must have met him somewhere. One of those parties, you know? Film people.' She spat the word 'film' as if it was an insult, as if it disgusted her in some way.

'You mix a lot with film people?'

'It's the only way to get by in this business. It's all about who you know and how much they like you. Talent has nothing to do with it.' Her voice sounded wistful, as if remembering a game she had once cared for but could no longer quite recall.

'When was this?'

'Ages ago . . . maybe a year.'

'And then what happened?'

'I don't know. I was star-struck, I suppose. Imagine that. By a dumb football player.' Her voice trembled, as though she might laugh, or cry.

'Is that how you met Salim Farag?'

'Salim the Creep. Salim the Cockroach.' She giggled to herself for a time.

'The film director.'

'That's a joke. It's something he tells people, but he hasn't actually directed a real movie. He's one of *those* people . . . you know. His father left him some money, I think. Anyway, he lost it all in one hopeless project after another.'

'When was this?'

'Ages ago.' Her brow wrinkled. 'Maybe even before I was born.'

'He must have had some success.'

'Oh, he worked with a few good people, but even then he had a bad reputation. He bribed his way in with the government. You know how it is. They put him on one committee or another. He made a couple of documentaries about ministers and army generals. I think that's what kept him out of prison.'

As she talked, Makana realised that Mimi Maliki was probably a good deal smarter than most people gave her credit for. She picked up details and stored them away.

'How did he and Adil manage to get together?'

'Oh, that's a whole other story.' Mimi fell silent for a moment, watching the smoke trickle up through her fingers. 'Everyone thinks Adil is so tough. They see him up there, larger than life, the nation's hero. But he's not really like that.'

'What made him interested in becoming a movie star?'

'Maybe he got tired of running up and down kicking a ball.'
She stared at him as if it was obvious, and maybe it was.

'Was he any good at it?'

'Acting? There's a lot worse out there doing fine.'

'True.'

Her eyes narrowed to slits. 'Why aren't you writing any of
this down?'

'I have a good memory. I write it down later.' Makana examined the knick-knacks on the white shelves over the television set.
'When is your uncle coming back?'

'Oh.' Mimi shook her head. 'I have no idea.'

'Why did you agree to shoot the screen test?'

'You saw that?' she groaned.

'You were the best part of it,' Makana assured her.

'Like I said, they had no real idea what they were doing.' She
sighed heavily and picked at the seams of her jeans with fingernails the colour of pomegranates. 'I was really disappointed. I
thought it was going to be my big break.'

'Nothing came of it?'

'Adil got strange. He stopped answering my calls. Just dropped
out of sight. I didn't want to call Farag because you never know
with a creep like that.'

'Where did they shoot the screen test?'

'One of those resorts. You know, by the sea.'

Makana put his hand into his pocket and touched the shell he
had taken from Adil Romario's desk. 'What resort? Do you
remember its name?'

Mimi paused to relight the joint. For a moment or two there
was silence as the herbal aroma suffused the air. The tension
visibly left her. She began to relax, slumping back in the sofa and
propping one foot up on the low table.

'The Big Blue. It's owned by this Russian . . . Vronsky. You know the kind of thing: terrace by the beach, full of fat Italian women and ugly Germans, waving their arms and legs in the pool. Stuffing their faces with food all day.'

'Is Farag the connection between this man Vronsky and Adil?'

'No, it's the other way round.'

'How did Adil come to know Vronsky?'

'Do you always ask so many questions?'

'I'm trying to find Adil. He might be in trouble.'

Her eyes closed and she seemed to float off into a dream for a moment or two. After a time, Makana bent down and plucked the joint carefully from her hand before she burned herself or set the place on fire. Mimi sat up and rubbed her nose, blinking and looking around the room as if she had no idea where she was, until she found him.

'Are you really a journalist?'

'No,' said Makana. 'Saad Hanafi hired me. He's worried about Adil.'

'I knew it!' She wagged a finger at him. 'The moment I saw you, I knew it.'

'Tell me about Adil. You said he's not like people think.'

'We're very similar, you know? I mean, neither of us really fits in anywhere. It's like we don't really belong.'

'But Hanafi took him in as a child. Treated him like his own son.'

'The family never accepted him, not really. They thought he was acting above his station. Especially that bitch . . .'

'Soraya?'

'She would like nothing better than for him to disappear for ever.'

Makana wondered if this explained Soraya Hanafi's outburst.

If she wanted Adil to disappear, did that mean she'd already known he was Hanafi's son?

'When was the last time you spoke to him?'

'About three weeks ago. He just stopped calling . . . wouldn't answer my calls.'

'Was this before or after you went to the family asking for money?'

Mimi Maliki pulled a sour face. 'That was that *kalba*'s fault. Always trying to push me out of the way. She wanted me out of Adil's life, and when I refused she started offering me money. In the end I thought I might as well take it. It didn't mean I had to stop seeing him.'

'Adil knew about all this?'

A quick nod. Mimi's restlessness had returned, as if she knew she had crossed a line by taking the money, and Makana wondered if that was the cause of the rift between her and Adil. Her fingers found the bag of hashish and she busied herself with rolling another joint, the first one forgotten. As she was lifting the lighter to her lips she stopped, the flame suspended in mid-air.

'You don't think he was kidnapped or something?'

'All we know is that he seems to have disappeared.'

'I wouldn't be surprised if *she* was behind it.'

'Soraya Hanafi?'

'She pretends to care for him, but it's all an act. The truth is, she can't stand him.'

'Did Adil ever mention receiving any threats?'

Mimi stared at Makana for a while and then laughed. 'Are you joking? He got threats all the time. There are some strange people out there. They hate you just for being successful, better off than them, better-looking, richer. Anything at all really.' She inhaled a lungful of smoke. The air in the room was thick with the sweet, organic smell. 'But he was never bothered by all that. Most people didn't have the courage to do anything but yell the odd insult or send him an obscene letter. Until that time he came back from Khartoum . . .'

Makana felt his heart lurch at the mention of his old home.

'What was he doing there?'

'I don't know, really. The details, I mean. It was some kind of exhibition match.'

Makana recalled the list from Gaber's file of matches the DreemTeem had played. They were mostly held to drum up sponsorship. Khartoum seemed an unlikely place to go for that.

'When he came back, that was it. He was afraid. He tried not to show it, but he behaved oddly. I asked him what it was about and he brushed it off. But he couldn't fool me. He would watch the mirror carefully when he was driving, always looking over his shoulder. He was . . . changed.'

Putting down the joint, Mimi held out her hand for a cigarette, fluttering her fingers in the air in the manner of a film diva. Makana shook out a Cleopatra and lit it for her. She exhaled into the air above her head.

'I think you'd better go now.'

'I thought you wanted the money,' said Makana, producing the envelope from his pocket.

Mimi chewed her fingernails. 'I've already told you plenty.'

Makana considered this for a moment and then dropped the envelope stuffed with notes on the table between them.

'There's more where that came from,' he said. 'Anything else you can tell me, it doesn't matter how insignificant it might seem, let me know.' He handed her one of his business cards. She took it from him, then stood up and went over to the dining table.

'You know, you're not bad-looking, for a cop.'

'I'm serious about the money.'

'I know. I just don't have anything more to say to you.'

'Maybe you'll think of something.'

'Maybe.' She sighed and began rolling herself another joint, the cigarette smouldering in the ashtray forgotten. She lit up and drew the smoke deep into her lungs, then slumped back on the sofa, her head back and her arms hanging limply by her sides. Makana watched her for a moment. She seemed at peace with herself. He hardly recognised her. Then he told himself he was a sentimental old fool, and turned and walked quietly out of the room.

Chapter Twenty-one

Possibly the last person on earth Guido Clemenza might have expected to see as he came out of the changing room at the club that afternoon was Makana. He was leaning against the wall, waiting.

Clemenza did a good job of pretending not to be annoyed. He snorted audibly and carried on walking. When Makana fell in beside him, he said with a sly smile, 'I take it you suffered no injuries the other night.'

'They seem to take your custom very seriously.'

'I am a regular client,' Clemenza sneered. 'It is only natural.'

'And I suppose, since you've started paying your debts, you are even more welcome than ever now.'

Clemenza flashed him a sideways glance but chose not to respond. He put his head down and began walking towards the row of cars parked against the side of the building, heading for a silver Alfa Romeo.

'Oh,' said Makana. 'It looks like you have a problem.'

The Italian looked at the flat tyre in dismay as Makana walked around the car.

'How could that happen?'

Makana ran his hand over the gleaming paintwork. 'They don't make them like they used to.'

'I'm calling Security.'

'Yes, that's probably a good idea, and I'll go and fetch Hanafi and you can tell him about your business with Vronsky.'

Clemenza pulled a face. 'What is it you want from me?'

'You can begin by telling me about your dealings with this Russian.'

The Italian scowled. He dumped his sports bag on the boot of the car.

'You don't want to get mixed up in this, believe me.'

Makana smiled. 'It almost sounds as if you are afraid of this man, Guido.'

He had meant it half in jest, but now he saw that he had struck home. Clemenza was scared of the Russian.

'Let me give you some advice, my friend. Vronsky's the kind of man it's worth being afraid of.'

'Why is that?'

'He's ex-Russian military. A black beret. Special services. He was in Afghanistan and Chechnya.'

'Sounds like you have some strange friends.' Makana was thinking about the rumours of Clemenza's involvement with the Italian Mafia over the match-fixing scandal. Was he now working with the Russian branch instead?

'And just what is your connection to him?'

'What do you think?' The Italian smirked. 'He throws great parties. The most beautiful women you can imagine, and they are willing to do anything.'

'I don't doubt you for a minute. And Adil introduced you to him. Why is that?'

'Business. Adil was looking for business opportunities. A footballer has to think ahead.'

'Forgive me, but you make a highly unlikely pair of business partners. You yourself made it plain there is no love lost between the two of you.'

Clemenza was looking round desperately for someone to change his tyre. 'Why is there never one of those clowns around when you need one?' Finally, as if summoned by his words, a uniformed security guard holding a teapot appeared on the far side of the compound. The team manager waved and shouted. The man disappeared around a corner, still clutching his precious teapot.

'This country will never achieve anything. Its greatness is behind it.' Clemenza gestured in the direction of the pyramids, far away in the distance, on the other side of the river.

While he was talking Makana kept silent. It had just come to him that he was looking at this the wrong way round.

'There's another over here,' he said, pointing at a second flat tyre on the far side of the car. 'Must have been kids or something.' Clemenza gave a cry of disbelief as he rushed round and began swearing loudly and profusely in Italian. He turned suddenly on Makana and pushed him against the car. There was a lot more muscle to his bulk than might have been expected. Clemenza hadn't gone completely to seed. 'You will pay for this! I don't care what Hanafi says.'

Makana held his gaze evenly. 'It wasn't Adil who introduced you to Vronsky, was it? It was the other way round.'

Clemenza's grip on his jacket loosened. Makana waited for him to step back.

'Why did you do that? You couldn't stand Adil, thought him a jumped-up prima donna, but you took him to see your friend Vronsky? What for?'

'You can't let personal feelings get in the way of business.' Clemenza brushed down his sleeves and straightened his shirt. He was sweating now. Damp patches had appeared under his armpits despite the cool weather.

'What did Vronsky want from him?'

'Take my advice,' Clemenza lifted his bag off the back of the car. He took one long look at Makana before turning away. 'You really don't want to get involved in this.'

Makana watched him walk away. What would a Russian businessman want with a football player and a second-rate film maker?

Chapter Twenty-two

There was something Makana had been putting off, something that he had been avoiding in his mind but which he now felt he had to face. From the stadium he took a taxi to Dokki. It dropped him outside the ash-grey building in the narrow side street crowded with cars that looked as though they had been fashioned out of mud. He climbed the stairs to the second floor and leaned on the buzzer, not sure what to expect. A whirling chirp sounded from within, but for a long time there was no indication that anyone was home. Just as he was about to turn away he heard something approaching – a soft shuffling sound. A bolt was pulled back and a lock turned. The door cracked open and a puffy round ball bearing a faint resemblance to a rotten melon appeared. It was streaked with purple and yellow. A large bandage covered the right temple. The eyes were familiar, ringed with black, like a panda, only this time it wasn't kohl that had run. They widened as she saw who it was. She fell back, letting the door swing open.

'What do you want?' Her voice trembled. She pressed a hand to her throat as if expecting Makana to throttle her. Speaking clearly caused her pain. Her left arm was in a sling and several fingers appeared to be bandaged and in splints.

Makana stared at her. 'Farag did this?'

She was having trouble breathing. Staggering back, chest heaving, she slumped down on to a narrow chair that gave an ominous crack but managed to bear her considerable weight. She gasped for breath, refusing to look up at him.

'What did you come for this time?'

Whatever Makana might have been about to say was cut off by an exclamation from further down the hall.

'Ya Allah! *Ya Allah!* What is this?'

A man in his fifties appeared, dressed in a pair of pyjama trousers and a vest. He brought a strong reek of hair oil with him. The husband.

'What do you want?'

'Aziz,' the woman pleaded, her voice no more than a strained sigh. She reared back as his hand lifted.

'Be quiet, woman! You!' He jabbed a finger at Makana. 'What is going on here? Somebody explain to me. Is this the one? Is it?'

'Look,' Makana began, 'I'm sorry about what happened . . .'

'What?' The man's narrow brows arched like bows, pointing up towards the oily patina of thinning hair combed close to his skull. 'Sorry?' he thundered like an actor on stage, frowning and gesturing. 'You stay away from my wife.' He jabbed Makana in the chest with a hard finger. Makana stepped back until he found himself pressed against a sharp metal protrusion in the door frame.

'Aziz!' his wife cried.

'You and your boss have done enough damage. You tell Farag. We will have nothing more to do with your dirty business.' He gestured at his wife, who sat crying quietly to herself. 'See what you have done?' Suddenly he was beside himself, wretched and helpless. 'We have done nothing . . . nothing, do you hear?' The emotion was too much for him to bear. His head slumped and a sob escaped from him. 'Just leave us alone,' he whispered. 'Go away and leave us alone. We've done nothing to you.'

'Look, I'm sorry about what happened.'

'Sorry?' the man sneered. 'I told Farag I will not have strange men visiting my wife at home and look what he did to her. Look!'

'Did you call the police?'

'The police? Do I need more trouble? She has lost her job. Look at her. You need to go. Now.' He pushed the door firmly shut in Makana's face. The hallway was dark. He stood for a moment. Fifteen minutes later he was leaning on the door buzzer of Faraga Film Productions, and kept leaning until there was a response from within.

'All right, I'm coming!' called a voice. Lumbering footsteps approached. 'Where's the fire?'

As the door began to swing inwards Makana threw his weight forward. The door struck Farag full in the face, causing him to let out a howl. He weaved about blindly, hands clutched to his nose, thumping into the wall behind him. Makana stepped inside and shut the door carefully, pushing the bolt across to make sure they would not be disturbed. Farag's eyes widened with confusion over the mask of his hands, blood spilling through his fingers as he saw Makana lift the chair that stood by the reception desk and smash it against the wall. Forgetting his bleeding nose for a moment, Farag let out a high-pitched cry of terror and sank down as the chair splintered above him. A picture frame containing verses from the Quran exploded, raining shards of glass and holy words over him. Farag squealed and began to crawl on his hands and knees towards the door to his office.

He wasn't moving very quickly and Makana had time to check there was no one else in the apartment before following him, pausing to separate a stout leg from the remains of the chair. A trail of blood smeared the floor tiles in Farag's wake as he crawled into his room, weakly pushing the door to behind him. Makana kicked it aside. At the far end of the cramped office, Farag was half out of sight behind the desk, trying to pull open the bottom drawer. He had his hand inside when Makana came round and brought down the chair leg on his wrist. There was a snapping sound and Farag, still on his knees, let out another howl, clutching his hand to his chest as he rolled away.

Opening the drawer to see what he had been reaching for, Makana discovered a 9mm Beretta with a cross-hatched grip. He lifted it out, slipping off the safety catch and pushing back the slide to check there was a round in the chamber. Then he moved closer, bending down over the fallen man and pushing the barrel into his fat and somewhat sweaty neck.

'Is this real, or just one of your film props?'

Makana didn't really need or expect an answer. Farag was breathing heavily, his eyes clamped tightly shut.

'Was it really necessary to hurt that woman? What were you afraid she might tell me?'

'What are you going to do?' he whimpered. 'Shoot me? You're mad, you'll never get away with it. I'm not just anybody, you know.'

'I wouldn't be too sure about that, but for the moment I need your assistance so I'm not going to kill you right away.'

'What do you want to know?' Farag stared up sullenly, pressing his good hand hopelessly to his nose, trying to sit upright. Makana put the gun barrel to his ear and shoved his head flat against the wall.

'Tell me about Vronsky?'

'Vronsky? He arrived here with money in his pocket. Don't ask me where he got it, because I have no idea. Where do any of those Russians get their money?' He sniffed, guarding his broken wrist against him like a wounded animal. 'They all come looking for a quiet place in the sun. Vronsky came here. Don't ask me why, I suppose it's safer than Spain, or somewhere in Europe where they still have policemen who do their job. So he settled for this place.'

'Then what?'

'What do I know? He builds himself a palace and prepares to die of old age.'

'What does he want from Adil Romario?'

'Nothing.' Farag tried to smile, his face a grotesque mask, nicotine-yellow teeth stained with blood. 'Vronsky likes to have fun. Parties, that kind of thing.'

'I heard about the parties, and the girls.'

'There's no harm in it,' Farag snivelled. 'It's just a bit of fun, that's all.' Makana realised he was trying to smile and gave him a kick.

'What was that for?'

'You looked like you were enjoying yourself too much.' Makana flicked the gun under his nose. 'What was your part in all this?'

'I filmed them, discreetly. It was all just for fun.'

'What kind of people attended these parties?'

'Ministers, aides, officials, people who could get things done. Businessmen. Vronsky wanted to invest his money.'

'Saad Hanafi?'

Farag shook his head. 'No, but his lieutenant was there.'

'Gaber?'

'Slim, white hair, looks down his nose at you.'

Makana couldn't resist bringing the chair leg down hard again on the man's knee. There was another howl of pain.

'You're insane,' Farag whimpered. 'I'll never walk again.'

'You should have tried acting instead of directing,' said Makana. 'You might have been more successful. Now get up.'

'What?' Farag licked blood from his lips, real horror in his eyes.

'You heard me. We're going for a drive.'

'Please tell me,' the man whined hysterically, 'are you going to kill me?'

'If I had wanted to do that, you'd be dead already.'

Farag didn't look reassured.

'Where are we going?'

'To see your friend Vronsky.'

'No, no . . . wait,' Farag implored. 'Please don't make me do this. You don't know what kind of person he is. I mean, he'll kill me, I swear.'

'Where's your car parked?'

Chapter Twenty-three

It took a while for Farag to hobble down the stairs and out into the street. He exaggerated his difficulties somewhat, which caused Makana to jab him in the ribs with the gun a couple of times. They got some odd looks on the street, but the car was parked in a narrow alley out of the way, an old beige Mercedes 200 that had seen better days. In the boot Makana found a length of electrical cable, among the rest of the junk that was in there. He pushed Farag into the passenger seat and tied his hands to the door handle.

'What's wrong with him?' asked a man in rags who had emerged from behind a heap of discarded office furniture to stand watching. He looked like he'd been shipwrecked a century ago.

'I'm taking him to the hospital,' Makana explained.

'Is that why you have to tie him up?' The man's trousers were in shreds and he only wore one shoe.

'He's not right in the head. He might hurt himself some more.'

'This whole city is full of crazy people,' said the man, shaking his head.

On Farag's directions they drove out south-east of the city in the direction of the sea. He remained silent for the most part, staring at the empty landscape they were driving through. A few times he asked if he could smoke but Makana ignored him.

The traffic eased up as the narrow streets gave way to open highways. They stopped to fill up the tank. Farag said he needed the toilet, so Makana untied him and led him round the back of the petrol station and told him to get on with it. There was no fight left in Farag, who was convinced that he was about to die. He was shaking so much he pissed on his shoes. They were back on the road in less than five minutes. Makana relented and gave him a cigarette.

The Mercedes was sluggish but powerful and had no difficulty passing the slow trucks and tourist buses lumbering towards the coast. It took them just over an hour to reach the Red Sea and from there the road wound south along the shoreline for another three hundred kilometres. It took them just over four hours altogether.

The Big Blue was located in a new tourist development just north of Hurghada itself, which was a sprawling mess of hotels and cheap restaurants. El Gouna was an old fishing village gradually being transformed into an upmarket alternative, a complex of luxury resorts. The construction work was in full swing, and the raw, unblemished shoreline was slowly but surely being whittled down to make way for more marinas and golf courses. In a few years' time there wouldn't be an inch of it that remained untouched. The Big Blue was placed on the tip of a peninsula that jutted out into the sea. You could see the walls, a pale turquoise colour, rising out of the sand against the sea beyond, capped with a wavy white strip along the top to make them blend in better. This was what distinguished it from the less classy places down the coast, supposed Makana as they turned in off the road and circled a roundabout that resembled a desert island, complete with palm trees. A black squad car was parked to one side inside the car park. The police officer inside it was asleep, snoring with his head thrown back. Makana pulled on the handbrake and reached over to untie Farag.

'You're going to behave yourself, aren't you?'

Farag nodded, weak and limp, nursing his bruised and bloody face. Makana hauled him out of the car. Then he placed the gun in the glove compartment and locked it.

'I'll hang on to these for a while,' he said, putting the car keys into his pocket.

The lobby of the resort had a sleepy feel to it, as if nothing of any great importance ever happened there. In its air-conditioned interior the quaint ceiling fans were mere decoration. They turned languorously, offering the change of pace conducive to a good holiday.

'Ah, Mr Farag,' the receptionist began. His smile faded when he got a closer look at the fat man's battered face.

'Tell Vronsky I'm here,' muttered Farag, trying to maintain some dignity.

'Right away, sir.' The receptionist nodded and fumbled for the telephone.

Makana leaned on the counter and surveyed the reception area. It was a wide open lobby, cluttered with furniture that seemed to have been set down with no real consideration of the space available. Open doors led through to a sunny inner courtyard. In the far corner two men lounged in rattan armchairs. One was snoring with his head inside a newspaper and the other was picking his teeth. In front of them were the remains of a meal and some half-empty glasses. They were SSI agents. A blind man could have spotted them a mile off. The second one nudged the first awake and they both stared sullenly at Makana for a time. Then one of them produced a telephone from his pocket and began to press buttons.

'Mr Vronsky will see you right away.' The receptionist snapped his fingers and a porter appeared. A slim young man still in his teens, he wore a uniform topped off with a red tarboosh. It was fixed to his head by an elastic band worn under his chin, which made him look like a monkey about to perform somersaults. Instead, he led the way across the lobby and out into a wide, shady courtyard. At the centre was a swimming pool. It was surrounded on three sides by villas arranged in a semicircle around a curving beach. They were linked by a series of terraces covered in teak tables and chairs, shrouded by large umbrellas. Along the beach straw sun shelters like large umbrellas shaded pairs of loungers. A few of these were occupied, mostly by middle-aged Westerners. They were dressed in swimsuits and sunglasses, and were reading books or sleeping. Over on the other side another set of guests were standing in a shallow pool up to their well-stuffed waistlines. A group of elderly ladies waved their arms in the air in enthusiastic if ungainly time to the disco music screeching from loudspeakers, while their eyes feasted on a young, muscular instructor who yelled orders at them from the side, like a sergeant major in a T-shirt and flowery bathing trunks.

The bellhop led them through to an area fenced off by a bamboo screen to prevent curious eyes from seeing into it. This part of the resort stretched all the way down to the sea and seemed to mark the beginning of an even more exclusive section of the property. The crowns of tall palms waved majestically overhead. A high green gate was set in an archway covered in glazed blue tiles. The porter rang the intercom and whispered something. A buzzer sounded and the door swung open to admit them.

The inner sanctum was almost as spacious as the main area, only there were fewer buildings and people. A wide lawn stretched out, ending in a neat file of palm trees lined up along the beach. There was another swimming pool, around which lounged a number of women in bikinis. These were younger and in better shape than the ones Makana had seen exercising in the pool next door. Some were Europeans, some not. A couple of them sat on the edge, kicking their feet in the water. Nobody paid much attention to Farag and Makana as they took the path towards a large Spanish-style villa. A wooden door heavy enough to guard a palace opened automatically as they climbed the steps. Someone somewhere had seen them coming.

The bellhop abandoned them here to a Filipino valet in a crisp white uniform. Without a word he turned and led the way across a wide hall with arches and doorways on both sides and a staircase leading upwards. Another arch admitted them to a large semicircular patio the size and shape of a small amphitheatre. It was cool and airy here. There was the splash of water from a pool of some kind, this time occupied by bright tropical fish flitting about in it like coloured darts. Water spilled into the pool down a wall of rippled brown coral. To the right of the steps was a long bar equipped with high stools, another Filipino waiting attentively behind it. Beyond this was a gym area. Fans blew cool spray into the air over their heads. All manner of running machines and weight-lifting equipment were spread about on a rectangle of artificial green turf, which brought to mind Hanafi's golf range.

Vronsky, or the man Makana took to be him, was lying face up on a bench, lifting a bar loaded with weights. Beads of sweat rolled down his forehead as he concentrated on his workout. The two men standing beside him seemed to serve no purpose other than to provide him with an audience, but when he'd finished his routine they stepped in to take the heavy bar from him and set it on its stand. It didn't look easy, even for the two of them. Vronsky sat up to reveal a torso covered in tattoos. Both shoulders were decked with feathers that descended down his back and along his arms as far as his elbows, giving the appearance of wings. On his forearms were words in Chinese and what might have been Sanskrit. Makana would have put his age at close to fifty, though a man ten years younger would have been happy with that body. There was no excess fat. It was all muscle. Someone handed him a towel and a bottle of water. Someone else handed him a shirt, which he pulled on but didn't bother to button. He was wearing tracksuit pants and flipflops on his feet.

One of the bodyguards stepped towards Makana and Farag, and indicated for them to lift their arms. He ran a quick, expert hand over them both and stepped back with a nod.

'What happened to your face?' asked Vronsky, amused, peering at the blood caked around Farag's nostrils. He murmured something inaudible. Vronsky stepped forward for a closer look before turning to Makana.

'Did you do this?'

'We were having problems communicating.'

A quizzical expression crossed Vronsky's face as he studied Makana for a moment before turning back to Farag.

'So, my fat friend, have you been playing games?'

'No! Really. I have done nothing . . .'

'Always trying to make a little extra money for yourself. You know what that's called? Greed. That's what. You can't trust a man who doesn't know when to stop.'

'I swear on my mother's life, I never told him anything,' Farag whimpered.

Vronsky turned to Makana.

'And what is your game?'

'I don't have a game. I'm looking for someone.'

'And what leads you to think I know anything about your friend?' Vronsky clowned for his audience, rolling his eyes. The two bodybuilders, or bodyguards if that was what they were, didn't smile back.

'He's looking for Adil Romario,' explained Farag, trying to be helpful.

The Russian circled a finger in the air. 'What part of this story am I missing?'

'I work for Saad Hanafi,' Makana said.

Vronsky tilted his head to one side, and his eyes seemed to light up.

'Hanafi? Why didn't you say so?'

He wasn't a tall man, but what he lacked in height he seemed to make up for in presence. The smile was unconvincing on that rigid face. Without taking his eyes off Makana, Vronsky said something over his shoulder in a language that Makana assumed was Russian. One of the other men stepped towards Farag, who tensed.

'It's okay.' Vronsky had reverted back to English. He ran a hand over the smooth bristles of his silver-flecked hair. 'Go with them. They'll fix you up. That looks nasty.' He winced in exaggerated fashion, pointing at the wound on Farag's nose and patting him on the shoulder. 'It'll be fine. They will clean it up and you should get some rest. Have something to eat.'

Clearly unhappy, Farag was led away, head hanging, like a condemned man on his way to the gallows.

'Why did you really do that?' Vronsky's pale blue eyes seemed to radiate their own inner light.

'I don't like men who beat up women.'

The Russian's eyebrows lifted in mock astonishment. 'What are you? The avenger of the poor and abused . . . restorer of justice?' He led the way over to the bar and ordered a glass of juice which appeared in front of him in no time. 'What can we offer you?'

Makana declined with a shake of the head. He looked around him, taking in the glass tables, the trickling waterfall, the vulgar display of opulence. Vronsky's wealth was of a different order to Hanafi's, but the two men had a lot in common. They were both ruthless and uncompromising, both determined to win. The difference was that Hanafi had put killing behind him. Vronsky looked like he still enjoyed hurting people who rubbed him up the wrong way.

'Shall we go into my office?' he suggested.

Makana followed him up a short flight of stairs and through a door into a large, L-shaped room on the corner of the building. Glass walls on two sides provided a panoramic view of the sea. When you looked back towards the shore the full extent of the development under way there became apparent.

'In a few years this will be one of the most exclusive resorts in the world with a luxury marina, pools, golf courses, fine restaurants. It will be a world unto itself.'

Makana could not shake off the feeling that there was something ominous about the fact that as soon as people had some money, the first thing they wanted to do was cut themselves off from the rest of the world. Maybe it was just human nature. But whatever it was, there was no denying the fact that it was happening here.

'And who is going to come to your little paradise on earth? Fellow Russians?'

'People of the world,' Vronsky announced proudly, as if he had just discovered a new class of the human race. 'The new global citizens. Yes, there are already Russians here, and there will be more probably. They have money, they want somewhere quiet to live. Is that so much to ask?'

Makana turned to look in the other direction. Along the shore to his left he could make out a collection of dull brown dwellings of quite a different sort, simple houses and shacks. Vronsky followed his line of sight.

'That's what it used to look like,' he said. 'The past and the future, side by side. That's all there was here a few years ago, a few fishing villages. This is the last one. People find that they can make more money working in a resort than they do fishing.'

'Convenient for you.'

'It's the way of the world.' Vronsky sized Makana up again. 'You don't look like the usual kind of clown that Hanafi hires.'

'Am I to take that as a compliment?'

Vronsky allowed himself a smile.

'Why have you come to see me?'

'I'm trying to find Adil.'

'And how can I help?'

'Well, it might be useful to know what kind of business you and he were engaged in. Was he thinking of going into the tourist trade?'

That brought a laugh from the Russian. He moved behind the large glass desk to sit himself in a swivel chair so big it made him look like a midget. He sat with his back to the view.

'It may surprise you to know that I don't feel I have to discuss my business with you, Mr . . . ?'

'Makana.'

He was busy examining the office. The furniture was modern,

all black leather and stainless steel. A lot of glass. A row of lacquered black cabinets lined up along one wall upon which stood an array of fax machines and printers, telephones and monitors of one kind or another. On one of these a series of black-and-white images showed various aspects of the complex on a split screen. Makana leaned down to peer into it. Vronsky was obviously concerned about security.

'Farag told you I have some kind of business arrangement with Adil?'

'It wasn't Farag.'

Makana straightened and turned towards the Russian, whose dull flat gaze struck him as being almost reptilian in its stubborn, unflinching intensity. Then Vronsky appeared to relent.

'Okay, all right. Adil is simply an acquaintance. He comes to visit sometimes. He likes it here. And the staff all get very excited when he turns up.'

'When was he last here?'

'You ask questions like a policeman. Is that what you are?' Vronsky's muscle-bound neck lolled against the chair back as he peered along the bumpy ridge of his nose at Makana.

'I told you, I am just helping Mr Hanafi.'

'I am always happy to be of service to a man like Hanafi.'

'I understand that you know Gaber, his lawyer?'

'Our friend has been talking too much.'

'I wouldn't blame Farag. He didn't feel he had much choice.'

'People always have a choice.'

Makana turned his attention to some sketches hanging on the wall. One showed a figure on a balcony overlooking the streets of Cairo; in the distance the Citadel rose up out of the hillside.

'Is that Napoleon?'

'During his Egyptian expedition. Did you know that he rewrote the Quran?'

'No,' Makana said over his shoulder. 'It's true that he tried to persuade the Egyptians to rise up against their Mamluk rulers by claiming that the French were the "true Muslims", and he also enlisted the learned *ulema* to support his cause, but I don't think there is any evidence that he actually went so far as to rewrite the sacred book.'

Vronsky got to his feet and came over to join him as Makana moved on. The next print showed French troops in 1798 in front of the pyramids.

'Quite a collection you have here.'

'It's a hobby of mine. I have been fascinated by Egypt since I was a child.'

'I thought your interest was in the building of empires?'

'Perhaps I have misjudged you.' Vronsky smiled. 'You are an observant man. I like that.' It was the satisfied smile of a predator peering down on his helpless prey. He leaned forward to examine the print. 'It is true that there are certain parallels. When Bonaparte arrived in this country it was ripe for the picking. The Mamluks were in a state of decay. It was a brilliant move.'

'I've always thought the history of the French occupation greatly exaggerated.'

'Oh, how so?' Vronsky frowned.

'Well, it was really no more than a sideshow for Napoleon; a diversion from the war with the English. It lasted a mere three years. The Mamluks, it is true, were over-confident. According to the historian al-Jabarti, who described visiting the French *savants* to see their scientific studies, the country's rulers had overestimated their own abilities and thought they could defeat any number of the *Franj*.'

'There are few men with the vision and courage of Napoleon.'

'Hanafi's empire is your Egypt?'

'Perhaps.' Vronsky smiled, liking the idea. To people like him the French expedition was symbolic, it seemed to Makana. It was a way of saying that the Egyptians didn't really appreciate everything they had; only a European could do that.

'Have you ever come across a man named Daud Bulatt?'

The change in Vronsky's mood was unmistakable.

'Why do I get the feeling you are just shooting in the dark?' he snorted impatiently and turned away, waving a hand in the direction of the sea. 'Let's take a walk.'

They went out across the lawn towards the beach. A cool breeze whipped in from the sea where the choppy water was dashed with white caps. The sea was such a brilliant colour that to Makana's eyes, used to the browns and greys of desert and city, it looked slightly unreal. They reached the water's edge and paused in the shade of a tall palm that swayed majestically in the breeze.

'You know what I like about the sea?' Vronsky asked. 'I like its clarity. It gives away nothing. It is transparent, and yet beneath it all manner of horrors take place. Nature draws a veil of water over its own cruelty.'

'What can you tell me about Adil Romario?'

'When he first came to me, I thought he was interested in doing something spectacular. Football is a way into the hearts of the people. For an outsider like me it is important to have a profile. To be seen to be doing something good for the country.' Vronsky glanced over at Makana as if wondering if he might understand this. 'Great men are born, not made. Napoleon had it in him from the start, that urge to achieve something. I was wrong about Adil. I thought he was special, but he is a small man. You know why? Because he lacks vision. He has had a fairy godfather holding a hand over him all his life, protecting him. When Alexander was his age he had conquered most of the Levant, Egypt, Persia and a good piece of Asia. Adil Romario wants to sit smiling on television every night. Where are the men of vision in this country?'

'That's a good question,' said Makana.

Vronsky drew back his arm to reveal the foreign script there. 'When I was seventeen years old I was sent to fight in Afghanistan. The place to me is synonymous with death. I saw a lot of it there. Many men died. Brave men. They died in terrible ways, in great pain, crying like children for their mothers. I was lucky to survive in one piece. It was not our country. We tried to fight the Mujahideen on our terms, but they knew the terrain in a way we could never hope to do. All the dips and hollows where a man with an RPG could hide.' Vronsky turned away from the sea to face Makana. 'And they had a weapon more powerful than any in our sophisticated armoury: faith. They truly believed that they would prevail, and we did not.'

He produced a pair of sunglasses and turned back to the sea, the lenses reflecting the line of blue water. He spoke without turning his head.

'I have nothing against you, Mr Makana. I survived the war because I knew how to learn. I think you are also a man who learns, which is why I am letting you go. You came a long way for very little, I'm afraid, but don't make the mistake of coming back here again unless you are invited.'

'What about Farag?'

Vronsky lifted his chin fractionally. It was impossible to tell for sure, but he seemed to be smiling. 'You don't need to worry about him. You delivered him to me. His fate is now in my hands.'

As Vronsky moved away, Makana reached into his pocket for

his Cleopatras and lit one, heaving the smoke into his lungs gratefully. A shadow fell over the ground in front of him and Makana turned to find one of the bodyguards standing next to him. Tall, broad-shouldered and silent. Without a word he gestured over his shoulder with a thumb.

Chapter Twenty-four

Back on the road Makana found himself glancing at the empty seat next to him in the Mercedes. It seemed he had played straight into Vronsky's hands. Despite everything, he felt bad about leaving Farag behind with the Russian.

Vronsky had great ambitions. That much was plain. What he wanted out of Hanafi was anybody's guess, but money and power would probably not be far off the mark. Why did he need Adil, then? And what did Adil gain from helping the Russian? It wasn't much, but Makana was pretty sure he was getting closer. And there was something else. Vronsky had reacted when Makana had brought up the subject of Daud Bulatt. The name wasn't unknown to him. Bulatt was the key, the piece that connected them all together: Hanafi, Liz Markham, Vronsky. And Adil? Was there a link between him and Daud Bulatt?

Makana hadn't been driving for more than about two minutes when his anxiety and frustration got the better of him. He swung the wheel and pulled off the road, to be greeted by the blast of a powerful horn and a rush of hot air as he was buffeted by the slipstream of a huge articulated lorry, rushing by so close it might have taken off the wing mirror had there still been one on that side of the car. Farag's Mercedes shuddered like a frightened animal.

Below him, Makana could see the sea, the calm rhythm of the breakers beating against a flat bay. He recognised the little cluster of houses he had spied from Vronsky's office, their brown mud walls almost invisible against the earth. It was not difficult to imagine that not so long ago, when the road was not so busy, this would have been an idyllic place. Getting back in the car, Makana engaged gear and carried on along the rough edge of the hard shoulder until he reached the unsurfaced track that led down to the village. Stones crunched under the wheels as he swung in a long arc that brought him bouncing towards the little hamlet about two hundred metres away. As he rolled down through the narrow streets towards the water he saw not a single soul. The houses were simple and rundown. Many appeared to be abandoned. Roofs had fallen in, window shutters hung off like broken wings.

The road came to an abrupt end in an open bay cluttered with rubbish, smashed bricks, battered fishing boats and heaps of nets. A black donkey tethered to a solitary telephone pole stood twitching its ears. The sea rolled into the small arc of the bay in long graceful furls, like silk being thrown out in reams. Makana parked the car in front of what looked like a restaurant of some kind, a house with a low terrace shaded by a trellis thatched with palm fronds. There was a meagre collection of stacked plastic chairs and tables. The place looked abandoned. An open doorway led to the interior. A man stood bent over in the far corner, sweeping away sand with a frond brush.

'*Salaam aleikum.*'

The man straightened up slowly, broom in hand. He seemed to be in his forties and had an unkempt, distracted air about him.

Beyond the house was a compound of some kind. A stray dog was sniffing at the ground. A small green fishing boat lay there. It was overturned and covered with nets and buoys and didn't look like it had been used for weeks. The scruffy yellow dog had a hole where one eye should have been. It came closer and began barking at Makana.

'No fishing today?'

'It's too rough.'

Makana reached for his cigarettes as the man bent down to pick up a stone. He threw it and the dog loped off, pausing to look back with its one mournful red eye from a safe distance.

'I think I'll just take a little walk around, stretch my legs.'

'Suit yourself.'

The man went back to his sweeping as Makana wandered along the beach. At close hand it was a mess, cluttered with the tide's harvest of cans and rusty wheels, broken crates, scraps of nylon fishing line like long blue and orange worms, driftwood. Away in the distance he could make out the elegant crowns of the tall palm trees around The Big Blue. It was like looking at the frontline in a battlefield, only in this case there seemed little doubt which side would prevail. The fishing community already appeared to have hoisted the white flag. Many of the houses looked to be unoccupied but he saw a handful still had rags flapping at the windows and nets hanging out to dry or for repair. By the water's edge two men were unloading straw baskets from a boat that looked as if it had just come in. Makana strolled over to them.

'A good catch?'

'No, there's nothing left for us out there,' the older man said, heaving his basket into the back of a rusty pick-up. The basket contained a meagre assortment of fish, none of which looked particularly appetising. He was white-haired, wearing a pair of baggy trousers and a vest that was more holes than cloth. His hair tilted in the wind like a miniature sail.

'The big trawlers take up everything. Most of it they throw out, but that's too late for us.'

'It looks too windy to fish.'

'Windy?' The man laughed, looking over at his companion, a younger fellow who might have been his grandson. 'This is nothing, just a light breeze.'

When Makana turned to walk back up to the car he noticed that the one-eyed dog was trailing behind him. The fight had gone out of it, just as it seemed to have gone out of everything around here. When he got back to the terrace, he saw the broom propped against the wall and the man was no longer to be seen. Makana had been hoping for a cup of coffee before he set off for Cairo. He walked across the terrace and leaned through the doorway.

'Hello?'

No answer. There was a counter and some shelves, a couple of battered wooden tables and chairs but nothing else. A door led further inside to what looked like a kitchen, but that too was deserted. On the terrace the wind ruffled the palm fronds overhead, making them hiss angrily. Makana reached the end and peered round the side of the building. He went past the heap of abandoned fishing tackle: nets threaded with cork floats, buoys with flags, cans that once contained lubricating grease or kerosene, and had a closer look at the boat. It lay underneath a mountain of green and blue webbing like a dead turtle. A cracked oar was tossed on top of the heap for good measure. It all looked forlorn and forgotten. On the far side of the compound was a simple building, like a warehouse. Makana went up and peered through the gap between the two corrugated-iron doors. Holes in the roof allowed narrow shafts of light to illuminate something that gleamed faintly.

'Hey, what are you doing?'

Makana turned to see the man from the terrace.

'Ah, good, I was just looking for you.'

'Are you from the government?' His look of suspicion deepened.

'No,' said Makana.'Nothing like that. I was just hoping for a cup of coffee.'

The man's expression seemed to say that if Makana had just crawled though the desert and offered him a million pounds, he still wouldn't have a glass of water for him. He stared back morosely.

'No gas. I forgot to change the cylinder.'

The light was already fading as Makana thanked him for his time and got back in the car. The coast road was clogged with slow vans and ancient trucks that lumbered along at a snail's pace, gushing thick clouds of black fumes. Heavy juggernauts rumbled towards him, making the solid German car tremble as if made of cardboard. Three hours later, when the road finally turned inland towards Cairo, it was pitch dark and Makana decided he needed a break to calm his nerves. Up ahead the lights of a café loomed out of the darkness. A simple breeze-block construction pitched in the dust by the side of the road. The neon lights were cold and unattractive but Makana was too tired to be fussy. He drew up alongside and killed the engine.

There was nothing else out here but desert in any direction you cared to look. The tables outside were unoccupied. For a long time he sat there smoking as he waited for his tea, watching the traffic buzz by like a stream of insects. A faded green Datsun rolled over the dust towards him, circling round to park right beside Farag's Mercedes. As he watched, the door creaked open and a familiar figure climbed out. He straightened his shirt, shut the door and walked straight towards Makana.

'May I join you?' And without waiting for an answer, Sami Barakat sat down.

Chapter Twenty-five

'Before you start threatening me, I should tell you I have seen enough to be able to go straight to the police with everything I know.'

Sami Barakat was so nervous he was shaking. The lighter in his hands clicked over and over like an enraged cicada. Finally Makana leaned forward and struck a match, the flame bobbing between them as Barakat bowed his head to light his American cigarette. He sat back and signalled for the waiter to bring him a glass of tea.

'So,' Makana said, 'what exactly do you know?'

'I thought you were working for the government. Then I thought you were working for Hanafi, and now it turns out you're with the Russian.'

'You sound confused.'

Sami Barakat pushed a hand through his ruffled hair and smoked nervously. 'Okay, look, I admit it, I'm out of my depth here. I don't understand what is going on.'

Makana laughed. 'What are you doing here anyway? I thought you had finished with this story. Why don't you go home and make up the rest like you did last time?'

'I didn't make it up.' The reporter looked genuinely offended. 'Well, the majority of it anyway.'

'The mystery man was a nice touch.'

'I have you to thank for that.'

'Kind of you to say so.' Makana studied him for a moment as the waiter arrived and poured the tea. 'You followed me all the way down there and back?'

Sami Barakat nodded as he leaned forward to spoon a thick white layer of sugar into his glass which he then stirred into a syrup, never taking his eyes off Makana the whole time.

'Why is your editor so interested in Adil Romario?'

'He isn't.' Sami Barakat hunched his shoulders. 'I was fired.'

Makana whistled. 'I thought you were their star reporter?'

'Hanafi gets what he wants. If he pulls his advertising like he threatened, the paper could be closed down in a week.'

'Then what are you doing here?'

Sami Barakat puffed on his cigarette for a time. 'I'm not sure. I just have a feeling about this story.'

'What kind of feeling?'

'The kind that tells me this is *the* story, the one I have always dreamed about. A story big enough to catapult me out of the reach of any small-minded editor.'

Makana thought this over. Sami Barakat struck him as genuine.

'Hanafi is that important to you?'

'Hanafi, and people like him, are the reason this country is in such a mess.'

'You could wind up in prison talking like that, or worse.'

Sami Barakat sat back, one leg crossed over the other, his foot tapping to a nervous beat in his head somewhere.

'Why are you telling me all this?' Makana asked.

'Because there's something about you . . . I can't put my finger on it, but you're not like the rest of them.'

'Hanafi hired me to find Adil. Whatever I think of the man, it's a job, and in my position I can't afford to be too fussy about who does the paying.'

'I hear what you are saying, but still. Maybe it's because you're not from here, but you know what I'm talking about. You're not in this to protect Hanafi's interests.'

'All I am concerned with is finding Adil Romario.'

'This is about more than that.'

'That's what you say.' Makana sipped his tea. 'Let me ask you a question.'

'Go ahead.'

'What is so fascinating about Adil Romario?'

Sami Barakat leaned back and looked up at the sky where a few faint pinpricks of stars were visible beyond the glow of the neon above their heads.

'He's an icon, I suppose. The classic case of a poor boy who got lucky. He's done what we all dream of, gone from rags to riches. It's too good to be true. The papers all repeat the same platitudes and clichés about him.'

'Not you?'

'Not me. To me this story is about dignity. We all dream of becoming rich, but what does that actually mean . . . how does it change us inside? And how much are we willing to compromise ourselves in the process?'

'You're writing a moral tale?'

Sami Barakat leaned forward, his gaze fixed on Makana. 'This is a fairy tale come true. Poor boy born in a village gets picked out one day and put on a pinnacle. He's up there, a star, a legend. But the question is, how did he get there? And how does he feel about that? Adil Romario is a smart man. No matter what he does in life, he knows he will always live in the shadow of the man who pulled him out of the mud. How does he live with the knowledge that he owes such a debt to someone who embodies all the corruption and dishonesty which is ruining our country?' He sat back in his chair, his case made. 'For me, it's all about dignity.'

'You should listen to yourself sometime, you're a dangerous man,' said Makana slowly.

'I have to tell it the way I see it. I can't lie.'

'A lot of brave men have lived to regret similar sentiments.'

'Sure, I know that.' There followed a long silence. Finally, the reporter said, 'Why exactly did you come to this country?'

'It's a long story, and it's late.' Makana's eye fell on the Mercedes and his mind went back to Farag. 'Who are you writing this story for if you don't have a paper to go to?'

'Oh, I'll find a way to be published.' Sami shrugged. 'If I believe in this story, then I am sure there are countless others who feel the same. Old Hanafi can't tie up all of the press, in his pocket. But like I said, there's a lot going on here I still don't understand.'

'And you think I can help you?'

'Maybe we can help each other.'

Makana considered the idea. Sami Barakat nodded over his shoulder, tapping his useless lighter against his knee.

'The owner of that car. What happened to him?'

'I don't know,' said Makana quietly. 'But I have a bad feeling.'

'And the guy you went to visit, the Russian. How does he fit into all of this?'

Makana looked Sami Barakat over once more, and decided that, for whatever reason, it made sense to trust him for the moment.

'Adil was working with Vronsky, or for him. Doing what exactly, I don't know.'

'I could look into the Russian, if you like? I know people who work for the development company out there.'

'Well, he's a bit of a mystery. But what seems clear is that he is trying to build himself an empire in this country.'

'You think he's competing with Hanafi?'

'He could be.'

'So he's using Adil to get at the old man?'

Makana stared off into the darkness. Could that be it? Was Vronsky using Adil to get a foothold inside Hanafi Enterprises? He watched a large black Toyota SUV pull off the road and park in front of the café. The driver got out and hitched up his trousers, then walked around the side of the building following an arrow scratched in charcoal on a whitewashed wall, indicating the direction of the toilet. Another got out of the passenger side and stretched his arms above his head.

'It's funny how the disappearance of one person can send everyone around him into disarray. It's like astronomy or something,' Barakat continued.

'Astronomy?' Makana frowned.

'You take one piece away and the whole system becomes unstable.'

'You think you can find out about Vronsky?'

'I'll make a few calls. I know some people.'

'Okay,' nodded Makana. 'If we're moving towards the idea that this has less to do with Adil Romario than with Hanafi himself, we will need to know the state of his company. You must have contacts or former colleagues with some insight into the business world. Perhaps you can find out something about the state of Hanafi Enterprises . . . what their situation is, who their enemies are.'

'I think I can manage that.'

The two men from the black Toyota nodded a greeting as they moved past them to settle at a table behind, up against the wall. Both ordered coffee. One of them called for a shisha.

'Does this mean we are working together?'

'It means we are cooperating.'

'How do I know I can trust you?' Sami asked.

'You don't,' Makana said. 'That's the nature of these things. And there's something else you need to bear in mind,' he said, getting to his feet. 'I'm not trying to scare you, but you need to realise that some of the people in this game are pretty ruthless.'

'Don't worry about me,' grinned Sami Barakat, 'I can take care of myself.'

'I hope so, for your sake.'

It was well into the early hours before Makana arrived home. He parked the Mercedes under the eucalyptus tree and stumbled down the slope towards the river, barely able to keep his eyes open. The *awama* was silent and dark. He stepped on board, pulling the Beretta from his belt. Then he went through every room. When he was sure he was alone he set the gun down next to the answering machine. The red light was flashing to tell him that he had a message. He punched it and heard Soraya Hanafi's voice. Her nervousness was plainly audible as she tried to affect a light tone.

'I feel I have been unfair to you. I'd like us to start afresh.' She wondered if he would mind meeting her the following morning for a game of tennis at the Gezira Club. Makana couldn't help smiling. Tennis? He would have to watch himself. Before he knew it he would be hobnobbing with the best of them.

Chapter Twenty-six

T he guards on the front gate of the Gezira Club did not appear overly convinced of Makana's qualifications to join the well-to-do members inside. They detained him, asking him to pull over to one side as they waved every other car through. Stern looks were thrown Makana's way in passing as the well-heeled sons and daughters of the city wondered what deviousness he might be guilty of.

Makana waited patiently. In the distance he could make out the giant finger of the Cairo Tower rising into the air. Modelled on a lotus flower, symbol of life in Ancient Egypt, it was built in the late fifties to transmit the *Sawt al-Arab* radio signal. The legendary broadcasts united the Arabs around the bold leadership of Gamal Abdel Nasser and his defiance of the West. In his determination to remain independent, Nasser symbolised Arab pride and dignity. Nowadays, people looked back upon that era with fond nostalgia. Where had it all gone, they wondered, all that hope? He was said to have built the tower with a $3 million bribe the Americans threw his way before refusing to finance his construction of the High Dam. It had never struck Makana as a particularly attractive object. There was a restaurant up there

233

which revolved while you ate. Spinning around in the air trying to eat struck him as a strange idea. Was that what had become of Egyptian independence?

One of the guards approached, looking as officious as a presidential aide, fiddling with something that looked like a children's toy but was some kind of walkie-talkie. He waved Makana through with a distracted gesture, as if, now that he had been given permission to let him in, he had something more important to do with his time. Peer into any sentry box and you'll find a little dictator in the making, thought Makana. Who said that?

Soraya Hanafi was waiting for him. Even when she dressed casually she managed to look more elegant than most people did when turned out in their best clothes. She was wearing a white tracksuit that was slim-fitting and immaculate. In the bright sunlight her hair looked lighter, tied back in a pony tail that peeked out of the back of an American baseball cap. Her face was radiant though largely obscured by a pair of sunglasses. Makana instinctively straightened his jacket, even though he knew it would make no difference. He made a mental note to go shopping for a new outfit one of these days. Presuming he ever managed to finish this case, he might actually have the money to purchase something. Soraya Hanafi tapped her racquet against one hand impatiently.

'You didn't come ready to play.'

'I'm sorry. It completely slipped my mind.' Makana had never played tennis in his life and he wasn't about to start now. Soraya Hanafi gave him a knowing look.

'No need to apologise. It's my fault for insisting. Come, let's sit down.'

It was early and the air was cool and fresh as they proceeded along a path to a terrace where a table with a parasol over it was reserved for them. Despite her attempt at disguise, if that's what it was, they were stopped several times by people wanting to say hello. She acknowledged all of them with warmth and grace. Makana felt as if he were in the presence of royalty. She might have been a princess or a film star. What she was, of course, was heiress to one of the largest fortunes in the country. She handled herself well in the role. A waiter appeared the moment they sat down and she ordered freshly squeezed lime juice. Makana asked for tea.

'I suppose you come here a lot.'

She nodded. 'Since I was a child. There are more exclusive places nowadays, but one would hate to abandon one's friends.'

Somehow, Makana doubted that friends played a huge part in Soraya Hanafi's life. She carried herself with the confidence of one who is at ease with solitude. Work was her life, which might have explained why she hadn't married yet and why, so far as he knew, there were no obvious suitors on the horizon. Cairo's socialites must have been buzzing with potential marriage prospects for such a valuable catch, but Soraya Hanafi wasn't the kind of woman to throw it all aside and settle down as Mrs Somebody Else. What husband, after all, could hope to fill old man Hanafi's shoes?

'I take it there have been no major breakthroughs in the case?'

'No,' said Makana. 'I'm afraid not.'

'It's unbearable. Not knowing, I mean.'

'What do *you* think has happened to him?'

For a long time Soraya Hanafi said nothing. She stared at Makana, as if still unsure whether he represented a source of hope or a threat. Then, folding her arms together on the table, she spoke almost in a whisper.

'I wanted to apologise to you for my outburst the other day, I know you are doing your best to find Adil. As you will understand, I am very concerned about him. I am afraid something terrible has happened.'

'What makes you say that?' he asked.

'Adil would never go away for this long without calling, or leaving a message, or . . . I don't know, just something. He would tell me . . . one of us . . . someone.'

'What about the theory that he went abroad, to seek a contract with a European club?'

Soraya was adamant. 'He would never do something like that without discussing it with me first. Everything he needed was here. Why would he go to Europe?'

The tea arrived in a fancy pot with a cup and saucer. Makana silently kicked himself for not asking for red tea in a glass with mint.

'It must be difficult, trying to find someone you've never met.'

'It's not the first time I've done this, but it's strange . . . the more I learn about Adil, the less I feel I know.' Makana reached out to pour his tea. It dribbled down the spout on to the table and a drop even scalded his leg. He replaced the pot on the table, inwardly cursing the idiots who designed objects that were completely unsuited to the purpose for which they were intended. He would have liked to have lit a cigarette, but since he knew she would disapprove he refrained. Makana was on his best behaviour today.

'Might I ask you a personal question?' he said.

'That depends.' She laughed lightly. 'How personal?'

'How did it feel to discover after all these years that Adil was your half-brother?'

'I think I explained to you once before that there is no rivalry between myself and Adil. There is no need for it.'

'But surely this changes things. He now has a claim to your father's wealth.'

'We must wait and see if my father wants this to become public knowledge.' Soraya leaned across to reach for the pot. She poured his tea carefully, filling the cup nearly to the brim without a drop out of place.

'Milk?'

'Thank you.'

Soraya replaced the milk jug on the table and was still for a moment.

'You're saying he may not publicly recognise Adil as his son?' Makana considered their surroundings, among the socialites of Cairo. Admitting to an illegitimate child would not go unremarked in these parts.

Soraya shook her head briefly. 'Adil would not be a popular choice as my father's successor.'

'Why not?'

'Many people are already aware of the extent of his influence over my father.'

'You mean, inside the company?'

'Inside and out. Bankers, sponsors. There is even a rumour that several senior managers have threatened to resign if Adil were ever put in charge.'

'How would you feel if he were given the job that you probably deserve?'

A trickle of laughter escaped her. 'You flatter me! Until a few years ago I really had no idea what I wanted to do with my life. But I have worked hard since then. I earned myself a place in the company. I have my own ideas. Hanafi Heavens, for example, is mine.' She paused, untying the band that held her hair in place and tossing it down on the table. 'If Adil were to be put in charge I think he would have to adjust.'

'Do you think he could?'

'We all have to make adjustments.' Soraya allowed herself a smile. 'My father and I are very alike, though I don't agree with everything he says. Even Gaber doesn't stand up to him the way I do. He calls me his toughest rival.'

'That still doesn't make you the son he has always dreamed of.'

'Nothing will ever do that.' She laughed again, sounding almost unconcerned. 'I never forget that I am a woman, and in this country that counts for very little. I grew up the daughter of a wealthy man, but I am not blind. I see the way most people in this country live. My father never let me forget how hard he had to struggle to get to where he is. Adil represented something I had never known. In the beginning I used to feel I had to be extra nice to him for that reason.'

Soraya still hadn't touched her lime juice. She stretched out her hand to touch the glass and a bracelet bearing her name winked on her wrist.

'I don't believe this is just about Adil,' she went on. 'My feeling is that someone may be trying to destroy the company.'

'How easy would it be?'

'To take us over?' She frowned. 'Right now we are in a vulnerable position. The financial climate of the last few years has been difficult. The Gulf War hit the economy hard. We have made mistakes, overstretched our resources. The stadium is an expensive, prestigious project, and this is the wrong time for it. Once Hanafi Heavens is completed our situation will greatly improve. It will be the first of many such projects. It will draw in a lot of investors, national and international.'

'What does Gaber say?'

'Oh, Gaber.' She made a throwaway gesture with her hand. 'Gaber never, ever admits that anything is wrong. He is very loyal to my father.'

'They go back a long way.'

'Yes, they do.'

A breeze picked up and fluttered her hair around her face like a veil. It made her look more alluring than ever. There followed a lengthy silence. In the distance the cacophony of the traffic was interrupted by the grinding two-tone siren of an ambulance and then, as if in response, the triple-tone horn of a taxi struggling through the gridlock.

'Adil is my father's weakness. It's where his judgement goes awry. He sees his younger self in him, in his recklessness. The older he gets, the more he indulges Adil.'

'In what way?'

'Well, Gaber and I have a hard time persuading him not to entertain Adil's business ideas.'

'Is he the one who thought up the new stadium?'

'I'm afraid that was my father's idea to begin with. Something he has wanted to do for years. And it could be done, just not on the current scale. But Adil played upon my father's vanity, pushing him to make it into the dream of a lifetime. He has no head for business. Adil's strength is his charisma, his ability to draw people in, to persuade them to go along with him. He thinks that's all that matters, getting people to go along with him.'

'Is that why you paid Mimi Maliki to disappear?'

Her attractive almond-shaped eyes hardened instantly. 'You spoke to her, of course.' Soraya's chest heaved. 'She is not the right kind of girl for him.'

'I don't know.' Makana smiled. 'I thought they might make a handsome couple. And besides, isn't Adil old enough to make decisions like that for himself?'

'You have to understand.' She tried another smile, and almost succeeded. 'All kinds of women throw themselves at Adil, but at heart he is quite a simple soul.'

'You look out for him, then.'

'All the time.' Soraya seemed to relax visibly. 'I've known him since I was a child.'

'It must have been a difficult time for you. I mean, after the accident?'

'Yes. My mother and elder brother died. Out of that little family my father and I survived. It created a special bond between us.'

Makana wondered how far that special bond went. It was true there was something tough and independent about Soraya, which he could see would appeal to a man like Hanafi.

'It was a long time ago. I suppose you don't remember much about it.'

'Very little. I was only small at the time.' She bent her head to sip her lime juice.

'How young exactly?'

'About three and a half, almost four.'

'How much do you actually know about your father's past?'

'I hear the rumours, of course. He came from a very disadvantaged background. It wasn't easy getting to where he is today, and so he made a few enemies along the way. But rumours have a habit of growing deeper and darker with time. People like a good story.'

'Of course they do,' said Makana. 'Does the name Daud Bulatt mean anything to you?'

Soraya shook her head blankly, then she smiled. 'My father has always shielded me from the worst of it. I remember very little. I don't really recall my mother at all. If she were standing right where you are now, I wouldn't know her. He never talks about her. When I was a teenager I would go to him in tears after hearing some of the things I heard in school. The other girls would talk. They would repeat things they had heard their parents say. You know how kids are?'

'Sure.' Makana nodded.

'I was my father's youngest daughter. His golden princess, he used to call me. And, like a princess, I lived a charmed life, kept out of harm's way, protected. I was spoiled rotten as a child, given anything I asked for. I was brought up by my elder half-sisters. The age difference between us made me think of them as aunts. The house was always full of people and I felt safe there, that was all that mattered to me.'

She leaned back and took a deep breath. 'I'm glad we've had this chance to get to know one another a little better.'

'I am grateful to you for being so candid.'

'I think I understand now why my father hired you. You're a complete unknown. There is no danger of your having any connection to his past.'

There followed another prolonged silence. Makana turned his head to watch people go by. Some glanced in their direction, being casual about it; others were less discreet. He felt like a visiting dignitary. It was a strange feeling, and although disconcerting, not altogether disagreeable. A little girl, about thirteen or so, went by with her father.

'What are you thinking about?'

Makana had been lost in his thoughts. He looked over at Soraya Hanafi.

'I'm sorry, I was thinking about something else. A woman was murdered the other day. An Englishwoman.'

'How terrible.' Soraya stared at him. She seemed about to say something more, but hesitated. Finally, she got it out. 'Gaber told me about your family.'

'It was a long time ago.'

'Seven years is not that long. You lost your wife and daughter. I can imagine how that must feel. I'm sorry.'

Makana toyed with his cigarettes. There was only one left in the packet. It seemed the moment to light it anyway.

'They say when someone close to you dies, they stay with you in your heart. It's true at first, but it doesn't last. Like everything else, they start to fade, and then you realise you are really alone.'

'Yes,' she agreed. 'That's how it is.'

They were silent for a time. The breeze changed direction and the soft wind ruffled her hair around her face again. For a time Makana thought about the strange path that had led him to this place, but that diverted him down a line of thought that was almost unbearable. Instead he turned his mind to the woman sitting in front of him. There was something about her that he couldn't quite put his finger on. But even that thought led him nowhere. So he smiled at her and she smiled back and for a while he tried to think about absolutely nothing. They sat there in silence, watching the people who went by, some of whom greeted her before moving on, no doubt wondering who that strange man Soraya Hanafi was sitting with could possibly be.

Chapter Twenty-seven

When he walked into the dusty junk shop Makana saw no sign of the old man. He stopped just inside the doorway and cocked his head to one side, listening to the sounds of the centuries echoing in the obsolete objects around him. The door stood open; the rickety chair with the mended leg stood forlornly outside like an abandoned sentry post. As he ventured deeper into the interior, edging his way forward, he became aware of a growing curiosity to see this place without the old man standing over him. Ahead of him was the little doorway, illuminated in the gloom by the light beyond. He had almost reached it when the wizened figure appeared out of nowhere, moving with sprightly ease to block his path.

'I thought it was rats I heard moving about,' he said, challenging Makana with a look.

'I can't imagine they would dare.'

They stood in the gloom, face to face. The airy space below opened up like the deck of a well-equipped ship while they, secluded in the crow's nest, whispered like mutineers. A crescent of light found the edge of the old man's cracked spectacles.

'I wanted to ask you a question,' said Makana.

'A question?'

Smoke flared from his nostrils, turning blue where it picked up a fissure of light. He made no move to invite his visitor to descend into the basement. This intrigued Makana. Where was the former hospitality, the offer of coffee and a chat? He recalled the brusque dismissal of the woman and her son the first time he had spoken to the old man.

'Have you told anyone about me?'

'About you?' The old man tilted back his head.

'About someone coming round here asking questions about the old days?'

'What makes you think I would do a thing like that? What would make you say a thing like that?' In the dim light he resembled an old and wrinkled tortoise. Beyond that he was a mystery.

'Is there anyone you can think of, from those days, anyone who might still hold a grudge against Hanafi?'

'I can think of hundreds . . . thousands.' A shudder seemed to run through the man's frail body.

'How about Daud Bulatt?'

'I heard that he was killed in his pursuit of jihad. You're hunting ghosts.' The bony face creased with amusement. 'Anyway he would be insane to come back. He declared war on the state.'

'But is it possible?'

'That he didn't die?' The old man stared into the darkness. 'Who knows?' he said finally, his voice hoarse. 'It's in the hands of our Lord.'

'Would you tell me if you knew?' Makana called as the shopkeeper turned away and out of sight. But there was no response from him.

Walking back out through Sharia al-Muski, past the stalls, the spice merchants who sold everything from rough black pepper-corns and bright strands of saffron to sacks stuffed with starfish, Makana wondered about the change in the old man. Perhaps he was busy, in the middle of some tricky piece of forgery. No, it wasn't that. He was worried about something. Makana walked on, deep in thought. The ground was littered with discarded leaves and scraps thrown to the scrawny hordes of cats which skittered about underfoot in search of a feast.

When he arrived back in the busy thoroughfare where he had left the car Makana found Okasha leaning against the side of the Mercedes. Sunlight gleamed off his expensive sunglasses and the inspector was wearing a rather pleased expression, his square jaw jutting out at the sky. Nearby a police driver sat behind the wheel of a battered blue sedan, picking his teeth with a matchstick.

'If I didn't know any better, I would think you had informants all over this city.'

'*Wahyat Allah*, you are the most suspicious-minded person I have ever met.'

Okasha opened the rear door of the police car and motioned for him to enter. Makana climbed in while the inspector went round to the other side.

'What's this all about?'

'I care about you, Makana. Don't you know that? When I say I'm the only friend you've got in this town, I'm not joking.'

The upholstery was shot and Makana felt the hard metal frame digging into his back. The car was hot and uncomfortable and smelled of raw onions and vomit, the stale odours of men in fear. Okasha sat back and folded his arms, taking a moment before speaking.

'I had a phone call. Guess who from? That's right, your friend and mine, Colonel Serrag. And while I was wondering what I had done to deserve such an honour, he told me what he wanted.' He paused, taking his time, easing his bulk in the seat, adjusting the tight belt around his waist. 'You know what they want to do? They want to send you back.' He nodded solemnly. 'That's right, my friend, home. Now why would they want to do that? More importantly, what would your old friend Mek Nimr say when you landed back there in handcuffs?'

'Why would they want to do that?'

'Who knows? I'm just a humble inspector. It is not my place to question the motives of my superiors. A gesture of goodwill, they say, to help repair relations with our brethren to the south.'

Makana was silent. Someone had been eating *tasali*. The floor was littered with the husks of roasted melon seeds that had been spat there.

'You know what I think he might do?' Okasha went on. 'I think he might just drive you out to a quiet spot in that godforsaken *khalla* you call a country, and put a bullet through your empty head, because that is what you deserve. It would be quick and simple and it would leave nothing to worry about. No loose ends.'

'Why would Colonel Serrag take an interest in me?'

'It's not so strange. You're an interesting case, Makana, as I have pointed out many times. You are . . . what do you call it? An enigma. That's it, a puzzle. You hang in the balance. We don't really want you here, but at the same time we don't like regimes that try to kill our President.' Okasha grimaced, referring to the assassination attempt by a group of Sudanese militants on President Mubarak in Addis Ababa three years earlier. 'You know what that makes you? No? Well, I'll tell you. It makes you a hostage.'

'Are you going to tell me what I am supposed to have done, or do I have to guess?'

'I'm going to tell you what you are not going to do again, okay?' Okasha lifted a warning finger. Then he threw out his hand and slapped the driver in the front seat on the back of the head. 'Go and smoke a cigarette, Mustafa.'

'I don't smoke.'

Okasha rolled his eyes heavenward. 'Well, go and arrest somebody then, and keep your eyes peeled for any bearded assassins.' Grudgingly, the policeman climbed out of the car and went over to stand by the wall and smoke a cigarette. Okasha turned back to Makana.

'What you are not going to do is bother Alexei Vronsky. He is a guest of the state.'

'Ah.'

' "Ah" is right, my friend. You step on his foot and I feel the pain.'

'The two gentlemen in bad suits in the lobby.' Then Makana remembered the car at the roadside coffee place on the way back. The black Toyota.

'SSI. Their job is to protect our Russian friend.'

'He didn't strike me as the kind of man who needs a lot of protection.'

'Vronsky's connections go all the way to the top.'

Makana leaned back and reached for his cigarettes. 'Just why is he so important?'

'That doesn't concern you.' Okasha held his breath for a moment and then decided to press ahead anyway. 'He is co-operating with our security forces, if you must know, providing valuable information. Vronsky is ex-Russian Military Intelligence. He was Special Forces. He knows the *Afghanis*. He fought against the bastards and their jihad.'

Afghanis was the term for Egyptians who had left to join the holy war in Afghanistan after the Soviet invasion of 1979. When the Soviets retreated and the war was over they were left with nothing to do. Instead they looked for other holy causes to fight. Many of them turned their attention to the people who ruled their own country. They'd returned home battle-hardened and victorious. They made a formidable enemy.

'Where does Serrag come into it?' pressed Makana.

'Nowadays he runs a special counter-terrorist task force. He answers directly to the Minister of the Interior.'

'He called you?'

'Out of the blue, and it's not so much a call as a summons. To Lazoughly, the last place on earth I want to go and I am an inspector of police. My hands are shaking. But there he is, all smiles. He starts telling me what wonderful progress I am making. He enquires about the case of the Englishwoman, Markham. Of course, he had heard that we had a visit from Scotland Yard.'

Makana was about to correct him again, but he didn't bother.

'That was why he summoned you, to congratulate you?'

'This is SSI, Makana, they don't call you in to pat you on the back. That was just the preamble. He tells me that he is always on the lookout for bright officers.'

'He wants you to work for him?'

Okasha stroked his moustache. 'Not bad, eh? This dead Englishwoman could be a blessing in disguise. There's only one fly in the ointment and that's you, my friend.'

'He wanted you to warn me off Vronsky?'

'Which I have duly done.'

'You'll go far in this world if you carry on betraying your friends like that.'

'Come on, you're out of your depth with this Russian. He's a state asset.'

'Did Serrag remember any more details about the Alice Markham case?'

Okasha dismissed the question with a curse. 'SSI doesn't care about that lord and lady nonsense, especially when the English are so keen on reminding us of the fact.'

'So what is Colonel Serrag interested in?'

'He is interested in Daud Bulatt.' Okasha heaved a sigh. 'It turns out you did me a favour by asking me to look into the guy. It brought me to Serrag's attention. He's asked me to join his team.'

'So, Bulatt's alive?'

'Well, let's put it this way, he's not just part of the old folklore around here any more.'

'What's the connection to the Russian?'

'Vronsky apparently tangled with this particular snake back in Chechnya,' said Okasha.

Makana sniffed and stared out through the grimy windscreen, the outside world obscured by scratches and smears. He was trying to think, only half listening as Okasha went on.

'Anyway, I wanted to let you know, we have a tip-off. Colonel Serrag's unit is going to be hitting a possible hide-out tonight. I'm going with them.'

'Where is this?'

'I'm not supposed to tell you, but it's an old farm about ten kilometres out of town. We have to hit them soon and fast, before they get a chance to organise themselves and disappear. Want to come along, it might be fun?'

Makana's impression of this kind of paramilitary assault on supposed terrorists was that it was a very dangerous place to be. Civilian casualties tended to run high and the idea of being in the company of a band of trigger-happy policemen with semi-automatic rifles held no appeal for him.

'Thanks, but I'll sit this one out. Serrag thinks Bulatt is there?'

'If he is, he's going to wish he'd stayed dead.'

'One last question. Who made the connection between Liz Markham and Bulatt?'

'How do you mean?' Okasha glared.

'Was it you or Serrag who made the link?'

'The only person who made that link was you.' Irritated, Okasha waved a hand as if brushing away a fly. 'Go, do your detecting thing. But don't forget to keep me informed. I need to know what you are up to before Serrag hears about it, and if you think I have eyes and ears everywhere, you should see what *he* has. I can't protect you from them now. If you cross the line you'll find yourself on a plane with a one-way ticket to paradise.'

Makana cracked open the stiff door of the police car and made to get out. Okasha leaned out after him.

'By the way, where did you get that car from?'

'A friend.'

'I told you, Makana, you don't have any friends except me. You would do well to remember that . . . and remember what I said about staying away from the Russian from now on.'

'Believe me, I don't want to get any closer to him than I have to.'

'You know, we're supposed to be on the same side,' said Okasha. 'It might be an idea for you to act like that from time to time.'

'The law is only as strong as those who police it.'

'Always with the philosophy,' chuckled Okasha. 'If only I could remember to write down some of the things you say . . . I would die a happy man.' But the joviality in his voice was tempered by a note of unease that Makana hadn't heard in it before.

He should have been excited. The news that Bulatt was alive and in the country backed up his notion of a connection between Hanafi's past and Adil's disappearance. The link to Vronsky was also confirmed. But what really disturbed him was the sound of Okasha's laughter, which still rang in his ears long after the police car had turned the corner and vanished from sight. Makana couldn't put his finger on why it was that it disturbed him so. It was like hearing a songbird that was off-key and instinctively knowing something was very wrong. It took him a while to realise what it reminded him of: a faint echo of something which took him back in time, back to the old days.

Chapter Twenty-eight

The moment Makana's life had jumped off the rails and departed along a new and very dangerous track was burned into his memory. All at once he had found himself in a universe where the once familiar was suddenly strange.

He should have listened to Muna. Back then, when he still had a chance to change things, he should have listened to his wife, but he didn't. He was afraid of giving in to his own fears. So he did what any husband would do, he tried to calm her. He reassured her that they were safe, that he was a police inspector and that they would always enjoy a certain degree of protection, even when he was no longer sure how long this would last. Muna saw things more clearly than he did.

'You can't see it, can you?' She spoke softly in the dark. 'Or maybe you don't want to see it.'

'You're upset.'

'No.' She rolled her head from side to side in exasperation. 'I'm insane! Or maybe I am sane and the whole world around me has gone mad.'

'Muna, please.'

'You don't understand. These people care nothing for your

rules, your sense of duty. They want power, and to get it they will sweep you away . . . you and your department, even the law itself. None of that means anything to them.'

'You're wrong. There is such a thing as the rule of law. There is a constitution.'

'They will rewrite the constitution to suit themselves.'

He could argue endlessly but was never going to convince her; he could barely convince himself. She was right. He wanted to believe in the system, in justice winning out in the end, because wasn't that the whole point for him? He had served it, fought for it, defended it with his life. Now he was supposed just to step aside and let them do with it as they wished?

'People like you and me, they hate us,' she corrected him gently, 'because we can read and write, because we can see through them. Because we choose not to live our lives according to the norms of the seventh century.'

Then there was victim number four.

On the veranda outside his office one day Makana bumped into the bearded man again. The big-shouldered brute with dark, nervous eyes whom he had met under the bridge all those months ago. The discovery of the teacher who had turned out to be the first in a series of murdered women. It was this man, and his unit of the People's Defence Force, whom Makana suspected of the crime. The bearded man, still dressed in his peasant clothes, carried himself with the same swagger, moving around the police department as if it was his own personal domain, a battered AK-47 slung over his shoulder. His fierce black eyes glared malevolently as he brushed by. When Makana turned, he found Mek Nimr standing there.

'One of yours?'

Mek Nimr was rising fast in the Revolutionary Security Force.

There were rumours he would soon be offered a post high up in the National Intelligence and Security Services. He no longer wore a blue police uniform but instead dressed in paramilitary fatigues with a camouflage pattern, as if in preparation for deployment in the jungle somewhere.

The RSF answered to no one. They did as they pleased. He peered over Makana's shoulder and smiled.

'People transfer in and out of the unit all the time. You know how it is.'

Makana knew how it was. The ways of these new militias made little sense but they were here to stay and he had better get used to that.

'How is your wife by the way?' Mek Nimr asked then.

'My wife?'

'I heard she had been taken ill. Was it the pressure of having to take over the department at such short notice?'

'You almost sound as if you care.'

'Come now, we old colleagues have to stick together.'

They talked as equals now, but even this was a pretence. While Mek Nimr's career was in full flight, Makana's had stalled. The CID department had gradually been whittled down to himself, a clerk and an adjutant who doubled sometimes as his driver. Everything else had gone, including filing cabinets, type-writers and all the rest of it, commandeered or seconded, whatever the term was. Makana now occupied an out-of-the-way room that had once been a storage space for stationery and office equipment. One side of the room was piled high with tables, chairs and filing cabinets nobody wanted to see again, all of which threatened to topple over on him at any moment. Still, it served a purpose. He had selected a new table and chair from the clutter of broken and abandoned furniture. The telephone rarely worked and the ceiling fan either ran at an insanely high speed or not at all. He had two windows, one of which was entirely blocked by the clutter. Nowadays he spent most of his time staring out of the other one.

'Muna's fine,' said Makana quietly.

'I'm glad to hear it. We must take care of our women, the mothers of our children. You should consider asking her to resign her post. After all, it's not a decent job for a woman.'

'What are you talking about? She's a botanist. She studies plants.'

'Exactly.'

The self-righteous look on Mek Nimr's face might have been comical if circumstances had been different. It had puffed up like a blowfish. 'I was concerned,' he said.

'Concerned about my wife?'

'Well, obviously, concerned that anyone should want to teach that we are descended from monkeys. Aren't you?'

'Darwinism. I forgot you were something of an expert.'

'An expert, me?' Mek Nimr looked embarrassed, glancing along the veranda as if worried someone might overhear and take what was being said seriously.

'Of course, it's just a theory.'

'Ah!' Mek Nimr's face showed relief. 'So it's not proven?'

'There are those who believe it is true.'

'Believe?' Mek Nimr grimaced, getting back into his stride. 'Come now, you make it sound like a religious faith. Is that what it is, a faith? A religion that worships monkeys, eh? That must be quite something.'

'It's not a religion. It's a science.'

'That must be where I got confused. I was never very bright at school, you know. I didn't have the benefit of having a teacher for a father, like you did.'

Mek Nimr's laughter echoed along the veranda as he walked away. It was the laugh of a man who never questions the fact that he is on the winning side of history. Makana watched him go. Over the balustrade he watched Mek Nimr emerge from the stairwell below. His men were waiting for him in the compound, standing in the dust, leaning against the pick-ups. A change seemed to come over him as he addressed them before getting into the lead vehicle. The little man's inner fury seemed to stir up a storm that swirled about him. The men cheered and raised their guns in the air. Makana realised that he was witnessing a remarkable transformation. He was one of the few people who had known Mek Nimr in the old days, when he was just another ordinary policeman who lacked the resources to go far. Then times had changed. He had seized his opportunity and profited from it. The militia men jumped on to their pick-ups and raced out of the compound, horns blaring and guns waving.

Muna used to bring home with her stories about the 'morality police' who would roam the campus advising students and staff alike that their clothing was un-Islamic. A campaign was launched from time to time, targeting lecturers. One day a student handed her a pamphlet that was being distributed around the university, urging people not to attend the lectures she was giving on evolution, filling in for her late professor. These lectures were denounced as part of a 'zionist *kafir*' plot to undermine Islamic morality and replace it with the modernist ideology of the unbelievers. Both she and Makana tried to dismiss the campaign as nonsense, but Mek Nimr obviously knew about it.

Makana carried on in the old ways, trying to solve the new wave of murders. They were vicious, cold-blooded crimes that someone was covering up, he was sure of it. Some person or persons unknown had launched themselves on a bloody killing spree and they were acting with impunity, which probably meant they were protected.

The second murderered woman was found in the scorched yellow grass near a dusty patch of ground where the boys played football. Metal goalposts without nets were the only indication of what went on there. The girl was naked. The students who had found her had covered the body with sheets of newspaper that they had weighed down with stones. They seemed outraged about having to witness such a sight, as if the dead girl had decided to have herself raped and murdered just to cause them personal offence.

Her name was Awatif. She was nineteen years old and her father was a prominent lawyer, known for his opposition to the regime. A close friend of Amir Medani's, Awatif was in the third year of an architecture degree. There were one hundred and ten students in her class and most of them described her as a hard-working, decent girl. Most of them. Gradually another picture emerged as some claimed that Awatif was opinionated. That the clothes she wore were not always as decent as they should be. That she refused to cover her hair properly. They said she was stubborn and proud, and that it was no doubt her own vanity which had led her to her awful fate. Makana stared at the girl who told him this, her plump cheeks pressed out like ripe fruit by the tightly wrapped grey headdress that covered her hair. 'People like that think they are better than the rest of us.' Her smug, self-satisfied expression betrayed no sympathy for the dead girl.

The third victim turned up in the old war cemetery, among the headstones of British airmen who had died half a century ago defending this corner of their empire from the Italians, who flew in across Abyssinia in their Fiats to dump their payloads on the flying boats stationed on the Nile. It seemed symbolic, leaving her there, particularly as the victim, Layla Awadallah, twenty-seven years old, was of mixed blood. She had an English mother. Her father was a doctor who had trained in Durham in the sixties. She worked in a travel agency. The body had been ravaged by the dogs that roamed the cemetery at night. It was hard to reconstruct what had been done to her before she died from the damage inflicted by the wild dogs afterwards. Like the other victims she had been raped repeatedly. There was no connection between her and either of the other two.

Aged between nineteen and thirty-five, the victims of this wave of killings were educated, professional women: a teacher, a university student and the manager of an airline agent's office. They were all subjected to sexual assault by multiple attackers. All were left in plain view, in places where they would be found quickly. No attempt was made to bury them, or to hide the bodies in any way. It was as if they were being left out as a warning. Finally, they were all gagged, and in their mouths, when the gag was removed, a piece of chalk was found. A stick of classroom chalk. Nothing more. The message was obvious: keep your women at home or they will end up like this.

Makana worked alone. He didn't talk to anyone, didn't submit a report to his superiors. Major Idris took no interest in what he was doing; so long as things were quiet he made no objections either. Nobody really cared except Makana, or so he told himself until one day when he began to notice a small white pick-up following him around. Wherever he went it would be right there behind him. Whenever he came out of a place he would spot it parked nearby, a man sitting behind the wheel reading a government newspaper. They didn't even bother to hide any more.

Chapter Twenty-nine

As he drove south along the six-lane carriageway of Sharia al-Haram, Makana's mind was in free flow, turning over the facts in his head as he understood them. By his very absence, Adil Romario seemed to be unravelling the world that had revolved around him, like a black hole that appears in a corner of the universe and sucks all the light into its void. Maybe Sami Barakat was on to something when he talked about astronomy. On his way out, Makana had stopped by to speak to Hanafi. It was inconvenient, he was told, as Mr Hanafi was on his way to an important meeting in Amman. But Makana insisted and in the end five minutes of the magnate's precious time was conceded to him in the subterranean garage. The door of the white limousine was held open for him and Makana climbed inside to find himself perched on a fold-down seat facing Hanafi and Gaber.

'What is this about?' snapped Hanafi's right-hand man, clearly irritated.

'I need to know,' said Makana, addressing Hanafi directly and ignoring his lieutenant, 'if you have any reason to believe that one of your old enemies might be behind this?'

'What is he talking about?' Hanafi growled. In the uneven streaks of light from the neon strips illuminating the basement, fury made his face look stark and cruel. His eyebrows were arched and his nose flared. The lines of his face were all drawn together as if he were about to implode.

'I am talking about Daud Bulatt.'

'Bulatt is dead,' said Gaber. 'He died years ago.'

'Yes, where was it?' A touch of pleasure lightened the dark expression on Hanafi's face. The thought of the death of his old rival seemed to amuse him. 'Afghanistan? One of those places Allah has forgotten about. Of course, that's why he went there, to fight for the glory of Islam. Well, good luck to him.'

'Bulatt may not be dead,' said Makana.

The smile faded away slowly and Hanafi sat straighter. 'Not dead? What are you talking about? Of course he's dead.'

'There are rumours that he is here, in Egypt.'

'Do you have any idea what you are saying?' asked Gaber.

Makana glanced at him. 'I'm sure you have plenty of contacts inside the security and intelligence services. It shouldn't take much to confirm this.'

'I should have killed him when I had the chance,' muttered Hanafi. He sat brooding like a squat bullfrog, fists balled tightly on his plump thighs.

'Do you think that Bulatt would have any reason to take Adil?'

'Who knows what he might do? The man was insane, even back then. You think he has my boy? What for? What could he hope to gain by doing something like that?'

'Apart from the obvious?'

Hanafi frowned. Gaber leaned forward and pointed a finger. 'If he is in this country, the entire weight of the security forces will come down on his head. He will find nowhere to hide.'

'I wouldn't be too sure of that,' said Makana. 'Bulatt seems to be resourceful enough to have eluded them so far.'

'But what possible motive could he have for taking Adil?'

'The oldest motive of all,' said Makana, 'revenge.'

Hanafi's thick fingers closed around Makana's arm like an iron clamp. He leaned close; his breath had a cloying sweetness to it.

'Find him. Please, just find my boy and bring him back. If that man has him, I will bring the wrath of his god down on him so hard it will teach him the meaning of religion all over again.' Then he turned and struggled out of the car. Gaber leaned out after him.

'Where are you going? We have a plane to catch.'

'I'm not going anywhere,' Hanafi grunted, 'until this matter is resolved.'

'Why can't you just stick to finding Adil?' Gaber slumped back in his seat and glared at Makana. That look stayed with him, even now, like a point of darkness against the bright glare of the road ahead.

It was busy today, with vehicles of every shape and size vying for position. The road was a chaotic mudslide, crammed with all manner of jumble and debris, broken bits of metal junk flying down into the abyss. People took their lives into their hands to cross it, stepping between the lanes of traffic as if performing some ancient dance with death. They paused with cars rushing by in front and behind them, so close it made their clothes billow.

Ahead of him the pyramids emerged from the thick polluted air. Their perfect geometrical symmetry struck a note of clarity that had echoed across the centuries, to collide ultimately with the cacophony of chaos that was the present day. By contrast, the buildings lining the road seemed to have been tossed up as an afterthought, assembled like the doodlings of a distracted mind unable to concentrate long enough to draw a straight line. The drooping cables, the lopsided, crushed vehicles limping along amid the whine of sirens and brakes, the gasps of exhaust choking the light out of the air. Against all that madness the pyramids seemed as perfectly suited to this world as spacecraft that had arrived from another galaxy and set themselves down on this scrap of benighted desert. According to the papers, however, even their grasp on eternity was gradually being eroded by the vibrations created by the steady rumble of the nearby road. Little by little they were being shaken to the ground, to join the rising mounds of rubble to which this city was ultimately, inevitably, destined to return.

Makana turned west and the road became crowded with heavy articulated lorries laden with stone or shuddering iron rods. He fell in behind a truck filled with camels. They gazed out at their surroundings serenely, seemingly detached from the insanity through which they were passing. To the left was a canal, choked with bullrushes and reeds and discarded junk. Rubbish was heaped up in piles, interspersed with smoking fires and scavenging crows. On the right were intermittent rows of buildings, small, half-finished structures that looked as if they would fall down as easily as they had been thrown up. Here and there was the odd house, set back from the road. Once upon a time this was all open farmland dotted with the villas of prosperous landowners. But that age was long gone now and the old estates had been whittled down to pocket-sized plots, hemmed in by the proliferation of grey breeze-block walls that charted their insistent, meandering course along the side of the road – rising and falling, slumping here and there into heaps of rubble, only to totter inexorably onward again.

The village itself had been incorporated into this urban sprawl and now was barely distinguishable from the roadside strip. There were stalls dishing out plates of *koshari* and kebab, heaps of fruit and vegetables, aubergines the size of a child's head, pomegranates like cannonballs. Makana parked the Mercedes by a white wall scrawled with charcoal graffiti and for the next hour or so wandered the winding, untidy streets, looking for some trace of Adil Romario's past. The market was crowded with vendors selling everything from loofahs to bright orange acrylic blankets stamped with tigerskin patterns. Everyone seemed to have something to sell. The main street was crowded, the uneven ground littered with melon rinds and corn husks, nylon string, metal bindings, straw and sheep droppings.

When he reached the far end of the village the ramshackle houses surprisingly gave way to green fields that extended into the distance. Herons drifted overhead like scraps of stray paper caught in the breeze. Ibis stepped on dainty reed-like legs through the golden shield of flooded fields. All of this was presumably where Hanafi's beans and *bamiya* came from. Makana turned and kicked his way back through, his eye distracted by the omnipresence of his quarry: peeling and faded images of Adil Romario in his prime appeared everywhere, in windows and doorways, anywhere there was a scrap of glass free or an empty wall. Grubby and in many cases torn, the stickers testified to this claim to fame. The local boy who had done well. As he moved away from the noise and bustle of the market and into the quieter streets, Makana noted that the player's name had been scratched on the walls at regular intervals. A voice called out from nearby: 'Adil! Adil!'

Startled, Makana turned and began retracing his steps. The street was deserted. He rounded a corner and then another; here the houses were built so close together you could reach over in places from one balcony to shake hands with your neighbour across the street. An elderly woman, her skin yellowed by age and framed in a black shawl that had seen better days, leaned out of a window, yelling at no one in particular.

'I'm calling my grandson,' she explained. 'He must be around here somewhere.'

'Maybe you can help me? I am looking for the house where Adil Romario was born.'

'Ah,' she nodded knowingly. 'You must be one of those journalists. We get them all the time.' She leaned out of the window and pointed. 'You can't miss it. Of course the family doesn't live there any more, but everyone knows it.'

Makana imagined that there were a good number of boys around here who had been named after the footballer. The house was indeed impossible to miss. The whitewashed walls were covered with charcoal scratches and more elaborate painted caricatures depicting Adil Romario's career. There was an image of him as a little boy, bouncing a ball, then the figure seemed to be sucked into a vortex of goalposts and flying players. There were crowns and jet planes, even doves with olive branches, along with tournament cups flying one way or another. There were scores from memorable matches and the name Adil and the DreemTeem logo appeared in numerous forms. The quality of the wall art varied. Some of it was not bad, though many of the aspiring artists were blessed with more enthusiasm than talent.

Makana turned a corner and circled the block, coming up a narrow street across which two men were shouting at one another. It was impossible to make sense of their discussion which appeared to involve a number of in-laws, a defective car, the failure to fulfil one's promises, and so on and so forth. It was one of those public displays which had more to do with demonstrating one's presence than resolving any particular problem. They had succeeded in acquiring an audience, largely because they happened to be standing outside the entrance to a café. A simple hole in the wall. The unsurfaced street outside the entrance was sodden with damp layers of tea dregs and black coffee grounds like arcs of stubble which spread across the ground and even up the wall opposite. As he stepped inside, the customers' attention turned to Makana only briefly before moving on. When he mentioned the name Adil Romario, however, he was immediately surrounded. The two young men outside stopped trading insults and took up position to either side of him.

'You're a journalist? Or just a tourist?'

Makana examined them carefully; they were all eagerness and smiles.

'Would you like to visit the house? It's just around the corner. You can even see the room where he first saw the light of day.'

'And how much is this going to cost me?'

'Oh, well, of course the family are poor and would expect some compensation.'

'Naturally.'

Whatever animosity existed between the two men had been set aside in the common cause.

'I take it you knew him personally?'

'When he was a kid? Everyone knew him. Always kicking a ball, he was.'

'He used to sleep clutching a ball.'

'We used to play together all the time.'

Neither man looked the slightest bit athletic. Overweight and clearly out of shape, they looked incapable of jogging the width of the narrow street without running short of breath.

'What about his parents? Does he still have family here?'

'You see everyone in this place? We are his family. In this neighbourhood, we are all simple people. We care about each other. This village is like one big happy family. What paper do you work for?'

'Who said it was a paper? Maybe he's from the television, or the radio?'

'So his parents are not around?' Makana ignored their speculations.

'They were old. They died years ago, may Allah show them compassion.'

They leaned closer, trying to outdo one another now.

'Ask us anything about him, anything at all.'

'Yes, ask, please. Adil is one of us.'

'One of us, exactly. May Allah preserve him.'

'Why don't you cut out that lying nonsense?'

All heads turned towards a man in the corner. He was about fifty, and so immobile Makana hadn't even noticed him. Thin and dark as an axe, he wore baggy pants and a threadbare shirt that hung loosely over his bony frame. On his feet were plastic sandals as thin as sheets of newspaper.

'You're all in such a hurry to tell your lies because you can smell money. Or maybe it's because you've been lying for so long you don't know what is true and what's not.'

'Don't pay him any attention,' murmured the first of the two young men, making a gesture with his plump fingers. 'He's not right in the head.'

One scrawny elbow was propped on the beaten metal top of the counter as the man stared morosely at the three of them. His face displayed the drawn features of a long-term substance

266

abuser; hashish, alcohol, whatever. If that elbow slipped he would probably fall flat on his face.

'You come here asking questions, and you're not the first one. And like those who came before, you will not tell this story to the world. You know why? Because no one wants to hear the truth.' He pointed at the battered little portable television that stood on a shelf in the corner. 'We don't expect the truth to come out of that lying thing. They tell us who the President is and we smile and clap our hands. They tell us the people of Egypt are rich and we cry tears of joy. They tell us Adil Romario was born in this village and that his mother and father were a good couple who worked in the fields, and we feel our hearts soar.'

A rumble of discontent stirred in the little café, but no one made any serious move to dispute his claim. An uneasy silence settled and the two young men stepped back. Makana moved closer to the newcomer, reaching out to offer him a cigarette which he took without a word.

'Nobody wants to talk about what really happened because they don't want to annoy his lordship, the Great Pasha.'

'You're crazy!' muttered the first young man.

'He's insane,' concurred the second, who had already taken up position by the door, the game over, looking down the street in search of other distractions.

'I'm crazy enough to tell the truth, that's what you can't stand. You call yourself men? Look at you! Scared to say anything that might upset *him*. The fact is that the rich can have what they want and you all bend over to give it to them, whatever takes their fancy, even your own mothers.'

This insult duly provoked some shouting and shoving and for a moment the café descended into pandemonium. Then the young men decided it wasn't worth their time to protest and moved off with a few choice insults thrown over their shoulders. The skinny man didn't move a muscle throughout all of this. He remained where he was, elbow on the counter, smoking steadily. Finally, he turned his gaze on Makana.

'You're worse than they are. You come sniffing round here to find a story you can sell.'

'This pasha you're talking about is Saad Hanafi, right?'

'Were you born a donkey or did you go to school to get that way?'

Howls of laughter rang out from the gang of children crowding round the café's entrance.

'Hanafi owns all of this and more.' The thin man jabbed Makana in the chest. 'He owns our souls. That's right. We sold them to him years ago.'

'What has this got to do with Adil Romario?'

'It's all part of the legend. They want us to believe in him, like an idol, a god.' He picked up a scrap of coloured paper from the counter, an advertising flyer for Coca-Cola or bubble gum, featuring the inevitable image of the football player. Screwing it into a ball, he tossed it at the television screen.

'Hey, cut that out,' yawned the proprietor with a tut of annoyance.

'What for? You can't see anything on that thing anyway.'

The screen displayed little more than a howling sandstorm of grey particles. From somewhere inside it came faint rumours of a man and woman talking. Shadows shifted vertically at irregular intervals, like agitated clouds.

'Lies, all of it. Stories to cheer us up while we rot down here like rats. Everyone round here hates him. They watch him up there on the screen, thinking that it should be them up there.

What a great dream . . . but that's all it is, a dream. And *they*,' he wagged his finger again, '*they* own all the dreams.'

'Adil was born here, though.'

'Sure, he was born here, just like we were. He kicked a ball around these streets. But he isn't like us. He never was. How could he be?'

'You knew him?'

'Look, I'll tell you a story and you can go away and do what you want with it.' He paused to drop his cigarette butt on the floor. Makana held out his packet and offered him a fresh one. The man was overtaken for a time by a fit of coughing. He went to the door and ejected a long brown stream of phlegm before returning to his place at the counter.

'There was this young man, and like most young men he was itching to make it big. So he went to Cairo to seek his fortune. He didn't have much luck at first. He fell in with the wrong crowd, let's say. But then he came to the attention of a powerful man who helped him, gave him a chance. And the young man was grateful and became his loyal servant. One day he turned up here, driving a big car, wearing fancy clothes, handing out gifts to everyone. He brought with him his benefactor, a big, fat man, and they strolled around the village like King Farouk and his dog.'

'The big man was Hanafi?'

'I knew you were smarter than you made out.' The bony finger wagged in Makana's face again.

'What happened next?'

'The same old story they've been writing since Sayidna Musa first heard the Word of God. Hanafi's eyes fell on the picture of innocence that was the boy's young sister and he lost his head. Pretty soon that fancy car was coming round here on a regular basis.'

'What did the brother do?'

'Well, of course, he didn't find out until it got too obvious to hide any more.' The man curved a hand over his belly. 'We all know who Adil's father really is, but we don't talk about it.'

'You're sure about all this?'

'Why would a man like me make up a story like that?'

'People make up stories for lots of reasons.'

'The girl was fourteen. That's how those dogs are.' There was a pause, as if his own words had dredged up something he thought long since extinguished.

'You didn't say anything either, did you?'

The bloodshot eyes avoided Makana's. The voice dropped to a hoarse whisper.

'I was one of the lucky ones – Hanafi bought up land here. He put local people to work on it. Many families depend on him. We can't turn against him.'

'And the brother, what did he do when he found out?'

'He went mad. He swore vengeance.'

'He killed Hanafi's wife and child?'

The bony finger again jabbed the air in front of Makana's face. 'He would have killed more but they caught him and threw him in Tora, and that was the end of that. We never saw him again. Nobody wanted to talk about it after that. Now Hanafi owns all this land and we all love him. The thing about a lie is that if you repeat it often enough, people mistake it for the truth.'

With that he pushed Makana aside and staggered towards the exit.

'One last thing,' Makana called after him, 'Adil's family name is Mohammed Adly. Is that the name of the brother?'

'No.' The man turned back to answer him. 'That was on the mother's side. Adil took his mother's name, since officially there was no father. The brother used the family name: Bulatt. Daud Bulatt.' Then the gaunt shadow shifted and the doorway cleared.

Makana heaved a deep breath and turned to find himself facing the proprietor, who stared up at him from where he sat behind the counter.

'You don't want to pay too much attention to what that one says. He's as mad as they come.'

Chapter Thirty

Aswani's was crowded by the time Makana got there. He decided he couldn't be bothered to wait for a table and eased himself into a free space at the counter. He wasn't really even hungry, he decided, examining the trays of raw meat in the cold cabinet.

'Just bring me some salad and things. Pickles. Maybe some *taamiya*.'

Aswani wagged his head disapprovingly. 'You've lost your appetite? What's the matter? Are you in love? Who's the lucky girl?'

'You tell me when you find out.'

'It's a bad sign when a man goes off his food. When a man loses his appetite, he is opening the door to invite death in,' said the cook, stroking his moustache pensively before waddling away to deal with his other customers.

Sami Barakat appeared just as Makana had started to eat.

'The Hanafi DreemTeem is falling down the league tables like a rat down a sewer,' he declared, tossing a newspaper on to the counter. Makana glanced at the headlines. Without their leading star it seemed like the team was in serious

272

trouble. The article speculated about what might happen if Adil Romario's disappearance was in fact linked to his transfer to another club. There was a quote from a new 'star reporter' about the continued rumours of Clemenza's involvement. 'Is someone trying to bring the DreemTeem down?' ran the headline.

'Star reporter? They managed to replace you pretty fast.'

'Don't rub salt in the wound.' Sami dropped his satchel down on the counter as Aswani came up. 'No, it's all right. I'm not hungry.'

'Another one?' The cook raised his eyes to the heavens. 'They're trying to ruin me.'

'I can't afford to eat,' Sami said, lighting a cigarette.

'So what's your theory?' Makana asked, tapping the newspaper.

'What, you don't have time to read?' With his foot Sami hooked himself one of the high stools nearby to perch on. He looked more unruly and unkempt every time Makana set eyes on him. 'The rot was already visible, even when Adil was still playing. Now their rivals are closing in for the kill. The legend is cracking under the strain.'

'You must be overjoyed.'

Sami ignored the comment, reaching over into the basket in front of Makana for a piece of bread, still holding his cigarette and spilling ash on the counter. Tearing off a strip, he soaked it in the bowl of tahini dip. Looking thoughtful, he chewed for a while in silence.

'And there's another thing. I talked to a couple of people about the Hanafi finances. The company is hanging by a thread. They are overstretched financially. Too much expansion, too quickly. They can't cover their costs and there is little coming in.'

'That must leave them very vulnerable?'

'One source told me that if Hanafi weren't a personal friend of the President he would have been out of business months ago.'

'What about rumours of a takeover? Any mention of our Russian friend?'

'Whenever I brought up his name people got nervous. Nobody wants to talk about him, but the feeling is that he is big,' said Sami, dabbing his mouth with a napkin and reaching for more bread. 'One of my contacts at Bank Misr told me that everything is riding on this luxury residential project they have planned.'

'Hanafi Heavens.' Makana remembered Soraya Hanafi talking about it. 'I thought you weren't hungry,' he said, observing that Sami looked as if he hadn't seen food in days.

The reporter's eyes widened in surprise. 'I'm not, not really. But these *taamiya* are good.'

Makana slid the plate along the marble counter towards him. 'Maybe it's worth going out to take a look at this star project of theirs.'

'Fine by me. Oh, and I may have located an accountant who was fired three months ago.'

'So? What did he have to say?'

'Nothing as yet.'

'What's the problem?'

'He's scared,' said Sami, trying to swallow and talk at the same time.

'Do you want me to come with you?'

Sami frowned. 'No, no, I can handle it. I think he's just after more money. You have some sort of inducement to offer, I take it?'

'I didn't realise I was going to be sponsoring your efforts too.'

'This is just to loosen him up a bit.' Sami rolled his shoulders. 'Surely Hanafi can spare a bit of cash?'

'Sure he can, I'm the one who can't,' said Makana, thinking about the fact that this case was taking much longer than he had anticipated. He noticed that Sami was looking at him in a strange way.

'Forget it. I'll give you some cash, but I want a full account of who you are giving it to.'

'You're the boss,' said Sami, reaching for another *taamiya*. 'You should really try these, they're great.'

'I'll take your word for it,' said Makana, watching his lunch disappear into the other man's mouth. 'Remind me not to eat with you when you're hungry.'

'What about you? Any thoughts on what this is all about?'

'Somehow it is all linked to Hanafi's past. I just don't see how,' said Makana as he waved Ali over and handed him some money, trying to remember something. 'There's one other thing you can do for me. I need to know everything I can about Vronsky.'

'Everything? Meaning . . . ?'

'Well, mostly his military record. Where he was stationed. I think he was in Afghanistan and later in Chechnya. It shouldn't be too hard for you. These things must be on record.'

'I'll do my best,' Sami said. He nodded at the bundle of notes Makana pressed into Aswani's hand. 'Don't you even count how much you pay?'

'If you knew how much I owed this man, you wouldn't ask,' said Makana.

'There's a phone call for you,' said Aswani, jerking his thumb at the big old black telephone that rested on the counter by the wall. It was a museum piece that dated back to the days when the British were here, or almost. As he crossed the room, Makana recalled what it was that had been nagging at him. Okasha had said that Vronsky was helping them with their fight against terrorism. Vronsky knew Bulatt from Chechnya. But how did Vronsky know that Bulatt was alive and that he was back in this country preparing to create havoc?

Chapter Thirty-one

'Is that your office? It sounds awfully noisy.'

The caller was Mimi Maliki. Makana glanced around him. 'It's a busy day,' he said. He had included Aswani's number on his business card because he was generally by at some time on most days and there was as good a chance of catching him here as anywhere. 'What seems to be the trouble?' He suspected this was going to be another request for money.

'I've been thinking about what you said.'

'Which part?'

'You said that if I remembered anything that might be useful, I should call you.'

'And did you?'

'Did I what?'

'Did you remember something?'

'I might have done.' She broke off and Makana was beginning to wonder if she had passed out on him when she spoke again. 'Do you think you could come over here?'

'Right now?'

'As soon as possible, yes.' She sounded worried.

'This isn't about money, is it?'

277

'No, unless you've got some. I mean, for me?'

Makana fingered the envelope in his jacket pocket. It was already thinning out from what he had given to Sami, and he was beginning to suspect that this might be all he would ever see from Hanafi by the end of it all. The chances of finding Adil alive now seemed to be diminishing by the hour.

'I'll see what I can do.'

'Then you'll come?' She sounded relieved, like a gleeful child, though why he couldn't think.

'I'll be there shortly.'

This time a young man in his twenties opened the door when Makana rang the bell on the eighth floor. He was barefoot and wearing a scruffy beard, jeans and a black T-shirt bearing a picture of a long-haired man playing a guitar, which he scratched as he stared sullenly back at Makana.

'What do you want?'

'I came to see Mimi.'

He looked Makana up and down before turning abruptly and walking away, calling out over his shoulder as he went.

'Mimi, your boyfriend is here . . . or maybe it's your father.'

Makana stepped inside and wandered through to the big living room where the boy threw himself down on the sofa. Ignoring the visitor, he carried on watching television. The room was, if anything, more of a mess than it had been on Makana's first visit. A good deal of what was strewn about the sofas, the wide coffee table and the floor appeared to belong to the man who had opened the door. A brown sports bag lay cast to one side, with clothes spilling out of it like a ruptured intestine.

'You live here?' Makana asked casually, glancing at the screen where a bare-chested man wearing a bandana and covered in bandoliers was spraying bullets at a group of Orientals in a jungle somewhere. There was a lot of high-pitched screaming.

'What?'

'I asked if you lived here?'

The young man stared insolently at him but said nothing.

'Who is this?' he asked as Mimi came into the room. She had her hair tied back today and looked clean, her pale face almost translucent.

'*Ya* Ramzi,' she screamed. 'I told you to tidy up your things! I told you!'

'Hey, whose house is it anyway? Eh?'

Still, he took his feet off the table and moved about the room trying to look like he was doing something. He tossed a few shirts in the direction of the bag, managing to miss with all of them. Then the effort seemed too much for him and he sank back on to the sofa, muttering to himself. Mimi reached for a packet of cigarettes on the table and lit one.

'I can't stand this,' she said. 'I can't take it any more.'

'Calm down, will you? I'm trying to watch this.'

Mimi gave a high-pitched scream. She picked up the remote control and threw it at the wall where it came apart with a loud crack, dropping in pieces to the floor. While the boy screamed at her, Makana took the girl's arm and led her out of the room, through to what turned out to be the kitchen. Here the debris was an accumulative log of what had been consumed in the house over the past week or so; plastic bags and boxes from various takeaway restaurants in the neighbourhood added up to a diet of pizzas, *fateer* and roast chicken. Empty bottles testified to a high consumption of sweet fizzy drinks and beer. Mimi leaned on the counter and chewed her fingernails.

'Is he the reason you wanted me to come over?'

'Can't you get rid of him?' She paced up and down. 'Make him go away?'

'Who is he?'

'He's my cousin, so I can't kick him out, but he's a real bully.' She was fighting back tears. Ramzi appeared back in the doorway, holding up the smashed pieces of the TV remote.

'What are you going to do about this, eh?'

'Go away!' She put her hands over her ears. He moved towards her menacingly and Makana stepped into his way. Ramzi scowled.

'Who are you anyway, and what do you want? Why are you defending that *sharmuta*?'

'That's no way to talk,' said Makana. 'Go back in there and calm down.'

Ramzi did the opposite. He reached for the front of Makana's shirt and thrust him back against the wall, pushing the broken plastic pieces into his face.

'Who's going to fix this, eh? Who?'

Makana hit him as gently as he could. A quick punch to the solar plexus which brought Ramzi to his knees, doubled over and gasping for breath. Makana pushed him out and closed the kitchen door behind him before turning back to Mimi.

'Your uncle is still away on business?'

'He's not away on business. He fled! The police are after him. He was involved in some kind of scandal. A building that collapsed. He cheated everyone. A whole family died. Anyway, Ramzi thinks he's going to sort all that out.'

'He seems very spirited.'

'He's a psychopath.' She carried on chewing her nails as if she hadn't seen decent food for a week which, judging by the state of the kitchen, was a distinct possibility. Makana lit a cigarette and then looked for somewhere to tip the ash. The only available space that might not catch fire was the sink, which was already cluttered with glasses and plates.

'After you left it got me thinking, about me and Adil and everything.' Mimi pushed herself away and crossed the room, clearing some of the discarded packets and bags and lifting herself up to sit on the counter. 'I remembered how it was when we first met. Adil spent his entire life trying to live up to other people's expectations . . . trying to prove that he was somehow worthy. But he never did . . . never got used to it, I mean, not really.' Mimi tapped ash into the sink and straightened her back, suddenly assertive and sure of herself. 'It's what we had in common, the sense of playing a role, of constantly having to be something we didn't feel we were, not really.'

'Who were you trying to be?' Makana enquired softly.

'A thousand people, all rolled into one.' She spoke in a dreamy way, as if talking about the world where she really belonged. 'I thought my looks meant everything would come to me easily. And when it didn't, I was lost. Acting was the only way forward that I could see. I had some early luck but then it all just seemed to slip away. My heart wasn't really in it. I was set on becoming one of the golden ones. Those celebrities who shine – dazzle the world just by their presence. But that's a tough act, all alone up there on the high wire. And I toppled off and came down hard in the wrong place. I would have come down harder if it wasn't for Adil.' The way she spoke, Mimi seemed to be looking back on her own life as if from a great distance.

'I have this terrible feeling I shall never see him again,' she finished.

She helped herself to one of Makana's cigarettes. 'Do you

think there's any chance for us . . . I mean, of us getting back together?'

'I don't know,' said Makana.

She smoked in silence for a moment, watching him, before going on.

'The film business is full of people trying to convince you that they are important. It's all about bluffing your way through. Adil spent a long time telling people what a big fish he was going to be. How he was going to invest all these millions in new productions. At first people listened, the way they do. After all, Adil is not just anybody, he's a national treasure. People like to be around celebrity like that. It makes them feel special.'

'Then what happened?'

'What always happens.' She shrugged. 'Nothing. People lose interest. When there was no sign that any of what he was saying was going to happen, they moved on.' Mimi exhaled in an absent fashion. 'I think Adil was hoping that all his talk of the future would somehow make somebody take an interest in him. You know, give him a part in their movie? But film people don't work like that.'

'It had nothing to do with Hanafi, then?'

Mimi drew back. 'What an odd thought. You mean the old man might not want him to go into the movies? I never thought of that.'

It made sense. If Hanafi had known about Adil's plans to go into the film world, he would have known that control of Hanafi Enterprises could never pass to his son. Had he then used his influence to close all those new doors before Adil?

'Tell me how he ended up with Farag.'

'That reptile belongs under a rock somewhere! He was the only one Adil could turn to, and he was already up to his neck in sordid business. Everyone knew that, except,' she leaned her head to one side and pushed her hair behind her ear, 'Adil, naturally. He's always been naive that way.'

'How did they meet?'

'At Vronsky's place, at one of his fabulous parties.'

'It was Clemenza who introduced Adil to Vronsky, do you know why?'

But Mimi was already back in her own reverie. 'The thing no one understands about Adil is how obsessive he is. When he wants something, he doesn't take no for an answer. That's what it was like for him with film. He was determined to get into the business, which is what led him to take up with Farag. And it was the same with me.'

'He was obsessed with you?'

'Some people are like that. Men in particular. Obsessed with everything. First it was football. I suppose when he was a kid Adil was mad about that. Then he lost interest and it was movies. He went to every director in town and begged and pleaded and offered them money, anything to get himself into the business.' She stared at Makana as if she had just made a discovery. 'It's a disease, this obsession thing. It's got a name.' Her voice tailed off, then resumed. 'Anyway, after that, he wanted me.' She pressed the back of her hand to her mouth to stifle a sob. 'I imagined this whole life we would have together. Such a glamorous couple, going to all the parties. That's how it works in this country. A director or producer sees you and that's it. The doors open.' She laughed, a hollow, empty sound that echoed up from some place deep inside her. 'I guess I was a little obsessed with him too. Now I just want to leave, really. It's all I dream about. Just get out of this country. This city. I can't breathe here.'

'What's stopping you?'

'I told you, I spent all the money. And besides, what would he do without me?'

A crimson beam from the setting sun caught Makana's eye and he glanced out of the window. He could see a thin plume of dust whirling across the empty square below. A jinn, they used to call them, whipping itself round and round and away into the distance.

'Tell me more about what went on at Vronsky's place?'

'Vronsky has contacts with Russians all over the place, girls willing to do anything. And so he organises these parties. Wild, lavish affairs. Legendary. Very exclusive. He invites top people.'

'What kind of people?'

Mimi aimed the ash from her cigarette into a Styrofoam box and tapped. 'Politicians. Businessmen. The kind with lots of money. They would come down to the coast and lie around for three days, drinking and screwing.'

'Where does he get the girls?'

'He flies them in. Costs him nothing. Contacts, you know. Actresses, he calls them, but they don't act in any films I've ever seen. They walk around like glamorous princesses, but there is nothing innocent about them. I mean, I don't mind talking to people, having a bit of fun, but these girls, they were dirty.'

'What was Farag's connection? Was he filming at these parties?'

'If he did so, he did it secretly. I mean, I never saw him with his camera, except for that first time when he persuaded Adil that he was going to turn him into a star.'

Makana thought it over. If Vronsky were looking for ways of blackmailing politicians and businessmen, then Farag would be just the man to provide the evidence. Vronsky wanted to build an empire and there was nothing he wouldn't stoop to to get what he wanted.

'Adil used to say that Vronsky was going to get him what he deserved.'

'What did he mean by that?'

'I don't know,' she said. 'He wouldn't tell me more than that.'

'When did it all go wrong between them?'

'I told you last time – after he came back from the exhibition match in Sudan.' Mimi gnawed some more on her fingernails. 'Everything changed after that.'

'Including his relationship with you?'

All she could manage in response to this was a brief nod.

'It all got out of hand: the parties, the drinking, the drugs. One of the girls who worked there, at the resort, died. I heard that she killed herself, but maybe it wasn't that. Maybe she was killed. That's what I'm thinking now. What if she was killed because she knew something?'

'You think Vronsky might have killed her?'

'Dunya, that was her name. She was really popular. Just this simple *baladi* girl. The funny thing is . . . she had a thing for Adil. She was really fond of him, like a little puppy following him around. And he . . . well, he didn't do anything to discourage her. It annoyed me. He said he couldn't help it.'

'You think that's why she killed herself?'

'Like I said, maybe she didn't. Maybe she was murdered and that's why Vronsky was so angry with Adil. He knew who did it.'

'You're saying Vronsky had the girl killed?'

'Sure. Why not? All they would have to do is get rid of the body.' The way she told it made it sound completely obvious.

'How would they do that?'

'Probably they took her out and dropped her in the sea. There are sharks out there, you know, and all kinds of other things.'

'Who was she?'

'Dunya? I don't know, she just worked there.' There was something about his response which made her lose her temper. 'You don't believe me,' she said, upset. 'Why would I make up something like that?'

'I don't know. Maybe you'd like to get your revenge.'

'I told you, I'm finished with all of them, finished with this country. All I want is enough money to leave. You're like the rest of them. You think I am just a mixed-up girl whose head needs examining, making up stories for the hell of it.'

She was scared. Makana kicked himself for not having seen it before.

'You need the money because you're afraid? That's why you want to get out of the country?'

'Vronsky is a very dangerous man.' Her voice had dropped to a whisper.

Makana decided it was time for him to go. He moved towards the door to the hall, hoping to avoid the psychopathic cousin. He reached into his pocket for the envelope and handed what was left to Mimi.

'Buy yourself a ticket. Get away somewhere. It doesn't matter where, just out of this town.'

'I have relatives in Beirut.'

'That sounds good. You have my number. You can call me when you're there.'

'What about Adil?'

'Let me know where you are, and as soon as I know something I'll call you.'

Mimi looked down at the envelope and Makana told himself he was a fool. Most likely she would waste it on whatever she was smoking or sniffing and that would be the end of it. Still, sometimes you had to take a chance on people, otherwise where would we all be?

As he stepped out into the hallway there was a cry from his left. He jerked back instinctively as a tall vase narrowly missed his head. There was a rush of air as it went by and then a crimson flower of enamelled porcelain exploded against the wall. Turning, Makana put his hand to Ramzi's head and thrust him back and round, using his own momentum to send the youth spinning into the wall. Ramzi's face crashed into a mirror which splintered, silver shards of glass raining down on him as he fell.

'Ramzi!' Mimi screamed.

'He'll be all right.' Makana turned to look at her. 'What about you?'

'I'm fine. Just go. Go!'

Makana took one last look at her, and then he turned and stepped over the groaning Ramzi. The boy, his face streaked with scarlet, pointed a finger at him.

'I'll kill you, I swear it! Next time I see you, I'll kill you!'

3

The Invisible Caller

Chapter Thirty-two

Come and fetch me. Muna called him one morning, urging him, pleading. He tried to stay calm, his hand clenching around the receiver in his hand as he listened helplessly to her sobs, as if to the sound of her mind unravelling down the line. She was crying hysterically, unable to get the words out, and there was nothing he could do.

'They are coming for me,' she said.

'Calm down,' he repeated. 'Nobody is coming for you.'

There was a thump as the receiver clattered down and hit what might have been the desk. A desperate few seconds rolled by with no other sound. Then, finally, the scraping of the phone being lifted again.

'Makana?' It was Ikhlas, Muna's colleague who shared the office with her, a small, timid academic with horn-rimmed spectacles. 'Can you come over here?'

As he drove to the university Makana had wondered if another girl had been killed. News of murders no longer automatically came to his attention. He was out of the loop, ostracised, shunted aside like a derelict locomotive into a forgotten siding. They could have fired him, of course, or killed him. There wasn't a day when he didn't ask himself why they didn't save themselves the trouble and do just that. An accident wasn't difficult to arrange these days. But maybe that was too easy. Eventually, he concluded that they enjoyed toying with him, watching him suffer in obsoletism.

The department was crowded with women when he arrived, all trying to console Muna with cups of tea and words of comfort or advice. They clogged up the doorway to her office and Makana had to push his way through. Muna's eyes widened when she saw him. She reared back as if in disbelief. Her hair clung to her face, which was swollen and wet with tears. She couldn't get the words out, stuttering and starting over and over.

'They are coming for me.'

'No one is coming for you.'

Unable to speak the words, Muna raised a shaking hand and pointed at the door. Makana glanced back. She nodded insistently, so he got up and went over to examine it. There was a large cross marked in chalk on the outside.

'This was waiting for me when I came back from my first class this morning.'

On the desk was a piece of chalk.

'It doesn't mean anything.'

'Don't say that!' she screamed. 'Don't try to make it go away. All the other victims had pieces of chalk on them, didn't they?'

'They're just trying to scare you,' he said, as calmly as he could. What did the chalk mean? Was it even supposed to make sense?

'You have to find them! You have to make them stop!'

'I will. I swear. I'll see to it,' he promised. 'But first you need to rest.' He got her to lie down on the sofa and sat with her for a time, holding her hand, until her eyes closed. When he finally emerged from the room Makana realised he was shaking. Ikhlas came towards him, eyes fixed on him like pins through the thick lenses.

'She must see a doctor.'

'Yes,' agreed Makana, like an automaton, a sleepwalker, still shocked by the scale of his wife's mental collapse. 'You're right, of course.'

'My brother teaches in the School of Medicine. I can get him to come over.'

'That would be a great help.' Makana was distracted, becoming slowly aware of the world around him again. The idea of his wife losing her mind suddenly seemed very real to him. He walked the length of the upstairs veranda, trying to clear his own mind, trying to think. If the chalk was a warning, what did it mean? How far were they prepared to go?

When he reached the end of the veranda, he leaned his hands on the iron railings and looked down. Beyond a short strip of neglected yellow grass a road ran between the faculty buildings. Just to his right, under a large banyan tree, was a white Toyota pick-up. Makana turned and headed for the stairs, bumping into a man who was coming running with urgent news.

'Not now,' Makana said, brushing him aside. He took the stairs two at a time, ran the length of the ground-floor veranda, pushing through the crowd of students, and walked, rather than ran, the fifty-odd metres to the pick-up. He saw the man sit up behind the wheel, slowly begin to fold his newspaper. There was an old half oil drum standing nearby, acting as a rubbish bin. Kicking it over, Makana emptied its contents on to the gravel and lifted it high. The windscreen splintered on impact. Then he wrenched open the door and hauled the driver to his feet, pushing him against the side of the pick-up.

'Stay away from my wife, do you hear!'

The man stared at him impassively. Makana recognised him as the bearded militia man from that day by the river. A long, long time ago, it seemed.

'Why are you following me?'

'We're just doing our job,' said the man indignantly. 'Like you.'

He did not resist as Makana thrust him back once more against the side of the car.

'Take it easy,' he said. 'It's all over anyway.'

'What are you talking about?'

'They're arresting the culprit right now.' The bearded man smiled knowingly, then jerked his head. 'Why don't you go and take a look?'

'What are you talking about?'

'Professor Manute. He's the one who murdered those immoral girls.'

Releasing his grip, Makana shoved the man hard for a final time and stepped back. Folding his arms, the man watched him walk away, laughing and shaking his head to himself.

Professor Manute was being dragged from the history department as Makana arrived. A southerner, he was tall and dark-skinned. He was also old and frail. In his sixties, his head a shock of bushy white hair as he came into view, walking with the uneven gait of a man who had suffered polio as a child. It was patently absurd to suggest this man could overpower a healthy woman in her twenties. He was met by a torrent of abuse, racial and otherwise. A hail of stones flew from the crowd of outraged onlookers, students who had gathered quickly with more coming by the minute – running across the sun-scorched lawns, leaping over low hedges and railings in their haste. Terrified, the professor raised his manacled hands to his head in a bid to protect himself. The militia men who flanked him seemed more concerned with standing out of harm's way than protecting their prisoner. A chunk of brick found its target, striking the old man's forehead. Blood gushed from above his left eye. He was pleading with his captors to take him away from this place, but they seemed in no hurry to do so. They prodded him forward so that he walked ahead of them along the path which had now become a gauntlet, lined on both sides by boys and girls yelling taunts and throwing stones and pieces of brick heaved up from the borders of the flower beds.

As Makana watched, something else flew out of the crowd and the professor crumpled. His two escorts made no attempt to help him up. They watched as the crowd charged in. If something wasn't done the professor would be kicked to death on the spot. Makana waded in, confident that his uniform would be enough to deter most of the crowd. It worked. They fell back.

'You're supposed to be escorting this man, not throwing him to the dogs.' Makana addressed the militia men, helping the bewildered professor to his feet.

'He's a murderer and a rapist,' said one of them.

'That remains to be seen. You have to present your evidence.'

'Why are you defending a *kafir*?' spat one of them.

'As far as I know, he's not on trial for his religious beliefs, unless you know otherwise.'

'He must answer for his crimes. He has defiled and murdered good Muslim girls.'

'A proper investigation will decide that. We still have the rule of law in this country.'

'You have no right to do this,' said the other man, stepping into his path.

'Well, go and lodge a complaint.'

Just then, two pick-ups of the Revolutionary Security Force roared round the corner, coming to a halt at the end of the drive. Twelve men, all armed with automatic weapons, dropped to the ground. The crowd fell back, their euphoria replaced by fear. Mek Nimr climbed from the lead car.

'This is none of your business, Makana. This man is in our custody.'

'Even if he is a murder suspect, he still has some rights.'

One of the militia men slipped his AK-47 off his shoulder. Makana pulled his revolver from its holster and levelled it at the man's head. Mek Nimr was smiling now in that strange, unhappy way of his.

'You've gone too far this time, Makana. You leave me with no choice.'

Chapter Thirty-three

The light sand swirled across the bare tarmac like smoke, as if the wind were intent on swallowing up the road, wiping away man's futile endeavours to tame nature and return this place to the wilderness it was meant to be.

Makana had been awake most of the night, certainly long before Sami turned up in the faded green Datsun early that morning, his thoughts tossing back and forth. Sleepless nights had become commonplace over the past seven years. He appeared more than usually distracted as he got into the car, wrestling with the door to no effect until Sami leaned over and gave it a thump from the inside.

'Patience.'

'You're sure this thing will get us there?' Makana glanced over at the Mercedes parked under the eucalyptus tree. It looked a lot more reliable.

'*Inshallah.*' Sami shrugged philosophically. Detecting something in the other man's voice, he glanced over. 'Is something wrong?' he asked.

'Why should anything be wrong?'

'It's just a question.'

'Nothing wrong.' Makana stared straight ahead. 'I slept badly, that's all.'

Hesitating only for a moment, Sami started the engine and began pushing the gearstick into place. They crawled patiently through the early-morning traffic and turned south in the direction of Giza until they picked up the road towards the Fayoum Oasis. Once the city fell behind them and the traffic eased, the land opened up on both sides and they were soon driving through flat empty country, the dry air blowing through the open windows already warming up. The thread of tarmac stretched off into the distance. The bulk of the traffic that day consisted of cramped little minibuses carrying commuters to and from distant satellite towns, along with rusty old trucks struggling along, overloaded with livestock or heavy machinery or enormous walls of sacks.

Off to their right was evidence of what the future held in store for the city as it expanded, growing like some unsightly tumour into the unblemished desert. Clusters of buildings scattered along the roadside provided housing for workers employed in the isolated industrial complexes built by the government to relieve pressure on the capital. Eventually all these dots would be joined up into one big sprawl. New colonies were springing out of the desert like strange oases of brick and cement. For the moment these were just isolated pockets, like remote islands dotted in a vast sea of dust, but that wouldn't last for long. Ten years from now the skirts of the metropolis behind them would have spread out to swallow up all of this, drowning the silence and emptiness in snarling traffic and ugly concrete overpasses.

Makana's hand went out to the dashboard to steady himself as the car swung wildly. Sami was twisting round, groping for a newspaper that was flapping wildly on the back seat. Makana hoped he would toss it out of the window, and was surprised when instead it dropped into his lap.

The paper was folded to reveal a small article on an inside page. A man named Mohsen Taha had died of a heart attack, a senior aide to the President. The government lamented the loss of such a respected figure who had faithfully served his country for so many years.

'Why am I reading this?'

'It wasn't a heart attack. He took an overdose of sleeping tablets. The papers are keeping that side of it quiet. It would bring dishonour on the family, and by implication on the government. Nobody wants to upset the President, so it is described as an accident, and buried on an inside page.'

'They will be rewarded in the next world for their discretion.'

'What it also doesn't tell you is that Taha was being blackmailed.'

'You know this for a fact?'

'Facts are overrated.'

Makana raised his eyebrows. 'Coming from a journalist that doesn't sound reassuring. Who was blackmailing him?'

'Ah, that we don't know, yet. What might interest you is that Taha was involved in buying out Hanafi's debt on behalf of a third party.'

'Vronsky?'

'Possibly. According to a friend in the Ministry of Justice, Taha was being threatened with losing his post. There are rumours that a certain weekly journal that specialises in scandal was about to break some big story about him.'

The warm desert air blew through the open windows, bringing with it the scent of lost kingdoms. Of armies that had marched out into that nothingness and never returned. The traffic had thinned to the odd vehicle in the distance, dwindling to none at all in places.

'Underneath the beaming smiles,' Sami continued his account of Hanafi's financial situation, 'there is a dark yawning hole. Everyone's finances took a dip after the Gulf War. No hard currency was coming into the country. People were poor. And the terror threat has been hitting tourism, so that source has dried up as well. Hanafi was as hard hit as everyone else. He just managed to make it look like he was doing better than most.'

'How does that square with the expansion, the new stadium?'

'It doesn't. Some say that there were some other odd business dealings going on, with money coming in from investors in the Gulf. Without the outside funding none of that would have been possible. You just don't make that much out of frozen vege-tables, and the property market had plummeted. It was a good time for buying land, but at the same time Hanafi's credit wasn't what it used to be. Then, about a year ago, the banks started to call in their investments.'

'Do we know why that happened?'

'No, I can't find out what made them change their minds, but it sounds like one of their major clients in the Gulf was unhappy.'

'Was this after our Russian friend had entered the picture?'

'I don't know. Maybe the accountant will be able to tell us.'

Makana was now sure that Adil's disappearance had to be related to Vronsky in some way. Vronsky and Daud Bulatt. One seemed to lead to the other and round again in circles. To gain what he wanted Vronsky needed to secure the assistance of government functionaries. Most would be susceptible to old-fashioned bribes. The more stubborn ones, like Taha, say, might have needed more aggressive forms of persuasion. Was that where Farag and his cameras came in? And where was Farag anyway? Makana had called the man's office several times and nobody ever answered.

After a time they began to slow down. Sami swung the wheel and they turned roughly eastward and began going back in the direction of the river. This road was even more isolated. Here the wind blew the fine-grained sand directly across their path. It settled in soft pale sheets upon the grey, sun-cracked asphalt whose edges had been crumbled into tarry pebbles by the occasional heavy lorry.

Neither of them really had any idea what they were going to find. The further they drove, the harder Makana found it to reconcile what he was seeing around him with what Soraya Hanafi had described. Luxury residential estates, safe and secure. Remote enough from the crowds to put you and your money at ease. Stations on the road to happiness. A little chunk of heaven at an affordable price. They drove past a few similar developments, their titles displaying naked ambition: Paradise Oasis, Green Lands, Happiness Valley, Sunny Park. All the names were invented in English and then transcribed to make up words which made no real sense at all in Arabic, language being another notch in the gap between those who could afford such places and those who were not welcome. Hanafi and others like him were busy constructing another world out here. One which bore as little resemblance as possible to the rest of the country. A bowl for exotic fish to swim about in. And so the wealthy classes abandoned the city to the poor and the less fortunate – the wretched of the earth. More lush golfing greens and swimming pools popping up out of the ground like fairy-tale castles, complete with perimeter fences and security guards to keep the riff-raff out.

'It should be somewhere up here,' said Sami, turning on to what was really not much more than a single track. Makana was not convinced. The wind had picked up and sand had built into drifts that covered the road almost completely in places. From time to time the wheels caught and began to spin freely, slinging the rear end of the battered Datsun from side to side. After about ten more minutes of this they climbed a small rise and found themselves gazing down upon a dusty bowl at the centre of which was a compound, or rather the beginnings of one.

As they got out of the car, the wind wrenched the door angrily from Makana's hand. He wrestled it back into place. Squinting, he shielded his eyes with one hand, both feet sinking into the soft ground as fine sand poured into his shoes. Sami was pointing at a hoarding, now flapping back and forth as if a demon was shaking it. *Hanafi Heavens*, it read.

'This is it?' yelled Sami.

Beyond the high fence, however, there wasn't much to see of the promised bliss. Out of the ochre landscape a faint glimmer of green drew the eye, but it was a circle of windblown and withered palms, fronds snapping in the air like switches. Makana could make out the beginnings of some construction. Sami indicated a place where there was a gap in the fence for them to duck through. The barbed wire hummed in the air over their heads as if charged with electricity.

The houses were no more than empty concrete shells. Most of them were unfinished and even those that did have four walls were lacking a roof or some other essential component. They wandered through what felt like the ruins of a forgotten city, already half-buried in the sand. A vanquished empire.

Staggering up a slippery dune, stumbling and cursing before he reached the top, Makana turned to survey the development. He remembered the model he had seen back at the offices of Hanafi Enterprises and could roughly make out the lie of the land. At some point the first phase had been marked out. The tops of wooden stakes daubed with red paint protruded from the ground here and there. Many of them had fallen over, or been swallowed up by the drifting sand. It wasn't easy to imagine what it would look like when it was finished. The parks and ponds, the connecting paths, the cinema and shopping mall, a funfair playground for the kids . . . This place was meant to be complete in itself with no need for contact with the outside world. Sami had reached him by now and flopped down on the burning ground, gasping for breath. Makana stared down the hill for a moment then started off. With a sigh, Sami dragged himself to his feet again and followed.

As they made their way back along the curving path that traversed the undulating landscape, Makana said, 'At least you have a title for your article, when you eventually write it.'

'And what would that be?' Sami asked, squinting through the stinging dust.

'Paradise Postponed.'

Sami laughed all the way back to the car, partly with relief that they were leaving. But there was more work to come. The Datsun was stuck in the shifting sand. The more Sami pressed his foot down, the deeper the wheels spun themselves in. They climbed out and stood contemplating the buried tyres.

'Now what?'

'Now we start to dig,' said Makana, dropping to his knees.

Chapter Thirty-four

The accountant's name was Mustafa Debbous and he lived in a shabby block of flats underneath a flyover in Bulaq. Makana and Sami climbed the stairs in the gloom, stumbling over discarded bones and empty cans that had been scattered from a bag of rubbish, probably ripped open by a stray cat. On the fourth floor Sami leaned on the doorbell until a tremulous, excitable voice spoke from within.

'Who is it?'

'It's me, Sami Barakat.'

'What do you want?'

'I have a last question for you.'

'But I've told you everything I know,' insisted the voice plaintively.

'I've got someone with me. A friend.'

'I . . . uh . . . thought I made it clear, I can't be seen talking to people.'

They both turned as a door opened behind them to reveal a solid-looking woman wearing a black *gellabia*.

'If anyone wants an apology here, it's me!' she shouted. 'What right do you have, coming here and conducting your business in the middle of the hall so that everyone can hear you?'

'I'm sorry,' began Sami.

'Am I talking to you? I'm addressing the rat hiding behind that door!'

'I've told you before,' squeaked the rat, 'you have no right to involve yourself in my affairs.'

'Why are you afraid to come out and show your face?'

'I'm not afraid, certainly not of you.'

The door opened to reveal a small fellow with a narrow, elongated face and tiny eyes behind round spectacles. He did bear some resemblance to a rodent. He peered round them to address his irate neighbour.

'*Khalas*, we leave you in peace.'

'Peace? You don't know the meaning of the word. There won't be any peace in this house until our Lord gives you what you deserve.'

With that the door opposite slammed shut and Debbous stood aside to usher them in, glancing quickly round the outer hall before closing his own door. He stood wringing his hands as if trying to drain them of feeling. Producing a large handkerchief, he proceeded to wipe his brow.

'That woman is unbearable. She murdered her husband, I'm sure of it!' he hissed.

Then, like a caged mammal, he scurried away down a narrow, unlit corridor, leading the way into a shuttered salon that was cluttered with all kinds of antique objects: heavy standing lamps, chandeliers, ornate mirrors, gilded chairs and tables. It looked like a cave stuffed with treasures salvaged from the long-gone days of the pashas. The fact that it felt rather like a museum perhaps explained why the three of them remained standing in the middle of the room.

'Quite a collection you have here,' observed Makana. 'Are these all yours?'

Debbous clutched Sami's arm. 'Who is this?' he demanded in a faint whisper.

'This is my associate, Makana.'

'Oh,' said Debbous, his mouth locked into a circle. 'Another journalist?' He nervously fingered the tip of his shirt collar. 'Perhaps I should insist on raising my fee?'

'And perhaps you have already been paid quite enough,' said Makana.

'Well, it's not easy,' fretted the accountant. 'I could get myself into a lot of trouble.'

'You're a brave man,' said Makana. 'There aren't many who would steal from Hanafi.'

'Well, I didn't steal exactly.' Debbous's voice was a plaintive whine that sawed on Makana's nerves like an out-of-tune violin. 'I just sort of borrowed it.'

'Borrowed it for what?'

'Oh, to buy things.' Debbous gestured around the room. 'You know, bargains like these were not going to be available for long. Once sold they are gone for ever.'

'How did he catch you?'

'It wasn't Hanafi. He has no idea what is going on. It's all Gaber.' Debbous clenched his little fists together. 'He's like a snake, that one. You can't get anything past him.'

'What about the daughter, Soraya?'

'What about her?'

Makana spelled it out. 'How does she fit into the Hanafi empire?'

'Oh, she's smart.' The accountant tapped his temple with one finger. 'But she's a girl, of course, so nobody takes her seriously.

In this country, if you want to be in charge of something you need to be a man.'

'She's her father's daughter . . . his heiress.'

'It makes no difference to some people.'

'So Gaber is running things?'

'In theory, yes, but his hands are tied. He still has to follow the old man's orders. If Hanafi insists he wants a new stadium . . . what can he do? It is like a ship being steered by a blind man,' Debbous insisted. 'Sooner or later it's going to hit something.'

'How easy would it be to take control of a company that big?'

'You mean, buy it out?' The thin eyebrows twitched. 'Well,' Debbous folded his arms and shot a glance towards one corner of the room, 'I'm not sure I ought to share this with you . . .'

'If the information is good my associate will be happy to compensate you,' said Sami, which cheered Debbous up some- what. He cocked his head to one side.

'If somebody really wanted to take control, it would be easy enough. If you bought up the bank debts. I mean, there's nothing wrong with it as such,' he added. 'If you made a few adjustments, there's no need for the business to fail.'

'What kind of adjustments?' queried Makana.

'Some projects would have to be put on hold.'

'Like the stadium?' suggested Sami helpfully.

The accountant threw up his hands. 'It would be cheaper to build a pyramid. The company is over-extended. The housing projects, the stadium . . . it's too much. All you need is for someone to step in and offer to take the loans off the bank's hands. They would be more than willing to part with them.'

'Even though Hanafi is an old and trusted customer?'

'Old is the right word. He could die at any moment and where

307

would that leave them then? There's no one to take over. Who wants to be saddled with loans that size? They could bring down the bank. The government would be forced to step in, and everyone knows they don't have any money.'

'It's like one big house of cards,' whistled Sami.

'Theoretically speaking, who might be capable of stepping in and taking over loans that big?'

Debbous folded his arms. 'It's not so much the size of them. You'd need government approval, of course, but that can be taken care of . . . for a price.'

'Then what is the problem?' asked Makana.

'You'd need to have guts to take on Hanafi. He has a lot of enemies, and a lot of friends. Anyone who tried a hostile takeover of his business would be sticking their head in the lion's jaws.'

'So tell us about this Russian, Vronsky.'

'What about him?' The accountant's eyes began to wander nervously again.

'Has he been buying up Hanafi's debt at the bank?'

'Well, yes, but only in the last few months. Maybe six at the most.'

'Is there someone else?' frowned Makana.

'Oh, yes.' Debbous rubbed his hands together as if washing them.

'Who?'

'Well, I'm not sure who's behind it. It's a bank I'd never heard of before: Green Nakhala Reserve Fund.'

'And you don't know anything about them?'

Debbous shook his head. 'They seem to have unlimited funds. There is a suspicion that it is one of those Arab princes who has decided to put his millions at the service of Allah.'

'How much of Hanafi's empire is in their hands?'

'I couldn't tell you, not without making a few calls, but a good thirty per cent, I would say. The banks aren't keen for people to know their business. But you know what this country is like. Everyone wants a chance to talk.'

Makana was silent for a long time. So Vronsky had a rival. Another bank with Arab connections. Who was behind it, he wondered, and was Adil involved with them? The accountant was still talking.

'Between them, Vronsky and the Arabs own over fifty per cent. If they combined their resources they could take over tomorrow.'

As he turned towards the front door, Sami tried to reassure the nervous accountant.

'It's all right, you've done well.'

'I thought there was some talk of further compensation,' Debbous whined. 'I mean, I could get into a lot of trouble . . .'

Makana left Sami to negotiate and wandered back down the hall, his mind turning over the possibilities. The flat was a private museum full of ugly, useless objects from a bygone age. In the days of the pashas he himself would have been a Nubian servant who came and went at the beck and call of people like Debbous. Perhaps that was what the little accountant dreamed of: his own glorious reign. Everyone wanted to be king, it seemed. That was why everybody loved Hanafi, wasn't it? They dreamed of having the life he had. And what of Adil Romario . . . who did he dream of becoming?

Makana was bothered by a thought that had been nagging at the back of his mind for some time. There were too many coincidences linking Adil's story to his own. He needed to find out where the Green Nakhala Reserve Fund was based, but he had an idea he already knew. The course of Adil's life appeared to have changed after his trip to Khartoum for the DreemTeem exhibition match. What had happened there exactly? Who had he met?

Finally, Sami finished counting notes into the accountant's hand and the two men took their leave. As they stepped out of the apartment they were met by a hail of abuse from the strident neighbour. The building reverberated to the sound of her raised voice as Makana and Sami descended the staircase.

Chapter Thirty-five

The door to Faraga Film Productions stood open. Even as he stepped inside, Makana could see that the place had been emptied. A tall man wearing a striped *gellabia* and a sullen look on his face was walking out of what used to be Farag's office, cradling a television set in his arms. Makana recognised him as the *bawab* who usually stood listlessly on guard in the front hallway downstairs.

'What happened here?'

'Oh, they left.' The man blinked, replying with an unconcerned air that seemed to imply there was nothing odd about him walking out holding a television set that clearly wasn't his.

'Left how?'

'Some people came to pick up the films and stuff.'

'Not everything.'

The man looked down as if he had just noticed what was in his own arms. 'They said I could hold on to this. It's just as well because they never paid me for the last month.'

'Who exactly were these men?'

'How should I know?' He made to move by and Makana blocked his way.

'What did they say?'

Irritation crossed the man's face. He was annoyed at having his getaway delayed.

'What's it to you anyway?'

Makana flashed him Okasha's card, fast enough for him to see the police insignia and not much else. The man groaned.

'I've done nothing wrong. They told me I could keep it.' He hefted the set in his arms. 'It's for the children.'

'Who told you?'

'The ones who came. They said Mr Farag was moving his office to another place and that everything was arranged with the owner of the building, so there's nothing wrong with that.'

'Who were these men?'

'How should I know?' The *bawab* stared at the wall. 'They sounded foreign. And they work fast. If I hadn't come back from my breakfast early, I might have missed them.'

'Did they say where? I mean, where they were taking Farag's things?'

He edged towards the door again. 'Oh, no, and frankly, I don't make it my job to interfere in other people's business. Could you pull the door closed on your way out?' He gestured to indicate that he didn't have a free hand, and then he was gone. Makana listened to his slippers slapping their way down the stairs.

If a plague of ravenous termites had fallen upon it Farag's office could not have been stripped more efficiently. Nothing was left. Table, desk, chairs, the stacks of papers, the dusty computers and decrepit printer and fax machine, even the telephone, were all gone. It wasn't a bad room once the clutter had been removed. Makana went over to the window and peered down at the street below where a woman in black with a tray of guavas on her head stood on one foot while she chewed the strap of her slipper. Then she dropped it to the floor, stepped into it and shuffled on her way.

Makana tried to imagine Farag on an extended holiday by the sea, splashing about in the pool with Vronsky's stable of beauties, but somehow the image did not convince. Would he have been foolish enough to keep all of his incriminating tapes here in his office? Knowing Farag, it was quite possible. Whatever they thought he had, they wanted to make quite sure nothing was left behind. Makana was surprised they hadn't stripped the walls. Now it was gone, furniture and all, spirited away by the Russian bodybuilders. It didn't bode well for Farag.

On his way out Makana paused by an open doorway that led into a tiny room under the stairs where the doorman and his family lived. The *bawab* was thumping the top of the television set with one hand while frowning at the kaleidoscope of colour that fluttered before him but refused to settle into a picture. Behind him a flock of grubby urchins screamed and hit one another while a small, round woman, who looked no older than eighteen, reclined on a large bed, her head against the wall and her eyes closed in exhaustion.

'What about Farag's secretary, has she been around?'

'It's not my job to keep an eye on them,' the *bawab* answered, unable to spare Makana even a single glance. 'They come and go as they please.'

The old man's junk shop was closed. Makana was standing there peering through the window, trying to see past the layers of dust and the heaps of useless objects, when a small boy went by carrying a large alabaster cat clutched to his chest. It towered over his head.

'If you're looking for Old Yunis, he's drinking tea in the Coppersmiths' Street.'

A couple of minutes later Makana stepped into a café in Sharia al-Nahaseen to find the old man playing chess with a giant who loomed over both table and opponent as if they were toys. He was staring at the pieces on the board with fixed intensity while the old man glanced about him, looking for distraction. He seemed relieved when he looked up to see Makana.

'Ah, there you are.' He smiled as if he had been expecting a visitor.

'I was told I might find you here.'

Excusing himself, Yunis got to his feet and gestured towards another table across the room. The hunched man didn't even look up, his attention still completely absorbed by the challenge posed on the board in front of him.

Makana sat down and tea arrived almost immediately. He plucked a sprig of mint from the glass on the table and dropped it into the amber liquid.

'I owe you an apology,' said Yunis.

'Don't worry about it.'

'No, I insist.' The old man bowed his head for a moment before looking up. 'Shortly after you came to see me the first time, I was approached by a man on behalf of someone I knew a long time ago. They wanted documents made up – identity cards, passports. I didn't want to do it. I didn't want to get involved. These people are very dangerous. I told them I couldn't help them. I said it wasn't safe. I told them people were asking questions.' He tilted his head to one side. 'I told them about you.'

'This someone . . . was Daud Bulatt?'

Yunis gave the briefest of nods. 'Make no mistake, he and his associates are very desperate men.'

314

'I know,' said Makana. He lit a cigarette. 'I found out.'

Yunis bowed his head. 'I'm sorry. I didn't mean to put you in danger.'

'Bulatt is alive. But why has he come back?'

'That I don't know,' said the old man. He reached for a newspaper lying on a nearby table and unfolded it. 'But you can tell your inspector friend they are not going to catch him as easily as that.'

His finger rested on an account of the raid on the supposed terrorist hide-out. The raid Okasha had invited Makana on. It had been something of a disaster. Sixteen civilians died in the assault. And there was no mention of Daud Bulatt, which meant they had found no trace of him.

'My friend?'

The old man pushed the dark glasses up on to his forehead and rubbed his strange-coloured eyes. 'One should always be wary of people who are keen to impress.'

'You're saying I shouldn't trust Okasha?'

Old Yunis leaned back and folded his arms. He looked away at the street for a while. When he turned back his tone seemed to have softened somewhat.

'Perhaps I am being unfair. I have a feeling you don't trust many people. You prefer to be on the outside, never on the inside, like me.'

The street was crowded with people bustling along, carrying their wares. Two men rushed by, their backs bent under an impossible weight of sacks, like ants bearing an enormous burden. A slim boy on a bicycle elegantly weaved his way through the crowd, balancing a long wooden tray laden with flat round loaves of bread fresh from the bakery.

'Did you know that Bulatt was quite a rich man when he went

315

into prison? He gave it all away. Renounced all material possessions. Houses, land, cars. All of it.'

Makana studied the old man. The strip of worn Sellotape fluttered like a moth over the bridge of his spectacles.

'If a man can change once, he can change again. Maybe he's tired of being poor.'

'Aren't we all?' Yunis's hollow cheeks sucked in smoke from a cigarette. 'There are some men it is dangerous to know, and others it is dangerous not to know.'

'I seem to be caught between the two kinds.'

Their attention was distracted as the giant crouching over the chessboard let out a cry of triumph. With a sigh, the old man stubbed out his cigarette and got to his feet.

'Then you must be very careful which way you move.'

Makana watched him get up and move to the other table. Old Yunis surveyed the pieces on the chessboard for all of fifteen seconds before making his move. With a groan his opponent crumpled and slumped back down to hunch over the board again, brow set once more in fierce concentration.

Chapter Thirty-six

The light was already draining quickly from the day as Makana descended from the road. The entrance to the little shack on the embankment below the eucalyptus tree pulsated with bursts of white light and shadow as a television set played in the interior.

'Is that you, *ya bash-muhandis*?'

'Yes, it's me, Umm Ali. All is well?'

'*Ya sidi*, wait. I have something for you.'

From inside the hut came a good deal of scuffling, a few curses launched at children who placed themselves in the way. Makana stood attentively at a distance until the familiar figure appeared in the doorway. Umm Ali was wearing a long brown gown that was presumably her nightwear, which, although by any standards more than decent, was to Makana's mind somewhat more diaphanous than he was comfortable with. He imagined he caught a certain mischievous gleam in her eyes as she presented him with a large envelope.

'It was brought by a policeman on a motorcycle. It must be important,' she cooed.

'Thank you very much, and good night, Umm Ali.'

'Have pleasant dreams, *ya sidi.*'

Makana beat a hasty retreat down the path and stepped aboard the *awama* with a sense of relief. In the kitchen he discovered a disc of bread as hard as a plate, and a small red onion. He ran the bread under the tap and then turned it over the gas flame a few times until it softened enough to resemble something approaching edible. He made coffee, bringing the water to the boil, turning the heat down, spooning in the freshly bought grounds carefully, then turning it up again. As the dark brown mass bubbled away happily in the brass pot he sliced the onion thinly, sprinkled it with powdered red *shatta* chilli and lime juice. He climbed the stairs with this veritable feast, the envelope under his arm, and settled himself in the big wicker chair. He tucked the Beretta, which he now slept with, by his side, next to the cushion. Inside the envelope he discovered a bundle of photocopied sheets, accompanied by another note from Janet Hayden.

'It took a little longer than I had hoped,' she wrote. 'But I finally managed to get hold of a complete copy of Strangeways's original report into the disappearance of Alice Markham. It had been carted out to storage facilities in the middle of nowhere. Anyway, I hope it will be of some use in your investigation. I have taken the liberty of making two copies, one for Inspector Okasha, and the other for you.'

The letter went on at some length to explain how Hayden had managed to get hold of the report. Makana flipped through the photocopies impatiently, looking for what he needed. It didn't take long. Then he sat back and closed his eyes, suddenly exhausted. He should read the whole report carefully, but that could wait twenty minutes or so while he caught up on his sleep. He felt as though he were falling into a bottomless pit as his eyes shut.

When they opened again someone was calling his name. Umm Ali, her nightdress now covered by a more substantial *ibaya*, stood on the path looking fretful. Red and blue lights were reflected against the wall in front of him. She pointed wordlessly.

Wearily, Makana made his way up the path to find Okasha waiting for him. A police car was parked under the eucalyptus tree. It was early evening and the streets were busy with revellers heading for their night's entertainment. A continuous musical soundtrack of drums, strings and flutes echoed from the open windows of passing cars. In the ghostly orange glow of the street-lights, Okasha was visible, crouched in the passenger seat of the Mercedes, looking through the documents he had found tucked under the sun visor. He didn't look up when Makana leaned on the open door and lit a cigarette.

'You're an interesting man, Makana,' said the inspector, without lifting his head. 'I've said it before and I shall no doubt say it again. A lot of people in your position would have gone to pieces long ago, but not you.' Okasha glanced up at him. 'Nice car. Not really your style though. Where did you say you got it?'

'I borrowed it.'

'From a friend, yes, you said. And I told you that you don't have any friends.'

'Are you going to tell me what this is all about?'

Okasha dangled an object inside a transparent plastic bag in the air. Makana took it and held it up to the orange light. Inside was a large and somewhat cheap gold watch. He turned it over in his hands.

'You don't recognise it?' Okasha climbed out of the car and tossed the vehicle registration at him. 'That's funny, because it belongs to the same man whose car you've been driving.'

Makana lifted the bag again. The wristwatch was a copy of a

Rolex. Most of the fake gold plating had come off and a patina of rust now decorated the edges. Turning it over, he found a name engraved on the back: *Salim Farag.*

'Where did you find this?'

'It was attached to an arm,' said Okasha. 'Well, actually it was only part of an arm.' He indicated his own elbow. 'It turned up in a net full of fish that was hauled in by a fisherman, working in the timeless way we like to think still exists.'

'Where was this?'

'A dump just north of El Gouna. Perhaps you know it? It's close to Hurghada.' Okasha scratched the back of his neck. 'Funny, isn't it? I mean, if he hadn't been so fat it would have been lost for ever. And just imagine if the creature that ate the rest of him had swallowed this bit instead.'

Makana recalled the wind blowing off the whitecaps; the fishermen tugging their boat into the beach.

'Why are you telling me this?'

'Gouna used to be nothing. A lagoon with a little fishing village. A few houses. No one ever went there before the developers moved in. Now it's a luxury resort, a little more upmarket than neighbouring Hurghada. Come on!' Okasha leaned forward and stabbed Makana in the chest with his forefinger. 'You're going to tell me this is all a coincidence, right? Vronsky's resort is at El Gouna. You went to see him, and now you just happen to be driving the car of a man whose arm washed up on a beach without the rest of him attached to it. Tell me it's not connected. Anybody else would already have arrested you on suspicion of murder.'

'It sounds like a terrible accident to me.' Makana handed the watch back.

'I can see you're devastated by the news.'

'I'm sorry, I didn't really know the man.'

'Which brings us back to why you are driving his car.'

'Farag was in business with Adil Romario.'

Okasha hefted the watch in his left hand. 'So you went to see Farag, then what?'

'Then we both went to visit his business associate, Alexei Vronsky.'

'I warned you about this.'

'I'm telling you what happened. I left Farag at Vronsky's place.'

Okasha cast Makana a warning glance. 'If you're trying to suggest that our esteemed Russian friend of the state might have something to do with this Farag becoming fish food, you need to think again, my friend.'

The long tendrils of the eucalyptus tree swayed above them in the warm breeze, leaves trailing like slender fingers, tracing patterns in the dust.

'I borrowed his car to get home. That's it. I told you, I left him with Vronsky.'

'And I told you that Vronsky is out of reach. I don't want to hear about him.'

'You're treating this as murder?'

'And make myself the laughing stock of the entire police force? He was eaten by a shark. I can't call that anything but an unfortunate accident.' Okasha hefted the watch in his palm. 'This could spell a lot of trouble for you, though. You're driving his car. I could make a case out of that alone.'

'Why would I kill Farag?'

'Who knows the mysteries of your life, Makana? Why do you live on a sinking old heap of firewood?'

'Sounds like stalemate to me,' said Makana, turning to face

the river. Okasha sighed and folded his arms. Both men leaned back against the car, side by side.

'I'm serious, Vronsky is out of your reach. He's out of everyone's reach. He's a national security asset, I told you that. He has protection in high places.'

'I gather your raid wasn't a complete success?'

'It was a disaster,' sighed the inspector. 'They were waiting for us. The place was like a fort. No sign of Bulatt.'

'But you have evidence he is in the country, right?'

'Oh, he's here all right, and we'll get him. But he was warned we were coming.' Okasha turned to look Makana in the eye. 'Nobody knew about the raid. It was top secret.'

'You told me.'

'But you didn't tell anyone else, right?'

'What do you think?'

The air went out of Okasha's lungs like a slow puncture as he turned away. 'Sixteen civilians dead, twenty-seven wounded. It was a massacre. Serrag's men just let loose like there was no tomorrow. We lost two of our own.'

'Another great victory for the state.'

Okasha thumped the side of the Mercedes with the palm of his hand, so hard that the driver who was dozing in the squad car jumped.

'I don't need lessons in morality from you, Makana.'

'You know you're never going to win the war this way, don't you?'

'*Ya salaam!* Now you're going to lecture me about how to win the war against the fanatics.' Okasha thrust his face towards Makana's. 'The last I heard, you came running to us for help.'

'For every one of those killed, you create ten more jihadists.'

The two men stared at one another, realising perhaps for the first time that they were set on different courses, as if facing one another from the decks of two ships that had just veered apart, avoiding collision, watching the gulf widen between them.

'Maybe I should do what they keep saying and send you back,' said Okasha finally.

'Every man has to know his own limits.'

The policeman levelled a finger at him. 'You've been spending too much time up in that fancy apartment of Hanafi's. Don't forget that when this is all over and done with, you'll have to come back down here and live among the rest of us.'

'Did you read Hayden's report?'

'No.' Okasha kicked the dust with the heel of his boot, looking for all the world like a little boy who hadn't done his homework. 'I haven't got the time to read a report about the disappearance of a girl twenty years ago.'

'If you had you would know that Alice Markham was Bulatt's daughter.'

The expression on Okasha's face turned from rage to incredulity. He straightened up.

'His daughter?'

'The young man Liz Markham met when she originally came here on holiday was Daud Bulatt. He was hanging around the hotels, looking for foreign girls in need of hashish. He is the one she came looking for five years later with their little girl.'

'So who took her?'

'Hanafi's young wife and son had just been gunned down by Bulatt's thugs. Who do you think took her?'

'Hanafi killed her?' Okasha thumped a fist against the side of the car. 'But there's no evidence. Nothing to prove it.'

'Would you act on it if there was?'

Okasha's eyes swivelled round to fix on Makana. If there was ever a moment when the two men might have come to blows, thought Makana, this was it. But Okasha simply shook his head, then turned and walked away. 'You're like a drowning man,' he called over his shoulder, 'clinging to the wreckage. Only pride prevents you from taking the hand that's reaching down to save you.'

Makana watched him go. He was thinking it would be a shame to make an enemy of this man. After a time he realised Umm Ali was calling to him. In the distance the telephone was ringing.

Chapter Thirty-seven

The stadium was floodlit. From high up in the office building it reminded Makana of a cemetery. Instead of tombs, of course, it had statues of Hanafi, resplendent in the dark, their golden visages gleaming in the harsh glare. It seemed a fitting monument to the great man himself. A symbol of the heights to which he had lifted himself, and of the absurdity of his desire to rule the world, building his empire literally in the sand. Off in the distance the skyline was split by the rigid angularity of Kheops' pyramid, lit up itself against the ripped net of stars by white beams that raked the sky like luminous trees swaying in a storm.

Soraya Hanafi was a whisper, a sliver of a shadow, over by the window. The conference room where they had first met was unlit but the glow that filtered in from outside was bright enough to see by. She turned to face him as he stepped over to the window alongside her.

'Thank you for coming.'

'It looks like a temple.' Makana nodded down at the half-finished stadium. 'Something a pharaoh might have been proud of.'

Something about her had changed, almost as if she was

dissolving into the shadows around her. Her hair was loose and unkempt, curling around her face as she seemed to sway in the shifting light.

'I'm sorry to ask you to come out here so late.'

'Why are you still here?'

'Oh, I was working, and suddenly none of it made sense any more. Don't you ever get that feeling?'

Makana glanced at her. 'I have bad days.' He was aware that she was staring at him intently. When his eyes mets hers she turned away, looking back out at the stadium and the darkness beyond.

'You would be able to see the stars if all those lights didn't block them out. Doesn't that sum up the foolishness of man?'

'To obliterate the very heavens your towers are meant to reach?'

'Yes, something like that.' The planes of her soft, unblemished face caught the light in a way that gave her the regal air of a Nefertiti – wife of the heretic Akhenaten.

'You told me once about an Englishwoman who was murdered . . .'

'Elizabeth Markham.'

'She came here to look for her daughter, isn't that correct? Did you ever find out what happened to her . . . the little girl, I mean?'

'Everything points to her having been killed.'

'Why would anyone kill a little girl?'

'Revenge. An eye for an eye. That kind of thing. She was caught between two very dangerous men.'

'One of them was my father, wasn't he?'

Makana hesitated for a second. 'Your father did a lot of bad things in the old days.'

'It's all right,' Soraya said, her face breaking into an uneven smile. 'I am no longer a child. I think I am finally beginning to see my father clearly for the first time.'

Makana had debated with himself how much to tell her. What proof did he have that Hanafi had killed Alice Markham? None. He suspected that little Alice had been a casualty in the war between Bulatt and Hanafi, but he knew nothing for certain. What he did need, however, was for Soraya to see things clearly, to see her father as he really was.

'I wanted to speak to you because I feel that perhaps I am the cause of all this. Of Adil's disappearance.'

'What makes you say that?'

She began to speak and then stopped herself, turning away instead.

'What happened to that girl, by the way, the actress?'

'Mimi? I'm not sure. I hope she went to Beirut.'

Makana reached into his pocket for a cigarette. He recalled, briefly, that last time he had tried that she had stopped him. This time Soraya Hanafi seemed to have other things on her mind. There were no objections as the thin blue smoke filled the room.

'To Beirut, to start a new life? How I envy her. Isn't that strange? I know it makes no sense.' She turned her back to the window, leaning the side of her head on the glass while she surveyed him. 'You gave her some money, of course.'

'Some,' conceded Makana.

'You're good at that, aren't you? Helping people in need, I mean.'

'I don't make a habit of it, if I can help it.'

'I envy her for being able to leave it all behind and start again.' Soraya Hanafi held his gaze for a long time before she spoke again. 'I'm pregnant,' she said quietly.

Makana spilled ash on the polished window sill. The fine sediment curled like scattered petals on a sheet of grey ice.

'It doesn't show yet, but it will soon.' She attempted a smile. 'I thought you would understand, as a father.'

'It's Adil's child?'

Unable to trust her voice, Soraya gave a quick nod.

'Who else knows?'

'Nobody. I couldn't tell anyone. I knew what it would mean.'

'What would it mean?'

'My father would kill him.' She spoke matter-of-factly, as if there could be no doubt. 'Especially now that we know . . . about Adil, I mean.'

'But you told Adil himself?'

A brief nod.

'So when he disappeared, you naturally thought that he was running away from it?'

'I thought that maybe he needed a little time to get used to the idea.'

'When did all this begin? I mean, between the two of you.'

There was a long pause, and when she spoke again Soraya's eyes were closed. Her face was averted, almost as if she was addressing the window or the darkness beyond.

'It started when I was very young. He would make me do things. He made it sound like a game, like something children do together, but I knew it was wrong.' She stopped, sighing deeply before going on. 'I lived like a princess in a palace, completely isolated from the world. I suppose that in time it felt natural. In any case, it continued.'

'Isis and Osiris were brother and sister,' Makana said, stubbing his cigarette out in a large crystal bowl, presumably meant for flowers or fruit. There was nowhere else. He watched the blue wraiths of smoke circling within the glass halo.

'That doesn't make it right.' Soraya sniffed, rubbing the back of her hand across her nose like a child. 'When I found out . . . the other night, that he was my . . . half-brother, I . . .' She broke off. More than fear or terror there was self-loathing in her voice. 'What am I going to do?'

'Was that the last time you spoke to him?'

'When I told him? Yes.'

'What happened then?'

'He took a phone call. Something urgent, he said. Then he got into his car and drove off. I haven't seen him since.' Her voice cracked and subsided into gentle sobs. Makana watched her bowed head resting against the glass. He had the sense she was leading him around by the nose. What she said explained certain things. She had paid off Mimi because she thought she wasn't good enough for Adil, because no one could ever be good enough for Adil, except Soraya herself. Still, there was something about her story that didn't sit right with Makana. He couldn't say what it was, but something was wrong.

'How does all this relate to the stories you have been spreading about Hanafi Heavens?'

'Hanafi Heavens?' she said, wiping her nose.

'Yes, all this elaborate hoax about the new development that will bring in a fortune. Was that just to keep the company afloat?'

'We are on the verge of collapse.' Soraya straightened up. 'It would kill my father if he ever found out.'

'Don't worry, he won't hear of it from me.'

She dabbed at the corners of her eyes. 'What has this to do with Adil's disappearance?'

'I'm not sure.' Makana's gaze returned to the stadium below.

It was a fascinating sight, man's ego let loose with no limits. All it took was cash. What was it that history taught us about the downfall of kings? 'All I know is that Adil was working with a Russian named Vronsky.'

'He's been causing all kinds of problems for us, for months now.'

'I think he planned to use Adil to help him take control of Hanafi Enterprises.'

'Adil would never do that.'

'Wouldn't he? Why not?'

Soraya cast around her desperately, looking for an answer. She came up with the nearest thing she could find. 'He didn't need to do that, he didn't need to do anything. He had me.'

'Look, Soraya, this company appears to be in serious financial trouble. There are at least two interested parties trying to take it over. You have been telling banks, investors, sponsors, advertisers and anyone else who will listen that it will all be redeemed by the completion of the Hanafi Heavens complex, only that's far from being ready. I was out there. I saw it. No work has been done for months. It won't be ready for years.'

'Your job is to find Adil.' Her tone was suddenly much more controlled. This was the Soraya he knew, in complete command once more. 'Right now, nothing else matters. That is why my father hired you. You don't need to concern yourself with the state of the company.'

Makana mulled that one over for a while.

'What are you going to do about the child?'

'I suppose that depends.'

'On Adil?'

'On everything.'

Chapter Thirty-eight

Makana opened his eyes the next morning to find Umm Ali's cross-eyed little girl crouched beside him on the upper deck, tearing strips from a pile of fresh newspapers. She rolled the strips into balls and tossed them into the river to watch them float away. When he wasn't working, Makana was in the habit of reading the front pages of the copies spread out on the pavement by street vendors, without troubling actually to buy a paper. But these days, now that he had a little money, he had asked for the papers to be fetched every morning. Seeing he was awake she got to her feet and came over, placing the heap of newspapers carefully down beside him. Makana struggled upright in the wicker chair where he had slept, and stretched, Strangeways's report falling from his lap as he moved. His back hurt from where the Beretta had been digging into it. He had overslept. The sun was already up and rising fast. He counted out a couple of notes to pay for the papers and then added an extra one, which the girl deftly tucked away into a secret fold in her dress before vanishing down the stairs. She was cross-eyed, not stupid.

Adil Romario's disappearance had now become an affair of

state, to judge by the level of commentary. The story was gaining momentum. The press scented blood. The Hanafi DreemTeem had lost another match the previous night and one columnist suggested that perhaps Romario had been kidnapped by a rival team. 'Where is their hero in their hour of need?' ran one caption, beneath a photograph of Clemenza looking despondent after this latest humiliation. If they carried on like this, said the paper, their closest rivals would win the season without difficulty. An inside page was devoted to the honourable Mohsen Taha. His death was already being buried underneath a shroud of honourable tributes and venerable tears. A state funeral was being planned, with full honours.

Downstairs while the coffee was boiling he connected the decrepit television set and the VCR and pushed in the tape that Farag had given him, praying it would work. With a bit of aggressive nudging it did. He ran through the now familiar scene with Adil and Mimi. He recognised the view of the sea from Vronsky's villa, the palm trees in the distance. He rewound the tape as the camera panned around the room, waiting for the moment he'd remembered. He heard the coffee pot boiling over just as he froze the image on a woman standing in the background. She was dressed in what looked like a black uniform and Makana wondered if this could be Dunya, the girl Mimi had mentioned. Makana went to the kitchen to salvage his coffee and came back. The camera had picked her up by accident, but there was no mistaking the look of desperation on her face. It was the look of someone who was utterly lost.

An hour later Makana was behind the wheel of the Mercedes. If Farag's death had not come as a shock, it was because Makana had known deep down that something bad was going to happen to the man he had abandoned there. He was annoyed with himself for not having reacted sooner, though. Once on the road he felt relief that he was at least going to face Vronsky again. But how do you put things right for a man who has been fed to the sharks? It didn't make much sense. Seeing Vronsky would probably mean the end of his own understanding with Okasha, but there seemed to be no way of avoiding that now.

Traffic was slow, and it took him an hour to get out of town, but then the long open road was soothing and the wind felt cool. Grey clouds peeled off the khaki earth and drifted across the blue sky, veiling the burning eye of the sun, rendering the world a pallid, dusty monochrome. He had set off late, but still forced himself to stop at a roadside shack and eat a couple of *shwarma* sandwiches, standing up. By the time he reached El Gouna, the sun was already past the meridian and the afternoon heat was gently waning. This time there was no sign of the SSI men in their shiny suits. They were probably in their room, sleeping off a large lunch. The lobby was deserted. He walked through it, and round the outside of the complex to the arch at the far end where the high green gate marked the entrance to Vronsky's inner sanctum. When he leaned on the doorbell the release clicked and the door swung in. Just inside were the two heavies Makana remembered from his last visit, wearing sports pants and T-shirts to show off their muscles. They were also wearing neat little automatic rifles that hung on straps over their shoulders, and holsters round their waists with pistols in them. It seemed like a lot of weaponry for a sleepy resort. As they moved towards him, Makana stepped back and lifted his jacket to show that he was unarmed. He had considered bringing the Beretta with him, then decided it would serve no purpose against this kind of firepower.

'Tell Mr Vronsky he has nothing to fear from me.'

One of them kept an eye on him while the other stepped away and talked into a walkie-talkie. After a moment he motioned his hand to let Makana through.

They walked, one ahead of him and one behind, along the path that curved across the neatly trimmed lawn towards the patch of palm trees and the wooden jetty jutting out into the sea. The water was turning purple as the light settled. Vronsky was waiting at the far end, standing on the upper bridge of a big powerful motor launch. He was wearing a flowery Hawaiian shirt and white slacks. He waved a cigar in the air.

'Ah, Mr Makana, what a surprise. Come aboard and let's talk.'

Makana hesitated. The idea of stepping aboard a boat with Vronsky struck him as being not a particularly wise course of action, but he hadn't come all this way for nothing and didn't see that he had much choice. The diminutive Filipino valet smiled and held out a hand to help him down. As he took it Makana felt his own hand being seized in an astonishingly muscular grip and twisted behind his back. Something hit him hard on the back of the head and he blacked out.

When he came to, Makana was lying on the aft deck of the boat, up against the side. They were moving fast through the water and he could see Vronsky up on the bridge, his clothes buffeted by the wind. When he tried to sit up, Makana found that his hands were bound together with a well-knotted length of rope. Another loop had been slipped down over his shoulders, pinning his arms to his sides. As the boat veered in its course, he was thrown off balance, slamming against the deck. One side of him was in pain where he guessed he had landed when they had knocked him out. As far as he could see there was no one else in the boat with them. There was no sign of the diminutive valet, or the strong men.

Makana eventually managed to sit up again and made himself as comfortable as possible. He could feel the powerful engines reverberating through the wooden planks beneath him. There was nothing to do for the time being but reflect on the foolishness of his own approach. So he looked at the sky and wondered how this was going to end.

After a time he felt the noise of the engines slacken off and the vessel began to slow until it came to a halt, bobbing rather animatedly at first in the open water. Vronsky came down the ladder to the rear deck and looked Makana's bindings over before moving to the console. He pulled open a teak panel to reveal a refrigerator from which he extracted a couple of small glasses and a bottle of vodka.

'A lot of people like to complain. You know how it is.' He poured the clear liquid into the two glasses with practised ease, not spilling a drop despite the bobbing deck. 'A foreigner living like a king. People say, why him and not us? They are right, of course. But if life teaches us anything it is that life is not fair.' He smiled and drained one glass before coming over with the other. He kneeled down in front of Makana and held it out. 'I never trust a man who doesn't drink.'

'That can't leave many people around here.' Makana ached from the fall, and he was having trouble feeling his fingers. He flexed his shoulders.

Vronsky smiled and leaned forwards to remove the rope pinning Makana's arms to his sides. Then he tilted the glass to Makana's mouth so that he was forced to drink. His lips and throat burned as the alcohol made its way down. Makana rolled his cramped shoulders to get the blood moving again. He wondered if this was some kind of Russian tradition, a final act of mercy to the condemned man.

'I'd rather have a cigarette,' he said.

'A terrible habit.'

Still, Vronsky reached into Makana's shirt pocket and found the Cleopatras and the lighter. Placing one in Makana's mouth, Vronsky lit the cigarette and then stepped back towards the console. He poured himself another drink and swallowed it down like water.

'We have to make the best of what we have. Take yourself, for example. What do you have?' Vronsky looked Makana over. 'Not much. You have no home. No real profession. You manage to make ends meet by snooping into people's private affairs.' Vronsky waited, puffing on his cigar, as if expecting a response. 'The last time I saw you, I told you I would kill you if I saw you again. And yet, here you are. You possess a stubbornness which I admire. You persevere. Most people give up much too easily, but not you.' He wagged a finger at Makana as if he were a badly behaved dog. 'I could make you a very rich man,' Vronsky was saying.

'Is that what you told Farag?'

Vronsky's head dipped. 'Is that the reason you came? A sense of decency? Surely you don't really care what happens to a man like that? Frankly, I found him distasteful. You want to take a bath after shaking hands with someone like him.'

'Not any more.' Makana leaned back against the rear of the boat. With his hands still bound he reached up to remove the cigarette from his mouth.

'You think this life is some kind of a game? Do you imagine that Farag was not aware of the stakes he was playing for?'

'What I don't understand is why?'

'Why?' Vronsky leaned his head back to look at the sky, where streaks of crimson and indigo flared like banners. 'Why? Why? Why?' He picked up the bottle and his glass and moved to sit himself down on the built-in bench opposite Makana.

'The last time we spoke, you asked me about Daud Bulatt. A man most people believe to be dead, but not you. How could that be? I wondered.'

'Yet you knew he was alive, and I wondered about that.'

'I have my sources, some of them just across the border in your home country, as a matter of fact, which is where Bulatt has been hiding for the last few years. You didn't know that, I suppose?'

Makana said nothing.

'And I suppose you have no explanation of who tipped him off about the raid the other night? It wouldn't have been you, would it?'

'Why would I warn Bulatt?'

'I have no idea. Last time you came here, you told me you were working for Hanafi.'

'I still am, I think. Trying to find Adil Romario.'

'Well, good luck to you. He is the least of my concerns.'

'Is that what all the extra security is about? You're expecting Bulatt to come after you?'

'He will know where the information came from. He has ears everywhere. And when I catch him, I will make sure he tells me that and many other things.' Vronsky drained his glass and smiled, going over to refill both glasses to the rim. 'Now I'm asking myself why you returned. Was it to lead Bulatt to me? Is that why you came here today?'

'I came because I heard a story about a girl. A girl who worked here.'

Makana watched Vronsky's face carefully for any sign that he knew what he was talking about. Perhaps he was good at disguising his feelings, but he looked more bemused than anything.

'Dunya, her name was. She was fond of Adil as I understand it.'

Vronsky shrugged. 'A local girl, she came from that village you saw from my office.' He frowned. 'I would have thought that in your profession a lot must depend on asking the right question at the right moment. In this case, I am afraid you are off the mark.'

The light had now almost left the sky. A dark blue light glowed from the console. By Makana's feet was a coil of rope. Attached to one end was a large stone in a small net. He gave it a kick. Vronsky smiled.

'It doesn't take much to drown a man. Even quite a small weight is enough to tire most people sufficiently to get the job done.'

'And the sharks get rid of the evidence?'

'Not just sharks. Have you ever seen the teeth of a barracuda? They can take a man's arm off with a single bite.'

'You were using Farag to blackmail people in government, people like Mohsen Taha. You wanted the support of influential people. Farag made sure they wound up on film in compromising situations with your lady friends.'

'I encountered a lot of resistance. In some quarters there is still loyalty to Hanafi. Money simply wasn't enough. Perhaps it is some misguided sense of national pride. I thought Adil would become my Arab prince. He would step in and take over. He is a national hero and the country would accept him as a replacement for Hanafi. That was Farag's mistake, bringing Adil to me.'

'After that you didn't need Farag.'

'It was a messy, distasteful business.'

'Even for you.'

'Even for me.' Vronsky conceded a smile.

'What is there between you and Daud Bulatt?'

As he leaned forward for the bottle, Vronsky's head entered the halo of blue light. Night had fallen now and the Russian's voice rumbled through it, low and thick. 'I knew him, years ago, in Chechnya, in the hills outside Grozny. I was in command of an elite unit. Our job was to hunt down the Arabs and kill their leaders.' The last rays of daylight picked out Vronsky's eyes like lost islands in the darkness of the surrounding sea. 'Bulatt was smart and ruthless. It was a bloody war, as bad as anything I have ever seen. Worse than Afghanistan.'

'What happened?'

'We had them pinned down in a small valley. We even had air support. Mi-24 Hind helicopter gunships. They couldn't move, but still, it was like pulling fingernails. Every metre we advanced was drenched in blood. In the end a handful of them, including Bulatt, managed to escape higher up into the mountains. We thought they had gone. But they hadn't. They waited two weeks. When our ground forces withdrew they came back down and cut the throats of every man, woman and child in the nearby village. They thought someone there had betrayed them.' Vronsky drained another glass of vodka. 'They had no business being there. It wasn't their fight, but these were real fanatics. They didn't care about the people. They were just looking for a cause to die for.'

'He got away from you.'

'Twice. The second time he wasn't so lucky. That's how he lost his arm.' Vronsky read the expression on Makana's face. 'You didn't know about that? Interesting. Anyway, we captured two of his men. We cut the tongue out of one of them in order to get the other one to talk. He did, of course. Led us right to them. We had Bulatt surrounded.'

'This was what . . . three, four years ago?'

'February 1995.'

'Who were they, the two men?'

'Arab mujahideen. The Islamic Regiment.'

'You killed them, I suppose.'

'We let them go. Bulatt killed them when he learned they had betrayed him, but by then the trap was sprung.' Vronsky leaned his head back to gaze up at the stars. 'A mortar shell landed up above in a gully as they were trying to make their escape. There was a landslide, lots of rocks falling. A large boulder spun down and crushed his arm. By then it was late. We couldn't risk moving up in the dark, so we dug ourselves in to wait for first light. We didn't know he was trapped. He knew that at first light we would come for him. You know what he did?' Vronsky's voice was so low it was almost lost in the lull of the sea. 'He did what a wolf does when it is caught in a trap. It gnaws off its own limb. Bulatt cut his arm off with a bayonet. He cut through the flesh and sinew and amputated his left arm at the elbow.'

'That must take some courage.'

Vronsky's glass of vodka rested forgotten in his hand. 'He didn't cry out, not once. We would have heard. You know, in a valley like that, all sound is amplified.' His eyes sought out Makana's in the gloom. 'You can't fight that kind of madness. You can't reason with it. You have to exterminate it.'

The boat rocked lightly from side to side in the water. The lights along the coast were a sparse necklace of tarnished diamonds draped across the dark expanse of inland shadow. Vronsky got to his feet, somewhat unsteadily, and leaned over to attach the end of the towrope to Makana's bound wrists. The boat gave an unexpected lurch. Makana seized the opportunity and kicked out to scissor Vronsky's legs from under him. The

Russian came down heavily, the bottle smashing with a metallic tinkle. Makana rolled to his feet. Vronsky was on one knee by then. He was breathing heavily and there was a thick trail of blood running down his right arm. Makana hoped this might disable the man somewhat, since he was clearly the stronger and fitter of them. If this was the case, the Russian certainly didn't betray it. His eyes showed the steady calm of a man who is in complete control, of one who has killed with his bare hands before and is preparing to kill again.

Casting round him for some kind of weapon, Makana lifted the lifebelt off its hook against the side of the boat. It was the only thing within reach. There wasn't much room to manoeuvre. Vronsky reached down and seized the neck of the broken bottle, its jagged edge glinting in the console's blue light. As he lunged, Makana ducked away and then swung the lifebelt to hit him full in the face. The bottle clattered from Vronsky's hand as he staggered back towards the console. Makana stepped sideways to reach for it. As he bent down, Vronsky reached for the throttle and thrust both levers forward. The engine, which had been idling, surged into action and Makana was sent reeling backwards against the aft railing. Vronsky didn't give him a chance to recover. He stepped forward and Makana felt a heavy weight hit him full on. Then he was toppling over the railing and into the water.

Chapter Thirty-nine

The sea hit him hard and cold. Then he was sinking into nothing. The stone hanging from his wrists pulled him down. He struggled, the lifebelt wrenched from his hands in the fall. He kicked and pawed at the water. Then the rope attached to his wrists began to tauten. He seized hold of it with his hands as he was dragged along in the wake of the launch. The weight at his wrists kept him beneath the surface. As the boat gathered speed, Makana knew that he would drown soon unless he could get his head out of the water. He managed to tighten his grip and drag himself upwards until he could roll over and fill his lungs with air. He caught a brief glimpse of the running lights on the boat through the fluorescent glow of its wake. Almost immediately, he felt a change in its momentum. The boat was turning and he was being propelled sideways, out of the wake, swinging in a wide arc. What was Vronsky up to?

Makana found out soon enough. He felt himself strike something hard in the water. He would have broken his ribs except that the speed he was travelling at lifted him up and sent him skimming over the shallow reef. He felt the sharp pricks against his skin as his clothes were ripped by the coral. It was like being flayed by a thousand tiny razor blades. The sting of the salt water told him he was bleeding. The stone thumped against his chest, knocking the breath out of his lungs, then he was out in the deep water again and his weighted wrists were pulling him down into the darkness below. He felt his head spin and knew he was about to pass out. The rope slackened somewhat and he tugged at it to lift his head above water again. The boat was turning. It began to gather speed again, and soon they were once more running headlong towards the reef.

This time he was more scared, anticipating the blow but not knowing when it would come, trying to protect his head. Once again he felt the boat swing away and once again he felt himself begin to slip sideways, his body hurtling over the wake of the boat, bouncing hard against the water. This time when he struck the reef he felt coral breaking off against his bones, felt his skin tearing as he struggled to try to gain purchase. If he could wrap the rope around something, he thought, lock it into a crevice . . . anything. He pressed his wrists downwards, hoping the friction would wear through the rope, then he was off the reef and back into deep water. His whole body felt mangled and broken. Already he had swallowed a lot of sea water and Makana knew he was tiring and that he would not last much longer.

The third time around he felt something give in the rope that bound his wrists. Something had cut through it, or the water had loosened the knots. He pulled on the line, using the last of his strength to try and yank himself enough slack to work his hands free. Again he began to sink as the boat slowed. He clawed at the line with his fingers, aware of the darkness rising around him. But this time something was different. The line kept coming, even as the sound of the engine receded. Vronsky had cut him free.

Makana wrestled frantically with the loop of rope that

immobilised his hands, bound him to the stone that was pulling him down. As he sank deeper and deeper into the water, he used his teeth, tearing at the knot until finally he felt it loosen. Kicking his legs, he felt the weight fall away and his body rising. His head broke the surface. He gasped for air and felt the pain in his lungs ease.

As he looked around to find his bearings, Makana saw that his only point of reference was the line of twinkling lights which marked the shoreline. He was out in the middle of the sea. The only sign of Vronsky's launch was a dwindling fluorescence in the distance, then nothing but dark water. He wondered how much he was actually bleeding. He tried to remember how little blood sharks could detect. Was it a drop of blood in a million parts of sea water? That sounded ridiculous and he hoped he was wrong. How far away did they have to be? he wondered. The temperature of the water was beginning to make him shiver. Either he could start swimming towards the shore, or he could wait until his legs cramped up and he drowned that way.

Makana had never really been a strong swimmer. As a child he had splashed about in the river with his friends like all the other boys, but no one had ever taught him to swim properly. But he had no choice now. He began to kick with his feet and stroke the water aside, telling himself he needed to conserve his energy. The shore didn't seem to be getting any closer. As he swam his mind was turning back to the case. He was fairly sure now that Vronsky had killed Adil, probably the same way he'd killed Farag. Why, he couldn't say. Did Adil turn against Vronsky, refuse to do his bidding?

Rolling on to his back to give his muscles a rest, Makana stared up at the stars and marvelled at how clear they were out here, so far away from human habitation. It was remarkable, just how many there were. They felt comforting, despite his situation. They took him back to his life with Muna, the happiest time he could remember, when the world had been simple. Sitting out in the yard in the evenings, watching the sky revolve slowly around them. It seemed like another world.

He had been swimming for what felt like hours when he suddenly had the sense that he was no longer alone. Within the darkness around him a deeper, darker shadow was moving in the water. Reducing his movements to a minimum Makana stayed afloat, kicking as lightly as he could. The sea seemed to be alive around him, rising and falling like the breathing of a great animal. He consoled himself with the thought that it would be over in a minute. That was all it would take. A wave struck him in the face with the force of a hard slap, shaking him from his reverie. He began to kick harder again, cautiously at first, expecting the darkness to reach out and swallow him every time he extended an arm, then more firmly, determined to get to shore. His heart stopped when his hand finally struck something hard. He realised it was the reef. Dragging himself over it, he felt the temperature of the water rise and knew he was in the shallows. A few minutes later he collapsed on the beach, gasping for breath. The world looked different. The palm trees towering over him were still. He got to his feet and looked about him.

In the stark glare of a battery of floodlights, the high walls of The Big Blue stood out against the night sky as vividly as the whitewashed cinema screens Makana recalled from his childhood. He could see Vronsky's villa. Makana glanced back at the sea and heaved a sigh of relief. It was good to feel the earth beneath his feet. His body felt bruised and swollen, and he knew that if he stopped moving his muscles would seize up. He forced himself to move quickly, breaking into an awkward jog.

Approaching the complex along the beach, he was surprised that none of the guards appeared to be in sight, that he was able to get so close without being challenged.

There was a figure up ahead of him in the shadows, walking briskly along the path, away from the villa, heading for the same gap in the fence, the arched green door. The man paused, hearing something. He stopped and glanced back. Makana recognised him. It was the man who had been haunting his dreams, the man he had once glimpsed on a street in Cairo. The man in the beige chequered shirt. He looked at Makana and then turned away and increased his pace. Something was wrong. Makana called out and raised a hand. In the instant he did so there was a bright flash over to his right, coming from the direction of Vronsky's villa. A hand thumped into his shoulder, lifting him off his feet and into the air. Then everything went black.

The explosion was like a light going on and off in quick succession, a bulb exploding in the back of his head. The blast threw him a good ten metres. Then he was gasping for air, engulfed in a thick cloud that swirled about him, filling his lungs and choking him. After a time he became aware of the intense heat on his right side. He managed to open his eyes and turned to look in the direction of what remained of Vronsky's villa. It had been almost completely destroyed. The side facing the sea and the upper floor had been ripped right off, as though a giant claw had reached down from the sky and gouged them away. There were shouts and screams of horror coming from the hotel behind him. People were running, calling frantically to one another. Thick smoke billowed out from a fire that licked angrily from the black, cavernous mouth.

Makana rolled over and found himself lying beside the headless torso of the Filipino valet, still in his white jacket. A wave of nausea swept over him as he pushed himself away and fell back on to the grass. His head was ringing and he felt dazed. Everything around him was fuzzy and indistinct. His legs felt as if they were made of rubber, but somehow he managed to stand. He staggered towards the gate leading to the main resort area. A crowd was milling about on the other side of the fence. There were screams of panic and cries in a variety of languages asking what was going on. They parted pretty quickly when they saw the state he was in. Some of the staff appeared, and he fought off their efforts to help him, pointing back the way he had come. 'Help them,' he shouted, 'help them.' But he couldn't hear his own words. His mouth was filled with acid bile and he gulped down mouthfuls of air and then bent over and threw up.

He cleared the reception area in time to see a waiting car pulling away in a hurry, exhaust fluttering in the red glow of the tail lights. It looked like there were two men inside. Makana was sure one of them was the man in the beige shirt. Farag's Mercedes was where he had left it and the keys were miraculously still in his pocket.

His hands were sore and bleeding. They kept sticking to the wheel. His clothes were soaked through and his entire body ached from the salt and lacerations. Makana shivered as he drove with his lights off, humming through the dark, eyes pinned to the twin red darts of the tail lights up ahead. They went south, further down the coast. His head throbbed and his eyesight was blurred. The night air that blew through the open window was cool and dry. There was nothing else he needed to think about apart from those lights ahead. After about fifteen minutes they began to slow. They were approaching a junction. No houses or buildings of any kind in sight. They turned inland and headed west.

Away from the coast it was easier to see without lights. The open landscape seemed to absorb the glow from the distant stars. Makana's eyes could make out the edges of the road he had to follow. He let the other car get a good distance away, memorising the curves it made to help him see the road. There was nothing out here, nothing but blackness. No signs of human habitation of any kind, just the dim silhouette of hills rising in the distance. The road curved on, rising gently towards the looming shadow of a jagged ridge. A large boulder blocked his view of the road ahead as he went around a long curve. When he came out on the other side the car ahead appeared to have vanished. The road was deserted. No lights in sight.

Makana slowed, allowing the Mercedes to glide to a halt. He cut the engine and climbed out. He stood in the middle of the deserted road listening to the silence. Beyond those hills was the Nile and the Valley of the Kings. Then he caught sight of something. A brief glint. Headlights brushing against stone, like white paint being splashed across a canvas in the dark. It was off to the right. He started the engine again and nosed along the road until he found the rough track leading up to the right. Makana swung the wheel and eased the big car off the road.

The uneven track twisted and turned, winding up into the hills. The rocky walls drew in around him as the track led him deeper and deeper into the shadows. A few minutes later he came around a bend and saw a gently sloping ramp leading at an angle on to a circular platform that jutted out from the rockface. On the top of the promontory a large building perched on the hillside facing towards the sea.

The Mercedes coasted to a halt, engine off. There was no sign of the car he had been following, no sign of anything or anyone. No lights showed in the building. It looked abandoned, a toothless face with windows for eyeholes. Makana made sure the car's interior light was off and then clicked open the door, acutely aware of how sound travelled, echoing from the walls around him.

He didn't hear them come up behind him until it was too late. A slight crunch of stone underfoot and then the cold barrel of a gun was pressed against the nape of his neck. The muzzle prodded him to move forward. The gravel crunched under his feet as he climbed the track towards the empty building. It looked like a hospital of some kind. The hollows of the empty windows stood open like invitations. A flashlight clicked quickly on and off. So far no one had spoken a word. Hands seized his arms to steer him up the steps and into the building. Their footsteps rang hollowly through the ruined shell as Makana found himself propelled along. They led him deeper, along corridors where the flashlight bounced back off walls that closed in. The darkness shifted around him. Walls gave way, opening into rooms to left and right, shadows moving fluidly across them like malevolent spirits. The air was damp and cold, rich with organic rot. His shoulder, already raw from the reef, bumped into a wall, then he was bounced down a set of stairs, along a narrow corridor and finally into a room, where he was sent sprawling on to a heap of rubble. The flashlight flicked around the room and then clicked off. The footsteps withdrew. He heard a door slam and a bolt being shoved home.

The fear he felt then was a physical sensation. A memory locked into his body from another time. He had to fight the rising panic. Already he felt the claustrophobia that still haunted his dreams, brought him awake in a heaving sweat. It was all too familiar. The weight on his chest, the sense that he was suffocating. It had been so long ago, and yet here it was, coming back to him as vividly as if it had been yesterday. The unbearable physical memory of being imprisoned, locked away. His breath came in short quick stabs, his heart racing. He forced himself to take deeper breaths, fighting the impulse to scream. I've done this before, he told himself. I can do it again.

Makana crouched on his heels in the dark, drawing himself into a ball, taking up as little space as possible, making the room around him expand. He couldn't tell if the darkness extended above his head for hundreds of metres, or whether it stopped just in front of his face. It was as if he had slipped beneath the surface of this world into another, subterranean plane of existence that was wired into his memory. His whole body was shaking uncontrollably now. He had been shivering with cold in the car. Now sweat poured from him. There was no point in fighting it, he realised. It was coming to carry him back.

Out of the darkness, it was coming.

Chapter Forty

Help me! Please help me!

A ghost house. He knew it as soon as he opened his eyes. He woke up in his own filth, the filth of others who had passed through these narrow walls before him. The air too thick to breathe, fetid with the acrid reek of piss and shit. His own body waste mixed with that of countless, faceless others who had disappeared before him. This was where they became nameless. This was where they vanished. This was where men were reduced to nameless creatures, without families, or hopes, or beliefs. Their bodies scraped across these walls as they were pushed out of this world.

Save me, Baba!

He couldn't let go, he told himself. Not just yet. Heaving himself to his feet, he hurled his weight at the door, feeling the jolt of pain as the metal thumped back into his shoulder like a drum. Barely enough strength to stand up. 'Let her go!' he screamed, over and over, until his lungs burned. Then he fell back, silent, pressing his ear to the door, straining to hear.

Baba!

'Nasra!' he called. Silence but for the flies crowding round his face, trying to get into his mouth, buzzing at his nostrils, his eyes. His ears were alert to the slightest sound. A locust's wings. A leaf spinning on water. A cough, a sigh. Any change in the air that would signify that his daughter was safe, alive. Exhausted, his legs buckled and he sank down to the ground, back resting in the pool of filth. When they hosed out this room all trace of him would be gone, he thought. This is all I am, all that remains of me.

What were they doing to her? he wondered. His eyes scoured the wall of darkness for any crack, a hairline fracture that might promise light.

Baba, help me, please!

Night and day. At times he knew the voice was just in his head, screaming at him from somewhere inside, a part of him he could not identify. But then he would come awake in the early hours with a gasp, as if someone had poured ice-cold water over him. The days passed in a blur, shadows closing in on him from all sides. If he pressed his head down to the bottom of the door he could feel the cool night breeze brushing his face. A narrow slit, no more than a couple of centimetres. It was all he had to hold on to. A moment. A breath of air. A tiny increment of hope that told him life went on out there. That people lived and talked and laughed and loved. It was important to believe that there was more than this. Lying there with his face in the filth. The scrabbling of beetles and ants crawling over him. Worms wriggled, coiled over his eyes. A mosquito buzzed in his ears like a diesel engine. Just a single breath of air. It was all he needed to know this would end.

'Nasra! Nasra!' he called over and over. Silence.

At times there were other voices. Whispers coming through the door. Low and persistent. A babbling brook that seemed to be trying to warn him. But what were they saying?

Flinging himself to the ground, wriggling, trying to slide under the door to get closer to them, to hear what they were saying, convinced that they held the key to his fate.

'What? What is it?'

He slept against the wall, propped up against it for protection, feeling the plaster rub off against his skin, trying to dig himself inside. He would be woken at all hours. The door would open and the men would enter and start beating him. So many there wasn't room for them to lift their sticks. Heavy boots thudded into his ribs. Other times water would crash over him. Sometimes it was not water but the toilet bucket, the stench so powerful it made him gag, his eyes stinging.

Days passed like decades. Centuries, it felt like, his life withering into bile and then dust. Fever made his eyeballs ache, his head throb. He vomited when there was nothing left inside him, a thin green trickle running down his chin. He floated in a state of suspended animation, no longer sure of who or what he was. A cockroach? A beetle?

Some days, just to remind him of what the open air was like, they let him out. He hated that. It disoriented him. It was a taste of freedom, a reminder of the power they had to take it away again, any time they pleased. When they pushed him back into the cell, he would kick and scream. The walls yawned open to draw him in, sucking him back down into the waiting darkness and filth.

One night they flung him in and he stumbled. Something unfamiliar was occupying the floor. He fell silent, his heart telling him what he could not bear, that it was his daughter. Frantically, he fumbled for another explanation. Panic fought the logic which told him that the body was too big. A man's arm. A man's body. Not a child's. *Alhamdoulilah*. He wept with relief as he continued his investigation. The man's face had softened where his teeth had caved in. Cheekbone and nose broken. Makana's fingers found the halo of white hair around the crown of his head. Professor Manute. The man he had tried to save. Would he have lived if Makana had not intervened?

The rusty bolt squeaked itself open to reveal light. His eyes tried to adjust. Eventually, he saw dusty walls, the leaves of a tree in the distance. A world whose existence he had forgotten. Still, he did not move. He knew this game. A familiar outline appeared in the doorway.

'Bring him out.'

The cell shrank suddenly as two men squeezed in, grabbed hold of him and hauled him up, stumbling over the dead professor, and out, to dump him like an old mattress in the sun.

'Clean him off.'

A hiss of water stuttering in warning from a hosepipe before it hit him, making him gasp in shock. So cold. So clean. He scrabbled about, tumbling this way and that in his effort to get away. Then silence. Drops fell from his shivering head to the muddy pool that had formed beneath him. In that brown mirror he saw something resembling a monster which could only be himself. Another shadow clouded the sky.

'What are we to do with you?'

Makana recognised the voice without raising his head. Mek Nimr squatted beside him.

'You're a dangerous man, Makana. You know why? Because you put yourself before the common good. You think you are above the rest of us, but no one is more important than the salvation of the nation, not even you.'

'Salvation?' gasped Makana. 'Is that what you call this?'

Mek Nimr smiled. 'We're the same, you and me. The

difference is that you married a woman from the educated classes. That doesn't make you any better than me. But you've always behaved as if you were superior.'

Makana managed to lift his head. 'We're not the same.'

'You lack humility. You will thank me for this one day, for saving you from yourself. You would have wound up an atheist like that poor old professor, thinking that his learning put him above the rest of us. Is that what you want to do, corrupt good Muslims with your atheism?'

'I want to see my wife, my daughter.'

'In good time. Patience.'

With that Mek Nimr turned and walked away. The men who had brought him out of the little cell helped Makana to stand. His feet were swollen and he collapsed, seeking the ground again. It was too painful to stand. A large sergeant he remembered from a lifetime ago took pity on him.

'Carry him over there and put him in the shade. Give him something to drink.'

They put a hand under him on either side and dragged him across the yard to a bench set against the wall of an office. No sooner had they set him on it than he keeled over, collapsing to the floor like a sack of dates.

'Get him up again,' ordered the sergeant.

How long did he spend sitting there, the stench still on him? In his skin, his hair, his pores, inside his very being?

'We're going to take you home now,' said the sergeant, leaning over him, close to the wall, as he spat a long brown stream of tobacco against it. 'But bear in mind that he won't be satisfied until he is finished with you.'

Makana tried to turn his head, to look up, but the sun blinded him. The big shadow passed over him like wings and was gone.

He barely registered what was going on as they drove him across town, pushed him from an unmarked car into the road. Stumbling along the uneven street, his bare, broken feet shuffled over stones and shards of glass, sheep's jawbones filled with teeth, rusty cans. Neighbours stood in their doorways watching him go by. Everyone knew him. They drew back. Doors closed quietly. He didn't blame them. If a police inspector was not immune then who was safe? Still, the news reached his house before he did. Muna rushed out into the street. She threw herself at him, disregarding whoever might be watching, and led him inside.

'We thought you were dead.' Her eyes were red and puffy, her face drawn. He barely recognised his own wife.

'Our daughter . . . where is she?'

'She's fine,' sobbed Muna. 'She's asleep.'

'I must see her . . . now,' he said.

Taking his hand, she led him like a stranger through his own house, shuffling along, his feet leaving a bloody trail behind him on the veranda tiles. He didn't believe Nasra was going to be there. Convinced that somehow Mek Nimr had taken her, spirited her through the walls, back to the cell Makana had just vacated. But there she was, stretched out on the bed in their room, as if she was flying.

'She's fine,' murmured Muna soothingly. 'She's fine.'

That was when he broke down, sobbing helplessly in her arms.

'We have to get out of here,' he said finally.

'Why? What are you talking about?'

There was nothing here that he wanted to keep. It was all coming down around him now. Nothing that couldn't be better the next time.

'It's not safe for us.'

'What do you mean?' she whispered, stroking his forehead.

'Get as far away as possible, before they come for me again.'

'Go where? Why should they come again?'

'They'll come.'

As if in response to their fears, the telephone began to ring on the bedside table. Makana saw the terror in her eyes. He wished he could protect her, but he couldn't see how. Extricating himself from her arms, he rolled upright and placed his feet on the floor. The pain brought fresh tears. He stared at the telephone but couldn't bring himself to reach for it. Muna stepped past him and lifted the receiver, putting it to her ear.

'Hello? Hello?' She held it out. 'There's no one there.'

Makana stared into her eyes. They wouldn't leave his family alone. Not now, not ever.

'We have to go, now,' he said, getting to his feet and throwing open a cupboard. 'Get Nasra ready, whatever she needs.'

'But where? Where will we go?'

Makana stopped to think. 'North. We can get across the border to Egypt and head for Cairo.'

He took his spare pistol from the locked drawer beside the bed, a Tokarev 7.62mm automatic. He checked it was loaded. Then he remained still for a long time, just sitting there staring at the blunt-nosed weapon. If the time came, would he be able to do it? he wondered. Surely ending it all would be better than subjecting Muna and Nasra to whatever horrors were imagined for them?

'We're ready.'

He looked up and saw Muna standing in the doorway, the child cradled in her arms. She saw the gun and he looked away before she could see what was written in his eyes. Standing, he tucked it into his holdall before leading the way out. The car was parked on the other side of the narrow alleyway. An old

Volkswagen Passat, its bodywork bruised and scarred by count-less previous owners. He placed the suitcases in the back, the canvas holdall under his feet in the front.

'You drive,' he said. What made him choose not to drive? Was it the pain in his feet, or the fear that he might pass out, still weak after his ordeal? Or because that way he could keep an eye on what was going on around them, and then if he had to use the gun, both his hands would be free?

The streets were quiet. With curfew hour fast approaching the few vehicles left on the road were making their way home as swiftly as possible. They would have to hurry if they were to make it, but if they were stopped just after curfew they would probably be let through as last-minute stragglers. The guards on the bridge were regular army and despised the new militias. He still had his identity card if there was any doubt. The bridge was the noose through which the thread of their freedom passed. Beyond that the borders of the city were porous. They could slip out into the open emptiness and nothing could stop them after that.

The approach to the bridge was deserted. As the Volkswagen curled along the long open road Makana spotted the soldiers casually moving towards the centre of the tarmac, guns slung over their shoulders. One of them raised a hand. Makana stuck his out of the window and waved back.

'Slow down,' he said.

Muna began to panic. 'They're not going to let us go,' she whimpered. 'They will kill us!'

Makana glanced over at her. Muna's eyes were wide with fear.

'It'll be all right. We're just a family getting home late.'

They slowed and came to a halt. A couple of soldiers ambled slowly forwards. They were still setting up the barrier for the night, rolling oil drums into place in slow, lazy arcs, turning them on their rims, letting them fall into place. Then Makana saw something else. In the shadows beyond the arc of lights tracing the bridge were other shapes. Objects that his eyes slowly made out. The end of a vehicle. Two pick-ups, men moving around them like smoke in the fluid darkness. A trap, he realised, too late. He was reaching under his seat for the automatic when Muna gave a cry of panic and stamped her foot down on the accelerator. The old Volkswagen puttered and struggled, whining up the incline, trying to gain speed. She ground it up another gear. One soldier rushed forward, stepping into their path, only to go spinning off as the front wing brushed him aside, the wing mirror splintering.

They had almost reached the top of the bridge's arch. On the other side the road would be clear with nothing to stop them sliding down into the deserted, unlit streets, to vanish into the soft darkness beyond. The army lorry appeared out of nowhere. A huge Magirus Deutz lumbering up the incline towards them. The highbeams came on, blinding them both. Muna wrenched the wheel to the left. Makana heard a pop as one of the old, worn tyres gave out, then they bounced up the kerb and struck the railings. He was flung sideways, against the passenger door. It gave and he flew out, hitting the road hard. There were shouts and a siren, the thunder of boots approaching. His head was ringing, his sight blurry. He blinked furiously to clear his vision, scrabbling about for his gun. Then his sight cleared and he stopped.

The Volkswagen had climbed up over the thin metal railings which had bowed outwards, bending down towards the river like long, trembling stalks. The car was perched with its bonnet in the air, the front wheels still spinning. Through the open door

Makana could see his wife, stretched out across the passenger seat. Blood traced a line across her face. Extending one hand towards her, he struggled to get up. Muna lifted her head. She was reaching for him, trying to speak. What? What was she saying? He dragged himself over the road towards the car. Ten little fingers appeared in the rear window, reaching up, then his daughter's face as she raised herself to look out, dazed and bewildered by what was happening.

'Nasra!' he called, urgency increasing his efforts, trying to get to his feet.

It happened very slowly, or so it appeared in his mind, the countless times it had played itself out in his head over the years. The car gave a lurch that seemed to begin somewhere in the region of his heart. The metal bars groaned as the railings gave the final few millimetres which spelled the difference between life and death. Then the battered old Volkswagen began to tip, like an enormous set of scales. Makana flung himself forwards, but he was too late. He let out a cry that was lost in the rushing sound of the air as the car somersaulted through it, slowly turning over before plunging down towards the dark water. It struck the surface with a sound like a giant door crashing shut.

Then he was at the railings. Below he could make out the frothing water erupting in glassy bubbles from underneath the upturned chassis. Hands seized him from behind and pulled him back. He struggled, finding the strength to hold his assailants off for a brief moment as the car sank out of sight in the river. Kicking and punching, he tried to rip himself free and throw himself into the water after his family. But there were too many of them. They pinned him down. No matter how hard he struggled, he was unable to do anything but open his mouth and roar.

'Let him up,' said Mek Nimr eventually.

They hauled Makana to his feet, dragged him back to the railings. There was nothing to be seen. The dark water had closed over the car, over Muna and little Nasra. Like a veil falling over his life, all that remained was the smooth swirling black surface. Nothing more.

'I'm going to let you go,' said Mek Nimr quietly. 'Do you understand?' He turned and pointed off into the distance, beyond the bridge, the low houses, the streetlights like glowing matchsticks and the endless darkness.

'I'm doing this for old times' sake.' He paused. 'Go,' he said. 'And don't come back.'

Makana tumbled, fell, stood, fell again, got up and carried on. A solitary figure, already lost in the dusty road that lay ahead of him, limping down off the bridge, into the dark web of night that settled over him like a cloak. He never looked back.

Chapter Forty-one

A flashlight clicked on, the beam playing up and down, allowing Makana to see that he was actually in a fairly big room. The light was reflected back from walls still covered by white ceramic tiles. Here and there the broken shaft of a pipe stuck out at an odd angle. He was in an old bathroom, in an institution of some kind, he guessed.

'They used to bring the madmen here, back in the days when anyone cared what happened to madmen. Now they just let them run riot in the streets.'

The man's voice rumbled out of the cavernous gloom. In the glow of the flashlight's beam Makana could make out a solitary figure moving around the room. The reflected light revealed a gaunt silhouette. He appeared to be wearing a combat jacket over loose-fitting clothes. A tracksuit. The left arm of the jacket was tucked into a pocket. The beam moved, settling on a corner of the room. Shadows lengthened and stretched about it.

'You know who I am?'

'Daud Bulatt.'

The man came closer now, squatting on his heels in front of Makana. After playing the light over himself, he set the big torch down on the ground so that the beam rose up to spread across the ceiling like a fan. Makana could just about make out the other man's face.

'Looks like you managed to find me after all.'

'I was at the hotel when the bomb went off. I followed your men.'

'To act so impulsively, a man must be either very brave or reckless. Which one are you?'

'Does it matter?'

Bulatt tilted the beam to settle it on Makana's face.

'I feel as though I know you somehow.'

'You're the one who was following me?'

'Not myself. My men watched you.'

'One of them took a shot at me.'

'And you broke the ribs of another. That would make us even, don't you think?'

'Why the interest in me?'

'We weren't sure how much you knew.' Bulatt stood again and prowled around Makana in the dark. 'We have some mutual acquaintances.'

'What acquaintances?' Makana strained his neck to follow his movements.

'All in good time, my friend. Now tell me, what was your business with the Russian?'

'I am trying to find someone,' Makana croaked, his throat dry. 'Your sister's boy.'

'You're wasting your time, Adil is dead. Another good reason for the Russian to die.'

'You think Vronsky killed him?'

'What do you think? Adil went to see Vronsky. No one has seen him since.'

Bulatt moved away, leaving the lamp where it rested on the ground, the beam aimed up at the ceiling. Makana listened to him moving through the shadows, the sound of his feet stepping carefully over the uneven ground.

'You've been asking a lot of questions about me.' The voice receded into the darkness. Makana craned his head painfully, trying to follow it. 'Did Hanafi hire you to find me?'

'Hanafi thought you were dead. Everyone did.'

'Except you.'

'Adil found out the truth about who his father was. It didn't come from Hanafi. It could only have come from someone else, someone who was there back in the old days.'

Bulatt was silent for a time. Makana listened but could hear nothing. When the other man spoke again, his voice was so close he appeared to be standing right behind Makana.

'Years ago you tried to have Hanafi killed,' said Makana quietly.

'I was unlucky. The men I hired to do the job failed. Hanafi was too smart for me.'

'Did Hanafi take Alice Markham hostage?'

'She was his insurance policy. If I tried anything else, he would kill the girl. Not that I cared about her. I didn't even know her.'

'Liz never told you she was pregnant?'

'After she left this country, I thought I would never see her again. Some men went after foreign women like her, hoping they would marry them and take them to live in Europe. But I didn't care about that. I had a life of my own.' It might have been his imagination, but Makana thought he detected a touch of sentiment in Bulatt's voice nevertheless. Perhaps there had been more to his relationship with Liz Markham than simply a holiday romance.

'What did you do when you heard Hanafi had survived?'

'What could I do? I gave myself up, went to prison. Hanafi couldn't touch me there.' Bulatt's voice hardened once again at the memory. 'Inside, I realised the error of my ways. I made mistakes when I was young. I lived a bad life. I drank and chased women. I used to hang around the hotels for fun. The foreign girls were easy targets. They fell to us like doves.'

'Just like Liz Markham.'

'Yes,' said Bulatt slowly, 'just like her.'

'Why did you kill her then?'

'What makes you think it was me?' Bulatt looked down at the automatic held loosely in his hand.

'Who else?'

'Who was interested in finding me? Ask yourself that.'

'She was asking questions about you.'

'She was harmless. All she cared about was her daughter. Our daughter. Actually, if there is anyone to blame for her death, it is you.' Bulatt looked Makana in the eye as he went on: 'They saw her talking to you.'

'They?' But Makana already knew the answer before he asked the question. 'You mean Colonel Serrag?'

'Serrag was on Hanafi's payroll back in the old days when he was an inspector. He knows that I know that. He wants me more than anything in the world. He thought Liz would lead him to me, so he tortured and killed her.'

Makana closed his eyes. Suddenly the pain and the fatigue brought down a weariness on him that he couldn't fight.

Bulatt's voice loomed nearer. 'This is not about revenge, Makana. It's war. Our war to rid this country of the *kufar*, those infidels who have infected the Islamic world with their corruption.'

'Sounds like a nice speech, but I thought that all ended in Luxor?'

'Nothing ends. The war will not end until we are victorious, *inshallah*.'

The words sounded rehearsed, as if Bulatt had spoken them thousands of times before. He no longer needed to believe them. He stood up again and moved away.

'When Adil first came to me, I was prepared to kill him. I hated Hanafi so much.'

'But Adil was your sister's child.'

'I came up with a sweeter way of taking my revenge.'

'So when Adil came to seek you out in Khartoum, you decided not to kill him?'

'Adil was a lost soul. An illegitimate child who never knew his real father. He spent his whole life trying to please people. He played football for them, like a trained monkey. Then he convinced himself he could become a film star. All he wanted was to belong.'

'And you offered him a way?'

'I told him the truth about who his father was. I showed him how we could take our revenge and take over the company. We would destroy Hanafi.'

'You set up the Green Nakhala Reserve Fund to start buying back Hanafi's debt. In return Adil told you about Vronsky.'

'Things became complicated, mostly because Adil changed his mind. He was sentimental, couldn't bring himself to get even with the old man. He tried to persuade Hanafi to run away with him, on a safari or something, then he just disappeared.'

'That's why you came back here, for revenge?'

There was a slight shifting of weight as Bulatt moved round to squat in front of Makana again, his face looming out of the dark into the cone of light, thin and dark, bisected by hard planes.

'This is about more than personal revenge. Hanafi is a symbol of everything that is wrong with this country. If Hanafi Enterprises collapsed it would bring down the national bank. There would be an economic crisis.'

And crisis would lead people back to the mosques for assistance. Makana considered the possibility that Daud Bulatt was a very disturbed man. He was certainly very dangerous. It didn't matter to him that the majority of people in Egypt cared little for the Islamist militants. They only wanted to work, to feed their families.

'You want to make the whole country pay.'

'"Let evil be rewarded with like evil."'

'"But he that forgives and seeks reconciliation shall be rewarded by God,"' said Makana, completing the quotation. Bulatt smiled, his face still illuminated.

'The old man said you were smart.'

'Old Yunis?'

'In the old days he was a poet and a painter. A strange figure. But like the rest of us, he needed money to support his cause. So he turned his hand to forgery. He's good. One of the best in the business. Did he show you his work?'

'He showed me a scar you gave him.'

Bulatt chuckled. 'He was a lot tougher in the old days, and he used to drink. Did he tell you that? No, I didn't think so. Now, he says he's not part of our fight, but old ties are difficult to break.'

Bulatt leaned closer and lowered his voice to a whisper.

'In Tora they placed me in a hole in the ground. A shallow grave. I lay on my back and could not move. My arms touched the sides. My nose pressed against the cover. When they closed me in it was like being buried alive. I told myself that I was already dead, that I was in the ground awaiting Judgement Day, the end of time, and that on that day I would rise up with the dead and watch those who had condemned me burn in eternal hellfire.'

'Why are you telling me this?' asked Makana.

'You are a man who has known prison. Some men are broken by the experience. I grew stronger. I think you did too.'

'How do you know that? The old man didn't know I was in prison.'

'No, that came from an old friend of yours.' Bulatt was silent for a moment. The metal in his hand flashed dully in the light. 'You haven't forgotten Mek Nimr, have you?'

Makana was silent for a long time. 'No,' he said finally. 'I haven't forgotten.'

'Your country gave me a home these last three years. We were scorned here, treated like outcasts, after all the sacrifices we had made.' Daud Bulatt grunted and rocked back on his heels. 'When I came out of prison I was a changed man. I wanted to put my former life behind me. I wanted to cleanse myself, to do what was right. I wanted to defend Muslims everywhere in the world. First in Bosnia. After that Chechnya. I was prepared to die, to sacrifice my life in the cause of Islam, fighting the infidels.'

'Of course you were,' said Makana drily.

Bulatt's head jerked angrily at his ironic tone. 'You don't understand that kind of devotion. You are not a religious man.'

'I had a bad experience.'

'Mek Nimr took care of me. I was almost dead when I arrived there. I owe him a debt. He protected me, gave me a home when I had nowhere to go.' Bulatt paused, then added, 'I promised him I would kill you.' Makana stayed silent. 'But you are a lucky man,' Bulatt continued. 'The other day you saved my life.' Makana waited for him to go on. 'I was inside the old man's shop when you came by. One of my men followed you after you left and saw you getting into a police car.' Makana remembered the time, how Old Yunis had brushed him off. The day he talked to Okasha. 'It made me nervous. I changed my habits and that night I did not go back to the place where I was meant to sleep.'

'You weren't there when Serrag's men hit it.'

'Allah is generous to those who have faith.' Bulatt smiled. 'You should think about saying your prayers more often.' He stood up and stretched as if his legs were stiff.

'What will you do now?'

'Vronsky's death has served its purpose. By now tourists all over the Red Sea will be packing their bags and running for the airport to catch the next plane home.'

'They'll come after you.'

'They have been after me for years. We shall not rest until these *kufara* are removed from government and true Islam is restored to our country.'

'What about democratic means?'

'Democracy is like love, a lie invented to keep us content and in our places.'

'Some might say the same about religion.'

Bitter laughter trickled out of the darkness. 'You have a dangerous tongue, Makana. You should be careful. It might get cut off.' The empty sleeve of Bulatt's jacket had come loose. It dangled in front of Makana's nose, a reminder that things did not always go according to plan. Far above the sound of a helicopter ground its way urgently across the sky.

'Where will you go?'

'Back across the border, for a time. Do you have any message for Mek Nimr?'

'Only the kind you can deliver from that gun.'

'Go in peace, Makana.' Bulatt withdrew, taking the light with him. The shadows closed in over Makana.

Chapter Forty-two

*B*aba! *Wake up, Baba!*

Makana came awake with a start, jerking upright, convinced that Nasra was leaning over him, only to feel his heart fill with the bitter ache of disappointment. There was no Nasra, just faint scurrying sounds off on the other side of the room. The night was beginning to lift. Dawn had broken outside and a faint glow revealed a small window set high in the opposite wall.

His body was stiff and cold from the beating it had taken on the reef yesterday, compounded by an uncomfortable night on a hard floor. Getting slowly to his feet, Makana groped his way to the door. He pushed and it swung open of its own accord. He stepped out into a corridor, at the end of which he could make out a shaft of light. Stumbling along, he discovered the stairs he had come down the night before. Feeling his way up these, he came out on to an open floor. He made his way through corridors, past vast halls and rooms that were deserted, their windows boarded up. Doors stood open, or hung off their hinges. In places he found traces of the visitors. Discarded empty tin cans. A wall blackened with the sooty traces of a fire. Finally, he emerged into a wide room overlooking the valley below. He stood at the window and gazed down at a spectacular view, stretching down over a stony ridge to the plain below. In the distance he could make out the sea, sparkling bright and blue in the sun. Clean, as Vronsky might have said. The road threaded its way through a gorge from west to east, leading in the direction of the sea.

He was surprised to find the Mercedes still there. The key was in the ignition where he had left it. He drove slowly down the winding track, passing a metal sign that had been knocked to the ground and mangled. It looked like a tank had run over it. *Military Hospital for Mental Health*, it read. This was where they had once brought soldiers who had lost their minds. Maybe there weren't any insane people in the military any longer, Makana mused, or maybe they were running things these days. He followed the road towards the coast. A helicopter rattled heavily above the shoreline.

The whole area was inundated with military personnel and checkpoints. As usual, they were very excited about locking the stable door after the horse had bolted. Makana had to stop three times before he reached what was left of The Big Blue where a thick cluster of army and police vehicles blocked the road. They had razor-wire barricades and spiked chains dragged across the tarmac. When he tried to get into the driveway of the resort, he found a gun pointed into his face.

'No one gets in or out without permission.' The boy holding the AK-47 had the wild eyes of someone who was terrified of anything that moved.

'Who do I need to speak to?'

'Bring him over here!'

The soldier nodded over the top of Makana's car to one of the SSI officers Makana had seen in the lounge. The clumsy-looking fellow with dopey eyes was picking his nose as Makana came over.

'Inspector Okasha told me to look out for you. He thought you might turn up.'

'What's your name?'

'Marwan.' He hitched up his trousers, which seemed to keep falling down.

'How bad is it?'

'Eleven dead so far and they're still pulling them out of the rubble,' said Marwan, stepping neatly out of the way as a coach-load of tourists lumbered its way out of the car park, on their way to the airport. Pale, frightened faces looked out over the country around them with newly discovered horror. A day ago they had been paddling around in the pool, shovelling food into their faces; now they were scared.

'What are you doing back here? I thought Okasha told you . . .'

'Is he here?'

The SSI man nodded over his shoulder, taking in Makana's clothes, ripped and stained with blood, a little too late. 'What happened to you anyway?'

Makana went straight past him. A little too fast. Two armed men standing at the entrance to the hotel lifted their weapons in a state of panic.

'It's okay, it's okay.' Marwan waved to them to lower their weapons. 'He's with us.'

He chased Makana through the hotel lobby and out into the courtyard on the other side. There were field stretchers laid out and paramedics in orange jackets were moving the victims around. Most appeared dead, some were wounded. Someone was screaming somewhere off to the left. A doctor in a white coat waved them to one side as he came running through. Makana recognised one of Vronsky's muscle men lying on a stretcher. He was howling in Russian. His left leg appeared to be nothing more than a blood-soaked sheet.

'I thought I warned you not to come back here.'

Okasha was just inside the fence. The remains of Vronsky's villa were still smoking. The sickly smell of burning flesh hung in the air. The inspector was angry. Not necessarily at Makana, but he was the closest person to hand.

'Did you know about this?'

'How would I know?'

'I'm warning you,' Okasha jabbed a finger at Makana, 'if I find out . . .'

'You're not asking the right question.'

'Oh, no? Well, what question should I be asking?'

'You should be asking how it is that Bulatt can get across the border with such ease.'

'Well, I'm sure you have a theory. Why don't you enlighten us?'

Marwan was trying to keep them apart when a voice behind Makana asked: 'What is going on here? Who is this man?'

Okasha straightened his uniform. 'This is Makana, sir.'

He needed no introduction to know that this was Colonel Serrag. He was in full uniform, sunlight bouncing off the brass buttons. He was wearing dark glasses, which he removed now to reveal heavy-lidded eyes that surveyed the state Makana was in and found him wanting.

'Somehow, after all I have heard, I expected something a little more impressive.'

'Makana was just leaving,' Okasha said. Serrag ignored him.

'What are you doing here?' he asked Makana.

'I came last night to talk to Vronsky.'

'I see. And did you learn anything of interest from him?'

'He was scared.'

'Yes, and with good reason. You know who did this?'

Makana glanced at Okasha, wondering if this was a joke. 'I heard it was a man named Daud Bulatt.'

Serrag leaned forward to tap Makana in the chest with the arm of his sunglasses. 'A dead man named Daud Bulatt. It's as good as done.' A helicopter stuttered low over their heads, circling round, and Serrag turned towards it, flapping a backhanded wave over his shoulder as if shooing away a pesky fly. 'Get him out of here.'

'Yes, sir.' Okasha nodded to Marwan, who seized Makana by the arm to steer him away, but he broke free. Serrag's bodyguard stepped forward to block his way.

'Why don't you tell us what happened to Liz Markham?' Makana called.

Serrag didn't even pause. Glancing briefly in Makana's direction he slipped the sunglasses back on and turned away.

'Ask him, go on,' Makana urged Okasha, struggling as Marwan pulled him back. 'Why don't you ask him what he knows?'

'You've gone too far, Makana.' Okasha shook his head. 'Take him away.'

As he was dragged off, Makana watched over his shoulder as the grey helicopter touched down. The doors slid open and the Minister of the Interior stepped out, surrounded by security men in suits. Colonel Serrag walked over to him and saluted before holding out his hand. All around them flashbulbs went off and cameramen jostled for a clear shot. Serrag led the minister and his entourage off on an inspection of the ruins, with Okasha in tow. Then Makana watched as Serrag ushered the inspector forwards and Okasha stepped up to shake hands with the minister.

'Looks like he's destined for great things,' muttered Makana as he was led in the opposite direction.

'Don't be too hard on him.' Marwan shrugged. 'He's doing his best.'

The big, bumbling man hitched up his trousers and saw Makana safely back to his car. He then did what he was good at, yelling at people to clear the way and pull back the barricades. An air of terrified panic hung in the wake of last night's carnage. The soldiers were jittery, which was never a good thing in armed men.

Once back on the road, Makana felt relieved to be away from the organised chaos of it all. He felt sick to the stomach at what he had just seen. Liz Markham's killers would never be brought to justice. Everyone was happy doing their thing, even Okasha was too busy shaking hands with the minister to look for Bulatt. Exhausted and in pain, Makana felt dazed and angry. He had been driving for about ten minutes when he suddenly realised that in his haste he had missed something. Easing his foot off the accelerator, he pulled off the road on to the dusty hard shoulder. A heavy lorry whipped by like a house on wheels, the horn screeching. The car rocked, buffeted by the slipstream. But Makana barely noticed. He sat there for a time before putting the car in gear again and swinging round to drive back the way he had just come.

As he neared the turn-off Makana spotted the track leading down towards the sea and the little hamlet of muddy houses. The car slid off the tarmac, and bumped and bounced its way down the uneven, broken ground, springs squeaking and metal rattling. A cloud of dust rose up around him. Either the road was worse than he remembered or in his haste he was driving too quickly. When he reached the little semicircle of houses by the water the flat bay was deserted. Everyone was probably up by the road watching the commotion at The Big Blue. Makana left the car and walked past the restaurant's terrace and around the building. He went over to the heap of fishing tackle and nets and rummaged around until he pulled out a cracked oar. Behind him the one-eyed dog loped around the corner and began pawing at the sand around the boat.

Makana went over to the storehouse adjacent to the house. It was made of the same adobe material as the main building. He slid the oar in between the corrugated iron sheets that passed for doors and put his weight on it. The metal was so rusted that it took him little effort. The doors swung open to reveal a large SUV half-covered by a tarpaulin. Tossing aside the oar, Makana went inside and pulled this off to reveal Adil Romario's silver Cherokee Jeep in all its glory.

'Hey, what do you think you are doing?'

Makana ignored the other man. The car wasn't locked.

'Where is he?'

'What are you talking about?'

But already the man's haunted eyes had given him away. When he had first seen him Makana had taken him for an older man, but now he was sure that he was much younger, probably only in his thirties. The dog was still scratching away at the sand. Makana went across to the overturned boat. He started pulling nets and buoys off, tossing them aside. The dog was circling feverishly, looking for a way in, digging its snout under the side of the boat.

'Get away from there!' yelled the man, his expression turning from one of dull stupefaction to anger and disbelief. Swearing, he leaned down to pick up a stone. When he straightened up again, Makana placed a hand on his shoulder.

'Let him dig,' he said quietly.

The man looked up and the fight seemed to go out of him. The stone dropped from his fingers and he slumped down on his knees. By now they had something of an audience. A few faces had tentatively appeared in doorways. Some children had gathered at the corner of the terrace, clinging to one another and yawning, wondering, no doubt, what was up.

It didn't take the dog long to unearth something. The hand sticking out of the sand was a man's. It was rigid and some kind of nocturnal creature had managed to find its way into the shallow grave. The fingers showed signs of having been gnawed away. Bones protruded from the tips. Makana picked up a stone and threw it to scare the dog away.

'Crabs,' said the man, his voice pained. 'They come up at night. I tried using the nets to keep them out, but they dig under them.'

'Dunya was your wife?'

'She was all I had,' he said. 'All she talked about was him . . . about life up in the hotel. How glamorous it all was. But most of all she talked about him.'

'About Adil Romario?'

'How handsome he was, how smart.' He stared dumbly at his feet.

Makana looked down. The sand stuck to what remained of Adil Romario's face, making him look like a mummy dug up from an ancient tomb.

'He came here, after she was dead.' The man looked up, his eyes glistening. 'He said he was sorry, said he wanted to make amends. I think he really meant it.'

'How did Dunya die?'

Tears washed tracks through the grime that covered his face. 'It was the shame, you understand? The shame of being one of us, rather than one of them, up there in their fancy palaces. She despised me. She despised herself.'

'How did she die?' Makana repeated gently.

'There were enough people around here who told me I should kill her myself. It's all right for them, but for us . . .' The wind whipped the cotton clothes against his lean, worn body. 'But I couldn't bring myself to do it. I said, "You can't make a woman stay with you for love. If she dreams of being up there with those fine people then she will never be happy here."' He gestured around him before glancing at Makana. 'Was I wrong to say that?'

Makana said nothing. He looked out at the water. He thought how calm and beautiful it looked and he recalled his ordeal of the previous night.

'She walked into the sea one night and that was it. They fished her up in one of the nets.'

The tone of the man's voice changed. 'Then he came here, pretending to be concerned about her, trying to make things better . . . when he knew *he* was the reason she had died. "What a tragic accident," he said. He tried to give me money, as if that would make things better. What kind of a world is it where people think they can just buy whatever they want?'

'I don't know,' said Makana. 'Not much of one, I suppose.'

'We sat together, over there.' He raised a hand in the direction of the terrace. 'He told me he knew what it was like to love, that he was in love with another woman, an actress or something, which was why he had never touched Dunya. It mattered to him that I believed him. That's when I hit him.' He nodded at the broken oar lying on the ground. 'I didn't mean to kill him.'

Makana suddenly felt weary. It was as if Adil had finally emerged from the secrecy that had been obscuring him, to be

378

revealed as a simple man, trying to make amends – and paying for it with his life.

'I don't regret it,' said the fisherman. 'It won't bring her back, but I don't regret it.'

They walked back over to the restaurant and Makana righted a chair and table and sat down while the man disappeared inside to prepare coffee. Lighting a cigarette, Makana called the eldest of the watching boys over. He handed him some money and told him to run over to the resort and call the biggest policeman he could find. 'Tell him to come straight away and don't leave without him. You'll get the same amount when you come back here.' The boy disappeared in a puff of dust, his bare soles flying behind him as he ran along the beach as if his life depended on it.

Makana sat and smoked a cigarette, listening to the wind thrashing angrily through the sharp, dry fronds overhead and watching the sea patiently striking the beach, pounding as steadily as it had done for millions of years. It would be a while before the boy got back, but the coffee was taking longer than he'd expected. After a while Makana realised something was wrong. He got up and went inside the house. The kitchen was empty. No coffee pot was on the stove. He moved from room to room until he found him. The body swayed back and forth gently in the wind. The man had fashioned a simple noose from a length of nylon fishing cord and hanged himself from a wooden beam at the back of the house. The palm fronds above his head thrashed in a frenzy.

Chapter Forty-three

It was after midnight by the time Makana got back to Cairo. Gaber's office was in darkness save for the low halo cast by a desk lamp. Makana paused in the doorway for a moment, watching him. The neat waves of white hair were bowed over the paper he was writing on. A wraith of smoke curled languorously from the ashtray at his elbow. He seemed to sense Makana's presence rather than hear him for he looked up suddenly, the expression of vulnerability on his face immediately remoulding itself into the familiar, impassive mask.

'Ah, there you are. Come in, please. What a terrible business.'

His eyes swiftly took in the state of Makana. The torn and bloodstained clothes, the scratches on his face.

'You appear to have been in the thick of the battle.' Gaber cleared his throat awkwardly.

Makana settled himself down in a big, comfortable leather chair and it felt softer than a feather bed. He resisted the temptation to close his eyes and instead reached for the sandalwood box on the desk without asking. Gaber was there with the heavy gold-plated lighter shaped like a sphinx. Despite the luxury of the upholstery, it was difficult for Makana to sit comfortably.

Every inch of his body ached with pain. He sucked in the sooth-ing, rich, foreign tobacco.

'Have you told him yet?'

'As you can imagine, he took it badly. The doctor is coming to give him a sedative. I told him I would call him when you got here.' As Gaber reached for the phone, Makana raised a finger.

'You might want to wait a moment.'

'I'm sorry?' A faint, watery smile crossed Gaber's face.

'You need to consider Hanafi's reaction when he discovers what you were up to.'

In the long silence that followed Gaber aged visibly. He let the receiver fall.

'I met Daud Bulatt last night.'

Gaber sat back and folded his fingers together.

'You were there from the start. The ever loyal Gaber, cleaning up the mess. It was your job to make Hanafi respectable. You did it, you worked hard for all those years – and what did you get in reward? Very little. He still treats you with contempt. He humiliates you in front of people. Why? Because he can, because he always could, because he knows you will take it and never complain.'

Gaber stretched out a tapering hand for his own cigarette. He puffed at it for a moment or two before returning it to the ashtray. Reaching into a drawer, he produced a chequebook.

'You've obviously been through a lot. I am sure that Mr Hanafi would want you to be rewarded in full for your services.'

'That's it? I take the money and disappear?'

Gaber put down the pen he had lifted from the blotter.

'What is it you want from me?'

'Nothing. Just answers, that's all. I'm a curious man, and you're right, it's been a long night, so perhaps you will do me the favour of telling me the truth.'

'What do you want to know?' Gaber folded his fingers together again on the desk.

'When we first met, I asked you where you had got my name from. You were very vague, saying something about an old acquaintance. But you never said who exactly.'

'What are you driving at?'

'It was Bulatt, wasn't it? Daud Bulatt gave you my name.'

Gaber reached for another Dunhill from the box, the light bouncing off the mother-of-pearl inlay on the lid. Makana did the same. This time he lit it himself but it tasted just as good, despite the sharp pain that scored itself down his shoulders and back at the movement.

'You knew him from back in the old days, when he was with Hanafi.'

For a time Gaber sat in silence. A shadow had settled over his face and refused to budge. He lowered his head as if pondering a weighty dilemma. When he looked up it was as if the mask he wore had aged ten years.

'I devoted the best years of my life to serving Hanafi loyally,' he said, studying the glowing tip of his cigarette. 'When I first met him I was a young lawyer from a good family, and Hanafi, well . . . he was a *bultagi*, a simple thug from the wrong side of the tracks, but he knew more about the world than I ever would, or so it seemed to me. I was young and impressionable. He made his money through extortion. He was everything I had studied law to fight. I had led the pampered life of a middle-class child, spoiled by his parents. I was not as smart as they thought I was. I learned that at university. I knew I would never get the best jobs. But Hanafi gave me an opportunity.' Gaber sat back and looked at the ceiling. 'He had everything I lacked . . . power, charisma. He was afraid of nothing and no one. Not even death.'

'So you turned your skills to defending a criminal.'

Gaber dismissed this with a tut of impatience. 'He needed me. We were going to change the world, together. He needed someone to turn him into an honest businessman. He wanted to get out of the rackets. He took me under his wing, led me into the darkest corners of society, and I felt safe, protected.' Defiance glinted in Gaber's eyes. '*I* built this empire, not him. He has no business sense. He knows how to scare people, how to intimidate them, but he doesn't understand markets. He doesn't understand politicians.'

'But you do.'

'Yes,' said Gaber quickly. 'And now . . . his mind has gone. Age, illness, I don't know. It's all slipping away from him, but he won't let go. If I didn't act, he would take us all down with him.'

'You were trying to protect him from himself? Or trying to save the company for yourself?'

Gaber's head sagged low, as if he could no longer bear its weight, his face dipping into shadow. But you didn't need to see his face to feel the emotion in his voice.

'Hanafi started to get sentimental. I knew he was planning to hand everything over to Adil. He doted on the boy. You're right. He never saw me as anything but an educated fool. He would never let me take over.'

'So you decided to cut Adil out of the equation?' Gaber nodded. 'And you enlisted Soraya to your cause.'

'She saw what was going on. She understood the danger the company was in, and she knew that Adil was an obstacle and a threat.'

'You heard about Bulatt, that he was still alive and well and living just next door. Who told you, I wonder? Was it your friend Colonel Serrag?'

Gaber remained tight-lipped. Makana continued.

'You arranged a friendly match in Khartoum and sent word to Bulatt. You thought he would take care of things from there. Only Bulatt had other plans.'

Through the window behind him, Makana could see the trees on the terrace bending in the high wind. There was a storm blowing and the air swirled with fine dust which seemed to glow like particles of gold in the brilliant spotlights that illuminated the penthouse.

'You must have realised there was a certain risk, bringing Bulatt into the picture.'

'Of course,' Gaber snapped. 'But you must understand my position. I had no choice. I was convinced that if something wasn't done, everything would be lost.'

'So Adil came back, alive and well, and recruited into Bulatt's plans for revenge.'

'I know nothing of all that. All I know is that Bulatt tricked me. He didn't get rid of Adil. Instead he came here himself.'

'He came because Adil went missing. You didn't know what was going on. All you knew was that you had to deal with it as discreetly as possible. Bulatt persuaded you to hire me.' Makana paused. 'You were still on talking terms with Bulatt then. You didn't know that he had his own plans. You had no choice but to go along with him; with Adil missing you had nowhere to turn.'

'I didn't know what to think.' Gaber put his face in his hands. 'For all I knew the young fool had got himself into some other trouble. I just knew that if anyone started snooping around they might come up with all kinds of things. I couldn't risk that.'

'And Bulatt promised he would get rid of me when the time came.'

'Something like that.'

Gaber lifted his head and conceded the briefest of nods. Then his expression froze and his eyes drifted off to a spot somewhere over Makana's right shoulder. He turned to see Hanafi standing in the doorway. How long he had been standing there it was impossible to say, but from the look on his face he had overheard enough.

'What is this? What is going on?'

He stepped into the room. He moved like a drunk. Perhaps it was the medication they had given him, but there was something wild and deranged about him. The silk dressing gown he wore had come undone. Underneath, a vest and undershorts peeped through. He made no attempt to adjust his clothing, and seemed completely oblivious to his appearance. His hair stood on end as if he had been sleeping on it. Or tearing at it. He stepped closer to them.

'You killed my boy? You, of all people?' Hanafi was barefoot, his feet like pale mice creeping across the carpet in fits and starts. 'You were nothing, nobody, when I found you.'

Gaber began to rise. 'Now listen to me, Saad. Whatever I did, I did for the sake of all of us . . . for the company.'

'Listen to you? I have listened to you for long enough.'

By now he was upon Gaber. His open hands were swollen with age and rheumatism, but they came down hard like the wooden paddles of a steamer, relentlessly pounding Gaber to the floor. 'If it wasn't for me you would be out there peddling your ass! Selling insurance to old ladies . . .'

Gaber raised his hands to defend himself but sank under the blows. He tried to grab something to help him stay upright and pulled the fancy blotter, the telephone, the heavy cut-glass ashtray, on to the floor with him.

'He's dead! Do you understand that? You killed my son!'

'It's not like that,' Gaber protested, crawling back towards the bookcase, blood pouring from his nose and a cut over his left eye. Hanafi's strength seemed to belie his age. His fists drew back again and again to land on Gaber's head until it sounded like a pulped melon. Eventually he stood up and turned to face Makana. His hair and clothes were in disarray and his face was smeared with blood. Makana could hear a faint wheezing sound coming from behind the desk which told him the other man was alive, if only barely. Hanafi was staring straight through Makana, his eyes wild and unseeing.

'*Baba!*'

The haunted gaze lifted and Hanafi let out a cry as if he had seen a ghost when Soraya rushed across the room towards him. He threw up one arm to keep her back.

'No! Don't touch me!' Then he turned away, stepping blindly into the French windows behind him. The doors flew open as he crashed against them, letting in a gust of wind that sent papers flying.

Hanafi staggered out, carried by his own momentum. Makana watched as Soraya followed her father out on to the terrace, reaching out to him time and again. Each time he would brush her off and move further away. Finally, she stopped and watched helplessly as the strange figure pirouetted across the terrace as if upon a stage. Hanafi had the grace of an ageing ballerina, a drunk or a madman who manages to avoid, by some miraculous sense of balance, the most obvious traps and pitfalls. Staggering and somehow not falling, he made it across to the other side. With a little hop he stepped up on to a bench and then suddenly he was standing on the parapet of the terrace. The updraught from below flapped the hem of the gown around his plump legs so that he resembled a broken umbrella, or a large, ugly vulture whose wings had lost all coordination. He raised his hands and shouted something, as if addressing the world far below him. Soraya threw out her hand. '*Baba!*' she cried, one last time, and then he was gone.

Chapter Forty-four

Soraya Hanafi walked into the dining room of the Al Hassanain Hotel and looked around uncertainly. It was empty at that dead hour of the afternoon. The few guests staying there appeared to be out, busy struggling through traffic, no doubt, trawling for bargains in the bazaar, or trying to capture this vast, unfathomable city in a neat series of images inside a tiny box. Finally, gratefully, she spied Makana across the wide room.

He was sitting very still at one of the tables in the far corner by an open window, staring out at the square below and the old mosque. There was a timelessness about this place, he was thinking, that made all of our problems seem like brief shifts of the light. He didn't notice her until she was standing over him.

'I wasn't sure this was the right place,' she said.

Makana got to his feet, instantly annoyed with himself for feeling awkward around her. To his irritation he noted that once again she looked quite stunning. It seemed that she didn't even have to try, it came naturally to her. She was dressed casually in a dark suit with a black silk shawl swept around her upper body and over her head, as if she didn't want to be recognised. The light breeze stirred her clothes, adding to the impression of insubstantiality.

'You said it was urgent.'

'Yes, thank you for coming,' he said, gesturing at the seat opposite his. Soraya took one look at the furniture, the broken-backed chairs and the grubby plastic tablecloth, and shook her head. Her eyes were red and swollen, her face pinched and drained of colour.

'It has seen better days,' he sighed, looking around desperately for an alternative.

'All part of the charm, I suppose,' she said, glancing round the room as if on the off-chance she might spot some of that elusive quality lurking in a corner.

'I think it would be helpful for you to see the room.'

Soraya sighed. 'All right. But, please, can we get this over quickly?'

'As fast as possible, I promise.'

Makana led the way to the staircase. On the third floor he produced the key and opened the door. He gestured for her to enter. There was a moment when he thought she might not go through with it, but then she bowed her head and stepped forward. She stood just inside the doorway. Makana went past her and over to the window. He had to wrestle with the shutters for a time before they gave way, flying out with such force that they bounced back, almost slamming him in the face. Eventually, he hooked them into place and surveyed the view.

If there was any single reason why guests who found them-selves staying in this hotel by some accident of fate or necessity decided to stay on, this view was the most likely explanation. The authors of countless romantic novels would undoubtedly have been able to summon a thousand and one adjectives to describe it and none of them would have been adequate. An accumulation of centuries of history, jumbled up together in one glorious scene. This was the way it had always been, and anyone who thought otherwise was either insane or deluded.

'Why have you brought me here?'

He turned back to face her. The room itself exuded a dreary air. The heavy old telephone with its circular dial. The chipped and cracked walls. The raw bulb dangling from the ceiling on a length of stiffened electrical cord. Between them, the bed formed an awkward, uncharted sea of possibility. Uneven and listing to one side, with the headboard chipped and scratched, it told countless stories, most of which would not have been fit for children's ears. The room told another story, too, one that was more disturbing. It had been cleaned thoroughly but it still harboured the recent memory of Liz Markham's death.

'You know why,' he said.

Soraya stared at him. A flicker passed across her face and the stiffness in her manner seemed to dissolve. Once more she looked like a little girl, unsure how to begin this awkward dance.

'This is where she stayed?'

'She must have remembered it,' said Makana, turning to survey the view from the window once more. 'This is where she stayed when she came with her daughter, years ago.'

Soraya cast an eye over the room with renewed curiosity.

'At first I thought you couldn't possibly remember,' he said. 'The mind can play tricks like that. It is some kind of protective mechanism, I believe. It cuts out things we are unable to understand, or which our minds cannot absorb.'

Her gaze refused to meet his. It fluttered round the room like a trapped bird looking for an avenue of escape.

'The things we don't want to remember . . . things that are too painful to face . . . they get locked away, deep in our memory, so well hidden we don't even know they exist.'

Soraya took a tentative step forward, and then another, finally sinking down to perch herself on the edge of the bed. The springs erupted in protest like a chorus of hungry cats.

'One day something, or someone, triggers off a chain of events, a sequence of clues, that leads us back through the maze. In my case it was you.' Makana lit a cigarette and blew smoke at the window. 'The image I had of you as a child, running through these streets with nowhere to turn.'

'Me?' she asked.

'Little Alice managed to vanish without a trace. There was no ransom note, no demand for money. Nobody knew anything. Liz Markham didn't help matters. There was a big fuss. A little English girl goes missing in the Khan al-Khalili. You can imagine. They promised no stone would be left unturned. But none of their efforts turned up anything. Liz was hysterical. The police weren't sure they believed her story. Even her own embassy thought her an unreliable witness. She had a history of drug abuse. What was she doing here? they wondered. Had she sold the child?'

'You would need a lot of influence to make something like that go away.'

'Exactly. Somebody with a lot of influence . . . Someone like Hanafi.'

'How did you know?' she asked, stroking the faded coverlet on the bed.

'In the Gezira Club I told you about the murder. I didn't mention that Liz Markham had come here looking for her daughter. Yet the next time we met at your office you asked about the child. You knew.' He paused, watching her as she absorbed this in silence. 'In Hanafi's office there is a picture of you when you were small. Your hair must have darkened with age, but even when you were about thirteen it was still quite light.'

Soraya got to her feet and made as if to leave. Makana cut her off, swinging the door shut. She winced at the sound, instinctively raising a hand to protect herself. Slumping back, she sagged against the wall as if she might collapse.

'Do you remember any of it?'

'Bits and pieces, like a dream that I couldn't place. I didn't know what it meant.' She was facing away from him as she spoke. 'I don't think I wanted to know.' Her voice was vague and lost, eyes fixed dully ahead of her. 'In the beginning they kept me in this strange place . . . a house in the country. There were two women. The old one I called The Witch, she was evil. She hit me. But the other one was kind. When I cried at night, she would sit with me and whisper stories. I remember the palm trees at night, rustling overhead. I wasn't afraid though. I felt safe. I didn't miss my mother. I know that sounds strange, but I didn't want to go back to her.' She lapsed into a long silence. 'You learn to live with it. You eat. You sleep. And slowly, very slowly, you forget. I was four years old. In time I was brought into the family. I met the elder sisters. They took care of me. They accepted me as one of their own.' Soraya rolled her shoulders along the wall, first one way and then the other. 'We had so much in common, he and I. I'd never known a father. It was easy to believe he was the one. In time it becomes more difficult to face the truth than to live the lie.'

The sound of voices drifted up through the open window, the rhythmic intonations of someone reading a sura from the Quran. Makana moved to the window and looked down, leaning against the frame as he fished his Cleopatras out of his jacket again. Down below people milled about. A man bent over, resting one hand against the wall of the mosque in exhaustion. All of them, like busy little insects, striving to improve their lives, to move onwards and upwards, to find a place to rest, if only for a moment.

'When did you realise you were not Hanafi's daughter?'

'An Englishwoman who came back every year asking questions? It was only a matter of time before word got back to Gaber.'

'He told you?' A brief nod. 'And yet you never felt the need to go to her, to see her?'

'She sold me!' Soraya's voice was ragged as she twisted round to face him. 'Can you imagine what that feels like, to know that you were sold for money so she could carry on with drink and drugs and men?'

'You don't know that she did that.'

Soraya's hair had come loose, veiling her face. She brushed it aside. 'I did see her. I followed her one day. One of Gaber's men pointed her out to me and I followed her for a while. I thought I would feel something, but I didn't. She was a stranger to me,' Soraya moaned, pressing her hands to her eyes to stem the tears.

'You had a better life where you were. You didn't want to go back.'

'I knew nothing about her, except that she left me here. She abandoned me and returned to her life in England. I owed her nothing.'

'You wanted to be Hanafi's daughter. More than that, you wanted to be the heiress to his empire. And then Gaber told you about Adil and you knew Hanafi would hand the business to him. He didn't care about the stink it would raise. Hanafi wanted a son. All his life he had wanted one.' Makana brought his head close to the wall where hers rested. 'So you tried seducing Adil, thinking you could get rid of him that way, with a scandal. Only he turned you down, didn't he? His heart was set on another.

392

And when he told you about Mimi Maliki you decided to get rid of her, to pay her off and send her away.'

'She had no right to get involved.'

'You were going to tell me, weren't you? That night in your office. That was why you called me over. You were going to tell me that you knew you were Liz's daughter. But somehow you couldn't, so you made up some story about being pregnant. You thought that might throw me off track.'

'I was confused. I don't know what I wanted . . .'

Makana edged closer to her.

'The funny thing is that you and Adil were not all that different. You both came into Hanafi's family as strangers. You both wanted to belong. Adil wanted it more than anything. He knew he would never be accepted by you and Gaber, that once the old man was gone you would probably figure out a way to get rid of him.'

'What was she like?' Her voice was soft now, as if the fight had been knocked out of her.

'Your mother?' Makana looked around the room for a moment. 'I think she was a good person. Like most good people she wasn't perfect. She made one mistake and spent the rest of her life paying for it. She came here to try and make it right, and she died for it.'

'I can remember running through the bazaar,' Soraya's dreamy voice continued. 'I saw myself reflected in all the shiny glass and metal surfaces, like a star inside a world of mirrors. I've always kept that memory, deep down inside me, of that little blonde girl with pigtails.'

Chapter Forty-five

The sun was setting in the *maidan* in front of the mosque. Strings of light bulbs draped across the sky bobbed like glowing buoys, tying up the stars in nets. The sound of the muezzin floated through the quickening darkness as he sang out his melodic summons to the Maghrib prayer. The faithful arrived from every direction, slipping off their shoes as they passed through the arched entrance, while others carried on with their business, leaving prayer for some other time. Makana strolled across the square. He spotted the two men as he came in through the doorway. It was busy tonight, so much so that Aswani only had time for a brief greeting over his shoulder as he moved with remarkable speed, issuing orders left and right while threading cubes of meat on to long skewers, so fast that any lesser mortal would have done himself an injury.

'Ah, here he is.' Okasha looked up from the salad he was devouring. 'We were just talking about you.'

'Kindly, I hope.'

Sami intervened. 'The inspector was telling me how you managed to let a one-armed man get the better of you.'

'Not exactly the better of me,' said Makana. 'Seeing as he let me go alive, I think I acquitted myself rather well.'

Okasha held out his hand. 'I owe you an apology.'

'No, you don't,' said Makana. 'You were just doing your job.'

'So were you.' The hand remained awkwardly hovering in the air between them until Makana finally took it. Then he pulled out a chair and sat down.

'Has there been any sign of Bulatt?'

'Nothing. The general theory is that he has crossed the border to the south. Maybe we should send you home to find him.' It was delivered as a joke, but the only one smiling was Okasha.

'He came here to kill me.'

'But he had a change of heart. One day I'd like to hear how exactly you managed that.'

'And Soraya,' Makana asked. 'What happens to her?'

'She's helping us with our enquiries,' said Okasha.

'You have nothing to hold her on?'

'What am I going to charge her with?'

Perhaps it was for the best, Makana thought. Now she would take over Hanafi Enterprises and run it the way she wanted to do. He had no doubt that she would do fine.

Then Aswani appeared with the food and everyone's attention was diverted by their hunger. For the next couple of hours the three of them talked and ate, and ate and talked some more. They drank countless cups of tea and coffee. *Shisha* pipes were brought over and the sweet aroma of apple-flavoured tobacco filtered into the air. They compared notes, going back and forth, tying up loose ends, commenting on one aspect or another of the case. As the boy clicked his tongs and set fresh coals on the pipes, they turned the details over to view them from every conceivable angle. Sami wanted to clarify one or two points. Makana suspected that he was composing his book as they went along.

'The way I see it now,' explained Sami, 'I shall begin with the broad facts of the case, of course, setting everything out clearly right from the start so there is no confusion.'

'That, I'd like to see,' said Makana.

'But then,' Sami raised a finger in the air, 'I shall explore every aspect with a rational and scientific eye. Not too cold. There has to be room for poetry, of course.'

'Of course.'

'What would the human soul be without poetry?'

'How can you listen to him talk such nonsense?' Okasha demanded.

Sami was frowning fiercely. 'I see this as an epic battle between rivals. An ancient feud which has lasted decades. Both of them ruthless predators . . . born gangsters. One is made respectable by a society obsessed with wealth and success. The other turns to religion in order to save the country from the very things which have made his rival a national figure. What do you think?'

Okasha took the long waterpipe from his mouth. 'You will turn both of them into heroes.'

'Don't listen to him,' said Makana. 'You'll sell thousands. In fact, it will probably change your life for ever and you'll no longer have time for us. You'll be too busy hanging out with glamorous models and beautiful film stars.'

Sami frowned. 'You don't approve?'

'I didn't say that.'

'You don't have to say it. You condemn the whole enterprise with a single sentence.'

'My apologies. Please go on.'

'Apologies accepted.' Sami swept his hands in a wide arc before him. 'I can see it now . . . A series of character portraits. The princess in the tower. The evil father. The innocent young football player, the nation's idol.' He paused, lost for words momentarily as a serious thought occurred to him. 'It's really about the fate of this country and what is happening right now. It's about everything.'

Okasha rocked his head from side to side, letting a cloud of aromatic smoke out of the side of his mouth. 'He certainly has a way with words, you can't deny that. It sounds like something you might see in the cinema. Where does Makana come into it?'

Sami smiled. 'Oh, I think he remains the mysterious figure in the background.'

'Well, that's him, all right,' agreed Okasha.

'I don't think he can hear us.'

His eye on the open doorway, Makana's thoughts led him back to the day he'd first met Elizabeth Markham here. He would always be grateful to her, he realised, for bringing back the memory of his own daughter so vividly, if only for a brief time. He wished he could hold on to that feeling, just a little while longer.

'He doesn't even know we are here.'

'No, he's gone, carried off in the arms of jinns.'

A NOTE ON THE TYPE

The text of this book is set in Baskerville, named after John Baskerville of Birmingham (1706–1775). The original punches cut by him still survive. His widow sold them to Beaumarchais, from where they passed through several French foundries to Deberney & Peignot in Paris, before finding their way to Cambridge University Press.

Baskerville was the first of the 'transitional romans' between the softer and rounder calligraphic Old Face and the 'Modern' sharp-tooled Bodoni. It does not look very different to the Old Faces, but the thick and thin strokes are more crisply defined, and the serifs on lower-case letters are closer to the horizontal with the stress nearer the vertical. The R in some sizes has the eighteenth-century curled tail, the lower-case w has no middle serif, and the lower-case g has an open tail and a curled ear.

ALSO AVAILABLE BY PARKER BILAL

DOGSTAR RISING

A MAKANA MYSTERY

It is the summer of 2001 and in Cairo's crowded streets the heat is rising . . .

The unsolved murders of a number of young homeless boys are fanning the embers of religious hatred, and as tensions mount, Makana – who fled his home in Sudan a decade ago – has a premonition that history may be about to repeat itself.

Hired to investigate threats that have been made to a hapless travel agent Makana finds himself drawn to Meera, a woman who knows what it is like to lose everything and who needs his help. Meanwhile, Makana's troubled Sudanese past seems to be trying to lay claim to him once again, this time in the form of a dubious businessman who possesses a powerful secret.

When Makana witnesses a brutal killing he attracts the attention of both the state security services and a dangerous gangster family. His search for answers takes him from the labyrinths of Cairo to the ancient city of Luxor and an abandoned monastery in the desert, into a web of intrigue and violence.